Raves for the Jaded Gentleman Novels

Ecstasy

"Sensuality fills the page

Seduction *Sapphires*

"An amazing read. I enjoyed it immensely . . . Ashe and Caroline are wonderful characters that made me fall in love with them from the beginning of the story."

—*Night Owl Reviews*

"A fine book, well crafted, well researched, and an entertaining romantic novel . . . Historical romance fans will be delighted, I have no doubt."   —*The Book Binge*

"What a refreshing new take on two people who from first sight are determined to detest each other . . . I was immediately engrossed with the fiery, witty dialogue and the curiosity of how this couple, who loathed each other upon their meeting, would come full circle to a beautifully shared love in the end."   —*Fiction Vixen*

Revenge Wears Rubies

"Sensuality fairly steams from Bernard's writing. This luscious tale will enthrall you. Enjoy!"
—Sabrina Jeffries, *New York Times* bestselling author

"If you're a fan of spicy hot romances mixed with a bit of intrigue and set in Victorian London, don't miss this one!"   —*The Romance Dish*

"Galen's journey from emotional cripple to ability to love is a captivating, erotic romance."   —*Fresh Fiction*

continued . . .

Passion Wears Pearls

RENEE BERNARD

BERKLEY SENSATION, NEW YORK

THE BERKLEY PUBLISHING GROUP
Published by the Penguin Group
Penguin Group (USA) Inc.
375 Hudson Street, New York, New York 10014, USA

Penguin Group (Canada), 90 Eglinton Avenue East, Suite 700, Toronto, Ontario M4P 2Y3, Canada
(a division of Pearson Penguin Canada Inc.) • Penguin Books Ltd., 80 Strand, London WC2R 0RL,
England • Penguin Group Ireland, 25 St. Stephen's Green, Dublin 2, Ireland (a division of Penguin
Books Ltd.) • Penguin Group (Australia), 250 Camberwell Road, Camberwell, Victoria 3124, Australia
(a division of Pearson Australia Group Pty. Ltd.) • Penguin Books India Pvt. Ltd., 11 Community
Centre, Panchsheel Park, New Delhi—110 017, India • Penguin Group (NZ), 67 Apollo Drive,
Rosedale, Auckland 0632, New Zealand (a division of Pearson New Zealand Ltd.) • Penguin Books
(South Africa) (Pty.) Ltd., 24 Sturdee Avenue, Rosebank, Johannesburg 2196, South Africa

Penguin Books Ltd., Registered Offices: 80 Strand, London WC2R 0RL, England

This is a work of fiction. Names, characters, places, and incidents either are the product of the author's
imagination or are used fictitiously, and any resemblance to actual persons, living or dead, business
establishments, events, or locales is entirely coincidental. The publisher does not have any control over
and does not assume any responsibility for author or third-party websites or their content.

PASSION WEARS PEARLS

A Berkley Sensation Book / published by arrangement with the author

PUBLISHING HISTORY
Berkley mass-market edition / March 2012

ISBN: 978-0-425-24794-5

BERKLEY SENSATION®
Berkley Sensation Books are published by The Berkley Publishing Group,
a division of Penguin Group (USA) Inc.,
375 Hudson Street, New York, New York 10014.
BERKLEY SENSATION® is a registered trademark of Penguin Group (USA) Inc.
The "B" design is a trademark of Penguin Group (USA) Inc.

PRINTED IN THE UNITED STATES OF AMERICA

10 9 8 7 6 5 4 3 2 1

ALWAYS LEARNING   **PEARSON**

To Holly. There's never been a moment when I didn't look up to you in complete awe. As a sister, a mother and a "Happy," a teacher and a scholar, and as the voice of calm in any storm, you're one of those women who always amaze others without any effort at all. I know you don't like even a hint of mush, and maybe it's the hedgehog in you that makes us like you all the more. I love you.

To Heidi. What a heart you have! I can't even describe how much I admire you for your beauty and your humor. You make everything look so graceful; being a mom and being there for everyone around you. Martha Stewart would cry if she could see the beautiful house you keep . . . but only because she could never match the sweet spirit that you infuse in everything around you. I love you.

To Geoffrey and my girls. Let's stop time. Just for a while. Until I can catch my breath and get used to being this happy.

And finally, to Leslie Esdaile Banks, my Fairy Godmother. I miss you, your hugs, and your laugh. Heaven can't be beautiful enough for a soul like yours . . . but with your arrival, I'm sure it's been vastly improved.

Acknowledgments

I'm going to try to thank a new cast of people so that anyone paying attention to these doesn't get too bored hearing all over again about my wonderful editor, Kate Seaver, or my friend the media powerhouse, Sheila English, or my friends behind the scenes who made this book possible: Lisa Richardson, Sean Conley-Whiting, and Lia Boxwell. Or even yet another reprise to the ER staff at Marshall Hospital. (Has anyone done a study to make sure that children under the age of six aren't crazy? Because mine will do *anything it takes* to give me a heart attack—apparently for amusement. And for those stuffed bears they give out.)

But this time, I want to also thank my new agent, Eric Ruben, who is phenomenally brilliant and very funny. And on those days when all you want to do is cry and throw in the towel, it's nice to have someone with a great sense of humor come to your rescue (or at least offer to buy you a drink).

I want to thank Anne Elizabeth for becoming one of those amazing friends that you're sure you've never been good enough to deserve but you keep your fingers crossed that there will be enough opportunities to earn anyway. When I grow up, I want to be cool enough to hang out with Anne.

I want to thank Samantha Stoddard for being Samantha Stoddard. Sam was like a touchstone and while she pretended to need my help and advice, I swear I got more out of her internship than she did. My attempt at mentorship was probably laughable, but it was a joy just to be in her presence.

It's been a year of extremes, highs and lows. The low point was the loss of a dear friend, L.A. Banks, in August of 2011. It's not an original complaint but I'll waste my breath saying it. I hate cancer. I hate it. And a day hasn't passed when I haven't missed her or made an impossible wish about reversing fate. The worst of it is, I suspect, this will never change. The best of it is, every day is about being a better person to try to live up to the legacy she left behind. She's inspired me to try harder—at everything.

The high points were family weddings and quiet parenting milestones that made sure I was reminded of how precious every day can be. It's crazy to say that Fiona losing a tooth or Morgan touching the ocean made all the stress and long hours worthwhile, but there you have it. Life went on.

And again, just in case anyone is tracking these from book to book, you know I can't leave her out. My mother is still my biggest fan and strongest supporter. Geography makes no difference. I know she's right behind me and wherever this path takes me, my mother will be the first one to cheer me on.

I have to also mention the wonderful readers and booksellers in Australia who have been especially kind with their e-mails and Facebook friending (if that's a verb!). I'm saving pennies for the trip I imagine myself taking to the Far East and Australia. It's silly, I realize, but a woman must have dreams in these difficult times and mine is to see some of my favorite booksellers down under and "pop in" on a romance reading group or two. Australian Romance Readers Association conference in Brisbane in 2013, here I come!

To all my readers, wherever you are, I can't thank you enough. You're the reason I write. And yes, I'm writing faster.

Day and night I guarded the pearl of my soul.
Now in this ocean of pearling currents,
I've lost track of which was mine.

—RUMI

Chapter
1

London
January 1860

"Pinch your cheeks, foolish girl! You look like you're about
to faint!" Madame Claremont snapped open the shop window's drapes with a crisp efficiency that betrayed her terrible temper. "We've few enough appointments today without
you scaring my customers into thinking I employ sickly
girls!"

Eleanor Beckett dutifully pinched her cheeks and then
quickly moved to help rearrange the displays for the day.
Madame Claremont's dress shop was perched on the edge
of Mayfair in London, and while it was fashionable enough
to keep a few wealthy clients on the books, Madame Claremont was forever bemoaning the terrors of living on the
brink of financial ruin. Times were difficult for shopkeep-
ers, especially during the winter months when most of the
elite London residents had returned to their country homes
to escape the soot and disease of the city.

All four shop girls bustled around the room to begin
preparing for their first appointments, and Eleanor kept her

gaze lowered from her employer's face as she set out a new embroidered woolen cape. She had only earned her position six months before, and lived in fear of her imminent dismissal. But meager wages and endless hours over sewing tables were far more appealing than the icy-cold streets of London.

Madame Claremont sniffed her disapproval as she stood behind Eleanor. "And where is the red velvet evening dress? I wanted to have it out so that Mrs. Carlisle could see it when she comes in! That woman has a penchant for red and won't blink at any price I set!"

"It isn't ready, madame," Eleanor said softly, turning to face the consequences.

"Why ever not?"

"You told me to set it aside and finish Mrs. Belle's traveling dress. I stayed up all night to complete the hem work. She's picking it up this afternoon and I was sure you'd be pleased."

Except that Madame Claremont, who was really Mrs. Emmaline Smith of Cheapside, didn't look pleased at all. "I never told you to abandon that velvet dress! And don't you stand there like a superior little snit and think to inform me that I didn't expect you to manage your hours and energies and finish *all* your work in good time! I pay you honest wages for an honest effort. *Not* to play the clairvoyant and pretend to know my business!"

"Yes, madame." Eleanor took a steadying breath, hating the choking quiet that came over the shop as the other girls silently watched to see if she'd survive the morning's storms. "Perhaps, I could work on it in between appointments until Mrs. Carlisle arrives later? It is far enough along to make a good impression and I can work on the finishing to—"

"You'll finish it by the time she comes through that doorway, or by God, you'll buy that dress yourself in lost wages!"

"Madame!" Eleanor gasped. "I can't possibly afford the—"

The slap came hard across her cheek, effectively ending

Eleanor's protest. Madame Claremont's color improved as she stepped back as calmly as if she'd swatted a fly. "If you finish the dress, then Mrs. Carlisle will be the one to pay for it. And then you and I will put this unpleasant matter behind us. You will learn to deliver things to me when I ask, and I won't have to remind you of the consequences of your defiant attitude. Am I understood?"

It took all of her self-discipline not to reach up to touch the stinging ache on her cheek. Slowly, she nodded, miserable fury stinging like nettles inside her chest to match her injuries. *How am I here? Fallen so far that a woman like this has power over me and I'm going to nod and swallow injustice like a bitter tonic and tell myself how lucky I am not to be out in the cold.*

Oh, God.

"Understood, madame." She curtsied and turned to retreat back to the fabric room, fighting fury and humiliation. She was so hungry her hands were shaking, and worse, there'd be no remedy for a few hours yet. If she was pale, it had everything to do with the long weeks of sleepless nights and sparse meals that Mrs. Smith's generosity afforded her.

A tiny room was let to her by Madame Claremont's sister, and the rent deducted weekly from her pay. To make her finances even more tenuous, she'd discovered that Madame Claremont was quick to take out what she called "penalties" for infractions, real or perceived, in the shop.

I won't cry. I won't let her make me cry. I am a woman grown, and twenty-three is too old to allow it. The only consolation that kept her going was that the work was deemed respectable for a woman in her position. And respectability was the one thing she'd sworn she would never relinquish. No matter how dire her situation had become.

She closed her eyes and leaned for a moment against the shelves of fabric, determined to banish her emotions, ignore the complaints of her body and the terror of failure. *What would Father have said? Something about how a true lady never complains but wins her way through gentle resolve . . . or other words a bit more lofty he'd memorized from a book on social graces.*

She opened her eyes and squared her shoulders. Every second lost to self-pity was not going to be recovered. Eleanor accepted that the red velvet dress was simply the dragon she would have to slay to prove to her employer that she could hold her own. Mrs. Carlisle's appointment was at five fifteen so the impossible would just have to be managed. And in the meantime, there was dear Mrs. Lawson coming with her eldest daughter for a wedding consultation at ten.

She began to wrestle with some of the rolls of fabric, trying to pull the samples she thought might please her first customer.

"She's all thorns and thistles today, ain't she?" Maggie whispered as she came up to get her own fabrics and offer her coworker a bit of sympathy. Maggie was all of seventeen but had the grounded wisdom of a woman several times her years. "Don't mind her."

"I can't seem to do anything right!"

"'Course not! She's been off you from the start and there's nothing to be done about it."

"She'll dismiss me, then, for certain!"

"Never! She's so thrilled to have yer proper little ways mincing about the customers and making her look all high and mighty! Why, already her business has improved, and I'm not guessin' it's her insistence that horsehair petticoats will never go out of fashion!"

Eleanor put her hand to her lips to keep from laughing. Maggie was the only one of the other girls who'd warmed a bit to Eleanor's presence and demonstrated more than mere civility. From generally lower-middle-class families, the girls in the shop had eyed her with wary suspicion when she'd come to Madame Claremont's doorstep clutching her references. It was as if they had sensed that Eleanor was not necessarily one of their own. They'd accused her of taking on airs and holding herself above them with her reserved habits and precise manners. "You mustn't say such things, Margaret."

Miss Maggie Beecham shrugged cheerfully. "I'll say what I like, if it's true."

Eleanor shook her head and rebalanced a blue-striped gabardine on top of her pile. "I wish I had your confidence. I need this position too badly to be flippant, but I appreciate your sentiments. I only wish I knew how to make a better go of it. I'm working as hard as I can, and even so, I'm falling short each week."

Maggie's cheer evaporated as she nodded in sympathy. "It's a tangle, miss."

"I am as careful as a miser with every penny. I overheard one of the other girls talking about side work, but I cannot imagine how there can be more hours in the day!"

"You've only been here a few months, and you haven't seen the way of it, yet. But with your pretty looks and fine manners, there's no telling how—"

"Miss Beckett! Time is money, and when Mrs. Lawson and her daughter come, I want that first dressing room completely ready. If you have time for idle chatter, perhaps you can afford a few less shillings in your pocket at the end of the week."

"No, Madame Claremont. I shall see to it immediately." The bolts of weighted fabrics and silks were heavy enough to make her shoulders burn, but she wrestled them down the narrow hallway as gracefully as she could. The first dressing room was cheery enough, and Eleanor was glad to have the use of it since it had a small coal stove in the corner to fend off the wintry chill of January in London. Areas of the shop were always kept warmed for their customers' comforts during fittings, and it hadn't taken her long to learn the advantages of where to go to banish the numbness in her fingers.

Within minutes she had the bolts arranged attractively on a side table and all her fashion plates were preselected and in a good order to allow the young Miss Lawson to choose her trousseau for her spring wedding. She had risked one ivory satin and a stunning peach organza, just in case. Mrs. Lawson had already decreed that the wedding gown would come from Paris, and Eleanor didn't wish to argue against it. But it never hurt to let a young lady change her mind if she wanted to. . . .

Especially if it meant Madame Claremont might add a little money to my wages instead of constantly taking some away.

"Miss Beckett! What a pleasure to see you again!" Mrs. Lawson greeted her from the dressing room's doorway, ignoring the custom of waiting to be escorted into the shop's interior rooms. "You remember my daughter, Claudia?"

"Of course! Miss Lawson, thank you for gracing our showroom." Eleanor reached out to take her hand, genuinely happy to see the pair. "But have you come early? Or was I just caught daydreaming?"

Mrs. Lawson laughed. "We are early because Claudia cannot stop talking about preparing for the wedding, and undoubtedly, I am just as eager to see her happy!"

"Ah, Mrs. Lawson!" Madame Claremont came up behind them. "How rude of Miss Beckett to force you to wander back here alone!"

"Not at all! I knew we were several minutes ahead of our appointment and it is not exactly a labyrinth, is it?" Mrs. Lawson waved her hand in the air, carelessly dismissing the subtle accusation that she'd somehow trespassed. "I am an intrepid woman, madame, but perhaps you could offer me a cup of tea?"

Madame Claremont sputtered for just a moment before recovering her composure and remembering the promised business that Mrs. Lawson represented. "I'll have Bridgette bring you a tray."

Eleanor knew she'd pay for having witnessed Madame Claremont's comeuppance, but there was nothing she could do at the moment. "Miss Lawson, would you care to take a seat and look at a few sketches? I selected these with you in mind."

Claudia smiled, meekly taking both the offered seat and the fashion book. Plump and pretty, Miss Claudia Lawson was a shy creature with a mild disposition. Like a quiet foil for her mother's saucy wit and temperament, she was the living embodiment of a content and dutiful daughter. "Thank you, Miss Beckett."

Mrs. Lawson walked over to the table of fabrics, removing her gloves to finger the organza. Eleanor watched her out of the corner of her eye, praying she hadn't been too bold as Madame Claremont also noticed the unexpected choices.

Madame Claremont clasped her hands together. "A mistake, Mrs. Lawson! I specifically told Miss Beckett—"

"It's beautiful," Mrs. Lawson said quietly, her attention arrested completely by the shimmer and weight of the silk organza in her hands. "It's almost gold, isn't it? But in the light, then you can see that it's more peach. I am quite enamored, madame." She lifted the bolt and brought it to her daughter, settling down next to her on the sofa. "Isn't it divine, Claudia? Wouldn't it make a lovely wedding dress?"

Claudia brightened immediately. "I love it! But surely it's too grand for . . ."

"Nothing is too grand for you, dearest." Mrs. Lawson gave her daughter's hands a caring squeeze, then turned back to the business at hand to address Madame Claremont. "Can you manage a wedding dress, along with the travel clothes and day dresses we had planned?"

"Of course, Mrs. Lawson! I have the very latest designs for you to choose from, and we can deliver everything she needs as promptly as she requires!" Madame Claremont said, openly excited at the order. "I'll leave Miss Beckett with you for a few minutes while I gather some bridal samples for you to view."

She left and Eleanor did her best not to openly sigh in relief. "Shall we see the peach organza next to your skin, Miss Lawson? If you stand there, I can hold it up and you can see yourself in the mirror and better imagine how it will look."

Claudia stood eagerly, and then colored nicely when Eleanor draped the fabric over her shoulder and lightly around her waist.

"See? The color suits your skin and makes your hair look even more golden," Eleanor said. "You are so lucky to have such beautiful blond hair, Miss Lawson."

"Hair like an angel, her father says!" Mrs. Lawson sighed from her perch on the sofa. "His gilded girl. . . ."

"I like your hair better," Claudia countered, eyeing the strands of Eleanor's bright copper hair that had escaped to frame her face.

Eleanor blushed furiously, tugging on the lace caplet to hide her unruly curls. She disliked her garish red hair and had grown up with all the jokes about being a ginger top or a firecracker. "You couldn't." She smiled and tried to deflect her customer's attention with humor. "Not if you were the one to try to brush it into submission!"

Standing next to Claudia, their reflections couldn't have shown two more different young women. Where Claudia was petite, Eleanor was a good deal taller. Claudia was like a peach confection, with her pale blue eyes and blond curls. But Eleanor felt like a wraith behind her, wearing her dark plain work dress with jet buttons and black trim. Her figure was balanced and firm, but not voluptuous to lend itself easily to the desired hourglass effect of fashions. She was envious of Miss Lawson's petite beauty and respectable coloring. Eleanor was naturally pale, her face angular and lean with what her mother had once called "wild green" eyes. *She said I was a changeling from some forest fairy who thought it a grand jest to leave a red-haired child on their doorstep. And it somehow made me mind my hair less and daydream about doing magic to escape the nursery and acquire more sweets.*

Eleanor lifted the organza and then added some of the satin for effect, determined to steer the conversation toward firmer ground. "You must tell me about your fiancé, Miss Lawson."

"He's a barrister and Father says he's the fiercest debater in all of Britain."

"Mr. Lawson said he'd never seen a man bellow a court into submission like our dear Mr. Tupman! But you should see him around Claudia!" Mrs. Lawson began to thumb through the fashion plates, sorting through her choices. "He's as mild as a cucumber sandwich."

Claudia blushed on cue, then shyly looked up through her lashes. "When he called on me, I told him I was far too quiet to interest him . . . but he said he likes the quiet for a change."

Mrs. Lawson was beaming and stood up to come forward to squeeze her daughter's arm. "He *adores* you!" She looked at Eleanor. "He truly does! I thought it a ridiculous notion at first, he was such a growling thing and far too rough for my sweet girl. But the man is putty in her hands, and I've never seen a more dramatic change. I swear he starts to stutter every time she pouts."

"I do not pout!" Claudia protested softly, her bottom lip betraying her argument as it jutted out in a pink bow. "And Samuel is always well spoken."

Mrs. Lawson awarded Eleanor with a conspiratorial wink but held her peace.

Eleanor stepped back to let them admire the drape of the satin. "He sounds delightful, Miss Lawson, and how lucky he is to have you. See? You'll be the envy of every woman in England!"

A lump formed in her throat at the tender scene. What woman didn't wish for it? To be the choice of a man with a good future ahead of him and to know yourself adored and cared for? She had always assumed that her own plans would include having her choice of a husband and one day standing on a dais and being fitted for her new trousseau. There'd been a huge dowry and every luxury in her life—including an education to prepare for the management of a home.

But it wasn't the loss of fortunes and luxuries that stung now.

She missed her parents. She grieved their deaths and the death of her dreams. She would never stand with her mother at her back and see herself in a wedding dress or sit with her father and read aloud his favorite books.

Gone, all of it. Like a dream. So strange and stupid to imagine myself before—content and sure that nothing would change unless I wished it to.

"Miss Beckett? Are you unwell?" Mrs. Lawson's well-meaning question abruptly brought her back to the present.

"I'm fine, I just—"

Madame Claremont cut her off as she swept in from the doorway. "She is just overly warm from sitting so close to the stove. Refresh yourself, Miss Beckett, and I will finish attending the Lawsons and gather the details of their order."

The dismissal was too curt and firm to argue against in front of customers, and Eleanor was forced to retreat from the dressing room while Madame Claremont skillfully distracted the ladies with a flourish of ribbons and feather samples.

Too warm, indeed! I can't feel my fingers, you cruel bird!

Bridgette passed her in the narrow hallway with the promised tea tray and gave her a smug look. "The red velvet gown is waiting for you on your worktable, miss. But madame said to be sure to tell you to check first with the others to see if they needed a hand with their appointments. She said you had all the time you needed for the day's work ahead, so you could spare a hand with ours."

"Did she?" Eleanor bit off the sarcastic question, aware that antagonizing Bridgette would gain her nothing.

"She did. But then, I wouldn't worry if I were you."

"Why ever not?" Eleanor hesitated, dreading the girl's answer.

"Because"—Bridgette's smile was slow and frightening— "red becomes you." And with that, she continued on her way with a wicked saunter.

*   *   *

"Any more candles and you'll start a house fire, sir."

The houseman's acerbic comment lacked bite as he gingerly added another candelabra to the table at his employer's bidding. It audibly anchored onto the table with a wet *squish*, sinking into a quarter of an inch of melted wax as it joined dozens of other candlesticks and platforms all covered in candles of every height and width, all demonstrating proof of Josiah Hastings's eccentric demands for more and more light.

Josiah smiled. He'd hired the old man and his wife after returning to England, his wariness of servants and being seen as taking on airs yielding to their stubborn and incessant kindness. "I have a bucket of water and ash at the ready, Mr. Escher, and every confidence that you'd be at my elbow before I could sound an alarm."

"Right you are, sir." The affirmation rang with gruff pride as Mr. Escher left to return to his living quarters on the third floor, two levels below them. Josiah's apartments encompassed the top two floors of the brick building that had once served as a furniture maker's small factory and home. He'd bought the building and converted it for his own purposes as an art studio for his painting on the uppermost floor and a home below. The first two floors were abandoned, a fact that drove his friend Michael Rutherford insane with worry. Michael retained a soldier's strategic view of the world, and Josiah often jibed that the poor man thought of the defensibility of a host's parlor long before he bothered to notice the carpets.

But Josiah had had no interest in walls of security that would shield him from the world and no fear of its inhabitants. Surviving imprisonment in India had stripped away his regard for what he now considered minor threats like burglars, cutthroats, and assassins. The group of Englishmen who'd escaped that prison together with rags on their backs and jewels in their pockets in a ridiculous twist of fate—none of them looked at their world the same way they once had.

Time changes a man. Well, time and a few months of eating mush and brackish water.

Even so, recent events had forced him to accept that the

time for complacency had vanished. Ashe's wife had nearly died from poison intended for her husband—a direct attack on the Jaded that Rowan had narrowly averted. As of now, their plan to flush out their unknown enemy was close to execution. They had delayed only for Rowan's wedding, but as it stood, all of the men were anxious to see things under way.

He turned his attention back to the canvas on the easel next to the table. In practiced movements that had the solemnity of ritual, he cinched his waist with an apron and tied his long hair back with a strip of leather from his pocket. The additional candles gave the blank space a compelling glow even with the afternoon sunlight pouring in through the room's large multipaned windows. The smell of linseed oil and paint beckoned, and he retrieved a paintbrush from the bowl. The heft and diameter of it was comforting to him.

Very well, Hastings. Hell, let's paint a stick-figure dog and call it a triumph, but by all means, let's paint something, shall we?

Josiah Hastings closed his eyes and waited as the natural gray and black that danced there had settled into a reasonable calm slate that gave his imagination reign. Each deep breath was an invitation to inspiration, and he tried to be patient as nothing more than watery shadows of stale landscapes marched through his mind's eye.

He sighed.

Come on. If ever a man needed a divine push . . .

But nothing came. He opened his eyes again, disgusted at the elusive chase. For weeks and months, he'd found nothing to stir his soul and provide the courage he needed to paint. Josiah ran a hand over his eyes. "Gray, gray, gray. How is it even possible that all a man can think of and perceive in the world is gray?"

"Would a change of scenery help, perhaps?" Rowan West answered unexpectedly from the doorway.

Josiah wheeled around, nearly knocking over his canvas's frame. "Are you gifting people with heart attacks this afternoon?"

"I apologize. I never blink when my friends stroll into my library, so my social graces have grown rusty." The good doctor began to shrug out of his coat. "We're turning into hooligans, Hastings."

Josiah had to smile since it was all too true. The members of the small circle known as the Jaded had a terrible habit of informality and access to each other's lives. Rowan's study was like a hub for meetings and conversations, and they thought nothing of arriving or calling unannounced whenever need dictated. None of them bothered with the restrictions of etiquette or class when those rules threatened their bonds. The men were like brothers, and as a result, easily forgot things like knocking before entering.

Rowan laid his coat over a chair by the door. "Is this the immoral den of a painter? It looks just like an ordinary workshop, Josiah. Or does your man hide the empty liquor bottles and escort naked women into cupboards when you have guests?"

"Very funny. If Escher had time to do that, I'd expect him to have time to let me know that I had a guest in the first place."

"Don't blame him. I caught him on the stairs, and since you've no bell below, I told him it wasn't worth the trouble." Rowan walked over to the table, then stopped at a respectable distance. "It's the middle of the day, Hastings. Is there a reason you've got three dozen candles blazing in a room with afternoon sunlight pouring through the windows?"

"I'm experimenting with light." Josiah sounded defensive, even to his own ears, but he disliked being surprised and was instantly wary. "Was there a reason for this call? Has something happened?"

Rowan shook his head. "No. As far as I know, we're all safe and sound. Ashe is drafting the notice for the *Times*, with Michael's help, and then we'll meet when it's finished to discuss how to best proceed."

The plan was simple enough. They were going to respond to the anonymous villain who was stalking them by publicly challenging him in the newspapers. The time was fast approaching when the Jaded would take their futures into their own hands instead of hiding from the shadows. The treasures they'd stolen from their Indian warlord's hold during their escape had done more than provide for safe passage home to England. The gems had given each man a solid fortune and the security to build a new life for himself.

What they hadn't anticipated was that anyone would notice or care enough about a few handfuls of stones to cause all this grief. . . .

"I'm painting, Dr. West. I don't mean to be rude, but I'm . . . busy." It was a ridiculous thing to say. He was a man standing in front of a blank canvas without a single thought of what he was doing, but Josiah wasn't going to confess it. He was far too stubborn to admit that his battles had less to do with muses and more to do with the gray that pooled behind his eyes.

Rowan pointedly ignored him. "Odd, isn't it? It's a divine act, this quest for spiritual inspiration and the conveyance of beauty. The subjects I've seen at the museum seem lofty enough. So why is it that painters are seen as scandalous more often than not?"

"You mean, if we are instruments of the Maker looking to capture truth and beauty on canvas, how is it our reputations are so wretched?"

"Exactly."

"I cannot say. Something to do with society's dismay at our proximity to naked women for endless hours." Josiah recrossed his arms. "Granted, it's acceptable to look at a painting and appreciate a womanly form for a few fleeting moments, so there's the irony. It has something to do with the limits of time."

Rowan laughed. "So if I look at a painting of a naked nymph cavorting about, I'm an art lover. But if you spend weeks creating that same painting, you're a pervert?"

"Precisely." Josiah deliberately held his ground, waiting again for Rowan to either reveal his true purpose or give up the game and leave. "Are you here to commission a portrait or just to harass a friend?"

"The latter. I can't stop a growing concern about you from crowding my thoughts and—"

"You're newly married, Rowan, and blissfully so, if even my stern Mrs. Escher has heard tales enough to make her sigh about the house. Your thoughts should be completely occupied by your new wife, unless I've misunderstood the institution."

Rowan was a man on a mission. "Even so, Josiah, I'm not oblivious. Something's wrong. You didn't come to the wedding."

"I sent flowers." Josiah briefly wondered if he should call for Escher to force Rowan's visit to come to a close. "Travel doesn't agree with me these days, and I had things to do in the city."

"Travel doesn't *agree* with you? Are you ninety? Josiah, you've not been yourself and it's hardly like you to—"

"Go back to your bride, Dr. West."

"I'll go when I'm ready, Hastings. When we returned to England, you were as cavalier as Ashe and as easygoing. But something has changed. You've become guarded and reclusive."

"I haven't been in the mood for company. It's not a crime."

"Josiah. I brought my bag. Let me have a look at you."

The world seemed to hold its breath with Josiah as he realized that his dear friend was not backing down. "No."

"Whenever we gather, you're . . . tired. You lay about and cover your eyes as if your head is troubling you, and I would think you'd overindulged in some bacchanalian artistic frenzy, except that isn't like you. And you're not hung over."

"Aren't I?"

"No. I'm a physician, Hastings. I can spot a drunkard from fifty paces off, and you—I think there are monks that have more vices. You aren't hung over, but you're pretending to be whenever the others are around. What in the world would make a man do such a thing and risk his reputation so callously?"

"I'm an artist, Rowan. We just established that my reputation is already forfeit."

"Even now, you won't look me in the eye. So, let's have it. Are you ill?"

"It's none of your concern."

"It is very much my concern. You are not some distant acquaintance I'm going to abandon, and with so much at stake, we can't afford to ignore any critical detail as events unfold. So, is this really some sort of artistic malaise?"

"And if I say yes? Will you leave the subject and tell Michael to stop hovering?"

Rowan shook his head slowly. "Only if you let me take a look at you."

Damn it. Josiah felt cornered, like a child caught in a lie. Pride was not something he wanted to relinquish. It was his last defense and the only shield he had against the inevitable. "If you examine me, then you are my physician, Dr. West. Friendships aside, you'd be bound to hold my confidences to yourself, would you not?"

"I would."

"I have your word as a gentleman?"

"I just gave you my word as a physician, Josiah, but if you need a formal oath—"

"No, that was rude of me." Josiah walked to the windows and crossed his arms, composing his thoughts before he got into some ridiculous ramble. He'd imagined telling Rowan or even Michael, but in his daydreams, it had been some sort of brave exchange exemplified by its brevity in which he'd been in complete control and then merrily gone on with his day.

The reality, with Rowan in the room, was proving a bit more daunting. He turned back to slowly face his friend, the glare of the candles dancing like fireflies between them. "It's nothing. I'm not dying, Rowan. You have *my* word. Would that suffice?"

"No."

Hell, there's no diverting him! I've practically conceded

that there's something, so now he's like a terrier with a rat.
He'll shake it out of me if he has to. . . .

"I don't need an examination, Dr. West. It's nothing."

"All right, let's hear of this nothing, then, or let's have your shirt off and begin."

"I'm going blind."

"Hellfire!" Rowan exclaimed, the curse soft but heartfelt. "Are you certain?"

Josiah nodded curtly. "Ever since we returned to England, it's been getting steadily worse."

"How bad is it now?"

Josiah shrugged. "It's just good old London fog in my peripheral vision and a gray wash over the world. Like I'm looking out a dirty window, but I can still make out a room and faces and navigate the streets. Sometimes the fog solidifies into black spots in my vision that float about. I'm told that they'll only increase in size until it's all fog and darkness."

"My God!" It was almost a whisper, but Rowan took a seat as if all the air in the room had vanished. "And to think I was dreading diagnosing you with consumption. . . ."

Josiah smiled. "Poor man! Well, I'm glad to have spared you the agony."

"You're making awfully light of this, Hastings!"

"Appearances are deceiving, Rowan. It's a matter of time before the darkness wins and whatever life or achievements I thought to have will be lost. We escaped the pitch-black of that dungeon, but I somehow carried it with me, can you imagine? Embracing freedom only to realize that there are all kinds of prisons in the world? I'm not bemoaning it anymore. I control what I can, Rowan. The only difficulty is not knowing exactly how much time I have left." He shifted back to his canvas, hating the awkward weight of the air in the room while Rowan assimilated the news. "I manage well enough and I don't need you sighing over the tragedy of it."

"You've been examined by a professional? You're absolutely certain?"

"You're sighing, Rowan. Yes and yes. And, no, there is no cure or treatment and, no, to answer your next solemn inquiry, I am not going to waste time and energy seeking one." Josiah busied himself by rearranging the familiar objects on his worktable, unwilling to watch his friend's reaction. "If this is your best bedside manner, Dr. West, you've room for improvement."

"The mismatched buttons . . . I should have guessed it."

"Damn it! Why is everyone so determined to pick on a man for the state of his coat?"

"Hire a valet, if it bothers you."

"No! I don't need anyone else in the house! It's hard enough to concentrate as it is, and I'm not an invalid that I need someone else to tie my cravat or pull up my pants!"

Rowan smiled. "So the humble life of a disowned artist suits you. . . ."

Josiah began to smile, too, the tension easing as the humor of Rowan's line of conversation and his self-imposed poverty became clear. "I suppose so. Here I am, with fortunes to spare, and I'd rather see to my own buttons."

"At least you can afford as many candles as you'd like."

"There! You see! There's the silver lining!" Josiah waved off the bittersweet bite of self-pity that threatened to slip into his thoughts. "Now, leave me to my painting, Dr. West, and see that you latch the door on your way out. An artist requires privacy while he works."

"Josiah. There's not a man among us that isn't going to want to be supportive or offer a hand if you—"

"No, thank you. I don't doubt their friendship or their character. I don't have any questions about their loyalty, Dr. West. It's pride. I'm too proud and it's a sin, but I want to stand as an equal in the eyes of the Jaded for as long as I can. I don't want pity. I just want to be myself and paint and enjoy what's left me. I walk about London each afternoon and I am my own man, Rowan."

"It wasn't pity."

"No, but you'd coddle me all the same, if I allowed it."

"I wouldn't presume." Rowan stood to gather up his bag

and coat. "I'll keep your secret as long as I can, Josiah. But if it comes to the safety of the Jaded . . ." *Or your safety.* It was unspoken but understood between them.

"I'd have expected no less, Rowan. Thank you."

And then, true to his word, he left Josiah to his paints and candles without a word of pity.

Chapter
2

Eleanor slipped the tip of her finger into her mouth, drawing off the pain from what might have been the hundredth pinprick it had suffered in a single day. Exhaustion wasn't a helpful ingredient when it came to fine handwork.

"You'd best take a break, miss," Maggie whispered, tucking a warm roll into her friend's pocket. "You've not eaten and don't say you have. And pulling out them stitches is like to have me in tears, so be kind and just go stretch your legs to—"

Madame Claremont interrupted them. "The storeroom needs straightening, Miss Beckett."

Eleanor stood up from the worktable. "Yes, madame."

"I can lend a hand to make quick work of it," Maggie offered quickly, also starting to rise from the sewing table.

"No. You'll have that lace finished, Maggie. Miss Beckett will manage nicely alone, won't you dear?"

"Yes, of course." Eleanor headed for the storage room at the very back of the shop, glad for the bread in her pocket and any task ahead that didn't involve embroidery.

Since yesterday's fiasco, her spirit was still bruised and battered. Despite the lucrative appointment with the Lawsons, Madame Claremont's mood had never improved, and by the time the infamous red velvet dress had been laid out for Mrs. Carlisle's inspection, Eleanor's worst fears had manifested. A day on her feet racing to work on the dress in between other tasks had gone unrewarded. The gown had failed to capture Mrs. Carlisle's fancy and Madame Claremont had blamed Eleanor's rushed stitch work for it. So instead of getting paid like all the others, she'd received a scathing lecture at the end of the day and had an evening gown deducted from her wages as punishment.

I should be comforted to think if I starve to death I'll have the wardrobe of a queen at the rate I'm going.

The storeroom was quiet, and Eleanor found a box of tangled ribbons to sort to give her an excuse to sit down and eat the roll. Her situation had gone from bad to worse, and Eleanor marveled that a person could apparently work herself into such staggering debt. Between her room and board and all the "penalties" she'd incurred, she was a breath away from having nothing. As it was, all she had to show for her efforts was a tin box with her last few shillings and a strand of pearls her mother had given her on her eighteenth birthday.

Horror stories of the fate of a woman unprotected on the streets haunted her every heartbeat, and the specters of the workhouses or even debtor's prison added to her fears. She turned her hands over for a moment to study the pads of her fingers, still bruised and sore from her labors. *My hands are starting to show the worst of it. Odd to remember how my mother used to fuss about what a lady's hands reveal about her. All those creams and ointments to keep hers as white and soft as possible . . . I wonder what she'd say of mine if she were here.*

"Miss Beckett?" a male voice inquired, and Eleanor jumped up from her stool in shock. "I hope I don't interrupt and didn't mean to intrude. Perhaps you remember me? I was in last week with my sister, Mrs. Sherbrook." He was as unfamiliar to her as the man in the moon, but she wasn't sure how to reply. His expression was keen as if he absolutely expected her to recall him with enthusiasm.

"Mrs. Sherbrook? I don't think I waited on her. Perhaps it was another—"

"I was here to escort my sister, but I confess, it was you who caught my rapt attention. You were with another customer dawdling over fabrics, but I could have sworn you noticed my glances."

Eleanor's confusion was complete. "I beg your pardon? Is Mrs. Sherbrook here for another appointment?" She couldn't imagine what had brought him back to the cluttered storeroom or why any man would begin a conversation with a complete stranger with such odd declarations. She shoved the bread in her pocket and tried to recover her wits. "Was there . . . something you needed?"

"Yes, quite urgently."

"Why don't you wait in the front room, and I'll be with you shortly."

"I much prefer a chance to speak with you privately, Miss Beckett." He closed the storeroom door firmly behind him, turning the latchkey with an ominous *click*. "Or may I call you Eleanor?"

"I don't . . . think that it would be proper, sir. I don't . . ."

"Don't be coy, though I swear it suits you to play the shy little girl. From the first moment I saw you, I saw a woman who deserves only the finest things that life can offer—not living the life of a glorified servant."

Her mouth popped open in stunned surprise. He was speaking like a villain out of a penny novel and she wasn't sure whether to laugh or cry.

"I am Edmond Perring. Thanks to a large interest in a cartage company, I am a very wealthy man. And you are just the sort of woman that I can benefit! I think you'll find me very generous, Miss Beckett, and a very attentive patron."

Shock gave way to anger. "I do not need a *patron*, Mr. Perring, nor am I the sort of woman to seek one! You have overstepped! Kindly cease this unseemly conversation and leave this room immediately and I will say nothing of the incident."

He smiled, a slow, satisfied look that chilled her to the bones. "Your spirit does you credit, Miss Beckett. A little show of temper gives a man a glimpse of the passion you are capable of—and makes me look forward with greater anticipation to experiencing more of you."

She shook her head. "Do not mistake this for a demonstration intended to arouse your interest! I want nothing of you!" He took a step closer and fear intermingled with rage. "Leave, or I'll scream!"

Edmond put his hands up, palms out as if to demonstrate how harmless he was. "I apologize. A beautiful woman, like yourself, has every right to set her own price. Name your heart's desire, Miss Beckett, and you shall have it. Your own carriage? Jewelry and fine clothing? Or does the lady think to ask for a house of her own?"

"I desire you to leave. I am not a thing to negotiate for and—"

"Oh, there will be no negotiation! I shall give you whatever you ask for, without quibbling. But I will not leave empty-handed, Miss Beckett. May I call you Eleanor?"

"No! And you'll leave with a scratched face if you insist on it!"

"I prefer a willing minx, but if you would rather come scratching and clawing, who am I to deny you your traditional virginal protest?"

It was a nightmare. Eleanor became far more aware of how close he was, how there would be no getting past him if she wished to reach the sanctuary of the showroom, and worst of all, how all the fabric bolts and piles of boxes muffled all the sound in the tight space to null out any screams for help. It was almost a perfect trap.

Except for the delivery door that opened out into the alley.

She bolted for the door behind her, screaming in horror when he was almost as fast to reach her, his breath hot on the back of her neck and his arms strong, encircling and bruising her ribs, as he tried to pull her back.

"Come, miss! Let's have it easy!"

He tried to cover her mouth, but she twisted her face to avoid his hand. At the same time, Eleanor drove an elbow back with as much force as she could muster, pushing against the doorframe for leverage, and was instantly rewarded with Mr. Perring's grunt of pain as he loosened his hold on her.

She fumbled with the bolt lock, blinded by unshed tears, but was rewarded at last. When it gave way, she wanted to crow in victory at the sight of a slice of gray sky and narrow alley, the cool air on her cheeks promising sanctuary. It never occurred to her that the alley didn't signify freedom or an end to his assault.

At least, until he was at her back, and this time pushing her down the steps and propelling her down the alley toward the street and his waiting carriage.

"You wouldn't want to make a scene on the street, would you?" he growled in her ear. "You're a good girl, Miss Beckett. So let's not have any more trouble, agreed?"

For a single footstep, she quieted, her brain marveling that this monster knew her so well, knew she hated to draw attention to herself, and knew she wanted nothing in the world more than to be a good girl.

But that step was followed by another and her outrage returned in full force.

"No! No! No!" Eleanor kicked out and then relaxed her legs, becoming an impossible ungainly weight for him to maneuver. Mr. Perring growled in frustration but fought back, pinning her arms against her sides and gathering the leverage he needed to carry her down the alley.

She began to scream, wordless and mindless, like a terrified animal, and the sound of it frightened her more than anything else. Because Miss Eleanor Beckett, formerly of the Orchard Street Becketts, was not the kind of woman who faced rapists or lost her mind with panic.

And she was losing this fight.

* * *

The day was bitterly cold, but Josiah ignored it and tried to savor the energy of the market streets. Since he'd revealed his secret to Rowan, he'd been more restless than usual and anxious—as if speaking of a thing aloud made it more real. *Hell, I'm not any more blind today than I was yesterday! And there's still not a single smudge on that damn canvas. . . .*

But there was the fear.

The thought of childishly smearing paint on a canvas and playing "artist" made him shudder. Pride made him long to see one last creation of his own hands come together—but not just any creation. It would have to be the best painting he'd ever done. The culmination of years and one last painting to defy the gods and give him a final assurance that he hadn't wasted his life in the pursuit of beauty.

He'd sacrificed so much to have the chance to hone his talents and find his own path. He'd rebelliously refused to study the masters abroad, stubbornly sure that an Englishman could learn to paint just as well anywhere he wished—even if that meant staying in Devonshire.

Not that the decision wasn't motivated at the time by my empty purse and a—

A scream captured his attention, and he wheeled in the direction of the sound. A young woman was kicking out so violently there was a flash of white from her petticoats that even he couldn't miss in his fog. A man was gripping her from behind and now, with one arm around her rib cage and the other covering her mouth, he was struggling to haul her from the alley.

Clearly, the lady had other places she would rather go.

He didn't hesitate. The assessment was lightning fast.

Woman in trouble. Stop the bastard.

He ran forward, rage building in him with each step. *How dare you treat someone like that! She isn't cattle and I'm not the man to turn a blind eye to whatever shit you're trying to pull!*

"This is none of your concer—" The man started to try to ward him off with an explanation, but Josiah didn't allow him to finish. Josiah's fist connected in a quick, firm strike, relying on the sound of the man's voice and a moment of visual clarity to guarantee that he hit his target.

Josiah stepped back, instinctively angling himself in a boxer's stance to make it harder for his opponent to attack him in return. Rutherford's training kicked in seamlessly, and he kept his fist out of the man's line of sight to give him the element of surprise if he needed to hit him again. "Unhand her."

But the poor man already had, pain and shock working magic as he relinquished the woman so that he could cradle his face in his hands. "You bathard! You bwoke my nobe!"

"Did I?" Josiah smiled as if they'd just exchanged pleasantries. "I'm sorry. I thought you'd prefer a broken nose over a shattered kneecap. It would have been my first choice to incapacitate you, but I didn't want to risk muddying the lady's skirts."

"You are inthane! Do you know herh?"

"No. Do you?" Josiah's humor was bleeding away. One look at the pale and terrified face of his victim and the urge to punch the man again was almost overwhelming. "Go, sir, and mind that the next woman you touch gives you permission to do so."

"Bathard!" The man spit out one last curse but gathered himself to stumble as quickly as he could to his waiting carriage. The nearness of it made Josiah's heart race as he noted just how close the lady had come to disappearing into her attacker's clutches.

"You . . . struck him." It was less of an accusation than a statement, and he turned back to her—and London fell away.

Because there was no gray. In a world of fog and fleeting shadows that haunted his vision, she was color. A living, breathing pillar of all that his senses had longed for—a muse of beauty that defied science and logic. Her hair was copper bright, with thick, luxurious corkscrew curls. She blinked back tears, and he knew he'd found the inspiration that had eluded him. She was a flash of fire and color that had him hypnotized. Large eyes a shade of green that defied description made his knees feel weak.

"I did. I thought it prudent to strike first and apologize later if necessary." Josiah did his best to keep his voice level, aware that the lady might bolt like a frightened sprite at any sudden movement or noise. She was vibrating in a delayed reaction to the trauma of nearly being kidnapped, and the last thing he wanted was to add to her difficulties. "Was he an acquaintance?"

She shook her head, staring at him like an apparition, then managed, "His sister . . . a customer, he said. But I never . . . saw him in the shop. I never . . . met him."

"It's no matter." He looked at her and marveled that such a creature existed in London in the bleakest heart of winter, and he'd had the luck to finally see beauty again. "You're safe now."

She nodded, then shook her head. "I don't—I have to return. Madame Claremont—oh my!"

"Come let me escort you back." He held out his arm, and she took it as carefully as if he were made of glass. As he walked, he counted his steps and doorways so that he'd be able to find this place again if he needed to. It was a new habit, this counting, but he'd learned the hard way that he couldn't always look for landmarks to find his way. In this instance, the trick wasn't necessary. They didn't go very far, and he realized that she'd come from the back door of the dress shop on the corner.

Her hair had started to fall in a tangled mass down her back, and as they stopped at the bottom of the stairs leading up to the delivery door, she reached her hand up to try to restore her chignon.

"Are you all right?" he asked softly.

"I am . . . fine. Thank you."

"Please allow me to—"

"I must return to the shop. I have so much work to do. I'm sure Madame Claremont will wonder what has happened and . . ." She took an unsteady step back but waved off his offered hand. "I'm sure she'll be shocked to hear . . ."

Without another glance at him, she walked woodenly up the steps and went inside, no doubt composing how best to break the news to Madame Claremont that one of her customer's brothers was a notorious villain and should be banned from the shop.

Damn. I didn't even get her name!

Josiah watched her go and shook his head. The man's carriage had been openly waiting in front of the shop, and he had no illusions about how the drama had been orchestrated.

Which means her day is about to go from bad to worse.

Chapter
3

Eleanor felt numb as she walked back into the shop, swallowing a strange hiccup at the surreal turns of her mind. *That handsome man broke Mr. Perring's nose and I forgot to ask his name. I should have thanked him or said something—but I . . . He was like a panther striking out of nowhere.*

She walked past the workrooms, starting to shiver.

"Eleanor?" Maggie asked from the sewing room door, and began trailing after her. "Are you all right?"

Eleanor ignored her, unable to stop her feet.

"Madame Claremont!" Eleanor rushed to her employer's side, clutching at the woman's arm. "You cannot imagine what has happ—"

Madame Claremont slapped her hands away in disgust. "What are you doing in the showroom in such disrepair? Where is Mr. Perring?"

Eleanor shook her head. "I . . . He . . . left."

"He left?" Madame Claremont asked, the alarm in her voice making Eleanor grateful for a fleeting instant before she realized that the woman had asked for Mr. Perring before the story had been told. And then Madame Claremont continued speaking, and all her illusions of an ally began to melt away. "If he left, it's because you offended him!"

"I offended *him*? Madame, he tried to—he meant to . . ." Eleanor choked on the words, tasting bile as the twist in the conversation sank in. *She knew. She's angry. And not at Mr. Perring, but at me!*

"Don't be stupid! He's a catch the others would have scratched your face to get their hands on, and when he said he fancied you, I knew even you would see the opportunity of it. Side work is the easiest work there is, girl, so don't you dare stand there with your eyes agog and pretend you don't know what I'm talking about!" The woman seized Eleanor's elbow, her fingers like talons. "Now, what happened?"

It was as if the walls were closing in. "He cornered me in the storeroom. He tried to drag me out of the alley and I . . . kicked and . . . he . . . he broke his nose . . . but . . ."

"Out!"

"W-what?" It was a nightmare that had no ending.

"Out with you!" Madame Claremont propelled her back down the hall toward the storeroom and the alley door. "Useless baggage! Too good to spread your legs, are you? Too good to take a simple poke and allow a gentleman to pay for the privilege? You think you can insult me when I provide you the means to a good living? Well, we'll see how high and mighty you are when your ass lands in the poor house, won't we?"

She didn't fight at all, shock and horror helping to speed along her unexpected exit from the shop. It all happened in a fog. Somewhere Maggie was crying and shoving Eleanor's wool wrap into her unfeeling hands while Madame Claremont's vulgar screeching went on, and all she could think about was how strange it was to be propelled not once but twice in one day out the same door.

* * *

He'd positioned himself to watch the front of the shop, allowing that if she didn't come out of either the front door or the alley in a few minutes, he would go in and rescue the lady. He was nervous, because he didn't completely trust his senses and he didn't want to miss his chance.

His wait was all too brief, and once again, it seemed he could have just used his ears and lucked onto the scene. There was a flurry in the alley, accented by an older woman's screech of dismissal and the slamming of a door, heralding the inevitable. He jogged back down the alley to find her sitting forlornly on the steps, clutching a wool wrap. He'd have thought her a sad little blackbird, if not for the blaze of her copper hair and the sheen in her emerald green eyes. In a world of gray pigeons, she looked to him like a bird of paradise. Here was a miracle too spectacular to ignore!

"I take it Madame Claremont wasn't shocked?" He knelt on the back of his heels at the bottom of the steps, wary of frightening her off.

She shook her head.

"She dismissed you?"

This time the ruby curls bobbed as she nodded. Finally she spoke. "I'm a fool."

"You aren't a fool."

Fire flashed behind the green, and his breath caught in his throat at the sight of it. She was so crystal clear to him, and he couldn't tell why; Josiah wasn't even sure he wanted to know why. He just didn't want to stop looking at her, and lose his chance to see color again.

"She dismissed me because I . . . offended her customer! She actually *expected* me to—" Her cheeks darkened in embarrassment, and she was clearly unwilling to even give voice to the unseemly proposition of Madame Claremont and her client. "There was no side work! The other girls knew, and probably . . . oh my! Margaret was about to warn me and I was so distracted. . . ."

Her composure was starting to give way, and Josiah sensed that any woman who possessed her courage was entitled to a grand case of hysterics. *She is probably overdue, so this might be tricky.*

"May I have your name?" She stiffened, so he immediately added, "I've broken a man's nose on your behalf and it seems strange not to at least know your name."

"I am Eleanor Beckett." A single tear escaped down her cheek, and Josiah's hands clenched into fists at the amazing beauty of it, but also to prevent himself from reaching for her inappropriately to wipe it away.

"Miss Beckett." He kept as still as he could, trying not to frighten her. "I am Josiah Hastings, and at your service." Josiah held out his handkerchief. "Here."

She shook her head. "I'm not going to cry, Mr. Hastings. I am not the kind of woman to dissolve into useless tears."

"I see." He tucked the embroidered square of linen back into his pocket and tried not to smile. "Does Madame Claremont owe you wages?" He was hoping that the focus on practical matters might anchor her for a few minutes more.

He could see the panic in her face, but she said nothing. So he tried repeating the question as gently as he could. "Does she owe you wages?"

She shook her head slowly, but the tears began to flow silently. "I had hoped yesterday . . . I worked so hard . . . but no. . . ."

"You're certain?"

The tears turn into a torrent. "I . . . had to buy . . . the red velvet. . . . Mrs. Carlisle . . . wouldn't . . . There wasn't time . . . to finish. . . . She deducted it . . . but I . . ." It was mostly incomprehensible in between the hiccups and sobs, but he was able to gather that the poor thing was falsely indebted to her employer. This time when he held out his handkerchief, she took it without hesitation. "I've left the red velvet inside. . . . Now I've nothing . . . to show for my . . . labors."

"Come, Miss Beckett. You must get out of the cold." He escorted her out to the street and raised his hand to bring a hackney carriage to the curb. He addressed the driver and held up a sovereign to make sure he had the man's attention.

"The lady will wait inside your carriage while I attend to some business within. Please see that she is safe in your keeping until I come back, yes?"

"Aye, captain! You can count on John!" The coin disappeared into his coat pocket and he winked to seal the contract. "I'm your man!"

Josiah offered her a hand up, but she hesitated, eyeing him with some suspicion.

"I cannot . . . afford to pay you back for a carriage, Mr. Hastings," she said.

He shook his head. "I don't need repayment. But I do need you to wait here while I see to this. A few minutes, Miss Beckett, and I'll return. Promise me that you'll wait here inside the carriage where it's warm."

She nodded slowly and accepted his help up into the carriage. "I'll wait, if only to continue a debate on the impossibility of accepting your charity, Mr. Hastings."

"I look forward to it." He touched his hat and shut the carriage door to make his way back up the walk and up into Madame Claremont's lovely establishment.

* * *

His hesitation at the door had nothing to do with his conviction about Miss Beckett's cause, but everything to do with an attempt to summon the bravado of days gone by. Rowan was right. He'd once been as cavalier and worldly as any man walking, mocking Galen's dark moods and accepting any dare that Ashe had tossed out. But those days were gone.

Come on, Hastings. You remember the game! We'll play the lord and give this wicked creature a taste of humble pie.

He straightened his spine and walked in as bold as brass.

"Ah! May I help you . . . sir?" A portly woman in black came forward briskly, her tone changing from solicitous to suspicious in a single breath.

Damn. I really do need a new coat if even this bird is being put off.

"Madame Claremont?"

"Yes."

"I've come to collect Miss Beckett's red velvet gown and, of course, any wages you owe her in good faith." He heard a squeak of surprise from one of the other shop girls and thought he saw a bit of movement at the back of the showroom, but he didn't dare look away from his opponent. "Now."

The woman snorted in disbelief. "*Miss Beckett's* red gown?"

"I gather you deducted the cost of it from her wages, so that would make it hers." He folded his arms, settling in for the argument. "If you cannot produce the gown, then I'll expect her wages in full. It's a simple matter of math, isn't it?"

"And—who are you to Miss Beckett?"

He didn't even blink, giving her his coldest look. "It should give you pause, madame, that Miss Beckett may not be alone in the world and may not now be without resources. I am a wealthy and eccentric man, and whatever my relation to Miss Beckett, I recommend you pray that it's not too sentimental an attachment or I may forgo giving you this opportunity to settle your accounts amicably with the young lady and, instead, contact my solicitor and the authorities."

"Wealthy?" The snort returned with a bit less force, but the woman held her ground. "What man of substance quibbles over a shop girl's meager wages?"

"One with a distaste for bullies and a determination to see that you recall the day before you try to press another young girl into your service. My name is Josiah Hastings." He lowered his voice, the calm far more menacing than if he'd bellowed. "Don't let the state of my coat fool you, Madame Claremont. Mind your manners and obey your betters, or I'll take pleasure in what will follow when I call in the watch."

The woman's mouth fell open before she could close it, a fish out of water. "M-Maggie! The red opera gown! Bring it!"

He relaxed his stance and even pretended to admire a few of the dresses she had on display. The dim shop made it all colorless and lifeless to him, but he was enjoying the awkward presence of Madame Claremont as she tried to decide how best to get him appeased and out of her shop before another customer arrived.

"It's quite an expensive gown, sir. She didn't make enough to pay for it and I had planned to withhold her wages for the rest of the month as well. Naturally, if you'll pay the balance, she can have the gown. I didn't mean to quarrel with you, but you can understand I cannot absorb the cost for a girl I have just let go."

He ignored her and turned one of the hats on its display stand. "I don't care."

"I don't know who you are or what she's told you, but the girl is quite spoiled and prone to lies."

"Is she?" He turned back to the woman. "A liar, you say?"

"Here is the dress, Madame Claremont." Maggie interrupted the exchange, handing the dress directly to Josiah and betraying that she was well aware of the subject at hand and her own position on the matter. "Is Eleanor all right? I also brought out her reticule. Miss Beckett left it in the drawer by the sewing machine and I know it's her favorite."

She held out the small beaded bag, but Madame Claremont moved quickly to make her claim, glaring at the young girl. "I should see that she didn't help herself to anything else!"

"Is Miss Beckett also a thief, then?" He grabbed the reticule from the greedy woman's grasp. "You are a piece of work, woman. If so much as a farthing is missing from Miss Beckett's purse, I'll call the authorities and have you touted as the soulless flesh-peddler you aspire to be!"

"You have no—"

"Here, miss." Josiah pulled out his wallet from inside his waistcoat pocket, unfolding several pound notes without even trying to look at their amounts. "A gift for your trouble and your kindness to Miss Beckett."

Maggie took the money in astonishment. "Thank you, sir!"

As an afterthought, he also gave the girl his card, and then turned back to the modiste. "That same threat about calling the authorities applies to this young lady as well. There wasn't a penny of that intended for you, Madame Claremont, and if you punish her for the gift, I warrant she's smart enough to let me know. Aren't you, Maggie?"

Maggie bobbed a curtsy and tucked his card safely away. "Yes, Mr. Hastings," she said, and then vanished into the back of the shop.

Madame Claremont abandoned all affectation and put her fists on her hips, her accent suddenly as coarse as burlap. "You cannot just walk into my shop and . . . toss about threats and throw money at my . . . Whatever Miss Beckett told you is a lie and slander! It's her word up against mine, and I'll see to it that they hear how she invited that man's attentions and was eager for it. I'll say that's why I threw her out and who's to say otherwise?"

Josiah's breath caught in his throat, the weight of his anger and indignation making it hard to focus. For a few seconds, it had been like a game, swaggering in and getting the dress, even giving the other shop girl a chance to run. But this—he'd never wanted to hit a woman in his entire life—until that moment. "Your word will be worth nothing by the time I'm through. Your reputation will be forfeit, madame, and I wonder how many respectable ladies will cross your doorstep if they know how you encourage your girls to sell themselves for your benefit? I'm not sure"—he looked at her with contempt, before continuing—"but I don't think they'll want their day dresses pawed over by whores."

She gasped, her color draining quickly, and even in the shop's poor light, he could see the change. "You're a devil! Take her and good riddance! That little baggage thinks she's too good for it, does she? Well, I had no idea that Mr. Perring meant her any harm! He comes from a very good family, and any other girl would have been flattered. Hell, I was doing that chit a favor!"

And there it is. Spoken like a true pimp. God, what world is this and how do any of us survive it?

He turned to go, but the woman screeched out one last protest. "You're no better than the others! You're no saint! You've *saved* her for your own wicked pleasure, no doubt! And when you've ruined that strawberry and set her out in the cold, I hope you remember that I saw you for what you are! You're the Devil!"

His stride never slowed, but the words stung a bit. It was true his motives weren't as altruistic as one might hope. But he wasn't going to ruin her, and he sure as hell wasn't going to let the cruel badger of a woman see him stumble on his way back to the carriage.

Chapter
4

You're the Devil! Eleanor shuddered as her ex-employer's words echoed into the street. Her rescuer gave every indication of being a gentleman even if there was something of the buccaneer in the way he carried himself. Tall and rakish, she still wasn't sure what to make of her remarkably handsome guardian angel. Mr. Hastings might be Satan himself, but at the moment, she felt lost and wasn't sure what a lady would say to uncover the truth. *He may be a terrible fiend, and what have I to do? Politely thank him and climb out of this carriage so that I can honorably freeze to death?*

Even so, the sight of him coming down the shop steps with that impossibly red velvet evening gown was an arresting experience. He was being so heroic on her behalf, but the sight of the loathed garment made her want to start crying all over again.

Oh, God.

He climbed inside the carriage, setting the rescued gown down onto the seat next to her with as much care as he could. "I didn't manage to extort any funds from the woman, but I did manage to get the gown she'd forced you to buy."

"Th-thank you. It's . . . hardly . . . I'm not sure what to say."

"Where do you reside, Miss Beckett? I ask, only because I have a sinking feeling that your employer may have helped you secure those lodgings?"

It shouldn't have surprised her, but it was a horrible truth she'd managed to forget in the chaos of the moment. *Oh, God. Everything I have left is in that rented room.* "Yes! How did you guess? Her sister owns a boarding house at the end of the street. It's the one with the green trim at the corner. But, surely you don't think . . . ?"

"You need the rest of your things, Miss Beckett." He tapped the roof of the carriage. "Just to the corner for now, John!" The hack pulled away from the sidewalk and Josiah sighed. "Let's pay your landlady a visit before Madame Claremont thinks to send a runner and make your day more difficult."

"Oh my! Would she take my things?"

"There's nothing she wouldn't do out of malice at this point. But don't worry. We'll collect everything and I can contend with your landlady. I would offer to go in alone, but I'd rather not be arrested for burglary."

Eleanor's heart was pounding at the speed of her life's unmaking, but there was nothing to do except move forward. Her rent had been deducted from her wages, but with the hateful tone of her departure from madame's employment, she wasn't sure if Mrs. Smith would accuse her of being in arrears or not.

At the bottom of the narrow stairs inside the foyer, she stopped, praying for strength. "Mr. Hastings. Men are not . . . allowed on the upper floors, and so you'll have to wait here. I won't be long."

"Of course. Take as long as you need."

His patience was like a balm to her rattled nerves, but even so, she was a bit astonished that he would go to such trouble for a stranger. "Thank you, Mr. Hastings."

She climbed the stairs to the second floor and unlocked her door, relieved to see everything as she'd left it. It was quick work to empty the wardrobe and pack the two other dresses she owned.

Besides that impossible red dress we left in the carriage!

Slippers and her nightgown, sundries, and an extra pair of stockings were added to the small trunk, along with gloves and her lace caps. On top, she placed the well-worn small volume of *Lady M's Guide to Etiquette* she'd received on her fourteenth birthday from her father, and closed the trunk. Then she retrieved her bonnet from the dressing table to try to make a better showing for Mr. Hastings, and pulled her little jewelry box out from under the bed.

She checked the contents and was vaguely comforted by the sight of her mother's best pearls. Eleanor calculated her savings one last time. It was a paltry amount, but Eleanor closed the box and tried to summon the resolve she needed to avoid crumbling into a useless pile of tears. *I shall find new employment in just a day or two, and with any luck, a better place to live. I'll sell the red dress to add to my reserves and never think of Madame Claremont again.*

Selling the pearls was out of the question. She'd starve before she relinquished her mother's favorite keepsake and the last echo it represented of the life she'd once had—and the love of her parents.

"Running out?" Mrs. Smith asked sharply from the doorway. "It's a workday, isn't it? Does my sister know you're here?"

Eleanor stood, tucking her jewelry box firmly under one arm. "I gave her my notice today."

"More likely she tossed you out!" the woman scoffed, her piggishly small brown eyes brightening with malice. "I told Emmaline you were going to be more trouble than you were worth, coming from money, like you did."

"Well, I won't be troubling you any longer then, Mrs. Smith. If you'll excuse me," she bit off as politely as she could, attempting to step around the woman blocking her path.

"You think you're better than all of us, don't you?"

Eleanor shook her head, readjusting her grip on her jewelry box. "I have never thought such a thing, but at this moment, Mrs. Smith, I'm not sure why you care what I might think. I just want to leave—"

"The others are all good girls who know what it is to do back-breaking work to survive! But my sister sees to it that there's a bit of light work on the side and it's an easier life for all. They entertain downstairs when it's called for, and Emmaline takes care that it's only quality company, no rough trade. The other girls have the way of it, and no complaints!"

The other girls! Poor Maggie! "An easier life for you, perhaps, as you line your pockets!"

"Mind your tongue! A woman does what she can in this world, and you're no different. If that's Perring down there waiting in my parlor, then you owe us a finder's fee, Miss Beckett! And you're not leaving this house without paying your fair share for your little slice of good fortune!"

"That is *not* Mr. Perring and I am most decidedly *not* paying you a penny. I am an honest woman!" She tried to brazen her way past the larger woman, but Mrs. Smith didn't even blink. "Now, kindly let me pass!"

"Found a benefactor of your own, did you? I knew you were a brazen thing under those tight little laces! Well, you're not cheating us! We've put a roof over your head and kept you well enough these last few months when not another shop would have bothered with those soft hands of yours without a day's experience. You owe us our slice!"

A wash of rage flowed through her at the injustice of it all. "I've earned my keep, and then some, Mrs. Smith! I owe you nothing and wouldn't offer a prayer for your soul if asked, so for the last time, kindly step aside!"

"Pardon me." Josiah's deep bass resonated behind the older woman and he stepped casually in the room to pick up Eleanor's trunk as if there were nothing but pleasantries being exchanged. "I'll just carry this down, Mrs. Smith."

"I'll—I'll need to examine it, sir!" Mrs. Smith protested. "This chit might be carting off my finest silver!"

He hesitated and gave the woman a smile that was all charm, but also all knowing. "Do you keep your finest silver in your boarders' rooms, Mrs. Smith? I ask only because that would make you the most benevolent and trusting landlady I have ever met."

"I . . ." Mrs. Smith had the grace left to look embarrassed, but tried to recover. "You'll have her keeping and it's not my place to say, but . . . I'm due rent for the week, sir."

Eleanor squeaked in protest at the blatant lie, but Mr. Hastings shook his head, unfazed. "You're due nothing, but I can send for a policeman if you'd like. I'm sure they would love to hear more about this *slice* that you are owed for the trade of the unwilling Miss Beckett to your sister's client. Your sister has already confirmed that she doesn't want anything to tarnish her reputation since whoring isn't considered *fashionable*, is it? But you're running a trade house here, if I heard you correctly, so by all means, let's wait for the authorities and see what you're owed."

Mrs. Smith shook her head, her face growing redder and redder. "You misunderstood! Take her things and go, please. I keep an honest house here! I want no whores under my roof!"

"Come, Miss Beckett. I'll see you out." Josiah stepped back, and Eleanor was quick to seize the opportunity to escape with her handsome rescuer once again at her back.

Once they were at the carriage, he handed her small trunk up to the driver and helped her back up inside, where he joined her with an easy grace. "Well . . . that was"—he smiled at her—"an adventure."

"It's tawdry and—unseemly! All of it!" Eleanor shuddered, horrified to realize that she was already crying. "I am not one for tears, but . . . I . . . never knew . . . people could be so . . . cruel. . . ." She took a deep breath to try to banish the tearful hiccups, wiping her face and nose as discreetly as she could. "I've ruined your handkerchief, sir."

"Keep it for now. I have others, somewhere." He smiled, and made a show of looking for another handkerchief in his pockets. "Ah!" He pulled one out with a flourish. "A gentleman is always prepared for catastrophes."

"There is something so sordid about—having one's finances and personal struggles on display. I'm usually"— she took another deep, steadying breath, squaring her shoulders and doing her best to hold her own—"extremely independent. It was hard work, Mr. Hastings, but I wasn't complaining. If only . . . I had no idea that Madame Claremont was the sort of woman to condone . . . illicit behavior. And Mrs. Smith!"

Josiah watched in fascination as she began to work it all out.

"It all seemed so proper! The house rules were so strict about male guests that even when the other girls had uncles or male cousins visiting, Mrs. Smith would show them to the downstairs parlor for . . ." Eleanor stopped herself with a shocked hiccup. "Oh my! I'm so . . . blind!"

The world *blind* was a quiet, painful blow to his stomach, but Josiah marveled that the sensation was muted in her presence. "I have nothing but admiration for you, Miss Beckett, and you have nothing to be embarrassed about. Poverty tests you, but it doesn't define you, and whatever sins your housemates committed, it has nothing to do with you."

"You hardly know me! But I'm flattered all the same." She felt a little stronger, knowing that her benefactor didn't doubt her virtue. "Why have you done all this?"

"It was the right thing to do, wasn't it?"

"Thank you." She took one unsteady, trembling breath. "But you cannot be obligated to do more on my behalf. You have no cause and I cannot ask it of you."

"Where is your family, Miss Beckett?"

He had the delightful image of a cat puffing up to look larger than it is to scare away a potential threat as she stiffened her spine and gave the impression of a woman with an army of relatives within shouting distance. "If you mean to take advantage of my situation, Mr. Hastings, you have underestimated my resolve. I may not have family, but I have every intention of making an honorable life for myself."

"Of course," he conceded. "We share the same goal. Although, I've had a few strange turns on my journey. But I admire your pride and zeal, Miss Beckett, and I assure you that—you are safe in my company."

You are safe in my company.

Eleanor was having trouble focusing her thoughts in his presence. The confines of the carriage made his masculine company a bit overwhelming. The blur of her dismissal and rescue, the race to collect her belongings had finally slowed, but now, there was a man named Josiah Hastings sitting across from her, discussing her problems and offering polite support as if it was a perfectly ordinary thing to do. Every orderly and disciplined fiber of her being was completely off balance by the distractions of the most beautiful man she'd ever seen gently holding her hatbox on his lap.

But he'd corrected himself midsentence, she was sure of it, and Eleanor had to wonder what it was he'd intended to say. She felt safe enough, but he was so handsome and sincere that it was difficult to get her bearings. "Perhaps if you know of an establishment that . . . offers vacancies to women. . . ."

"I'm not sure, but West would know. With your permission, we could call on a friend of mine and seek advice on where to land. He's a physician and I'd like some assurance that you're uninjured." He leaned out of the window to give the driver an address but she stopped him.

"I'm fine." She could feel the heat in her cheeks, touched by his concern but alarmed at how efficiently he was managing her.

"Your cheek is bruised, Miss Beckett."

"Is it?" She reached up to touch her face, finding no tender places or signs of injury.

He leaned forward slightly, squinting, and then abruptly moved back against the cushions. "My mistake. A trick of the light."

"Oh." She dropped her hand, wishing she knew why he looked suddenly wary and wounded. "Mr. Hastings, as kind as you've been, I can't just . . . go with you. We have not been formally introduced and you could be . . ."

"The Devil?" he supplied, then let out a long sigh. "What do you suggest, then?"

Eleanor looked out the window and realized it was snowing. It would take most of the money she had left to secure a respectable room. She could sell the red velvet gown for a few pounds at the rag trades, but nothing felt certain.

There was always her mother's necklace. . . .

"I am ruined already, aren't I?" she whispered, her face to the glass. "I've climbed into a carriage with a complete stranger. I've not a friend in the world, and after months of struggling to find honest work and prove that I could keep myself from . . ." She turned to look at him, her cheeks streaked with tears. "I never used to cry, Mr. Hastings. And now—I can't seem to stop."

It was a miserable admission, and she was so sweetly pathetic making it. It was pure instinct that dictated his next move. Decorum be damned, she was so terrified and so sad, he couldn't help himself. He shifted over, set her hatbox aside, and just gently gathered her hands into his. She sobbed against his shoulder, sagging against him as the storm of her emotions took over. He said nothing, unsure of how to comfort her beyond softly squeezing her hands and doing his best to keep his attentions as brotherly as possible.

"You aren't ruined," he told her, his own heart starting to ache in concert with hers. "Far from it, Miss Beckett."

She sniffled a bit, the tears finally slowing, and pushed away from him, her cheeks stained with embarrassment. He released her instantly, retreating back to his side of the carriage to allow her to regain her composure. She was such a prim thing, in her bedraggled bonnet, clutching her jewelry box like a drowning woman would clutch at a life preserver. "Ruined or not, crying won't help and I intend to stop."

He nodded and held out the spare handkerchief he'd found earlier in his coat pocket. "Here. Take it."

She took it from him, careful not to touch his fingers. "Thank you."

He waited until she'd dried her cheeks and seemed steadier. "I may be able to help, Miss Beckett, with the matter of finding honest work."

"Truly?"

Tread carefully, Hastings, or she'll bolt from this carriage and you'll never see her again.

"Truly." Josiah decided that there was nothing to do but plunge ahead and hope for the best. "As for introductions, let me see if I can do better. My father is a titled country baron, and I say this only to reassure you that I come from a good family and had a fair enough upbringing to appreciate how difficult it is to forfeit respectability. I am a third and last son and the youngest of my siblings; together we number seven."

"Oh my!" She sighed. "I always wanted a sister, but you have four!"

He shook his head. "Yes, but here is where honesty must be applied. Miss Beckett, my family no longer claims me. I haven't seen any of them for several years. I was tossed out of the house when I turned nineteen because I had announced an intention to pursue my painting as a profession."

"Painting?" Her brow furrowed at the unexpected revelation. "You are a . . . painter?"

"Much to the lament of my father, yes." He waited a moment as she took it in. "Are you shocked, Miss Beckett? I can promise you, it's hardly the wild and wanton life that most people imagine. It's . . ." He struggled for the right words, wanting more than anything to make the muse perched on the carriage seat across from him understand. "It is hard to describe without sounding like an overzealous child, but I paint because I love it—the challenge of it, the craft, and even the frustrations. They're a part of me, as other men are inspired by the sciences or commerce."

"You've been so generous to me, a stranger, and I'm still

amazed at it. But are you not poor, Mr. Hastings?" she asked shyly, and he surmised it was out of fear that she'd added to his burdens somehow with her own troubles.

"No. Unlike so many artists, I'm not starving in my quest for beauty." He smiled. "Not that this has softened my family's opinions."

"How terrible! Success or failure, can they not be more supportive?"

"When I had no interest in the clergy or the law, as far as my father was concerned, to be a painter is to be a professional layabout." Josiah shrugged. "I never was eloquent enough to explain to him what it meant to me to paint. It's as essential as breathing, and when I was young, I was sure that I was just a few paint strokes away from immortality—and, ultimately, redemption in my parents' eyes. Exile was a fleeting threat and a small price to pay."

She nodded, and he took it as an encouraging sign.

"But it doesn't matter how far I've traveled to prove myself or how my fortunes have improved. I no longer strive for anyone's approval, Miss Beckett. But I do still strive for immortality, as vain as that sounds. I have a project to complete, and for some time, I've not found a model that inspired me—until today."

"I-I am no model, sir!"

"It's honest work, Miss Beckett. I will pay you fifteen thousand pounds if you will sit for me. Just that—sit for me. Nothing more. I'll even hire a chaperone, if it suits you, to guarantee that nothing questionable or improper occurs while we work."

She gasped. "Fifteen thousand pounds! You cannot be serious!"

"I assure you, I'm very serious. It's a small fortune, Miss Beckett, and the only reason I set such a price is that a woman of your character probably wouldn't even consider such a wild proposition unless the amount was notable."

"Notable? It's a heart-stopping amount and one that makes me question your sanity!"

"You'd be out of harm's way, Miss Beckett. With that

kind of money, you wouldn't have to worry about the Madame Claremonts of the world. You could live comfortably and independently and do whatever you wished."

"Oh my!" She put her hand up to cover her heart, and the trembling blades of her fingertips arrested his attention for a second or two before she spoke. "You are serious."

"I want to paint you, Miss Beckett."

"Are hysterical women so appealing, Mr. Hastings?"

He smiled. "I'll keep my reasons to myself only because if I say anything about the appeal of your coloring or the shape of your eyes, you'll misinterpret my intentions and I'll not have you freezing to death on the streets for a misspoken compliment."

She smiled back at him, and Josiah felt the first small hint that he might win the day. "I'd always heard that artists were odd. You are proving it true, Mr. Hastings."

"Should I provide character references, Miss Beckett?"

"Can you?" she asked, but there was a gentle teasing in her tone that made his blood warm.

"As many as you wish," he countered.

"I shall want several, but can I—have time to consider it?"

"As long as you need." He opened the window, leaned out, and gave the driver new instructions. "But it's getting dark, so let's get you someplace safe and warm so that you can regroup and think more clearly."

"I haven't enough money for a hotel, but perhaps—"

He cut her off. "It's unorthodox, but I have rooms to spare and a fierce housekeeper who—"

"Absolutely not."

"I beg your pardon?"

"I am not about to spend the night under a strange man's roof—even one who rescued me in a single afternoon from a lecherous man, a wicked dragon of an employer, and my horrible landlady. It wouldn't be proper."

"I see." Except he didn't really, but there was no chance he was going to set her down where he didn't have some connection to keep her safe.

West's is out. I can't impose on the newlyweds. Ashe is out. Caroline must still be recovering from her illness the way Blackwell's been behaving lately. Galen's alone in London with Haley at his estates in Stamford Cross, so that's no solution. Darius doesn't even have a house in Town, or I'd borrow it while he's in Scotland. Which leaves . . .

"Well, I know of a good inn called the Grove, and the woman who runs it is extremely kind; I know you'll be safe and the fare isn't bad." *Michael is going to give me a look and a lecture that would send a lesser man running, but I don't care. He can help me keep an eye on her until things are settled.*

"Very well." She smoothed out her skirts and rearranged her things. "If you think it suitable and reasonably priced, I will trust you to see to it, Mr. Hastings."

It wasn't the endorsement I was hoping for, but I'll take it, Miss Beckett. Every journey begins with a single step, and if my luck holds, you've just turned your toes in my direction.

Chapter
5

"Here! You've taken the apartment next to mine for a *woman*? What are you up to?" Michael Rutherford was not the kind of man that most people considered trifling with. Between his unusual height and serious demeanor, there were few men who had the courage to face him at all. But Josiah knew him as one of the Jaded and as their protector, and wasn't about to let himself be pushed around by Rutherford's growl. It was all a show when it came to his friends, and they both knew it.

"Miss Beckett needs a safe place to stay. I've arranged things so that I can discreetly pay for the apartment, and if pressed, Mrs. Clay has promised to quote a ridiculously low amount to the lady."

"Why would you go to all this trouble?"

"To protect Miss Beckett's pride, of course! This way her sensibilities aren't offended, her purse is barely touched, and I'll have a bit of time to convince her to . . . help me."

"That's not what I meant and—wait! Help you with what? And can you explain to me why I'm involved?"

Josiah took a deep breath, chafing a bit at the cross-examination. "Stop looking at me as if I'd kidnapped the girl, Rutherford."

"Did you?" Michael growled out, crossing his arms.

"No!" Josiah scoffed. "My God, man! What kind of idiot do you take me for?"

"Who is she?"

"I just met her." He held up a hand before Michael could fire off another question. "I didn't know her up until an hour ago, and I'd appreciate it if you'd give me the benefit of the doubt."

"How exactly did you meet her? Because as you well know, Mrs. Clay is not about to have some common—"

"There is *nothing* common about Miss Beckett, so mind your manners! She was in a bit of trouble, and I couldn't turn my back on her. *And* as it turns out, I'm indebted to the lady already or I will be if she'll agree to . . ."

"What is it that you want this Miss Beckett to do, Josiah, besides live next to me and make you sputter around like a fish out of water?"

Josiah rolled his eyes. "I want her to pose for me—and don't say it. I know there's a bit more going on right now than painting, but it's a priority for me, Rutherford. I can't explain it, but I don't care if the world is on fire. I need to paint and I need to paint *this girl.*"

"Is that all you want from her?"

"Don't be crass! The only reason I'm telling you all of this is that I wanted someone I trusted to be able to look after her. She won't hear of staying with me, so this was the best I could think of to keep her close."

Michael crossed the room to pour himself a drink. "I'm not guarding this girl. If she chooses to leave or chooses not to let you paint her, I'm not keeping her here against her will."

"Understood."

"Josiah, things could get very dangerous—for all of us—once the announcement is placed in the *Times.* Can't you wait a while to pursue your painting? There must a dozen women who could pose to—"

"No. I can't wait. And there aren't a dozen who would suit." He pressed his fingers against his eyes in frustration, and took a deep breath. "Rutherford." Josiah dropped his hand and tried to look his friend in the eyes. "I'm not asking you to babysit Miss Beckett. I just need you to be aware of her presence in this inn so that when you do see her, you'll keep watch to make sure she's safe. In other words, if you hear a scream in the middle of the night, you're not going to ignore it. Yes?"

"I wouldn't ignore it whether I knew the lady or not."

"No, but you'll move a little faster if I ask you to, won't you?"

"You never fail to surprise, Hastings. And so long as we understand that I'm not this young lady's bodyguard, then, yes, I'll strive to move a little faster if I suspect she's being murdered." Michael's humor was dry but impossible to ignore. "Or if some blighter is trying to take advantage . . ."

"You're a true friend." Josiah meant to clap him on the shoulder, but misjudged and ended up awkwardly patting Michael's elbow. "Well, I have to go. I don't want her to see me leave and think I've lingered for any unsavory reasons."

Michael followed him to the door. "I've missed something, haven't I? I've never seen you like this. Is there something else going on?"

Josiah shook his head, turning away because he wasn't sure if he could read Rutherford's expression correctly. "You're imagining things."

He left the inn quickly without looking back and never saw Michael Rutherford shake his head in dismay before shutting his door.

* * *

Eleanor circled the room again and then finally allowed herself to gingerly sit on the edge of a chair cushion embroidered with a rose pattern. It was all she could do to just be still and absorb the small wonders of a room that radiated cheerful comfort. After weeks of accepting peeling paint and lifeless, cold walls, this was nothing short of a miracle.

Chintz-covered chairs and thick wool rugs in muted colors bespoke of a home more than mere rented rooms. A smaller alcove held the four-poster bed with ruffled bed curtains and a plump feather mattress that promised the best sleep she'd had in ages. There was even an arrangement of dried summer blooms by her bedside to alleviate the press of winter. Linen doilies graced every chair, and glass curios sat atop the little table. And like something from a nostalgic dream of cozy warmth, there was a small sitting area by the fireplace where Mrs. Clay had told her as she stoked the fire that Eleanor was welcome to take her meals privately, if she wished.

"Not as fancy as some, Miss Beckett," the woman now announced, her hands folded in front of her as she surveyed her offering. "But I do pride myself on a tidy and well-tended establishment. The Grove sits on a quiet-enough street, and I confess, I love every creaking board of her."

The inn boasted country Tudor charm, and Eleanor had been entranced from the start, but the plump and matronly Mrs. Clay made the Grove a dream to her. Instead of suspicious questions about her lack of luggage or odd arrival in the middle of the afternoon, Eleanor had been swept upstairs in the warmest of welcomes. It made her curious what Mr. Hastings had said in making the arrangements—she wasn't sure of the details as he'd gone in ahead of her while she'd waited in the carriage. Mr. Hastings had indicated he wanted to make sure a suitable room was available before bringing her inside to protect her fragile sensibilities. While she'd have argued the point in different circumstances, her bruised spirit had allowed him to see to everything on her behalf this time. But now that she was inside the Grove, Eleanor wondered what she might have missed in the negotiations.

I was just hoping for a bed. But this! This is . . .

"This room is perfect for a lady and very quiet at this end of the floor," Mrs. Clay spoke, as if finishing Eleanor's thought. "There's just two apartments, and Mr. Rutherford is notoriously shy—don't let the man's size fool you! A

gentle giant, that bloke, and my favorite tenant, I must confess. When Tally accidentally dropped a can of fireplace
ashes in his room and the bucket just about exploded a
cloud of ruin over everything the man possessed, do you
know he didn't even fuss? Not one unkind word to my poor
Tally! We bashed his cushions for weeks, and I swear every
once in a while I still see little puffs of gray whenever I
walk over those carpets." Mrs. Clay sighed. "Bachelors are
usually such trouble, but I'm just letting you know that Mr.
Rutherford is no such man and my very own dear mystery,
so please don't pay him any mind."

Eleanor nodded, trying to follow the wonderful patter of
Mrs. Clay's speeches. "Yes, ma'am."

"Upstairs are my more temporary guest rooms, tourists
and the like mainly, but they'll use the west stairs off the
common room, and as you saw, the stairs at this end of the
inn are much better situated for you. And, of course, there's
the private parlor and receiving area there off the landing
for your use if you have callers."

"I'm not expecting any callers, Mrs. Clay."

"You can eat dinner there if you're shy of the common
room below. But I don't allow rough trade, so you're more
than welcome to come downstairs for your meals if you
wish the company of others. You'll be safe as a church
mouse among my guests, or I'll see to it and send them
packing!" Mrs. Clay stepped back, beginning her retreat to
allow Eleanor to settle in. "I'll send up dinner for you tonight, as moving always has a bit of a draining effect, don't
you think?"

"That would be so kind of you, Mrs. Clay."

"It's nothing really." Mrs. Clay started to put her hand
on the door latch, but then turned back. "You'll ring if you
need anything? Just give that bellpull a healthy yank. Tally
is always at the ready if you need more coal, and you
mustn't be shy about asking. I should tell you that Tally is
as deaf as a stone and just as mute. He's a sweet child of
twelve, and despite the bit about his hearing, I swear he's as
smart as a whippet. I found him on the streets starving and

filthy when he was the tiniest little mite you've ever seen, and I confess, I took him home for my very own boy! I've no children, but Tally is . . . well, you'll be kind when you meet him, I'm sure."

"Of course! He sounds very dear!" Eleanor stood, wanting to be polite and hoping that Mrs. Clay didn't think she was yet another stray to land on her doorstep. "I should pay—"

"Not until you're sure it'll suit! I couldn't take a penny before you'd decided it would suit!" Mrs. Clay waved her hand in cheerful farewell, and before the obvious argument against the illogical suggestion that anyone could manage to be uncomfortable in such a room, she'd gone through the door and was bustling down the stairs.

Eleanor leaned against the closed door, amazed. After the brusque treatment from her last landlady, Mrs. Clay was like a large, benevolent fairy godmother. No doubt, this Tally thanked his Maker nightly for his good fortune to land in such a woman's care. *I swear I don't remember my own mother being that solicitous. She's such a dear! But there is no possibility that I can afford these luxuries! The coal alone costs more than I have in my reticule.*

Eleanor reached up to touch her cheeks, not completely surprised to find them wet with tears.

I'm a practical woman and I do not cry!

But nothing she'd expected had happened today. Once again, her world had changed in the blink of an eye, and apparently, this time she had changed with it.

Her vow to never trust her care to another person ever again had evaporated the instant Josiah had struck Mr. Perring in the face. Her campaign for dignified independence had been sabotaged by Fate.

So how is it that I'm relatively unscathed?

Angels had intervened, even though she'd lost faith in their very existence when her parents had died. Or was it that the Devil had taken on the guise of a very handsome painter?

Had Mr. Hastings deliberately put her in a position where

she would be in his debt? It didn't seem likely. His every gesture had been extremely considerate and his insane offer of employment was still ringing in her ears.

Eleanor unpacked her things, drawing out the chore to give herself time to think and to try to make her dreamlike surroundings seem more real. The red dress was the last to go into the wardrobe, and she hung her coat over it to hide it just in case Mrs. Clay took a peek into her things and drew the wrong conclusions.

She closed the wardrobe doors and went back to the fireplace, feeling more like her old self with her things in order and her jewelry box on the table by the bed. "Home, sweet home."

The urge to cry had finally passed and she dried her eyes.

"Tomorrow, Eleanor Beckett," she told herself as she moved her feet closer to the warm grate. "Tomorrow, you will find less scandalous employment and be able to thank Mr. Hastings by paying him back for all of his generosity."

If not, I'm not sure what the future holds.

For then I may have to actually consider the remarkable promise of fifteen thousand pounds and decide if I should redraft my vows about not accepting any help to make an exception for insane artists with beautiful brown eyes.

Chapter
6

"Ah! There you are, Miss Beckett!" Mrs. Clay greeted her warmly as Eleanor tried to tap the worst of the snow from her boots before reentering the lodge. She had been out all day seeking employment and encountered only rejection and humiliation. She had no recent references, most glaringly none from her last employer. One agency had told her directly that she appeared to have no real skills when it came to domestic work and was too well mannered and too pretty for any woman to allow into her home. Unable to afford a carriage, Eleanor had walked the streets of London until the weather had finally turned her back toward the inn. She'd even begun to wonder if Mrs. Clay might let her work in her establishment to help pay for her room and board, or if a smaller room would suit.

She couldn't feel her toes and had to grip the wall to keep her balance. "Good day, Mrs. Clay. I shall do my best not to track in any water onto your floors."

"Don't mind that! Mr. Hastings has come calling for you

and is waiting in the upstairs parlor. There's a fire blazing there and it's nice and toasty."

"Mr. Hastings? Has he . . . been waiting long?" Eleanor wasn't sure what to say. Mrs. Clay seemed perfectly content to see her have gentleman callers, and instead of knowing looks, the woman was cheerfully gesturing for her to hurry.

"Awhile, I'd say," Mrs. Clay replied. "But I'm forbidden to say exactly how long as Mr. Hastings said you were sure to ask and he didn't want you to worry about it. Isn't he dear?"

"I don't know him very well, Mrs. Clay, but he seems very considerate." She glanced down at her cold, wet skirts and wondered if he were "dear" enough for her to keep him waiting until she'd changed. Eleanor sighed and decided to ignore her skirts. This wasn't a social call, after all, and no matter how disturbingly handsome he might be, she didn't actually possess the wardrobe to try to impress the man, so there was no point in trying. Nor was she willing to admit that she cared what the man thought about the state of her hem. "Thank you, Mrs. Clay."

"Shall I send up Tally to sit in the corner? As a sort of a chaperone, miss?" Mrs. Clay reached out to take her damp scarf and help with her coat. "He couldn't eavesdrop," she added with a smile, "but a good girl like yourself might be comforted to know he's there."

"Thank you, Mrs. Clay. If he truly wouldn't mind, I am so grateful for your thoughtfulness." Eleanor stepped up into the hall and headed up the narrow staircase.

The upstairs parlor was just off the stair landing and available for the monthly lodgers to use. It was a semiprivate space for conversation and even meals for anyone who preferred something more quiet than the bustling common dining room below.

As she reached the landing, she saw him standing in front of the fireplace, silhouetted by the orange glow. Broad shouldered and lean, she was struck by the long lines of him and the latent power there. His light brown hair was far too long and tied back in a loose queue with a strip of leather, but the old-world style suited him. It made him look more rugged and otherworldly, just as an artist should, she imagined.

She cleared her throat to alert the man to her presence. "Mr. Hastings," she said. "I've kept you waiting."

"You didn't know I was coming so how is that possible?" he countered with a smile. "It was only a few minutes."

Eleanor allowed the lie, flattered that he would go to such trouble. "I'm pleased to see you again, Mr. Hastings. If only to thank you once more for your kindness, but also to see if there is some way to rectify the arrangements."

"Is your apartment not comfortable enough? Mrs. Clay has a reputation for being accommodating, but if you're not happy here, I can look for something else."

"No, you misunderstand. It's very comfortable and far too luxurious for what I can afford."

"It costs you nothing. Surely that isn't too taxing for your purse?"

"Mr. Hastings, I cannot allow you to pay for my lodgings. It isn't proper."

His look was pure innocence, as if the concept was new. "Mrs. Clay is simply repaying me for a favor by offering you a room until you're on your feet."

"I do not like to feel cornered, Mr. Hastings."

All playful pretense fell away, and he squared his shoulders like a man facing sentence. "You aren't."

As if on cue, a small pixie of a boy appeared quietly on the stairs and came into the parlor to take a seat on a footstool by the fireplace with a shy smile. The small storm brewing between them lessened, and Josiah returned the boy's smile with one of his own. "I see our chaperone has arrived."

"Mrs. Clay suggested that she send her son along." Eleanor instantly recognized the humor of her diminutive guardian's presence but did her best to maintain what decorum she could. "I didn't think you'd mind."

"I don't. I don't mind it at all, Miss Beckett." He sighed and turned his attention back to her, and Eleanor had the odd fleeting notion that a woman needed a fire screen when standing this close to a man like Josiah Hastings. Even with cold, wet shoes and stockings, she had the urge to fan herself to keep a flush from her cheeks.

Eleanor took a deep breath to steady her nerves. "Let me be frank. I am at my wit's end, sir. My reserves are . . . if I described them as dwindling, it would be kind. I'm not ungrateful for what you've done, for what you're doing for me, but . . ."

"Say it, Miss Beckett."

"I need to know why. Is this some scheme to ensnare me? Have you an ulterior motive for your generosity?"

"I've kept nothing from you. I've never lied about my interests." Josiah sighed. "I only want to paint you, that desire is unchanged. But honestly, after getting to know you and seeing how determined you are to protect your reputation—I'm not sure if I've done you a disservice already. A thousand chaperones wouldn't protect you from the wicked imaginations and cruel tongues of people who will hear only that you modeled for me."

Eleanor couldn't hide her shock at his confession. "You're withdrawing your offer?"

"No." He shook his head. "I'm letting you know that I'm aware of the price you'll pay for agreeing. I'm letting you know that I'm not oblivious to the dilemma I've presented. But if anything, I'm renewing that offer, Miss Beckett. I am more determined than ever not to lose this chance. And as for the cost of your room and board . . ."

"Yes?" she asked.

"If you agree to sit for me, then if you wish, like your previous employer, I can deduct the cost of a room from your wages."

"And if I don't agree to sit for you?"

"I'll stubbornly insist on helping you. You can attribute it to a guilty conscience, since I'm the villain who lured you into a carriage and potentially compromised your reputation."

"You are hardly a villain! But I don't want to be in anyone's debt."

"Then don't be. You can simply repay me whenever it's possible. If you want, you can find something you like better and live wherever you wish. . . ."

There was a long pause as she nervously reached up to try to smooth down a cold, wet curl that had strayed onto her cheek. "I like it here."

"Then you should have your tea while it's still hot, and we can see about a satisfying dinner for us both."

"Dinner? I have never eaten dinner alone with a man, Mr. Hastings. I'm not sure if it's . . ."

"Proper?" he completed her sentence. "You have to eat, Miss Beckett. After all, we have a chaperone, so we're hardly alone. If you'd like, we can add to the party and see if Rutherford is home. Michael hates surprises, but I'm sure he won't mind this one."

"I fail to see how eating with two men I am unrelated to would improve things, Mr. Hastings." She shook her head slowly but started to smile at his obvious efforts to accommodate her sensibilities. "No, that was foolish of me. You've already saved my life and I can't keep insisting that it isn't proper to trust you."

He smiled. "Thank you." He rang the bell for the serving man, who answered the summons almost immediately. Josiah ordered for them both as if to give her time to gird herself for the next debate. Once they were alone, he leaned back in his chair. "May I ask you a personal question, Miss Beckett?"

"I suppose." She was wary, taking new measure of her handsome petitioner. His honesty was disarming, and she was struggling to come up with firm objections to a man who offered the solution to all her present difficulties.

"How did you come to work for Madame Claremont?"

"It's a long story and a bit complicated." Eleanor looked away embarrassed but then lifted her chin. "My father was quite successful in his business until things took a turn for the worst two years ago. He was a chemist and an inventor and came up with an array of new smelling salts that might be vaguely pleasing to the customer."

"Sounds like a clever idea. Not that I've ever been in the market for them, but I can see the appeal."

She gave him a skeptical look but continued calmly. "He'd invested everything in them, but his partner stole the formulas and patented them as his own to sell to a drug company all too happy with the potential profits. Keller's Gentle Smelling Salts have a display in almost every apothecary shop in England."

"Your father must have had some legal recourse."

She nodded. "He did, and the lawyers were also all too happy to take the last of my father's money in the pursuit of his case. He kept most of his troubles from us until near the end, borrowing money from disreputable creditors to shield us from any hardships. But then my mother died of influenza. It was too much for him. His heart failed and he followed her within the week."

"My God," he exclaimed softly. "When did all of this take place?"

"Last summer." She picked up her teacup, the illusion of her cool composure spoiled by her trembling hands. "The solicitors took everything to settle his debts, legal and domestic, and I was literally turned out. I have no relatives to speak of, and I refused to impose myself on family friends who had made their indifference clear by their silence when it was discovered that my father's fortunes had changed."

"You have no one?"

"I am very resourceful, Mr. Hastings. I've had a good education, possess some skills with a needle, and am not the sort of woman to sit helplessly on the floor and lament my fate. I'm not afraid of honest work."

"You continually amaze, Miss Beckett."

"Why? Because I sought work in a dress shop and discovered I'm as trusting as my father when it comes to other people and their true intentions?"

"Anyone with a good nature expects to find the same in others. You're no fool, Miss Beckett, and don't think for a moment that I'd mistake you for one."

Her shoulders relaxed and she smiled gratefully. "Thank you, Mr. Hastings."

"But it does make things more challenging if you don't trust your own instincts. I very much want you to sit for me, Miss Beckett. I can't hide my intentions, nor do I want to, but you will have to trust me."

"You really want to paint *me*?" she asked, lowering her voice at the scandalous subject. "You're sure?"

"Is it really so surprising a notion?"

"I am no great beauty, sir, and there is something—awkward—about presuming that I am worthy of . . . such attention." Her skin warmed at the thought of such a man openly staring and studying her for hours on end. It didn't seem possible to hold anyone's interest for that period of time, but even so, the way he looked at her now, hungry and wary, eager and cautious—as if he feared she would bolt from the room and spoil his plans—made her want nothing more than to let him look his fill. She wanted to do whatever she could to ease the ache in his expression and please him.

And that alone was reason enough to refuse him.

I'm not myself when he looks at me like that. I become another woman who would sit on a dais and preen and hide nothing from him.

"Tell me what you're thinking." His command was soft, but compelling.

"I'm wishing I were a stronger person. I'm wishing your offer didn't appeal."

"Why?"

"Because I think saying yes would reveal some great flaw in my character. It will make me less in other people's eyes."

"To hell with what other people think, Miss Beckett." He leaned forward, the intensity of his gaze pinning her in place. "Say yes and become more. Become your own woman, independent again and unconcerned with the gossip of small minds. You'll have the money you need to create any life you desire. If you never broke another rule again for the rest of your life, so be it. But don't deny me, Eleanor. Help me to achieve this work, and I'll spend an eternity in your debt."

Independent again. Any life I desire. It sounds too easy.

She took one deep breath, so aware of the sodden weight of her wet wool skirts, the tight, icy feel of her leather boots, and even the confines of her corset and clothing. She felt constricted and cold. To turn him down was to embrace a future without promise, as bleak as an English moor. To accept him was to let go of fear and pride and gamble her very soul for the hope of a life with security and comfort again.

"Fifteen thousand pounds," she whispered. "I am not for sale, Mr. Hastings."

"I'm not offering to purchase you, Miss Beckett. I would simply pay for the right to look at you, for as long as I wish—for the sole purpose of capturing your likeness."

And there it was.

The right to look at you, for as long as I wish.

"I'm not taking off my . . ." She swallowed hard, unsure of how a person delicately addressed the subject of nudity with such a man. "I won't pose without . . ."

"I'll not ask you to remove a thing against your will." His brown eyes blazed hotter than the embers of a fire. "And if that was your last objection, I take it that your answer is . . ."

"Yes."

God help me. Yes.

*   *   *

Josiah felt like crowing the instant she'd agreed.

Thank God.

It had been a long, miserable day, pacing and worrying about how best to present his case and secure her agreement before she thought better of it or simply disappeared. The shadows had been unstable and troubling, and he had gotten a headache trying to be patient and distract himself with a walk and errands. Finally, he'd just given up and decided to come to the inn, prowling in the sitting room and keeping Mrs. Clay and her staff on edge.

All worth it!

"You won't regret it, Miss Beckett. If I can make one more promise, I hope you'll allow me to make that one."

Her chin lifted, and she took another sip of her tea. "It's not necessary. I shall stand by my own choices, and if there is a consequence, then I'm not going to shirk it or blame you."

Proud. You're so marvelously proud, Miss Beckett. I think I'll personally want vengeance on anyone who tries to break that spirit of yours. Now if I can only trust my eyes to allow me to paint it. . . .

Josiah decided to waste no more time. "I took the liberty of visiting my lawyer today to try to assure you that you wouldn't have to trust my word alone if it came to it. As to payment"—he took out a contract from his coat pocket—"everything is arranged for your protection."

She took the folded paper from him, her eyes taking on a sheen of unshed tears. "You move quickly, sir."

"I had no wish to leave anything to chance, Miss Beckett." He waited, deliberately holding his place to avoid looking overeager. "The offer is honorable, and I thought if you saw it in writing, it would be reassuring to you."

"Thank you, Mr. Hastings."

The man returned with their dinners, and Josiah was grateful for the interruption. Eleanor tucked the contract into her skirt pocket and had a few moments to compose herself. When they were alone again, except for the young boy, who was now dozing by the fireplace, he poured her a glass of wine.

"I do not drink, Mr. Hastings."

"Oh." He stopped the flow of the ruby liquid immediately. "Of course you don't. I'll take this glass, then, and we can ring for more—"

"The tea is fine. I don't want to trouble Mrs. Clay's man more than need be."

"What trouble? I'll just move this over and—damn it!"

Josiah tried to catch the goblet before it tipped, but he'd misjudged the distance and instead of retrieving the glass, he'd knocked it over, splashing everything on the table, including his coat and shirt. He stood quickly, but his thighs struck the table's edge, and for a moment, he envisioned the entire dinner ending up on the floor. "I'm . . . so sorry. That was . . ."

"No harm done," she said, also standing to stem the tide with her napkin and come to his aid. Her young chaperone bolted up to hand her a towel, and between the three of them, things regained a semblance of order. "You are human enough, Mr. Hastings. I confess, I'm a little comforted to see it."

"Are you?"

"You've been bounding around corners and saving my life ever since I met you. It's a bit . . . overwhelming, don't you agree? Whereas this—makes me think you are just as subject to mortal woes as the rest of us!" She smiled at him, and suddenly he was lost in the column of clear lines and stunning color that was Miss Eleanor Beckett. "There, that's the worst of it."

The urge to bolt from the room faded as he kept his eyes on her. "If that's the worst, I can't complain. But I'd prefer not to demonstrate any more of my humanity, so let's hope I can keep my elbows out of the gravy boat."

"A reasonable goal, Mr. Hastings." She resumed her seat, and he took his.

It was humbling to think of all the social graces he'd lost and never mourned until this moment. The meal seemed far more daunting than it had a few minutes ago, but Josiah wasn't about to forgo her company. "Well, let's see if we can make enough of a mark on this feast so that Mrs. Clay is satisfied! She is a true favorite of mine, and my friends, and I hope you don't find her too . . . motherly. Rutherford growls all the time about getting too soft under her care, but he's not exactly rushing out to find another place to live."

"She mentioned him. She said something odd about him being her 'own dear mystery.' And since you spoke of him earlier, I take it that Mr. Rutherford is your friend as well, then."

Josiah nodded. "He is. One of my closest, in fact. But Rutherford would never forgive me if he found out that I'd made him the subject of conversation, much less divulged any of his secrets to please a lady."

"Do you know his secrets?" she asked.

"Mutton?" Josiah held up a platter, redirecting the conversation. "I'm starving, aren't you?"

Eleanor laughed and accepted the ceramic platter. "Very well. I will ask you about your painting and you can tell me when we'll begin."

"Agreed." He held out his hand. "I'll send a carriage for you in the morning."

She gasped in shock at the speed of the arrangement but took his hand shyly to seal her fate. Josiah shook it as solemnly as a bishop and allowed himself to hope.

Chapter
7

"*This* is your home?" She tried not to sound leery of the building as she leaned forward to peek out of the carriage window. For instead of the hackney carriage coming to some residential square and pulling up in front of a brownstone or house, the driver had traveled eastward into the city and stopped in front of what could only be described as an industrial brick ruin.

"Such as it is." He opened the carriage door and settled with the driver, tipping him generously for his patience. "I live and work on the top two floors, and my steward and his wife have a portion of the third."

He held his hand out to help her down from the carriage. "Please."

She took his hand, reluctantly leaving the sanctuary of the carriage behind. "You live here?"

He smiled. "I believe I just said that." He tucked her gloved hand into the crook of his arm, and then gestured grandly with his other hand like a man proudly showing off a local landmark. "Don't let her rough looks fool you! She's

seen better days, but she's as sound as Gibraltar and has a
good deal of character. Why would I want to live in an ordinary brownstone when I can have five stories of solitude?
Well"—he amended the description—"near solitude. As I
said, there's old Escher and his wife."

"It's . . . charming." It wasn't, but Eleanor wasn't sure
what to say. She'd never heard of anyone living in such a
place. She shook her head, newly concerned about his judgment. "Do all artists prefer—unique living spaces?"

He shrugged his shoulders. "I haven't asked my peers
what they prefer." He began to lead her inside through a
broken rusted gate and into a small paved brick courtyard.
"The bell doesn't work, but I don't have a lot of callers. Few
people know that's it's not still abandoned, but Rutherford
is insisting that I hire a man to stay on the ground floor for
security."

"A reasonable suggestion."

"It's not that rough! I don't need protection. You should
know that I met Michael in India while I was there, and he's
like a big, protective elder brother or a nanny—though I
would never say as much to him directly." He shrugged, as
if uncomfortable. "One of the benefits of being disowned,
Miss Beckett, is that a man can choose his family and af-
filiations as he wishes."

She nodded, her chest feeling tight with emotion. It was
a benefit she'd never considered, and as an orphan, it occurred to her that she, too, now enjoyed the privilege of
selecting the people she wanted to hold dear. But it seemed
a bittersweet reward, at best. "I look forward to meeting
him, then."

He opened a large, thick front door for her, and her
breath caught in her throat. Behind its plain exterior, his
home did possess a certain interest of its own. He'd lit a
great wrought iron lamp that hung from the massive beam
across the room's center, and she realized that the entire
front wall of the room was a series of large doors that
would have opened up to give the work floor light and ven-
tilation. Ornate old-fashioned touches of stonework graced

the arched doorways and spoke of more prosperous days before the structure had been damaged and scorched. It was the skeleton of a factory, with machinery along the north wall in disrepair all covered in cobwebs, and she began to hope that the upper floors were a little more livable. "Was there a fire here?"

"Yes, several years ago. It was a bit of a bargain because of the damage, but the top floors are restored and renovated. I just can't seem to decide what to do with the rest of it."

"There are so many poor laborers desperate for work. If you can afford it, you should do something, if only to help others feed their families during these hard times." She reached her hand up to touch one of the empty iron frames. "It seems a waste to do nothing."

She dropped her hand from the metal bars, horrified at the awkward silence that answered her thoughtless remarks. It wasn't her place to lecture any man on what he should or shouldn't do, and especially one who had rescued her from the edge of the abyss. "I'm sorry, Mr. Hastings. I spoke out of turn. It's a terrible habit."

"You spoke from the heart." He moved to the bottom of the stairs and held out his hand. "It's a habit you should practice as often as you can. But come, Miss Beckett. Let me show you the workshop above and you can see where we'll be working together."

The climb up several flights of stairs was invigorating enough to make her appreciate her first-floor accommodations at Mrs. Clay's, but Mr. Hastings made several diplomatic stops to describe a bit of architecture or point out the views from the windows set at each landing.

"And this is my studio," he said, pushing open a set of carved double doors.

Eleanor walked through, and found herself speechless. It was a vast unfinished room under the building's roof. It was empty of almost everything but a few tables covered with candles and a dais with a large upholstered fainting couch wide enough for two atop it, arranged near the garret windows. She eyed the couch warily but had to admit that it didn't seem out of place. Beautiful narrow columns of cast iron connected to cutout arched beams and steel girders that gave the room the look of an industrial Gothic cathedral.

Instead of feeling barren or lifeless, Eleanor marveled at the peacefulness and airy welcome of the space. Stacks of paintings leaned against the eastern wall, drawing her eyes to the unexpected splashes of color. She walked over to view them, the sound of her heels on the unpolished wooden floors echoing in her ears.

"Those are much earlier, some of them." He trailed behind her, his hands clasped behind him without any of the bravado that he'd shown downstairs. "Rough bits and experiments better left unseen, most likely."

She tried to hide her amazement and admiration for the strange and wonderful works of art. There were landscapes and still life studies unlike any she'd seen. Not that she had any vast education in fine art, but she wondered what a miracle it must be to see the world through the filter of an artist's eyes. There was a precision to some of the paintings that convinced the eye that the grapes on the glass plate were ripe enough to pluck and eat. But another stack of work was far more raw, as if color and undefined brushstrokes alone could convey the loneliness of a landscape or the texture of a drop of cloth.

There was even a bizarre portrait of a small child sleeping in a doorway, but every hue was a different shade of blue, like a melancholy dance of blue and gray that made her worried for that child and aware of how lost he looked. She'd never even imagined the world in one singular color, but there it was, as if emotion alone dictated vision.

She looked up at him with new respect and speculation. "I had no idea."

"What were you expecting, Miss Beckett?"

"Truthfully?"

He smiled, his stance relaxing a bit. "I prefer it when you speak directly."

"I thought there would be pictures of women. Naked women. I had lectured myself on the ride here on not being shocked if I were to walk into a room where I might struggle to find a safe place to rest my gaze."

"I see." He was struggling not to laugh, and Eleanor liked this side of him. He never looked at her with censure, and made it far too easy to say whatever she wished.

She did her best to steer the conversation away from such a scandalous topic, but her own curiosity outwitted her. "I'm simply pointing out that there are no paintings of women. Not a single one, Mr. Hastings."

"Isn't that better? Having a variety of safe places to rest your eyes?"

She shook her head. "I'm not sure." Instead of comforting her, the notion was unsettling.

"What are you thinking over there, Miss Beckett? You look as serious as a woman composing her last prayer."

"There are no women, even wearing clothes." She turned to face him, hating the blush that made her feel like a shrew for answering so honestly. "Or did you tuck away some of your paintings to protect my sensibilities?"

He shook his head slowly. "I'm afraid not. Although there might be a few downstairs in my apartments, but it wasn't to protect your delicate nature."

"No?"

He crossed his arms defensively. "I haven't painted a female model in a long time. And until I saw you fly out of the back doorway of that dress shop, I didn't think I would."

"Why ever not?"

He didn't answer her right away, his gaze turning back to the paintings sitting on the floor.

"I apologize. I've lost some of my social polish in these recent months," she said.

"I doubt that. But again, don't amend your ways for me. A veneer of good behavior rarely makes for great conversation, Miss Beckett."

"You are polite, Mr. Hastings, and I like your conversation very much."

He shook his head. "I'm not *always* polite, but thank you for the compliment. Now, there is a coat rack there, if you'd like to be more comfortable. I'll hang it up for you. I know the room is a bit chilly, but I have a brazier set up near my worktable, so I'll do my best to keep you warm."

Eleanor allowed him to help her with her coat, and then removed her bonnet. "How will this work precisely? Will I come every day or . . ."

"I'll send a carriage for you when I wish to paint, and naturally, provide one to take you back to the inn whenever a session is finished."

"When did you wish to start?"

"Now."

"Oh." She tried not to sound surprised. After all, the man had every right and she'd already agreed to everything, but Eleanor suddenly felt nervous at the prospect. "And how exactly do you wish me to . . . be?"

He smiled. "I have things arranged here, by the windows. I know it seems a bit odd, but I brought out a comfortable chaise lounge and some pillows. If you'll but sit there for a minute, I can better decide how to proceed."

"So, I just *sit.*"

"I'm not sure if you sound disappointed or shocked at the notion, Miss Beckett."

"No! I'm"—she tried to take a steadying breath, hoping she didn't look like some fearful little ninny—"relieved. I was afraid you'd ask me to dance about."

"I think I've challenges enough without trying to capture you in motion. But dance, did you say?" He looked at her as if considering this exciting new idea.

"I am *not* dancing."

"It would be modern, but we'll just have you sit, shall we?" Josiah did his best to pretend disappointment, secretly surprised at his body's reaction to the notion of the delightful Miss Eleanor Beckett shrugging off her proper ways and dancing just for him. It was out of the question, but a singularly wicked thought.

"It may take a while to find exactly the pose we want.

But I don't wish the portrait to be ordinary, Miss Beckett. I will have to wait for exactly the right moment."

"The right moment?"

"For inspiration to strike. But don't worry. It will happen."

"You sound so sure!" She nervously touched her hair, tucking yet another small stray curl back into place. "What if it doesn't?"

"Then we shall have spent a good deal of hours waiting for it, and I will pay you as a forfeit when time runs out." He wasn't worried in the slightest. Hell, he was already inspired and the woman was standing there in what was probably her better dress for a visit but it was clear that a forest green gabardine day dress wasn't the stuff of dreams that any artist would swoon over. Even so . . .

"Here, Miss Beckett. Just try sitting facing the worktable and my easel for a moment."

She dutifully stepped up onto the dais and took her place on the divan, landing as primly as a duchess. She smoothed out her skirts and then waited expectantly.

He moved the brazier, for her comfort but also to make sure he didn't forget himself and kick it over if he needed to cross over to adjust her position. Josiah dismissed the gray fog that had threatened to be particularly thick today in his peripheral, and instead concentrated on her face. He lit all the candles he could on the table and then looked back to assess the change in light.

It was astonishing.

Even with her hair pulled back, he could see the fire reflected in each copper strand, and her eyes radiated calm beauty. "If you don't mind, Miss Beckett, I'm going to move behind you and see if we can't improve things with a backdrop."

From the wall, he picked up a rope he'd been using for drapery and stretched it across from a latch on the window to a nearby column behind her. Over the rope, he tossed a length of black fabric like a loose curtain and then walked back around to survey her again.

"Am I improved?" she asked.

"It's helped quite a bit. Now the light is reflected back off the dark surface and isn't lost into the room." He tilted his head to one side, studying the way the light fell across her face. "Can you turn more to me?"

She turned obediently, and once more he moved behind her, this time at a much more intimate distance.

"May I?"

She nodded, and he gently pressed his hand between her shoulder blades, so that she was leaning forward a scant inch more. His hand brushed against her back, and his sensitive fingers detected what could only be described as a most industrial-strength steel-ribbed corset. He smiled behind her. This was not a woman who risked her virtue with light laces and whalebone. "What a lovely posture you possess, Miss Beckett."

"You're mocking me, Mr. Hastings."

"Just a little." He stepped back and caught her smiling in return. "If we're to spend a good deal of time together, I think it bodes well if we can laugh together."

"I thought art was a serious business."

"Now who's mocking who?"

She laughed outright, a proper woman shedding for just a moment the restraint of etiquette, and Josiah's breath stopped in his throat at the raw beauty of her.

"Do you just . . . begin painting when the mood strikes you?"

"I'll sketch you first. I'll make several sketches on paper until I'm confident enough to approach the canvas. I'll sketch a bit on the larger frame, and then, yes, I suppose, it's as simple as that. I just paint."

"I didn't mean to belittle the process. We had a neighbor that had his portrait made and I was always curious about it. He was such an . . . unattractive man, but that shouldn't matter, I suppose. For posterity's sake?"

Aren't you the most unique woman? I love how that mind looks out at the world. "If only people stopped to consider aesthetics before they insisted on their great uncle

Walter being painted." He sat on the edge of the table, leaning against it to stretch out his legs for a moment. "I've seen too many commissioned portraits of people now long dead that did little more than frighten their young descendants with eyes that followed you no matter where you stood. Hell, I think I even stooped to painting one or two myself when I needed the money!"

She frowned at his language, but the sparkle in her eyes told him she'd appreciated the jest all the same. "You never did! And I'll kindly ask you not to make me look too frightening."

"I'll do my best." He crossed his arms and tried to broach a more delicate subject while she was at ease. "Can you . . . bring what clothes you have tomorrow to see if we can choose something for the work?"

She smiled. "I warn you now, there's nothing of magic in my wardrobe. I have but three dresses and"—her humor faltered a bit—"and one of those is out of the question."

"Why?"

"It is that wretched red velvet dress, and I'm not about to be painted in scarlet!"

"I see." He bit his lower lip, mulling over the problem. "A shame, as you would look stunning in it, Miss Beckett. I know the color has its associations. . . ."

"I'll look like a harlot! That isn't an association, Mr. Hastings. That is a fact."

"You aren't a harlot. *That* is a fact. If someone puts you in purple, it doesn't make you an empress."

His logic was infallible, but Eleanor was having trouble accepting it or admitting that she was teetering on agreement.

"But," he went on, "if the red troubles you that much, we'll simply have to see about buying you some new clothes and—"

"No. Absolutely not! You are not . . . I will not have a man buying me clothes. The shopkeeper would insinuate— it isn't appropriate for a woman to accept such things from a stranger."

"The red, then." He nodded. "I understand and support your moral and courageous decision." He stood as if the matter were settled and moved to his table, arranging his tools and the sealed pigment jars, gathering some blank papers and looking for charcoal.

"Th-thank you, Mr. Hastings." She'd been outmaneuvered and they both knew it, and her modest blush in defeat almost made him forgo his small victory.

Oh, God, I'm already in danger of being besotted with this woman. Please just let me paint her and be done.

Chapter
8

Eleanor took off her bonnet inside the inn's entryway and made her way up the stairs, her steps lighter than the day before. Her first day under Mr. Hastings's scrutiny had proven that her fears were unfounded. There had been no leering or unseemly innuendos. He'd asked permission each and every time he wished to approach her or touch her to make an adjustment. And those touches were . . . fleeting, gentle, and never inappropriate.

She almost felt guilty for how exhilarated she was and how she'd forgotten to worry about being vain. He'd made it all too easy. She'd sat on that divan and never noticed the time. Instead, she'd been distracted by Josiah's hands as he sketched and the quick turns of their conversation. He'd sat several feet from the edge of the dais, and just as promised, looked at her as much as he wished.

It was his study of her that had proven to be the most challenging part of the day. She'd never had a man look at her as he did—and the strange heat in his gaze had kept even her toes warm in the chill of the studio. It was more than admiration. It was what she imagined worship would be if she allowed herself to conjure the wanton thought. After all, practical and independent women didn't encourage such whimsy.

Or enjoy the unexpected benefit of being able to study him in return as much as she wished. Josiah Hastings only became more handsome the longer a woman looked, so she'd done her best not to linger on his face too much. But the temptation was very real when he'd knelt next to the divan for a while to start a new sketch, close enough for her to absorb every detail of his delightful male form.

It's wicked for a man to look like that—like some refined yet rugged hermit. We're in the heart of London, and he looks like he's walked out of the Welsh wilds.

He'd worked until his fingers were black from his charcoal sticks and the winter light began to fade. He'd been lost in it, she suspected, until he'd finally noticed that the brazier had gone out and she was shivering a little. Then there was a flurry of apologies and he was bundling her up in her coat and scarf while his very grumpy Mr. Escher saw about hailing a carriage downstairs. And then Josiah escorted her down with assurances that they would begin again in the morning and offered one last reminder for her to bring the dress.

She reached her apartment door and pulled out from her coat pocket the key that Mrs. Clay had provided her, only to realize that it was already unlocked.

I locked it most carefully this morning!

A flare of alarm made her cautious as she pushed open the door and peered in for whatever intruder might be lurking or poised for attack.

A familiar blond head popped up from behind the chairs in front of the fireplace and Eleanor couldn't catch the yelp of surprise at the sight of him, but did her best to recover quickly and give him a smile of assurance. After all, here was Mrs. Clay's dear boy, and she didn't want him to think her rude or unfeeling.

"Oh! My chaperone! I wasn't able to formally say hello

last night to the very famous Tally I've heard so much about."

He was small for his age, if Mrs. Clay had placed him rightly at twelve, but his cheeks were rosy and full and his blue eyes shone with health, so she had no doubt that his size couldn't be blamed on a lack of nutrition or care. He came to attention like a little soldier, but there was no fear in him. She had less of an impression of a little rabbit and more of a small house elf caught in the act.

He gestured to the coal bucket, demonstrating how empty it now was, and then pointed to the bellpull and then himself, all the while smiling before turning back to finish his task.

She began to take off her coat and then nearly fell over when someone burst into the room.

"Miss Beckett? Are you all right?"

It was the largest man she'd ever seen, and if Tally hadn't just surprised her, she was sure she'd have fainted dead away. He was nearly seven feet in height, and lean with broad shoulders, a muscular giant, as intimidating a presence as any she'd encountered. But a practical woman could only put up with so much in an evening, and Eleanor Beckett gripped her coat in front of her like a shield. "I am fine! I was merely startled by—I didn't expect to meet young Master Clay over there."

"Oh." Michael Rutherford took an immediate step backward, retreating almost as quickly as he'd intruded. "Yes . . . Tally is . . . pardon me. So sorry to have . . ." And the door was closed behind him before she could even think of a thing to say.

Tally popped back up, oblivious to the brief drama behind him, merrily picking up the rag he'd used to kneel on to protect the carpets while he worked, and then bowed.

"Yes, thank you!" She spoke as clearly as she could, wondering if it made any difference at all. "Mrs. Clay said you were the man of the house. Thank you for the coal."

He nodded, then bowed again before leaving without making a sound.

For a moment, it was all she could do to sit down to catch her breath. But once her heartbeat slowed to a steadier pace, Eleanor decided that there was no time like the present if she wanted to repair things with her neighbor—and make sure the man wasn't prone to rushing in every time she stubbed her toes or Tally startled her.

She smoothed back her hair as she went out her door and crossed over to Mr. Rutherford's. Two firm knocks seemed appropriate to her, and she was rewarded quickly when he opened the door, his expression a little sheepish as he looked down at her apologetically. The giant wasn't nearly as frightening as she took in more details of her would-be protector. His hair was salt-and-peppered unruly curls, but he wasn't ancient at all. Rugged as granite, his dark eyes reflected nothing but humility at being called out for his misbehavior.

"May I help you, Miss Beckett?"

"I had eventually intended to ask Mrs. Clay to introduce us, as we are neighbors, Mr. Rutherford, but—since we seem to have just met, I couldn't let you retain a wrong impression of me. I didn't mean to seem ungracious at your attempted . . . rescue."

"Not at all. I was the one . . . You obviously didn't need a rescue."

"But you thought I did, didn't you?" she asked, a little puzzled. "Are you always so—quick to think of danger, sir?"

"A soldier's terrible habit," he conceded. "I'll strive to improve. I was out in the hall and had just come up the stairs when I saw that your door was ajar. Naturally when you cried out—I didn't stop to think."

"That was very chivalrous of you, Mr. Rutherford. But I hope you understand that I cannot be nervous about you taking it upon yourself to fight off invisible assassins if I prick a finger while sewing. May I—ask you to refrain from any future intrusions?"

He practically shrank in front of her into a very small, guilty child, nodding miserably. "Yes, miss."

A new thought occurred to her. "Has Mr. Hastings asked you to keep an eye out, or rather an ear out for trouble on my behalf, Mr. Rutherford?"

He paused. "Hastings may have said something about— I'm no bodyguard, Miss Beckett."

"I see. Well, that's good and since I'm not in need of one, Mr. Rutherford, you should be relieved. I hope you'll take your ease now that I've made it clear that I can take care of myself, sir."

He nodded in solemn awe. "I believe you can, Miss Beckett. I truly believe you can."

"Good night, then." With the awkward business out of the way, Eleanor relaxed. "It was a pleasure meeting you, Mr. Rutherford."

"Pleasure. Thank you." His expression was delightfully befuddled as he shut the door, and she almost starting laughing as she returned to her rooms.

Independence has its rewards. Apparently, I'm braver than I thought!

She closed and locked her door with a smile, marveling at her own cheekiness.

*   *   *

Michael Rutherford stared at the solid surface of his closed door for a few minutes and tried to absorb what had just happened. Hastings's little beauty had just given him prim and fair warning that she'd missed nothing of his friend's arrangements.

Not that I helped by nearly breaking her door down. . . .

I only hope Josiah has an inkling of what he's gotten into, because by the looks of it, that woman's not going to put up with any nonsense.

I think you've got a tigress by the tail, friend.

And you might not be able to let go—and survive to tell the tale—if you're not careful.

Chapter
9

Josiah looked at the red dress that Eleanor was holding gingerly out in front of her and instantly knew he'd made the right choice. The color was just as he'd remembered it, rich and ripe.

"Women with red hair usually avoid these colors, Mr. Hastings," she explained, absentmindedly stroking the soft velvet. "I'll look like a tomato in it."

"You won't." He walked over to the door and opened it to lean out and ring the bell he'd set on a table in the hallway, just outside. The building wasn't designed with a residence in mind, so there weren't bellpulls to allow him to get Escher's attention. Normally, he'd have just yelled down the stairwell, but he knew better than to demonstrate such rustic skills in front of the refined sensibilities of his lovely model. "I am not painting tomatoes today."

She laughed. "What a relief!"

"Miss Beckett, I loathe bringing up the subject of money, but it can hardly be inappropriate if I give you a modest advance on your sitting fee. You cannot be impoverished and without liberty to buy whatever your heart desires before—"

"No, Mr. Hastings. You are already paying for my room and board, and no matter what you say, it is a generosity that I am not accustomed to receiving. An advance would seem . . ."

"Fair?" he supplied mischievously, well aware she wasn't about to concede anything. "Ridiculously overdue?"

"Unnecessary. As you described them at dinner, the terms of my employment were very clear and I don't wish to muddle things. Please, Mr. Hastings, I have everything I need, and as I said before, I cannot allow you to provide for anything else." She blushed, a beautiful pink forcing his retreat from the battlefield. "A woman must adhere to her principles."

He bowed playfully but looked at her with a new respect. "As you wish."

"You rang?" Escher asked breathlessly as he came through the door, one hand on the small of his back.

"Can you ask your wife if she'll meet Miss Beckett downstairs and help the lady change her dress?" Josiah asked.

The man's facial expression was truly comical in his shock. "*My* wife? She'll not say no, but . . . there's no telling what else she'll say to that, sir."

"Thank you, Escher. I'm sure we can weather the storm. If you'll just ask her and tell her I'd be ever so grateful. . . ."

"Will do." The houseman turned and left to carry out the orders and Josiah watched him go, fully aware that stirring Rita from her kitchen was like luring a bear out of its cave midwinter. Not always wise, but there was no other way.

"Miss Beckett. I'll walk you downstairs and Mrs. Escher will come up and help you change. Then when you're ready, you can just come back to the studio where I'll be waiting." He held out his arm. "Does that sound acceptable?"

It wasn't an arbitrary question. The shy lady had yet to remove her gloves, and Josiah knew that it was a bit unsettling to discuss changing her clothes as the first order of business.

"Yes, although, I hate to cause trouble." She put a hand around his elbow and allowed him to escort her out. "From the way Mr. Escher was looking at you—"

"Don't pay that any attention. I know the Eschers may not be the most polished people in the world, but for all the growls and misplaced courtesies, I trust them both and they've become an odd kind of family for me. Just don't take anything Rita says to heart, and you'll be fine." He walked her down the stairs, secretly enjoying the heat of her hands through the cloth of his shirt and coat sleeve. He kept a free hand on the banister to make sure he didn't lose his balance and spoil the moment. "She's as sweet as a kitten when you get to know her."

Miss Beckett didn't look convinced, but she didn't argue so he decided that would suffice for now. Reaching the landing outside the doors to his rooms on the fourth floor, he heard the telltale faint sounds of pots banging and raised voices below before continuing inside.

"And here we are." He opened the doors, glad he'd remembered to have the curtains drawn so that the room appeared more cheerful. "My home, such as it is."

Unlike the unfinished attic floor above, the salon was tastefully furnished and outfitted to rival any manse in London. Even so, he knew that there was a vacant feel to the apartment because he spent so little time in its rooms.

Original art from his peers graced his walls, as well as a few works of his own, but he could hardly see them anymore, so her exclamations and sighs of approval were a good reminder that he'd once had a keen eye for setting out rooms. Now the layout of the room had far more to do with clear pathways and minimized clutter than comfort or care. The fourth floor had been beautifully renovated using his architectural designs and ambitious sketches. When they'd come back to England, he'd enthusiastically embraced change, intending to quietly thumb his nose at his life in exile. Before India, even with empty pockets, he'd always been welcome in many elite circles because of his heritage and because it was fashionable to have at least one or two artistic acquaintances who shocked and inspired good gossip. He'd spanned both worlds and enjoyed the game, even as he'd struggled to pay his tailors.

But he'd dreamt of having a place of his own without feeling like a trained monkey or a poor relative expected to earn an invitation by providing entertainment and witty conversation.

So when his adventures with the Jaded had ultimately lined his pockets, Josiah had built a luxurious home in an unlikely place, with the very latest in gas fixtures and indoor plumbing. His plans had even grandly included guest rooms, a music salon, and a small ballroom. He'd had visions of the parties and gatherings he would hold, turning this odd factory into a creative draw to the Ton, where artists and art lovers could mingle and enjoy a mutually beneficial association.

Then when his eyes had started to fail, he'd modified those plans very quickly and abandoned the rest of the renovation and construction on the other floors. His "hidden" mansion had transformed into a sanctuary from the world instead of a showplace to bring the world to his doorstep.

Hell, I don't even think I've ever had anyone up here—besides the Jaded—and they never needed an invitation, so I'm not sure if they count as guests.

The temptation to offer her a tour of the house and earn her approval was very strong. But he damped it down. He didn't want it to look like boasting or shameless self-promotion; and to what purpose? To feel like he had more worth in her eyes?

If wealth made a man more worthy or honorable, it would be a world of poets and kings, wouldn't it? But I don't think Eleanor Beckett is the kind of woman to bat an eye at a man's wallet or think more of him for showing off his assets.

She relinquished his arm and circled the room in a slow,

graceful stroll. At last, she returned to him. "You continue to surprise, Mr. Hastings."

"It's just a room."

She laughed. "If you insist!"

"It's a reception area and a salon. I once—had ambitions to be more social."

"But no more?"

He shook his head. "Ambitions change. It's just a room." He walked over to the inside doors leading to the hallway. "There is a guest room this way that you may use to change your dress. The third door down on the left. I'll send Mrs. Escher in to you as soon as she comes up."

"Thank you, Mr. Hastings."

He deliberately hung back, newly aware of the delightful Miss Beckett's sensitivities and adherence to etiquette. He didn't think she'd appreciate his very male presence within twenty feet of a doorway that led into a bedchamber. Ironically, the thought immediately evoked the image of his own large, empty bed and how remarkable she would look lying across it. Josiah caught himself before a hundred more erotic scenes flooded his mind, and bit the inside of his cheek hard enough to guarantee a redirection of his concentration to matters at hand. "You're welcome, Miss Beckett."

He turned back, already aware of the echo of Mrs. Escher's boot heels on the stairs as he moved to intercept her in the vestibule. "Ah, there you are, Mrs. Escher!"

"I ain't no ladies' maid," she gruffly announced, "but I suppose I could lend a hand if there's buttons."

"You are an angel, Mrs. Escher."

The words prompted the portly bulldog of a woman to turn into a giggling schoolgirl. "And you're a trickster to say such things!"

"I sent her to the blue guest room and told her you would follow. Thank you, Mrs. Escher."

She waved him off, bustling through the doorway to the hall, and he waited until he heard her brisk knock and the guest room door closing behind her before making his way back up to the studio.

Whatever her objections to the red dress, there'll be no dissuading Rita from her mission, but I just hope Miss Beckett isn't bruised in the process. . . .

* * *

Eleanor laid the dress out on the bed, turned up the lamps, and stood in new wonder as she surveyed the room. The walls and matching upholstery were a deep French blue, accented in gilt silver. The furniture was ornately carved wood that was almost blond in color, polished and graceful. It was a room designed for a woman, with a vanity table and every detail set out with elegant care. The bedding was sumptuous blue quilted silk and lace, and the bedposts were covered in flowers and vines carved in relief and painted with silver accents that gave it a fairylike appearance.

Even so, there were signs of dust and cobwebs in the corners.

It was as if the house had been decorated and arranged to perfection, and then abandoned. He lived here. But nothing echoed of his presence. Even the beautiful vestibule and receiving room he'd shown her had made the same impression. It had dazzled her senses, but then felt a little empty and unoccupied.

A knock at the door ended her reverie. "Come in."

"I'm Rita Escher." The woman at the door marched in, firmly closing the door behind her. "Mr. Hastings has it that you needed a woman's hand getting changed. I'll do what I can, mind. But I'm no ladies' maid, so if it's hair curling or frippery, you'll be left to your own, I'm afraid."

"Thank you, Mrs. Escher. Any help would be appreciated." She began to cross over to a dressing screen in the corner. "I'll just see about . . ."

"Oh, don't mind with that! Here, let me help with the back of that and let's see you out of it. You're a modest thing, aren't you, Miss Beckett?"

Eleanor yielded, blushing. "I suppose I am."

"Hmm." Rita's hands were efficient, if not altogether

gentle, as she tackled the buttons of Eleanor's dress. "Good enough quality in a lady, modesty, I'd say."

Eleanor helped the process along as best she could, smiling at the woman's gruff manners. *As sweet as a kitten, are you?* "So, you have the run of the house for Mr. Hastings?"

"I'm a cook, mind. And I do a bit of laundry and tidying up around here when I can. But it's twelve rooms on this floor and eleven of them generally empty, since himself keeps to his room when he's not painting upstairs—so who's to say when I dusted last!"

"Such a large house! All by yourself?"

Mrs. Escher reddened with pride. "It's not easy, but I manage—and Mr. Hastings is as easy as a pup. My own man is harder to pick up after in just two rooms, and what a lot of fuss! But Mr. Hastings keeps himself to himself these days. Too much, if you ask me!"

"Perhaps painting is such a solitary task, he prefers it that way."

Mrs. Escher grunted. "It's not healthy, prowling about up there, banging into the furniture and using enough candles to light half of London. But Mr. Escher worships him—besotted old fool!"

Mr. Escher isn't alone by the looks of you and the way you're worrying over him like a mother hen.

"Then Mr. Hastings is lucky to have you."

"He's off his beam. A gentleman, like that, with more money than God can reckon, I suspect, and my man and I are all he's got? He should have a house full of boot kissers instead of the likes of us. I can't keep ahead of a house this size as well as I'd like—and those stairs, mind! But we'd die for him, him giving Mr. Escher the work and paying like he does and then letting us live with him. Never complaining! I don't care if artists are supposed to be strange in their ways. Mr. Hastings can stroll about naked if he wants. I ain't sayin' a word."

"D-does Mr. Hastings stroll about naked?"

"Never! I'm just saying he could! He could put a cat on

his head and talk about the weather! You'll not get me to make a fuss!" Mrs. Escher's hands fisted at her hips as if this settled the matter. "Now, let's see about this dress."

Eleanor was down to her petticoats and undergarments, and lifted the evening gown to see how best to draw it over her head, but Mrs. Escher was shaking her head.

"The dress has stays, miss. Not that I stand to be an experienced maid or nothin', but I'm eyein' that hardware you've got on and I think you're not going to manage both."

"Oh." Eleanor blushed. Her corset was covered with thick ivory brocade underpinned with what the maker had assured her mother was a sufficient amount of steel supports to allow any woman to carry herself like a true lady. It was an endorsement she remembered her mother repeating when the garment was purchased, and it was one of the conventions she'd clung to. "Will it look proper without . . ."

"More proper than you tryin' to force it and tearin' a seam out. Let's see you out of it."

The corset was sacrificed, but the dress itself had light boning sewn in for structure, and Eleanor accepted the loss as the red velvet encased her slender figure, the heavy skirt drifting down and around her.

It was a sumptuous evening gown; the silk velvet was heavy and soft, giving the dress a softer shape than most fashions of the day. Unlike the lofty bell-shaped skirts and embroidered and beaded satins usually seen for London's evening revels, this was a fall of crimson glory about her. It was a full skirt, without any ruffles or flounces, and only the bottom had been hemmed in the simplest matching ribbon to protect the skirt's trailing edges. The décolletage was cut low off the shoulders, and again was edged only in a simple matching silk ribbon, without a single flower or bow. The color alone was the adornment of the gown, and it shamelessly drew the eye to Eleanor's creamy skin, ripe figure, and tiny waist.

I thought Miss Lawson looked like a confection in that peach organza. But I look like . . . a very wicked dessert, indeed. No wonder Mrs. Carlisle didn't buy it! It sighs of scandal, doesn't it?

But the silk velvet invited the touch of her fingers and elicited nothing but admiration. For all its decadent color, the dress was too beautiful to dislike.

"Oh, miss!" Even the gruff Mrs. Escher was overcome. "It's like a dream, ain't it? And you look like a ruby of a thing!"

The compliment was sincere, even if it did make Eleanor instantly color in embarrassment. "Well, we'll see if it will do for Mr. Hastings and his painting. Thank you, Mrs. Escher, for your help."

"You just call down the stairs when you need to change out of it, and I'll come up. No worries on that account, mind? I'll just meet you on the landing when you come in mornings, and we'll get a bit of a routine going so you aren't always asking and Mr. Escher can save himself a few steps."

"Yes, Mrs. Escher." Eleanor nodded dutifully, aware that she'd somehow passed an unspoken test with the woman and earned her help. "Thank you."

Mrs. Escher left, returning to her kitchens, and Eleanor stole one last glance in the vanity mirror at the odd sight of herself dressed for the opera in the middle of the morning. She nervously reached a hand up to smooth out her hair, tucking in a single stray curl. "He's waiting, Beckett," she reminded her reflection. "The sooner we begin, the sooner . . ." Her bravado faded at the unsettling new thought that she wasn't sure what would truly happen next, much less what her future would be shaped like after he'd laid aside his paints. She would be independent, that much was certain, but Eleanor had to push away a small burst of fear that the only thing she would possess would be money enough to be alone.

She shyly headed out to return to the stairwell and with each riser she climbed, she gathered her courage.

I feel like sin, walking about in this in the middle of the day.

But if it's a sin, why is it that all I can think to pray for is Josiah Hastings's approval?

* * *

Escher had brought up more candles, and Josiah was doing his best to arrange them to suit, using a small knife to scrape off some of the wax from the table's surface. The collection of candleholders and candelabras had taken on a life of their own, and he stepped back to admire the ornate little forest of white and ivory columns created by all the tapers. He could hear Eleanor's tentative footsteps coming up the stairs and he deliberately didn't turn, savoring the anticipation of her arrival.

"Mr. Hastings?"

Josiah pivoted to look at her, and almost forgot himself entirely. *Holy mother of . . .* Desire slammed into him with an unexpected force. His prim Miss Beckett was transformed into a siren, and there was no escaping the power of it.

She put a hand up to her throat. "I have no jewels for it. I hope you don't mind."

It was all he could do to nod.

"You hate it?" she asked, misinterpreting his silence.

"No. You don't need a single thing, Miss Beckett. You're flawless."

She smiled at the compliment but didn't drop her hand. "Thank you, Mr. Hastings. I'm not sure I've ever aspired to flawless."

He knew it was modesty that made her think to cover a bit of her bare shoulders and throat with her fingers, but the gesture only drew a man's eyes to the creamy expanse of her skin and the forbidden delights she tried to hide.

"Shall I sit as before, then?" Eleanor crossed the room and went around his worktable to the dais by the windows. "Here?"

He could tell she was nervous, so he did his best to damp down the boiling fire in his blood and approach her as professionally as he could. "Just as before, Miss Beckett."

He busied himself lighting the last of the candles while she settled onto the divan, until he was sure he had reined in the worst of his erotic thoughts. At last, he turned to survey her and take in the striking sight of Miss Eleanor Beckett in red velvet.

I'll have decided on the pose today, or I'm not worth the wax on the table, because if ever a man were going to be inspired by anything or anyone—there she is.

He approached her as reverently as a priest moving toward an altar, and then knelt on one knee next to her, barely aware of the sweet intake of her breath in surprise at his proximity. "Miss Beckett?"

"Yes, Mr. Hastings."

"Your hair . . ."

"I assure you this is the fashion." Again her fingers instantly sought to smooth any stray curls that may have disobeyed her desire for control.

"I'm sure it is entirely proper, Miss Beckett, but . . ."

"But? You have an objection?"

He shook his head. "More of a request than an objection. Will you take down your hair for me?"

"Oh," she whispered. "Truly?"

"Yes, please." *Please, woman. Because if I so much as remove a single hairpin, I think I'm going to fist those curls in my hands and kiss you past reason. Take it down, Eleanor.*

She nodded slowly, and he simply waited and watched as she reached up to gingerly take down the careful, tight-braided structure that restrained the wild mass of her copper hair. It took only a few seconds, but for Josiah, it was a beautiful display that unfolded in a glorious haze of pleasure. Her hair was far longer than he'd imagined, reaching her waist, and the reddish golden fire of it was fanned into life as each plump, satin-textured curl fell across her back and shoulders.

Here was an intimacy that made every part of him ache with hunger.

Here was a vulnerability that made something inside of him mourn a little.

For only a lover or a husband would ever have seen her like this—in a normal world, where poverty hadn't driven her into his sphere. The pride he so admired couldn't help but be stung by the act, but his conscience couldn't keep pace with his need to capture her on canvas—and behold the essence of her in his quest for color and time.

Mine, to look at . . . but if God is merciful, mine to translate onto that blank white space so that everyone can see what I see. One last time. Please, God. Let there be truth in beauty. Give me the time I need.

"May I?" he asked, holding as still as he could until she indicated her permission with the tiniest nod.

Only then did he reach out to carefully arrange some of the curls to trail over her shoulder, draping her bare skin with the molten fire of untamed tresses. He didn't want her to look mussed, but instead, like a woman unfettered by convention—unashamed and bewitching to behold.

She shivered in reaction when his fingers brushed against the nape of her neck, her pale skin marbling with what he imagined was a new sensation. It was a siren's magic that made him linger for a few seconds, absorbing the power of it.

There!

He shifted back a little, openly admiring the woman coming into his view. "Don't move."

She bit her lip in protest, but it was as if the restraint of his command took hold before she could even consider staging a rebellion. "Is it too late to point out the immoral implications of me sitting here in a red dress with my hair down, Mr. Hastings?"

"Far too late," he replied with a wicked smile. "Besides, there is nothing immoral about having lovely hair. If there were, would not people shave their heads and be done with it?"

"You have the irrefutable logic of a rogue, Mr. Hastings."

"So long as I win most arguments, who's to say? I could simply be right all the time, Miss Beckett."

She started to laugh, but then caught herself and sobered. "Or you could simply be wrong, but too clever to see reason?"

"Impossible! But moral arguments aside, what's troubling you, Miss Beckett? For I swear, if I have my way, I shall paint you as I see you at this very moment."

She sighed. "It's foolish to say it, but I . . . have never liked my hair."

"Why do women always say that? Is it to elicit compliments, since there isn't a man breathing who isn't fascinated by the elusive silk of a woman's hair?"

She gasped. "I had no idea that all men breathing held such fascinations, Mr. Hastings. I don't think women know this secret, or we would stop complaining and go about with our hair down all the time, wouldn't we?"

"To please us?"

"To please ourselves, probably."

"Would that not be the essence of immorality? Selfishly pleasing yourself? Or was it the quest for admiration that gave you pause?"

"There isn't a woman breathing who doesn't wish to be admired."

"Except you," he amended.

"Except me." Eleanor let out a long, slow breath, the last of her nerves fading before his eyes. "I've accepted my looks, Mr. Hastings. I overheard a friend of my mother's offering her sympathy that her only child had inherited some unknown ancestor's coarse Irish coloring. I have no illusions of being a refined English beauty, Mr. Hastings. But my father always wanted us to strive to improve ourselves and said that a lady is defined by how she acts, not always how she looks."

"Your mother's friend was either blind or just jealous that her own offspring were probably piggish little things without a hint of color." He gently pulled out another long curl, fingering it reverently before dropping it against her upper arm as carefully as he could. "But perhaps I was wrong about one thing."

"Were you?" she asked in mock surprise. "Truly?"

"Well"—he took a deep breath and retrieved a few of the longer pins she'd dropped on the floor—"perhaps not *wrong*, but let us see if there's a compromise here between my wishes and yours."

He stood to move behind her, loosely twisting up the bulk of her hair to pile it up on her head, artfully securing it in an elegant, careless style that allowed a few curls to frame her face and cascade down onto her shoulders.

"There. Now it is not exactly down, so perhaps you'll not mind it as much."

She reached up to feel the casual chignon, a bit unsure. "I'm not sure you would qualify as a ladies' maid, Mr. Hastings."

He walked back around to face her again, relishing his victory. "No man aspires to such expertise, Miss Beckett. After all, I'd say we look at women's fashions from a very different angle, and that's the truth." He bit off the balance of the thought, which was to confess that the only thought a man generally held when it came to a woman's clothes was how to remove them.

"I doubt women's fashions hold any mysteries at all for you, Mr. Hastings, but I shall continue to rely on poor Mrs. Escher." He could tell she spoke impulsively and without thinking as her words were immediately followed by a tell-tale blush across her skin.

Are you imagining what a ladies' maid I might make, my prim Miss Beckett? Did you read my mind and see it in my eye—the wicked turn of my imagination?

"Very well, Miss Beckett. Please don't move."

He'd pushed the table with the candles up against the dais, and set up his easel just in front of where she would sit. He was still a good eight or ten feet from her, but he knew it was closer than most of his colleagues would recommend. Even so, Josiah didn't trust his eyes and he wasn't about to squint and strain if he didn't have to.

The blank canvas was set on the floor, leaning against the table, and Josiah knelt to retrieve it, and out of the corner of his eye, he saw her and froze.

There. By all that's holy, there it is. The inspiration I'd have paid every penny I have to seize.

Without waiting for another breath, he moved into position and took up his pencil to touch it to the primed and ready surface of the canvas. He would paint her like this—like a mortal looking up at beauty. She was a goddess. Adorned with nothing but a crown of glorious copper curls tumbling down from that loose chignon like a woman without cares. And in that red.

He'd lied to her. That red evoked everything she feared it would. She looked wanton and touchable in that velvet. But she also looked so sweet and vulnerable. He had intentions of painting her as if she were nothing less than a grand lady, but the color added drama and lit a man's imagination so that he looked at her and dreamt of what it would be to possess such a woman.

Her eyes were the most incredible green he'd ever seen. Not emerald, and not jade. They were a shade that defied description. Fey green that he'd already spent a night mixing and remixing variations of green to practice capturing.

For now, he sketched as quickly as he could, a man possessed by the moment.

"Can I talk?" she inquired shyly, after several long minutes of watching him work. It was fascinating to see the strange intensity of his efforts, and she likened it to a dance between the warm fire in his eyes and the confident sweep of his hand.

"You may. Just don't move."

A few more seconds spun out between them, and Eleanor was suddenly reluctant to speak at all. After all, conversation was one thing, but this was an odd suspension of every social rule she'd ever known. This was small talk with a man whose every look sent sizzling arcs of heat through her while she sat on a divan in a silk velvet red dress pretending that nothing was extraordinary. Where did such a conversation begin?

"Well?" He stopped drawing and gave her his most piratelike smile from his place below her. "Was that a question of capability or desire?"

"I was paralyzed for a moment with the freedom to express myself and . . . wondered if I should have thought of what to say first before asking."

He shook his head and went back to work. "Say anything you like. You are in no danger of misspeaking here, and I'm sure to be entertained no matter what, Miss Beckett."

"There is *always* the danger of misspeaking, Mr. Hastings. But, surely you don't intend to . . . kneel there? I meant—you are . . . on the floor, sir."

"I take it that you are unused to men sitting at your feet?"

"No. Are you suggesting I should be?" she countered.

"I'm saying that you will be before this is over, Miss Beckett, as I'm very content where I am. Now, be still, woman." The last command was patently playful, and Josiah smiled as he felt her nerves begin to quiet.

Eleanor knew without a single doubt that she would never be used to Josiah Hastings kneeling at her feet, gazing up at her with his mahogany-colored eyes.

"I feel like you're looking up my nose from down there." She blurted the words out, blushing miserably.

He laughed, a warm, rich rumbling sound that sent a shiver of pleasure down her spine. "I am *not* looking up your nose. I promise."

"Well, if you *promise* . . ." His humor was contagious, and she settled into the strange work of sitting for an artist. The candles behind him dazzled her eyes, pressing stars into her vision so that it was impossible to look anywhere else but at the Adonis perched next to her toes, sketching onto the canvas in broad, graceful strokes. After several minutes, a natural curiosity dictated her choice of conversation.

"When did you first realize that you were an artist?" Eleanor asked.

"Ah! I think it was when I was ten. Our governess had punished me for some transgression—I can't remember what I'd done but I'm sure it was well deserved. In any case, I was made to sit in a bare little room until I'd repented. But there was the most remarkable light coming through the old bubbled glass windows onto the floor and the dust was dancing in the beams and it changed." He smiled at the memory. "It changed and shifted constantly. From one minute to the next, it was like a slow dance of a hundred prisms of light and color and I was mesmerized."

"I take it you weren't very quick to repent."

"I was in there for hours. My governess and my family were convinced I was the most stubborn and willful boy ever born. I was too embarrassed to tell them I'd just lost track of time watching sunbeams track across the room—but an artist was born."

Eleanor tried to imagine it. Something as simple as a sunbeam was surely a thing she'd seen countless times, but she couldn't remember ever really noticing it, much less spending any time remarking on its colors or movements. If she'd been punished with her pert little nose in a corner, she'd fumed at cobwebs and tapped her little foot in frustration. "By the way you tell it, you'd have deliberately done your worst to get back to that room."

"On the contrary," he said. "Once I saw the light, I found it everywhere! It was—" The joy suddenly drained from his expression.

"It was . . . ?" she prompted gently.

He shrugged, far too somber for her liking. "A discovery I carried with me, wherever I went."

"How fortuitous." It seemed like the thing to say, but she wasn't sure.

"Don't move too much, Miss Beckett."

She caught herself and leaned back as she'd been, and allowed the silence to fill the space between them until his eyes were clear again and the sound of the pencil against the canvas restored the growing connection between them.

Chapter
10

Eleanor returned to the inn that evening by carriage, settling into her room as her mind turned over the strange surprises and delights of the day. Conversation with Josiah Hastings was like playing a thrilling game of chess. After an awkward start or two, the hours had flown by and she'd forgotten to fear boring him or saying something wrong. And despite Mrs. Escher's firm announcement that she wasn't to be bothered with anything to do with artistic frippery, it was Rita who'd insisted on bringing up a lunch tray and fussed at Josiah for not giving his model any respite breaks.

By the end of the day, the first signs of a routine had emerged, and Eleanor wanted to pinch herself for her luck. There had been nothing scandalous in the process, and even in an evening gown without gloves, she'd come to think that all her fears were groundless.

I have modeled for a painter and am none the worse for it!

He'd covered the canvas with a cloth at the end of the

session, explaining that he would prefer her not to see the work in progress. "An artist's prerogative, Miss Beckett, to avoid criticism until after the last brushstroke." Eleanor's curiosity about the portrait was tantalizing, but she trusted him enough not to push, or peek. After all, she told herself, it hardly mattered whether she approved of the painting or not. The sitting fee would give her almost any future she desired, within reason, of course, and the arrangement even with the wicked red velvet dress was very agreeable.

It was perfect.

Except, there was something about Mr. Hastings that piqued her curiosity. Beyond the obvious fascinations and moral dangers of a wickedly handsome man with a soulful nature and questionable profession, she was convinced that he was shielding something from her, diplomatically avoiding certain topics and steering things away from himself.

There was no Mrs. Hastings. She'd boldly reconfirmed as much with Mrs. Escher while she'd helped her undress back into her day clothes to leave the red gown behind. And while Rita had growled something about him briefly tomcatting like a fool when he'd first gotten back to England with someone by the name of Blackwell, he'd apparently mended his ways and taken to staying home more often than not.

Perhaps he's addicted to opiates or some terrible tropical vice that has kept him to himself all these months. But his countenance seemed clear and unblemished to her, and everything Eleanor knew about such things had hinted that those who suffered from such afflictions were marked by it.

Perhaps he's just—

A knock on the door interrupted the direction of her thoughts, and she went to door, habitually checking to make sure her chignon was secure before opening the portal. "Ah, Mrs. Clay!"

"I took the liberty and brought you up a spot of tea. It's late for it, but I thought it might warm you up, Miss Beckett." Mrs. Clay held out her covered tray, and Eleanor very naturally stepped back to allow her dear landlady entrance.

"You spoil me, Mrs. Clay. It was a bit chilly on the ride home tonight. Thank you."

Mrs. Clay set the tray down on the little table in between the chairs by the fire. "I hope you're making yourself right at home here."

"How could I not? Mrs. Clay, the room is delightful." Eleanor uncovered the tray and almost sighed at the beautiful little biscuits and cream drops on a plate. "Won't you join me?"

"I will! What a darling you are to think of me!" Mrs. Clay took the seat across from her, and both women settled in for their first official visit. "I'm so glad to hear you say you like the room! I'd started to lament ever finding a lovely tenant who would suit, and then there you were. Tally's gotten quite fond of you!"

"And I of him, but . . ."

"There's a but?" Mrs. Clay finished pouring the tea. "About my Tally?"

"No. Tally is as sweet a boy as you described. My hesitation is . . . you must tell me how much the rooms cost, Mrs. Clay. I wouldn't want you to think I was taking advantage or that I am in Mr. Hastings's keeping."

"Not at all! You're a fine lady, Miss Beckett, and I would never be a villain and think ill of you! Not if I had my shoes in a fire!" Mrs. Clay cheerfully dropped five sugar cubes in her cup. "I pride myself on my ability to read a person, and in this business, it has served me well."

"I know that Mr. Hastings is paying you for my room and board. But I wish to make it clear that he is doing so only out of . . . a professional courtesy. There is nothing unseemly in the arrangement, Mrs. Clay. I intend to pay him back, you see. I don't want to be beholden to anyone."

"What a good girl! Of course you don't. And I promise, I'll write up a lovely draft so that you can see every penny."

"Thank you, Mrs. Clay! That is exactly what I'd hoped."

"But it can wait, can't it? You wouldn't want to bruise a poor man's ego like that by being too efficient, would you? I know your arrangement is as innocent as apples. Mr.

Hastings was quite firm about the matter when he took the room and knew I ran a respectable house. Miss Beckett, you are the most proper young lady I've ever had the pleasure to meet. So don't you fret! I'll make sure you have a bill so that Mr. Hastings isn't out of pocket and all will be well."

"Thank you, Mrs. Clay." Eleanor felt a little better but suspected that Mrs. Clay's idea of a lovely draft might not match the amount that Josiah was paying—since the woman clearly was in on his scheme to keep her oblivious to her living expenses. "May I ask . . . how long have you known Mr. Hastings, Mrs. Clay?"

"Hmm, let me see." Mrs. Clay sipped at her tea to consider the question. "I knew of him years ago, but only because there'd been a bit of a splash in the papers. Nothing unseemly! But the story was lively enough to catch my eye and I remember remarking to my husband that I'd remember the name Hastings for it!"

"What was the story?"

Mrs. Clay laughed. "He'd done a portrait for some rich old titled goat, and when there was a house fire, the owner had grabbed his nightcap, a stuffed trophy of a pheasant, and the painting of himself! Out the man ran, only to realize he'd entirely forgotten to put on a single piece of clothing! But there he was, holding his portrait to hide his altogether on one side and a feathered bird to cover his backside—and well, I'll confess it, I still get the giggles when I recall it in the *Times*."

"How infamous!"

"It was! And when I met Mr. Hastings some time after that, well, I knew I'd never forget him for a much better reason."

"And what was that?" Eleanor asked, completely intrigued.

"I had a dear friend who had a market stall over near Whitehall. And one day, while a group of very well-heeled gentlemen were strolling by, her entire cart was overturned onto the road. I was there, just by chance, and saw them all start to laugh and mock us on our knees scrambling to pick up her goods. It was her livelihood in the mud, but all they saw was two silly women in a panic, ruining our petticoats and looking for all the world like sodden rats."

"That's terrible!" Eleanor exclaimed.

"It was, indeed. But then, there he was. Every inch the young gentleman himself in a silk blue coat, if memory serves, dressing down those fools for being so coldhearted, and then he lifted the cart and began to help, as if it were every day for a man to squat in the muck and pick up rags and lacework."

That sounds exactly like the man I met behind Madame Claremont's—except for the silk blue coat. His clothes are plain, at best, and all so dark!

"I made a point of getting his name and was so delighted to think I knew the artist from that article!" Mrs. Clay continued, setting her teacup down. "I told him about the Grove and he's been good to stop by now and again. And when he came back from India, he introduced Mr. Rutherford, who was in need of a home, and the rest is as you've seen."

It was far more information than she'd had before. It was the second mention of India, tantalizing and exotic, but Eleanor wasn't sure how to press for more details without appearing far too interested for the wrong reasons. Asking Mr. Hastings himself would be the proper course, if her nerves held for it.

"That's quite a story, Mrs. Clay."

"You're almost out of coal!" Mrs. Clay exclaimed, starting to rise.

"Oh, please don't bother yourself," Eleanor said. "I saw what a full dining room you have tonight and there's some in the bottom of the bucket to see me through until tomorrow."

"Nonsense!" Mrs. Clay yanked the bellpull vigorously. "You'll catch your death in this weather if you don't stay ahead of it. And as for the crowd below, I agree, and probably better to stay above stairs and eat here if you would.

I've a French theatrical dance troupe in the house, of all things! Decent artistic performances only, but still—I can't tell ballet from ballyhoo, so I've given them quite a firm speech on minding themselves. Mr. Clay, rest his soul, had a soft spot in his heart for theatre people and so I occasionally let them come if they have references and can pay in advance. One can never be too careful, Miss Beckett, with entertainers and gypsies."

"I suppose not." Eleanor was a bit bemused at the idea of this down-to-earth landlady befriending painters and providing a haven to colorful circus performers and wandering minstrels. "I've never met a gypsy."

"Mr. Clay, rest his soul, when he was deep in his cups, used to claim to be a distant relation to a gypsy king, but I think it was a bit of wishful dreaming on his part, for I don't think the man ever went north of Old Street Road in his entire life. So I think he envied them their freedom a little." She set her cup down to take two of the biscuits. "But why travel when the inn brings a world of travelers to me? That's what I always said to cheer him, and it always seemed to work."

There was a quiet knock before Tally came in, shyly bringing more coal. Then to Eleanor's astonishment, he wiggled his fingers and made odd little gestures with his hands as Mrs. Clay nodded in comprehension. "Yes, dear. I'll tend to Mr. Reeves. That man's far too quick to fuss!"

"He spoke with his hands?"

"He did! Mr. Reeves is swearing his room's too drafty, but the man's a bit absentminded and keeps leaving his windows open, so what's to be done?" She brushed her hands across her apron and stood to leave their impromptu party. "He's a professor of something or other, but I just agree with him and then close it when he's not paying attention. He leaves on Tuesday, so there's a relief! I only hope he didn't leave his windows open at home in Glasgow all this time while he's been in Town! Can you imagine? There'll be a snowdrift in his bedroom!"

Eleanor was still enraptured with the two levels of communication happening in front of her, as Tally and Mrs. Clay watched each other in perfect comprehension. "I've never seen such a thing. It's so clever to use signals like that!"

"We've come up with a bit of a system, Tally and I. I read about it in a newspaper article and what a blessing! Mind, I don't think we're doing it the way those expensive deaf schools are doing it, but I just started when he was little, pointing out things and making up a little sign. We'd practice together and that's when I knew my Tally had as keen a mind as any! And now when we find a need for a new word, why Tally is the one to invent how he thinks it should look and he teaches it to me! Isn't he brilliant?" Mrs. Clay moved her hands as she spoke, including her adopted son in the conversation and in the praise.

Tally immediately blushed and retreated from the room.

"It's truly remarkable, Mrs. Clay."

"It's nothing, at all. He's my son and I simply can't run the house without him. Although, I do worry. When he's old enough, he'll need a girl bright and patient who can run the inn with him and see to the customers, but that's years off!"

"Years," Eleanor echoed softly. "But what a future he'll have!"

"He's a keen eye for the business and can track a penny. Mr. Clay would have loved him for it! It's not charity to leave things to Tally, I can tell you that! It's good sense and a good guarantee that my little inn will outlast us all." She brushed off her apron again, a habit that betrayed the leaving of one topic for another. "But, as I'm exiling you to your rooms for dinner, I'll arrange for a bath to be brought up afterward."

"Oh!" Eleanor trailed after her toward the door. "So much trouble! Just a bit of hot water in a basin will do for now, and I can—"

"A bath! A lady must have her bath and what's the trouble? I love a good hot soak myself. Nothing banishes a chill or sets one right like a nice warm bath, don't you think?"

"Well, yes! But—"

"All settled, then!" Mrs. Clay smiled, the matter decided. "Finish your tea, dear, and I'll have dinner up in just a bit. Then we'll see to the bath and leave you to your evening. Good night, Miss Beckett, and thank you so much for your hospitality."

Eleanor laughed. "*My* hospitality!"

"Well, it's as I see it. It's so nice to have a bit of female companionship, and I'll admit, I love the way you treat my Tally." She smoothed out her apron once again. "So that's that!"

"Mrs. Clay, you are a treasure and I have the distinct feeling that I should just yield to your judgment and stop arguing."

Mrs. Clay began to let herself out, chuckling. "There! At last, you have the way of it, dear! Mr. Clay, rest his soul, used to say he could get the moon to do what he wanted easier than steering yours truly. So, you just have that soak, and I'll see you in the morning!"

And with that, she was gone and Eleanor was left to wonder if any force of nature was as unstoppable as her kindhearted landlady.

Later, as the copper tub was brought up and filled with hot water from the kitchens, Eleanor had a little time to contemplate the new luxuries of her life. She'd had a lifetime of relative ease and never realized it, but months of hardship had provided a quick and brutal lesson on the costs of every common item she'd ever touched.

Eleanor picked up the pink bar of French-milled soap that the housemaid had brought up, turning it over on her palm. *There's a few shillings spent for rose-scented vanity after months of hard lye soap.*

Everything had its price. She sighed and set it back down in the little dish hanging off the side of the steaming bathtub. She began to disrobe quickly but still folded her things and set them aside carefully to avoid needing a pressing. Finally, she was able to step gingerly over the edge and settle slowly into the water until she was up to her chin in the indulgent sensation of silky heat.

As soon as the painting was finished, she would have money of her own, and the idea coalesced around her like the steam of her bath. The terrors of poverty could fade away and Eleanor would be able to celebrate the consolations that came with surviving with her honor intact.

Easy to pay Josiah back for coal and soap, but there's more to it, isn't there?

He sat at my feet and I was transformed somehow.

How do you pay a man back for that?

Chapter
11

That evening, most of the Jaded had gathered once again at Rowan's, each man finding his favorite chair or vantage point in the doctor's first-floor study and taking comfort in the familiarity of West's odd eclectic collections and artwork. The men had never known each other or even crossed paths in their different social spheres before they'd been thrown together by their experiences in an Indian dungeon. Surviving it and returning to London had strengthened the friendships between them, and now, the bond of brotherhood was unmistakable. Theirs was a circle that defied any enemy to break through.

"The advertisement for the front page of the *Times* is ready," Ashe announced, raising his glass in a mock toast. "Though I still say the language is too subtle for my mood."

Michael crossed his arms defensively. "Blackwell's mood suggested simply calling him out as a weak-boned, cowardly, murderous bastard along with a few other choice phrases I'm fairly sure the *Times* won't allow on the front page due to the decency laws."

"God be damned if this villain has—"

Galen moved to put a gentle restraining hand on Ashe's shoulder, interrupting him. "Ashe. Whoever it is, they'll pay for what they've done. And no one belittles your fury or sees it as unwarranted. If it were Haley . . . I think I'd have parted ways with reason."

"He did for a while," Rowan teased, also doing his best to decrease the tension in the room. Ashe's beloved bride had nearly lost her life, and while his rage was understandable, the game was too dangerous to allow any one of them to be blinded by emotion.

"How is Caroline faring, Ashe?" Galen asked.

"She insists that she is as hale and hearty as ever," Ashe replied, the brittle anger in his ice blue eyes giving way to softer sentiments at the mention of his wife. "But she tires very easily and I—worry. She's not herself."

The doctor in their midst took note. "I'll make it a point to stop by more often, Ashe. Gayle and she are thick as thieves, so I promise it will seem social enough to keep Caroline from suspecting that we are hovering."

"Thank you, Rowan," Ashe answered gratefully.

"Very well, then, let's see to this weak-boned, cowardly, and murderous bastard, shall we?" Michael suggested, unfolding a paper from a leather holder in his pocket. "Here it is."

Rowan took the paper and read it aloud:

Our patience is gone. Nothing is clear and you failed to signal as promised before you struck. Incompetence of your hired man is no excuse. If you want it, we are willing to talk. Place a message on the front page of the Times *within a fortnight if you're listening, Jackal, and we'll let you know where and when. In the meantime, be on guard. We'll end this one way or another.—The Jaded.*

"What do you think? Challenging but not too belligerent, without straying into outright libel, wouldn't you say?" Rutherford asked them.

"It's only libel if it isn't true, Michael," Ashe growled.

"The Jackal seems a catching nickname." Rowan handed the paper back to Michael.

"Why not do this in one go? Issue a challenge with the place and time and be done with it," Josiah asked. "Why give him two weeks to reply, if we're not waiting anymore . . . ?"

Michael shook his head. "We need to make sure the fish is on the hook. I want this over with as much as the next man, but he's gone to ground after his misstep against Blackwell. We could end up losing far more than our time—we could lose our chance to get answers, and more lives could be lost if we end up floundering about and lose the advantage."

"Agreed." Rowan nodded, pouring himself a small brandy. "There's been no communication or sign of this Jackal since the poisoning. We want this on our terms, not his, and on our timetable. To hell with full moons and mystic signs!"

"The only detail left to decide is where we want to meet the villain after he responds." Galen took the paper from Michael to read over it. "I'm assuming we're staying within London for this."

"Hell, let's make it Hyde Park!" Ashe refilled his glass and found a seat near Josiah. "A public spectacle might make him think twice before pulling anything."

Most of the men immediately began shaking their heads, but it was Michael who spoke first. "No. It's too open with far too many places for an ambush—and in the weather we've been having this winter, there might not be much of a public strolling Hyde Park to witness anything—not that we necessarily want witnesses! No parks."

"Fine." Ashe sighed. "I'm not making any more suggestions since it's clear none of you trust me not to bring a pistol to meet this murderer. And for the record, Michael has already threatened to make me empty my pockets, so you can all rest easier when the critical moment comes."

"Hardly!" Josiah scoffed softly, a hand over his eyes as

if the glare from the lamps were bothering him. "What's to keep you from just strangling him with your bare hands?"

"Good point." Michael shifted back to lean against the wall of bookshelves. "Blackwell stays home."

"Blackwell will do as he damn well pleases," Ashe countered.

"Time enough to argue about that, gentlemen." Galen cleared his throat. "So where will we demand the meeting take place?"

"There is an old gambling house near the Grove. I know the owner and we can reserve a private room on the first floor. It's public enough, I think, without exposing us to an ambush, but still discreet enough so that we can have whatever conversation is required without worrying," Michael explained.

"A gambling house." Rowan repeated the words, as if mulling it over. "Let's just be careful that our next message doesn't read like an advertisement for treasure. It already sounds salacious enough to catch every casual reader's attention. The last thing we need is an unexpected flock of curious pigeons showing up and muddling the plan."

"Agreed." Galen took a sip of his barley water. "Damn it, what is keeping Darius in Scotland?"

Ashe shrugged. "He won't say. Something about a personal matter, which makes me wonder if there is a lady involved, but he did send word that one of his best contacts in the gem trade had heard talk of a 'sacred treasure,' but didn't have more details yet. Hopefully, he can find out what the damn 'sacred treasure' is so that we'll know what we're dealing with." Ashe held out the last letter from Thorne to Josiah, but Josiah waved it off.

"What does the scholar have to say?" Josiah asked.

Ashe unfolded the note and read it aloud:

I may have a lead on the sacred treasure. Dealers here value customer confidentiality highly so can't rush, but will press as best I can to get better information. My favorite, Mr. P., is sure to know something, and hinted recently that there was quite a tale connected to our mystery object. Trying to get specifics on vague phrase, since every stone hauled out of India might carry the same description if you had asked a local. In any case, when the meeting comes together or even before, if any description becomes available, please send courier immediately.

Will remain in Edinburgh for now.

D

"If there are answers there, Thorne is sure to find them." Ashe spoke with confidence, his faith in his best friend unshaken. "He has the keenest intellect of any man I've ever known."

None of them argued, but a few glances were exchanged as Galen's protest had gone unanswered. *What personal matter would keep Darius away from London—especially now, when everything felt like it was coming to a head at last?*

"We'll wait to hear from him, and in the meantime, I'm taking our ad to the *Times* for placement. Gentlemen, things are in motion, but from this moment onward, we'll be the ones with our hands on the helm," Michael announced.

The informal meeting seemed to break up, as Ashe was determined to return to Caroline's side. The men began to offer their farewells, but Michael caught Josiah before he could slip out.

"About Miss Beckett—I'm not sure if she mentioned it, but the lady has informed me that she doesn't need a bodyguard, Hastings."

Josiah smiled, shrugging on his coat. "So much for your subtle skills of observance."

Rutherford bristled a bit. "As if my nerves weren't already on edge! I can't help but worry that you've brought this woman into things at the worst time, Hastings. You're making light of it, but—"

"I'm not making light of anything." Josiah held his ground. "The work is begun, and it's going fast. I won't stop now."

Michael shook his head. "Two or three weeks and this will be behind us. Whatever this work entails, what is a fortnight? You're being selfish, Hastings."

"Perhaps I am. But I'll hire the man you provided references for as a guard for the ground floor. I'll take any measures you recommend to guarantee her safety or mine, but I *can't* stop now. I have to finish this painting, Michael. As soon as I'm done, she'll end our association and be out of harm's way, but I'm not relinquishing this until I'm forced to it! And you, Michael Rutherford, are not going to force me to do anything!"

Rowan stepped in between them. "Let the man paint, Michael. None of the rest of us have suspended our lives. We've become more cautious, but we haven't ceased our professions or our pursuits. You cannot single out Hastings."

Michael shifted back, and the tension began to ease. "I apologize. The mysteries of painting are beyond me, and it's a failing of mine to see things only in terms of defense and strategy. I didn't mean to single you out, Hastings. It's only that . . ."

"It's only what?" Josiah asked.

"Something else is going on with you. Something you're not saying, because the man I know would never be so cavalier about risking someone's life. You cannot be so blind as to think—"

"Peace, Rutherford!" Rowan interjected.

Michael turned and left without another word, the firm closing of the study door creating a pall over the gathering.

"What was that all about?" Galen asked.

Josiah pulled up his collar, shielding his face from his friends as he turned to follow Michael out. "Just an exercise in defense and strategy, gentlemen. Nothing more."

*   *   *

Josiah left the brownstone, as distracted by the furious twists of his thoughts as the dark shadows that had settled into the left side of his vision for the day. Michael's words had cut too close to the painful truth, and Rutherford, as always, was not a man to hold his opinion back.

But Josiah couldn't argue his case without giving secrets away and sacrificing the last of his pride. And he wasn't oblivious to the dangers of the threat to the Jaded. But Michael's point had been well made. There was no denying that in recent months Josiah had somehow decided that ignoring the matter equated to an ability to avoid it. It was difficult to imagine the drama of hidden assassins and sacred treasures even remotely existing, much less in the stark world of London in winter. It didn't seem real, even now, despite everything that had happened to his friends.

I should know better.

Or is it that I've already become a bit blind? I've been so caught up in my own frustration and the struggle to come to terms with the darkness ahead, I believed it would be a mercy if some knife-wielding figure had leapt from the shadows. . . .

Until I met Eleanor.

Now I'm blinded by her colors and her beauty and Rutherford is right—I'm selfish.

Damn it. I want this.

But there was something else circling his senses, and Josiah finally acknowledged it with one long, heavy sigh.

I want more than just to complete a painting.

I want her. Ravenously. Mindlessly.

The revelation didn't bring him any comfort. It was beyond impossible. He'd vowed not to touch her, and Miss Eleanor Beckett wasn't the sort of woman that would allow him even the hint of a liberty. Hell, it was one of the reasons she probably appealed so strongly. It was human nature to seek forbidden fruit, and she was a woman out of his reach. Even if he hadn't been teetering on the brink of uselessness, her firm sensibilities and adherence to all things proper made him a terrible choice for her, with his artist's reputation for wild aesthetics and erratic morals.

And now that he was going blind, nothing was simple.

It didn't matter if he had two king's ransoms at his finger-tips or an acceptable pedigree—ultimately he would be a burden to her.

If she learned his secret, she might come to him out of pity and misguided affection, or convince herself that it was her Christian duty to see to him since he'd "saved her life." Josiah shuddered at the idea.

His desire for Eleanor wanted nothing to do with pity. In his fantasies, he was whole and there was a conquest to be made—with no room for his failings or the lack of a future. But the fantasy never held for long, disintegrating into a tender tangle that he suspected was far more dangerous than any straightforward seduction a man could envision.

By the time he reached his own home, he knew only one thing for certain.

He could no longer afford to be cavalier about anything.

Nothing is worth risking her life. But there's a compromise if I'm careful. I'll add the security that Rutherford's been after, and more.

I'll push harder to finish this painting before this other business comes to a head, and guarantee that Miss Eleanor Beckett will be free and beyond the reach of any of it.

It was the worst kind of irony that he would have to rush to see things finished when finishing meant losing her company. But there was nothing else to be done. If he didn't finish it, he would never have another chance to see his work come to life.

The darkness was coming. Time was his relentless adversary and he'd already chosen his path.

He would complete the work as quickly as he could and pray that his hunger for Eleanor didn't get in the way.

Chapter
12

"You look like a man with the weight of the world on his shoulders, Mr. Hastings."

He tried to smile, and shook his head. "I'm pouting like a spoiled boy. It's snowing and the light isn't good today. I shouldn't have sent for you at all, but we'll push ahead with the candlelight and make do."

He wasn't ready to admit that he'd grown used to her presence, and after the foolish argument he'd had with Rutherford several nights before, Josiah knew it was his own stubborn pride that had insisted on continuing to summon her.

Besides, this morning he'd awoken to a nearly clear field of vision. Escher had already replaced most of the melted candles and even found two more candelabras to suit his employer's mood. Josiah lit one candle and then began to use it to light the others while she waited.

Eleanor walked over to the table. "It's beautiful, isn't it? I imagine ballrooms don't have this many candles, Mr. Hastings."

"Have you never been to a ball, Miss Beckett?"

She laughed. "No!"

"To a country dance, then?"

"No, I'm afraid not." Eleanor smoothed her hands gently against the velvet at her waist. "My father was a self-made man who always aspired to higher society. We read all the social pages and he used to memorize etiquette books because I think he was afraid of anyone thinking less of him for not being born with a fortune. He had great hopes for me. . . ."

"And what were your hopes?"

"Mine?" she asked in astonishment.

"You seem to have memorized all those etiquette books as well. Were you not hoping to attend a ball? Meet some wealthy industrialist or aspiring politician and join a ladies' social club or two?" he asked, deliberately keeping his tone light despite his keen interest in her reply. "Or did you aspire to the peerage?"

She laughed. "I have never met a titled peer nor do I expect to, Mr. Hastings. I am a realistic woman and it is not in my future."

He had to bite his tongue to keep from correcting her since the Jaded's inner circle included a future earl. "What did you want, then, Miss Beckett?"

"I wanted to please my father."

"Is that all?"

"No." She trailed a finger along the tabletop. "But what does it matter?"

His hand froze midair and a single wax drop fell onto the table. "Out with it, Miss Beckett. Or I'll threaten to paint a big wart on your nose."

"You wouldn't!"

"Tell me what you hoped for."

"Why?"

"Because guessing is going to keep me from sleeping for years to come, so I'm begging you to share your confidences with me. Let's call it curiosity, and leave it at that."

"What if my hopes are mundane?"

"Are they?"

She looked away from him, shyness overcoming her. "You dream of immortality and freedom. You've sacrificed everything in their pursuit, Mr. Hastings. I have no wish to suffer your derision if I say I wish simply to be respected and to feel a sense of . . . order and belonging. I was so frightened after . . ." She straightened her shoulders and looked at him again, her green eyes teeming with the ghosts of hunger and depravation. "I wish never to be at the whim of Fate again. I would master my own life, Mr. Hastings, and never be in anyone's debt or service."

"Ah, I can directly relate to that wish, Miss Beckett."

"Can you? I find that hard to believe." She smiled, her eyes clearing. "All my life I've strived to be conventional, Mr. Hastings. Is that wrong of me?"

"Not at all. Don't forget, you're a woman of means again, Miss Beckett. Once you're through with me, there is nothing to keep you from charting your own course, free of debt and the burden of scandal. Please, sit down, Miss Beckett, and let's get to work." He held out his hand to escort her up onto the dais, hating the lump in his throat.

She arranged herself, taking her position carefully. "How is it possible? I look at you and you seem so courageous and content—and none of the rules apply to you at all, do they?"

He sat on a low stool to work, the canvas sitting practically on the floor between his long legs. It was unconventional, to say the least, but he didn't seem to care. From here, he was so close she could admire the shape of his hands as he worked, the sinews of his frame, and even see the thrum and throb of his pulse when he tipped his head to the side. Here was a proximity that she had never dreamt of only weeks ago, but with Josiah, it was easy.

"They apply to me, Miss Beckett. But I hate rules."

"I love them. They make me feel . . . safe. I know what to expect and what's expected of me."

"But it's an illusion, Eleanor. Even if you follow every rule, you can never know what to expect in life. Never."

"I hadn't looked at it that way. But surely it's better to try. Isn't that what makes life more civilized? Our rules and social niceties?"

He shook his head. "It's what makes life appear to be more civilized, but I fear it's only a veneer. And so thin. If you scrutinize it too much, it gives way so quickly. And then you've earned yourself the heartache of disappointment."

"So melancholy!"

"Am I?"

"You are, indeed."

"And how would you describe it, then? Our true natures?" he asked.

"I don't know. But when I look at you—purely as an example of an Englishman, of course!"

"Of course."

"You don't seem . . . disappointing."

"I am relieved." He smiled, but the light of it didn't quite reach his eyes.

"You're a good man, Josiah Hastings."

The hand holding the brush froze in midair, as if her proclamation had stopped time. "I'm terribly flawed. Perhaps more than most, Miss Beckett. Besides," he said, as the brush once again touched the canvas, "good men don't break the rules, and since you've already learned of my penchant for rebellion, I don't think I can genuinely make that claim."

"But you rescued me from that dreadful Mr. Perring, and Mrs. Clay told me of your first meeting. Even when it isn't to your advantage, you help others. We are all flawed, are we not? But you seem to think nothing of helping others. In my opinion, that's very meritable."

"You, Miss Beckett, make a man wish to improve himself." He looked up at her with a smoldering glance that made her breath catch in her throat. "Helping anyone in need is merely the right thing to do. All that means is that I have a terrible habit of following my impulses—good and bad. I am far from saintly, and daily struggle to live up to the few rules I do have."

"Which ones?" she asked, genuinely interested in understanding him better.

"Don't move," he corrected her gently. "Miss Beckett, may I suggest a change of subject?"

She surprised herself by shaking her head, a new confidence and mischief surging through her. "Which rules are troubling you, Mr. Hastings?"

"My new rules, Miss Beckett, introduced just days ago when you climbed into that carriage. There is a rule about not touching you too much, or making up reasons to get too close, and most especially there is a firm and unbreakable rule about not kissing you."

"Oh," she exclaimed softly. "*Those* rules!"

"What are you thinking in that proper head of yours?"

"I'm thinking that it would have been better to make a rule that you couldn't even mention your rules since . . . now I find I am thinking of all kinds of unbidden things. . . ."

"And?"

The urge to lie was palpable and strong. The conversation had become far too intimate, but it had happened so quickly and so naturally that Eleanor wasn't sure what to say. He'd made a rule about not kissing her and now it was all she could do to imagine what it would be like to be kissed by such a man. For there was no doubt from the molten fire in his eyes and the tendrils of heat spreading down her limbs that he wasn't proposing some chaste version of a courtly kiss on her hand or cheek.

What would happen if I let myself simply say what I'm thinking?

Before her mind could summon reason, Eleanor did exactly that.

"I was wishing I was the sort of woman who knew what it would be like to break all the rules," she whispered.

At first, he didn't react at all, and she wondered if he'd heard her. But then the brushes were being set aside with a methodical calm that didn't match the blaze of desire in his eyes. The wait was pure torture as Josiah carefully cleaned the brush and then unfolded himself from the stool.

Alarm and anticipation warred openly inside of her, and Eleanor forgot which side of her nature she was supposed to root to victory. For he was close, all at once, and not to adjust a coil of her hair or politely ask her to tilt her head to one side or the other. . . .

"May I?" he asked softly, and Eleanor didn't need to ask what he meant.

A kiss. He'd made the rule, so he needed her permission—and Eleanor knew it was desire and not fear that made her hesitate. Because she wanted this little taste of ruin. Because she envied every reckless soul who had wandered into blissful sin without a glance of regret over their shoulders.

"No." The word was whispered, and Eleanor's eyes filled with unshed tears. "Whatever I may wish, I am not that woman, Mr. Hastings."

She braced herself internally for the anger or disappointment in his gaze, but it never came. He held perfectly still and everything in his countenance was calm and caring. He was so close that she could smell cinnamon and sandalwood from the soap he used, and again, the urge to do the unthinkable and touch his face or offer some physical link to reassure herself that the growing friendship between them was real and tangible was almost irresistible.

Almost.

"No," he echoed softly. "You are not that woman. You are more, Miss Beckett, than the rules could ever restrain or define. And for that, I am grateful."

He stood slowly, ensuring that his withdrawal wasn't abrupt or brusque to be misinterpreted as anything more than a gentlemanly retreat from the field. Josiah knew that one sigh or misspoken word of disappointment at the loss of that kiss could send her running.

Oh, but it had been close!

The red dress had a power all its own.

She'd never even been to a country dance, but as he looked at her, it was impossible not to indulge in fantasies of what it would have been like to escort Miss Eleanor

Beckett on his arm to a grand ball or two. She aspired to respectability, but it was tantalizing to think of flexing some of his social powers and being able to introduce her to a few titled peers and his wealthy friends, all the rules be damned!

Not exactly the respectability of an upper-middle-class soiree, but amusing to see her there. God, but she would have dazzled them all and I would have felt like a peacock strutting about with such a woman next to me! In another lifetime, I'd have been able to pursue her and show her all that London has to offer.

He stepped down off the dais and turned to move back around to the canvas, glancing back to assure himself that she was still in position, still with him despite the trespass.

But that was a mistake.

He misjudged the distance, his shin hitting the low stool and knocking his paint palette and brushes to the floor, a small jar of oil overturning to add to the colorful disaster.

"Damn it!"

He knelt instantly to try to stem the worst of it and heard her moving behind him, heard her sigh of dismay.

"Oh my! Can I—"

"Stay there!" He held up a hand to hold her in place. "Please, Miss Beckett." The flash of anger had been entirely directed at his own clumsiness, but he didn't wish to add to the moment's weight with another misunderstanding. "A man should have to clean up his own messes, and I wouldn't want you to get paint on the hem of that dress—especially since I'm forbidden to buy you another."

"As you wish. Was your work damaged?" she asked softly, as she sat reluctantly back down.

The painting! In his embarrassment and rush, he hadn't even looked to see if the canvas had been splattered or soiled, but luckily, a quick assessment assured him that it hadn't been touched. *Well, there's something to be thankful for. Providence is keeping me humble but apparently has decided not to destroy my dreams.*

"No, it's fine. The worst of it will be hearing Escher's lecture, but I'll shift a drop cloth and put it off for a while. If I'm lucky, it might be years." He sopped up the worst of it using a cloth he had for wiping off the brushes, wincing as the smeared colors merged together into an inglorious gray.

God, I hate gray. Almost as much as I hate black, but how ironic to think it's there, lurking behind every rainbow on a man's paintbrush.

He sighed again. *Enough pouting for one day, Hastings.*

He shifted off his knees to balance on the back of his ankles, and caught sight of Eleanor Beckett's face, calm and compassionate. The magic was intact, for there was all the color he'd been trying to capture—still there. It made no sense. But just as striking was the lack of judgment in her eyes when she looked at him scrambling about on the floor.

"Years? You're an optimist, Mr. Hastings."

He smiled, his humor impossibly restored. "I'm a pragmatic child, but I'll accept the compliment all the same."

He stood, the brushes retrieved and his palette set aside on the table. "I'll head downstairs to change out of these paint-covered clothes, if you don't mind."

"Since the light isn't good, would you rather—"

"I'm not ready to admit defeat, Miss Beckett." He'd meant to say it lightly, but it came out as an Olympian vow of some heroic effort. *That was ridiculous, but I'm not taking it back.* "I'll simply mix new colors and see if I can't make the most of the day, despite myself."

"I'm glad." She said it so quietly for an instant he wasn't sure he'd heard her rightly.

"Are you glad, Miss Beckett?"

She nodded. "Even if the light isn't as you'd wish, and your model is, well"—she blushed before continuing on—"less than inspiring, I would hope for a chance at a better day for you. I would miss your company, Mr. Hastings."

"Thank you for saying such things." He stepped back from the table, turning to head downstairs, but then hesitated. "Although, I have to correct you on one point, Miss Beckett."

"And what is that?"

"I would argue that my model is *extremely* inspiring. You undervalue yourself, Miss Beckett."

"And you flatter me too much, sir." She smoothed out her skirts and shyly studied her slippers.

He headed toward the doorway, shaking his head. "Hardly," he muttered under his breath as he left the room. "And the next time you dare a man to kiss you, you'd better watch yourself."

* * *

That night, after eating her dinner in the Grove's common room, Eleanor wearily retreated to the quiet sanctuary of her apartment. It had been an eventful day.

She distracted herself by trying to clean an already impossibly tidy room, straightening her small wardrobe and rearranging her few possessions. She'd shocked herself with her own behavior, and was still weak-kneed to think how easily he could have been angered by a woman who unwittingly flirted only to spurn his advances.

I was cruel without meaning to be, and then when the paints spilled . . .

She'd expected him to banish her.

But he hadn't. After weeks and months of living in fear of Madame Claremont's unpredictable temper, she'd braced herself for the worst only to discover that her new benefactor was extremely forgiving.

Eleanor changed into her nightclothes and climbed into the bed. Before she doused the light, she spotted the copy of *Lady M's Guide to Etiquette* on the little table by her bedside. It was pure sentiment that made it a favorite because of her father's delight in hearing his daughter recite the order of precedence or quote passages about a lady's deportment. His love for her had inspired his ambitions, and Eleanor had adored him for thinking so highly of her— even if she had always secretly feared disappointing him. Reading Lady M nightly had become a ritual between them, and even now, the act brought her comfort as she turned the weathered pages for advice.

But Lady M had said nothing of men like Josiah Hastings. Lady M had spoken of proper small talk when receiving calls and the reserved and polite affections expected from appropriate gentlemanly suitors. There'd been one tantalizing sentence about bracing oneself for the natural physical exuberance of one's husband after the wedding, but even that had made it all sound very one-sided and strange.

One-sided. Hardly! I'm on fire, God help me. He's done little more than look at me and I am undone inside, like a restless, hungry child. He speaks of impulses and all of mine are awakened to clamor for attention. He bids me be still and I ache to move. Every nerve ending serves him and I'm ignorant as to the course of it all. It's maddening.

She scanned the vague paragraph again about marital bliss, her brow furrowing in concentration. Lady M was proving less than helpful, and if the molten unruly storm of sensations Josiah evoked was any hint of the veiled mysteries between men and women, Eleanor's logical mind had already accepted that there would be nothing reserved or polite about the matter.

Not if Josiah Hastings were the object of a woman's affections.

Eleanor sighed and set aside dear Lady M, abandoning the ritual, plunging the room into darkness. After a lifetime of relying on her head, there was nothing more terrifying than realizing that her heart may not have been paying attention to a single word of good advice. "I should endeavor to keep my affections out of this," she whispered to the shadows.

Her contrary heart answered without hesitation. *I should have let him kiss me. I wanted him to and now I feel like a stupid child for refusing him. It's all such a mess of pride and principles, and everything that I always believed was clear isn't anymore.*

Because artists were rogues and reckless men without moral principles, given to wild creative abandon—weren't they? Except Josiah had never demonstrated anything but respect and restraint, even while admitting his own desire to cross the line.

He had allowed her will to prevail over his, and yielded at the first sign of resistance. There had been no arguments or hurt looks. If he were calculating and maneuvering to seduce her, then Eleanor had to concede his strategy was seamless—and apparently effective.

As she fell asleep, her last thought wasn't of the man and his rules.

Or even how wonderfully wicked it would be if he'd broken them.

It was to replay the moment when his palette had hit the ground, the colors splattering across the wooden floor, and to recall the lost look that had swept over him.

Chapter
13

It was another dismal day, even more overcast than the last, and Eleanor paced anxiously, praying that the carriage would come and that the lack of light wouldn't keep him from sending for her.

A long night of jarring erotic dreams had set her nerves on edge, but Eleanor was determined to put on a brave face. All their conversations about rules had shaped a dream landscape where everywhere she turned, Josiah Hastings was there—touching her with hands that trailed colors over her naked skin. She'd awoken with the startling irrational thought that there would be no hiding her sinful desire with his handprints in sapphire and violet on her body for all the world to see.

It had taken her a few deep breaths to accept that the power of Morpheus hadn't actually left marks on her skin, but one unsettling truth had lingered.

I felt no shame.

His company was affecting her in ways she hadn't anticipated and in ways she couldn't really understand. The only thing that was still absolutely clear to her was that the practical matters of her world had not changed. She had promised to sit for an artist in exchange for a life-altering amount of money. If she breached that contract now, there would be nowhere for her to turn.

And she had no desire to end things, even if a sensual nature she didn't know she possessed was coming to light. The hours she spent with him were flying by too quickly, and Eleanor dreaded nothing more than their end.

By the time she'd finished brushing out and pinning up her hair and dressing for the day, Eleanor was ready to face him. Every instinct insisted that as soon as she entered the studio again, the world would feel right and solid.

At last there was a knock on the door, and Eleanor opened it eagerly to find young master Tally waiting for her.

"Has the carriage come?" she asked, and held out a small brown bag of ginger candy she'd bought for him on the way home.

He nodded cheerfully, shyly placing his hands together as if holding the reins of a horse, and then accepted her gift. The blush that lit his cheeks rivaled any of hers, and she sympathized with him for it.

"Thank you, Tally!" Eleanor quickly adjusted her wrap and swept past him to head down the stairs. Within seconds, she was cheerfully ensconced in the carriage and on her way to Josiah's studio, waving farewell to Tally as the horses pulled away.

The ride was brief and uneventful, but it was time enough to try to refresh an internal lecture on decorum and the dangers of allowing her imagination to run riot and get the better of her.

She was too impatient to wait for the driver to help her down. She alighted on her own and walked briskly past the outer rusty gate into the building.

"Who's walking?" a man's voice growled, and she froze with her foot on the first riser. "I say, who's walking there?"

She turned to behold a brutal thug of a man in a rough woolen coat rising from his chair in the center of the room. "I . . . am Eleanor Beckett."

He nodded tersely. "I remember your name. I'm to let you pass with all courtesies, but you'll mind I don't know any. Good morning, then." He sat back down with a grunt and proceeded to ignore her, stoking a small fire at his feet.

"G-good morning." She took two steps up the stairs and then hesitated. "May I have your name as well? For courtesy's sake?"

He looked as startled as she'd been just moments before. "Creed. Roger Creed."

"Good morning, Mr. Creed. It was a pleasure meeting you." She smiled in satisfaction as the gruff man bobbed back up only to sit unsteadily back down on his stool. *Lady M's sixth principle of etiquette: Good manners are the best defense and can disarm any opponent.*

She climbed the rest of the stairs, pausing only once to catch her breath and leave her coat and bonnet on the coat rack on the house-floor landing, and then finally reached the door to the studio. Eleanor took one moment to straighten her skirts before breezing in, only to have another surprise awaiting her.

A cot with bedding was pushed against the garret wall beneath the windows, and it took seconds for her to surmise that Josiah had spent an entire night at his creative labors. There were a dozen small jars and dishes with paints and powdered pigments on one end of the table, and every candle on the table was spent to less than an inch of its life.

And, of course, there was Josiah himself, wearing the same clothes he'd changed into yesterday, albeit with new splashes of paint and red-colored smears on his shirtfront. Where another man might look deflated or rumpled, when he turned to face her, her heart skipped a beat at the keen energy that radiated from his frame. He looked refreshed and ready to take on titans, and she marveled at him as she had that very first day.

"I see you've taken your friend's advice and put a man downstairs."

He managed to look a little embarrassed. "Ah, I meant to send a note about that! I hope he didn't startle you."

"Mr. Creed is rather . . . intimidating, isn't he?"

Josiah smiled. "Mr. Creed? I see he introduced himself."

"He was most cordial," she lied sweetly, remembering the sight of the poor man nearly falling off his stool. "But why now? You were so insistent before about not needing anyone."

"There is a lady in the house. Perhaps not in residence, but at least, often enough to warrant it. I'm not going to risk your safety."

"But you would risk yours?" she asked.

"You're taking things out of context and redirecting the conversation, Miss Beckett. As I told you, I've been meaning to make improvements on the security of the house for some time. Your arrival simply prompted me to move a bit more quickly."

Eleanor wasn't sure why she wasn't willing to drop the matter. But there was something in the way he wasn't quite meeting her eyes that made her wonder what else was happening in his world. "So you're just following Mr. Rutherford's advice?"

"Precisely."

"Why is Mr. Rutherford so focused on security? And on your behalf, as well as mine? It's not as if you expect Mr. Perring to leap out of an alley and offer to let you break his nose again, or track me down to Mrs. Clay's and attempt to kidnap me, is it?"

He crossed his arms and gave her the look of a man amused by the debate. "Rutherford's nature is as mysterious and unknown to me as the Amazon, and as to the rest, I'm sure I haven't given Mr. Perring a single thought. Of course, now that you mention the idea of kidnappers and bandits, I feel like a fool for not putting a battalion of men downstairs."

"You're teasing me, Mr. Hastings." She crossed her arms to mirror his gesture, playing along. "Shall I change and see if we cannot allow you to make some progress before there is a dragon at the gates?"

He shook his head and her heart sank. "No, the light is impossible today."

"But the carriage . . ." She dropped her arms. "You sent for me."

"My optimism was misplaced, but perhaps we can still salvage something of the morning. I am in need of a change of scenery, Miss Beckett. Let's get out for a walk, shall we? The skies are gray but not immediately threatening, and a brisk stroll might stir the blood and help me focus." He gallantly gestured toward the door, but Eleanor kept her place.

"A walk?" she asked.

"There's a small private green nearby. We can see a bit of the streets and then stop in the park for some roasted chestnuts. What say you, Miss Beckett?"

The proposition flustered her for a moment. "You're asking me to walk out with you?"

He straightened his shoulders and then sighed. "Not like a suitor, Miss Beckett. I'm asking you as an artist, simply needing to clear his head and get a breath of fresh air. And naturally, we won't be alone."

"We won't?" Eleanor hated the disappointment that seeped into her voice at the revelation. It was only proper that they be chaperoned, but now? After days of sitting with him alone in his studio, it was jarring to realize just how much of the rules she'd begun to cheerfully forget while enjoying the pleasure of his company.

"Escher will tag along, at a respectable distance, of course."

"Mr. Escher?" She blurted it out before she could stop the incredulous words from escaping her lips. The man was a less likely chaperone than even poor Tally. "Well, as you've gone to all this trouble to preserve my reputation . . ."

Josiah smiled. "Delightful."

Eleanor had a fleeting urge to kick him in the shins. It was déjà vu, for the man was always getting her to agree and concede to things, as if the idea had been hers in the first place. Worse, so far, every defeat had been impossibly wonderful each and every time.

I'm going for a walk with him.
So much for my professional demeanor.

* * *

The path was muddy through the small private green, and even with his failing eyesight, Josiah could tell that there wasn't much green to speak of. But it was good to stretch his legs after a long night of mixing paints and working, and the warm imprint of Eleanor's gloved hand in the crook of his arm was enough to let him ignore the blasted gray fog creeping up from his feet. If he looked straight ahead, it was like peering over a wall. All morning before she'd arrived, he'd been fighting the surreal terror of not being able to see his own boots.

Yesterday's session had ignited his creative sensibilities, and he'd gone through a box of candles throughout the night in his pursuit of his muse.

It's going quickly. Which is good, if my eyes are going to fail just as fast.

But the fear was diminished with Eleanor at his side, and Josiah was determined to escape for a few minutes while he still could. At the very least, he'd have allowed himself time to see if his horizon would steady long enough to let him even attempt to paint today.

Escher's curses against the numbness of his toes and the aches in his bones were muffled but distinct behind them, guaranteeing an odd humor to the excursion as they both did their best to ignore him.

"May I ask, were you in India during the Troubles?"

"You may ask, Miss Beckett, and I was. But I'm not sure it's a topic I'm comfortable with. I was there in Bengal, but not in any famous sieges or battles. India was a dream until the moment it became a nightmare, and I don't like to relive it."

She nodded, silent for a moment. "Then I'll ask what an artist was doing in India in the first place."

He smiled. "Painting, Miss Beckett. I'd gotten the fantastic notion that a new and exotic locale would make me a superior artist. I wanted to see new things and be inspired by a strange and glorious ancient culture."

"And were you? Inspired?"

"I was. It was a spectrum I never knew existed. Although, it hurts now to think of those colors—lost forever to me." He spoke from the heart, unchecked, and immediately regretted it. "But who needs rainbows when I can enjoy the beauty of London!"

"Beauty, indeed, Mr. Hastings!" Eleanor laughed as he made a sweeping gesture that took in the fairly colorless and industrial landscape that ringed the park. Black bare branches scraping a narrow slice of steel gray sky offered almost no aesthetic respite from the wintry streets of London proper. "No wonder you think me a model!"

He stopped and studied her in earnest, his mood sobering. "Do you still doubt my taste, Miss Beckett? My aesthetic sensibilities? Or do you truly need me to argue once more how lovely I find you?"

"I wasn't . . . pressing you for compliments, Mr. Hastings. It was a foolish comment."

"You are one of the least foolish women I have ever known, Miss Beckett, but by far, the most modest," he said.

The smell of roasting chestnuts led him down the path, and Josiah steered her gently toward the diversion. He bought a small bag of the steaming treats, though not as gracefully as he'd planned. Even without gloves on, the cold made it harder to distinguish the coins in his purse, so he just shoved a few at the vendor and prayed it was enough.

"You're so generous!" she exclaimed softly when they'd stepped past the man's hearing.

His chest tightened, but at least the error was in a positive direction. "When you say it like that, it makes me want to empty my pockets altogether, Miss Beckett. But I imagine you've money enough now to enjoy your own philanthropy."

"Not yet, Mr. Hastings. The portrait isn't finished, remember?"

"Ah, well . . . if you'd just let me advance you some—"

"No, I will not take a shilling until I have fulfilled my end of the contract. It wouldn't be proper!" Eleanor chided him gently, but ruined the stern admonition with a smile. "Besides, I live the life of a duchess thanks to Mrs. Clay's care. She has spoiled me completely."

"I'm glad," he said, genuinely happy to know that his impulsive decision to take her to the Grove had been a good one. "Michael adores her, too, even if she does keep trying to put flowers in his room."

"Mr. Rutherford is very lucky to have you as a friend. Mrs. Clay shared that it was you who pointed him to the Grove and made sure he had a home there."

Josiah shrugged his shoulders. "It was the least I could do, and luck is something none of my friends believe in. We were an unlucky lot, but blessed to have met in India when we did. I wouldn't be here if not for Michael and the others, and helping him to find a place under Mrs. Clay's ample wings was a small thing."

"So, it's *you* who tries to look out for him, then . . . and not always the other way around?"

"Hardly! Rutherford's a bear! Trying to do a favor for that man can be dangerous, but I knew I'd be safe enough with Mrs. Clay's talent for finding a man's soft underbelly and taming him with pastries."

They walked on, and the stroll became like a pleasant dream to him. Her measured steps next to him and the warmth of her presence dismissed the cold, and Josiah would have sworn the sun was fighting to come out.

God, it feels so good. I'm the king of my own little world, with a prim beauty on my arm, and who's to say that all things aren't possible? And now I'm a kindhearted philanthropist in her eyes, and who cares? Nothing matters but—

His boot caught the edge of an uneven flagstone, and without warning, he lost his balance. He had to let go of her to prevent himself from dragging her down with him as he landed on his hands and knees, furious at the unseen ripple in the path and the horror of falling like a toddler onto his hands. The stinging pain of his skinned knees and palms was the least of it. Josiah closed his eyes at the humiliation and rage that washed over him.

"Mr. Hastings! Are you all right?" She was there at his elbow, kneeling in the mud and snow. "My goodness!"

"I'm fine." He bit off the words, leaning back to start to brush off his pants and try to recover what dignity he could before—

"Mr. Hastings! There's a tumble! My God, you're a sight, sir! Here, let me help you up, then." Escher was a force of nature that wasn't about to be dissuaded by Josiah's usual growls and protests.

"I'm fine!" Josiah wrenched his elbow out of Escher's grasp, and stood unaided. "Damn it, Escher! Stop hovering over me like I'm in swaddling clothes!"

"Hmm," Escher grunted, clearly unfazed by his employer's outburst. "I will if you stop bellowing like you are. Why not let me get you a carriage? No need to limp back all the way, and I'm sure Miss Beckett wouldn't mind a nice ride, would you, miss?"

"Goddamn it, I'm not an invalid, Escher! The factory's just there and we're steps from home, so enough! I'm embarrassed as it is!"

Escher sniffed in hurt disapproval. "Well, I'll just walk ahead then and get Rita to warm up some cider." He turned and stomped off, leaving the pair in awkward silence.

"Well . . ." Josiah sighed, facing a now solemn Eleanor. "So much for impressing you with my calm, even temper."

"Or retaining a chaperone for appearance sake," she added, a small smile giving him hope that all wasn't lost.

"I'm . . . clumsy these days. It makes for miserable outbursts, so I apologize. Not that I should be trying to impress you in the first place."

Her smile widened, a mischievous light coming into her eyes. "Thank goodness. It would be extremely improper of you, Mr. Hastings, as my employer."

But nothing of propriety applied, and when he looked at her, the last of his distress and anxiety for looking foolish in front of her began to dissipate. *What if I kissed her, here and now? Such a public place but who would know us? Who would pay any attention?*

He gathered her small hands into his, marveling at how diminutive they appeared. She trembled a little but didn't withdraw from his attentions, and suddenly, the craving to touch her was more than he could manage. He slid two of his fingers inside one of her gloves to caress the palm of her hand, cradling it like a bird. It was intimate and deliberate, and he loved the way she swayed against him as the power of this simple caress worked its magic.

"You shouldn't."

She said the words with great reluctance, and Josiah was amazed to realize that she couldn't locate the willpower to pull her hand from his.

Mine. Damn it. Tell me that you don't care, Eleanor, who is watching.

He looked into her eyes, and the last tendrils of the world relinquished their grip. There was only Eleanor in his field of vision as he held her in place with the heat of his gaze and the warmth radiating from his frame. All his fears vanished and Josiah reveled in the sensations she evoked inside of him.

"I love your hands. They are so small and soft."

"Not as soft as a lady's hands should be, Mr. Hastings."

"You must learn to accept compliments without argument, Miss Beckett."

"Are ladies used to compliments?"

He nodded. "They expect and demand them, in my experience."

She shook her head, then whispered, "I pray your experience is unique. What woman would require such a reckoning? When all she needs is to look into someone's eyes and know—"

"Miss Beckett? Is that you?" A woman's voice echoed across the bleak clearing and Josiah almost groaned aloud with disappointment at the declaration he'd lost.

"I say, Miss Beckett! Is that you?" the woman repeated,

and Eleanor stepped back, involuntarily surrendering the fiery-sweet contact of his flesh to hers.

"M-Mrs. Dunleigh!" Eleanor was astonished to speechlessness. On such a day and in bleak weather, on a private green far beyond the neighborhood she'd once called home, the sight of Mrs. Mabel Dunleigh was as unexpected as seeing a ghost. "Mrs. Dunleigh, what a surprise!"

"Yes, indeed. My friend Mrs. Stroud and I do charity work at a home for women seeking relief from an immoral life on the streets. It is nearby. I was just coming out with the new pamphlets to hand out to any lost souls in the vicinity. This green is often frequented by . . . prostitutes and questionable characters." She eyed Mr. Hastings as if she wasn't entirely sure of him. "And what brings you to this"—Mrs. Dunleigh struggled for a polite phrase before continuing—"industrious part of Town?"

"I . . ." Eleanor was sure that she'd have chosen a beating over the current conversation. It had all been innocent fun, to walk with Josiah and escape the confines of the studio for a while. She'd lowered her guard and flirted with him shamelessly, craving his touch and attention. But Mabel's beady eyes gleamed with malicious judgment and Eleanor's stomach churned in terror. "I was also visiting a friend."

Oh, God. What to say? I'm just out walking with the man who is paying me to sit on a couch in a red velvet dress?

Josiah bowed slightly, touching the rim of his hat. "Josiah Hastings, at your service. I own a factory building and home here, and Miss Beckett is a family friend."

"A family friend. I see," Mrs. Dunleigh said crisply. "I don't remember hearing your name mentioned by the Becketts."

"Nor I yours," he countered. "But what a small world London can be."

"You are a painter, are you not?" Mrs. Dunleigh sniffed.

"How astute of you, Mrs. Dunleigh." Josiah shifted his stance, a man completely comfortable in the midst of confrontation. "Thank you for not mistakenly offering me a pamphlet."

Eleanor's face was burning in embarrassment, but his attempt to shield her wasn't helping. It was all she could do not to burst into tears. "I should . . . call on you, Mrs. Dunleigh. It's been so long since—"

Mrs. Dunleigh's charitable nature didn't extend that far, and she cut Eleanor off. "My daughter is at an impressionable age, Miss Beckett. I'm afraid I insist on restricting callers at present. As you are unmarried and"—Mrs. Dunleigh's upper lip curled in distaste—"independent, I think not. Good day, Miss Beckett."

The woman spared her a single curt nod, and then walked away as briskly as a woman departing a building on fire. Eleanor watched helplessly as the middle-class matron effectively gave her the cut direct and sailed off back to Orchard Street to no doubt spread delicious gossip about the encounter.

"What must she be thinking? I was—letting you hold my hand and . . ."

"What does it matter what she thinks?" he interjected calmly.

"She thinks I'm your—*mistress*! She was looking at me with pity and disgust as if—"

"Eleanor."

His use of her first name captured her attention completely.

"Eleanor," he went on softly. "Was she a dear friend?"

She shook her head slowly. "An acquaintance of my mother's. We were at her house on a few occasions for tea."

"Has she corresponded or expressed any concern for your well-being? Ever?"

Once again, she shook her head. "No."

"She's nothing, then. You're standing there trembling and on the verge of tears because a woman of no consequence has crossed your path. Her opinions carry as much weight as a cobweb."

Eleanor shook her head, unsure of how to convince him

that fear wasn't a weightless thing; that she was sure it could crush her. "I'm afraid, Mr. Hastings."

"What are you afraid of?"

"I'm afraid that I'm not nearly as proper as I wish to be. It isn't Mrs. Dunleigh and her opinions—it's far more dire."

"Is it?" he asked gently. "Tell me. Tell me, what were you thinking before the old battle-axe came over with her pamphlets and dampened the green in your eyes."

She took one uneven breath before looking away. *I was glad that Mr. Escher had gone. I was hoping it meant you might ask to kiss me again. Even now, with Mrs. Dunleigh's looks of disapproval clanging across my nerves, I'm wishing you'd touch my hands as you did before.* "Why do you always ask what I am thinking?"

"Perhaps I'm hoping to hear the voice of reason I suspect is so eloquent in that beautiful head of yours—and praying it will drown out the voice in my head."

And there it was. He spoke openly of his desire and hers broke free of its prison.

"And what are *you* thinking, Mr. Hastings? What is your inner voice saying right now?"

"That I would be the Devil himself if I kissed you right now, in such a public place, and even so, I'm not sure I won't."

She looked back at him, and without so much as a whimper, the voice of reason was silenced. "You won't. But I, Mr. Hastings, will."

Chapter
14

"Eleanor—"

She moved closer, her head tipping back to hold his gaze. "I've never been kissed before. I don't want to be impolite, Mr. Hastings, so I shall use the word *please* and trust that you'll oblige me."

Josiah didn't hesitate to "oblige" her with a kiss. He lowered his mouth to cover hers, intending to gently taste the soft, ripe sweetness of her lips, satisfy his lustful curiosities, and be done with it. But at the first instant that his mouth met with hers, he knew he'd underestimated his hunger and need for the delectable and prim Miss Eleanor Beckett.

She instinctively yielded to him, inviting him to take all that he wanted, parting her lips to let him feast on the soft honey warmth of her mouth and tongue, feeding on his touch with a hunger of her own that made his joints feel strange. Here wasn't a proper tight little kiss, but a fiery passionate touch that melted into his and matched every move that he made, holding nothing back in shy reserve.

It was a dance of sensation with a rhythm all its own.

Eleanor's gloved hands slid up inside his coat against his back as she clung to him, and Josiah discovered that his maidenly Eleanor was a quick study in the ways of pleasure. If he'd half expected a spinsterly display metered out and dutifully followed by a ladylike slap . . . he was happily disappointed.

Only the knowledge that his hands would feel like ice kept Josiah from giving in to an impulse to touch her throat or explore the hypnotic contours of her face. Instead, he gripped the wool sleeves of her coat, capturing her and holding her in place as every kiss surpassed the kiss before, like a string of perfect pearls.

He left her lips for just a moment to bend over and trace the porcelain arch of her ear with his tongue, and was instantly rewarded.

"Josiah." She moaned his name, and it was a music he couldn't ignore.

He pulled her up into his arms, pressing her close until he was sure that she would be able to feel every thrum and pulse of his heart through the layers of winter clothing that separated their bodies. Desire lashed out across his skin, and Josiah's blood reveled in the fiery heat that surged out from his core, quickening his pulse and tightening his muscles. His cock was instantly rock-hard, and Josiah groaned at the unexpected pleasure and pain of its presence. He'd abstained for months, and Eleanor's kisses were proving to be unbearably powerful.

To Eleanor, it was a sweet, slow slide into heaven. His lips were hot silk against hers, and her breath caught in her throat at the raw beauty of his touch. It was unnerving. From the vague descriptions in literature suited for young ladies, every hint had made it seem as if she would be transported into an ethereal state. But this—this was transformation of a very physical and grounded nature. This was a new awareness of herself as a fleshly being, and if her spirit was involved, it was only to underline that there was nothing she wouldn't be willing to happily forfeit in a primal quest for pleasure. For this—this was bliss. Everything that had defined her before his lips touched hers fell away: etiquette and place, pride and presumptions, ambition and reserve.

It was a freedom she had never known.

Every delicate flutter of nerves newly awakened was followed with a gripping surge of need that jarred her very core. Her fingers dug into his back, contracting with the waves of hunger that shimmered through her body only to pool between her hips. She came alive as never before, and prayed that it would never end.

He suckled her tongue, the rough velvet of it making her knees buckle. Eleanor opened her mouth wider, greedy for more, yielding to him and the lightning storm inside of her his touch evoked. A curious fire poured down her spine and across her skin, and when his teeth grazed the sensitive swollen peak of her lower lip, Eleanor trembled at the searing flash of lust that whipped through her frame, and waited for the guilt that never came.

She felt light and hollow, and when his arms encircled her to lift her against the warm wall of his body, Eleanor nearly wept at the delicious ache between her thighs. She had a fleeting thought that no matter who had initiated this embrace, she was lost in it now.

It was only when she realized that her feet had left the ground to cling to him like a desperate vine that her eyes opened in surprise.

A lady wouldn't . . . forget herself. . . . My goodness, I've nearly . . . in a public park!

She turned her face away from his to try to gather her wits, and pushed against his chest to kick out with her feet and recover her balance.

He disengaged reluctantly, forcing himself to release her. His mouth hovered over hers, their breath comingling, and Josiah knew that whatever natural curiosity or innocent impulse had driven her to make her request—she would not appreciate him mauling her like a ravenous beast in a public park.

Josiah looked down at her, waiting until her eyelashes

fluttered open and the Eleanor he knew returned to her senses even while his body throbbed in protest at the sudden change in plans.

"O-oh my!" She sighed, openly startled. "That was . . ."

"Unexpected." He finished her sentence, unwilling to hear her express her regret at the act. "We should get back, Miss Beckett, and see what we can make of the rest of the day. I should be mixing paints and finishing the preparations."

She stepped back, nervously tucking a stray curl back up into her bonnet. "Mr. Hastings, have I ruined all between us?"

He shook his head. "No, Miss Beckett. But I vowed to behave, remember? Not to trespass or take advantage? So, you'll have to be patient with me, for I'm not sure how far honor extends or where the limits of my self-discipline will fall away. You are unharmed and I wouldn't apologize for that kiss for an emperor's ransom. But, Eleanor . . ."

"Yes?"

"How did Mrs. Dunleigh know I was a painter?" he asked, deliberately provoking Eleanor's laughter and easing the tension between them.

"You have paint on your shirt collar, Mr. Hastings."

He glanced down, opening his coat to inspect the linen of his cravat. "A few splatters, but it's a work shirt, so there's no harm."

A few splatters?

Eleanor reached out to touch his coat sleeve, holding up what could only be described as a ruined elbow of scarlet and black. "Josiah . . ."

He reacted to his name as if there'd been a gunshot, his brown eyes instantly blazing with an emotion she didn't recognize. He pulled his arm away and took a step back. "That's enough for today, I think. Let's get back and I'll get Escher to send for the carriage to get you home."

"I've offended you."

"No, God, no. You could never overstep, Miss Beckett." He took a deep breath. "But I'm not fit company for a lady today. I'm—we'll start work again tomorrow if the light allows. Please. Be merciful and let's end the day while I have a bit of self-control left, yes?"

"Yes, Mr. Hastings." She'd nodded and shyly allowed him to lead her back to the house. A quiet overcame them both until the carriage arrived and he was left alone in his studio with his demons.

Holy mother of bleeding fools . . .

She said my name and I nearly unmanned myself.

Hell, when was the last time a woman said my name and I felt like that?

Answer: never.

Not once.

Not even with the witch who broke me so many years ago.

He was determined to put the kiss behind him and reassure her that he was a man of his word. But there was more than that behind his retreat. That kiss had proven to him that his emotions were far from his control and that the danger of losing his heart was immediate and very real. The obvious tragedy ahead loomed, and Josiah wasn't sure he had the strength to weather more loss.

Lose your sight but keep your heart, Hastings. Hell, I can't think of anything more pitiful than a heartbroken blind man shambling about and mumbling over a woman he can't have. Use your head, man! Borrowing trouble is a fool's game.

"I've taken my last leisurely stroll outside of the house." He leaned over the table and put his head into his hands, then had to groan at the miserable irony of realizing he'd just smeared paint into his hair.

Damn! What a day to keep a man humble! Between scraping my knees and this—I'd say it's a lesson learned. I'm as fit for romance and suited for seduction as a bell-capped jester!

Josiah sighed, straightened his back, then finished sealing up his pigment jars for the next day's work. He rang the bell for Escher to try to warn the man that he'd need help drawing a hot bath downstairs, and left the studio without looking back.

*   *   *

"Ah, there you are Miss Beckett!" Mrs. Clay greeted her with her usual enthusiasm. "Was it a shorter day, miss?"

Eleanor removed her bonnet. "I cannot complain, Mrs. Clay." She could feel the heat flooding her face as the memory of her first kiss washed through her. Luckily, the cold had already colored her cheeks apple red so there would be no telltale signal for her concerned landlady to see.

"Will you eat in the common room tonight or—"

"Not tonight, Mrs. Clay. I think I'll just . . . read quietly and stay warm by the fire, if I can."

"Of course! Tally's got you all set for coal and cleaned the grate today. He's sweet on you, I'm sure of it! I'll send you up a nice hot tray later and see that you're not disturbed."

"Thank you, Mrs. Clay." Eleanor retreated to her room without looking back and leaned against the closed door for a few minutes, determined to shut the world out. She could see the familiar tome of Lady M's advice on her bedside table, the sight of it mocking her.

Because today she had accepted that she was not as mindful of her reputation as she'd long believed. Eleanor's worst fear had been faced and discarded in one single brazen act. All her life, she'd fought so hard to be correct in her behavior and careful of the rules. She'd believed that stepping over the line would lead to some kind of black oblivion.

But kissing Josiah hadn't been oblivion. It had opened a universe of sensation and desire that she'd never imagined existed. And she didn't want to retreat from the discovery. Eleanor wanted more.

She wanted Josiah Hastings.

"I am *not* a proper lady," she said softly, and then waited for lightning to strike.

Chapter
15

The next day, Josiah paced the wide, open floors of his studio, anxiously listening for her footsteps on the stairs. Despite reading that losing one sense heightened the others, Josiah didn't believe his hearing had improved in the slightest—or any of his faculties. Even so, he crossed the floor again, quietly praying that he'd be able to detect her presence on the stairs and have a few seconds to prepare. He wasn't completely confident that Eleanor would actually return after the previous day's intimacies, but he'd braced himself for an awkward morning.

He was anxious to use the rituals of work and avoid any further misunderstandings. She'd invited a kiss with the most innocent solicitation he'd ever heard, but Josiah knew what was at stake far better than Eleanor.

Escher had brought in a new box of candles, and Josiah began adding them to the waxen forest as best he could. Gaslight had a steadier glow, but renovations on the house had ceased before he'd added lines to the studio. Before long the smell of beeswax candles all merrily lit and flickering away permeated the room and made him wonder if he should heed his houseman's warning about setting his worktable on fire.

"Mr. Creed was almost cheerful this morning!" Eleanor's voice carried from the doorway as she breezed in, already dressed in her red velvet for the day. "I brought him some of Mrs. Clay's cheese muffins and I swear the man *almost* smiled."

His relief at her arrival was so sharp it took his breath away for a moment.

So much for those heightened senses of the blind!

"Did you know he worked in this very building before the fire?" she continued gaily. "He was a woodworker of some kind and helped maintain the milling machines. Poor man!"

Josiah couldn't remember ever being so on edge around a woman in his lifetime. All he wanted was to finish before his baser nature robbed him of his chance—or destroyed his peace of mind.

"You're not supposed to distract Roger with tins from Mrs. Clay's kitchen, Miss Beckett." Josiah straightened his coat as he came toward her. "The man is a watchdog, not a pampered pet."

"He is not a canine you've tied to a post!" she protested. "Be civil, Mr. Hastings."

"You are right, of course. But please don't spoil his surly disposition, Miss Beckett. How can Mr. Creed frighten away intruders if you ruin his wretched demeanor?" Josiah teased.

"Nothing will make Mr. Creed less intimidating short of dressing him in petticoats, so I will ignore you and bring the poor man gingerbread biscuits on the morrow." She held her ground.

"And none for me?"

"We shall see," she said in a very good imitation of a headmistress addressing an errant pupil. "We shall see."

He shook his head, aware that the humorous exchange had undermined all his plans to usher her directly to the dais without small talk to make a professional start to the day. "Let's get started, then." He held out his hand to escort her to the settee.

"Is the light better today?" she asked.

"No, not really, but I've mountains of fresh candles and I'm determined not to lose another day." A growing sense of urgency spurred him on. His vision was better today, and something primal in him needed to paint and put brush to canvas. Josiah was determined to work until he couldn't stand anymore. He would work by candlelight alone, if need be, and use his imagination to finish what his eyes couldn't convey.

She settled into position, smoothing out her skirts. "Then I will do my best to be still, Mr. Hastings."

"May I?" he asked, gesturing toward her hair.

She nodded. "As you wish."

He rearranged a few tendrils, loosening the silken mass at the nape of her neck and then resecuring it with a tortoise comb to recreate the inspiring effect of a woman not quite unbound. "There."

Josiah accepted that no amount of icy resolve was going to mute the impact his siren had on his senses, but it did hasten him to withdraw to his own position in front of the canvas.

"I am ready, Mr. Hastings," she said softly.

By God, so am I.

* * *

Yesterday's kiss was like a dream to her.

Eleanor did her best to sit quietly and imagine that the man sitting across from her wasn't sending spidery waves of heat through her with every studied glance of his intense brown eyes.

She'd begun to love the sharp smell of linseed oil and turpentine, and had long surmised the reason that his clothing always had touches of paint on them. Josiah's attention was so completely wrapped up in his subject and the immediate sphere of his creation that he apparently never noticed where his elbows were. *Perhaps he forgets his physical presence and loses himself in those oil paints, a mystical process that the rest of us cannot perceive, like those rainbows and shadows he described seeing as a child.*

The brazier next to her perch on the couch did little to ward off the chill in the room, but Eleanor was comfortable in the warm layers of silk and velvet that encased her. Not to mention the additional experience of fiery-sweet tendrils of pleasure that revisited her with every recollection of his kisses.

He'd asked her for mercy and she'd dutifully retreated in a daze to the sanctuary of the Grove. But with the morning's light, Eleanor had learned that despite her decadent proclamation, there had been no divine punishment, no strikes of lightning, and most shocking of all, no outward mark or change to reflect her inner transformation.

She was determined to demonstrate to him that she was not only "unharmed," as he'd put it, but capable of enduring as many of those wonderful kisses as the man could inflict. The challenge was to see if she could persuade him to it, without overtly being brazen or upsetting his pride and honor.

"Do you . . . mix all the colors yourself?" she asked, admiring the contents of the tiny jars spread out across the floor next to him.

"Every painter guards his formulas with great zeal. See this red? This is for your hair. I added gold dust to try to capture the luster of your curls."

"How horribly extravagant!" she gasped.

"Your coloring demanded it, Miss Beckett. We cannot cheat now."

She shook her head. "You will bankrupt yourself, sir. Between the cost of your model and her ridiculous coloring, I cannot see how this is a very sound financial enterprise."

"This is art, Miss Beckett. We cannot think of pecuniary matters when we are pursuing greatness," he said loftily, then gave her a wink. "Which is why artists are infamous for proudly starving, I'm sure."

"Poor things!" She sighed, then straightened her shoulders before he could correct her. "I am glad that you are not starving, Mr. Hastings."

"Thank you, Miss Beckett."

Time slipped away as Eleanor allowed herself to enjoy the sight of him swept up in his pursuit of greatness. Josiah's hands moved in a dance, from the palette to the canvas and back, and the wicked echo of her dream came back as she imagined that it was her skin he was painting, the cool of the oil touching her face and throat, or sliding down across the planes of her belly.

"Beautiful," he muttered under his breath. "Just beautiful."

"What do you find beautiful, Mr. Hastings? I mean, you said before about a woman's hair being so fascinating to a man, and I begin to wonder, what else . . . has that power?" She blushed. "I was curious, as to the general subject, of course, and not to you in particular. It is an—academic question."

"Of course." He smiled, openly amused at the topic. "Miss Beckett, for a woman who professes to adhere to decorum, you do bring up the most surprising things, but since it is *academic* . . ."

"Entirely academic, Mr. Hastings."

"In that moment, I was admiring the slope of your eyebrows, Miss Beckett. You are a geometric feast of curves and lines today, and I was merely grateful for it."

"Oh!" She sighed.

"You're disappointed?"

"A little," she confessed. "I've not given one thought in my lifetime to my eyebrows, Mr. Hastings, and I should be comforted by that fact. But if beauty is so entirely out of my control or perception, it's a frightening thing for a woman, isn't it? Since beauty is supposed to be one of my singular goals, is it not?"

"So they say," Josiah said, continuing to work as they

settled into the conversation. "But you have never professed any interest in such shallow pursuits as vanity, Eleanor."

"True! I'm not going to waste hours of my life in front of a mirror. But here I am and there you are—and even after all this time, it still feels strange to think that anything about me appeals. It is a mystery, Mr. Hastings."

"Describe a beautiful woman to me."

She began to fidget, but held still out of habit when he started to growl. "Very well. She has golden hair, smooth and lovely without a single rebellious snarl or curl, and gentle blue eyes. Her skin is porcelain and she is quite petite and dainty. She is fashionable and neat, and her feet are well positioned."

"Well positioned?"

"Yes. My mother said my feet pointed out like a farm hand's. I'm not sure she'd ever seen a farm hand, but apparently, a lady is not supposed to stand like she's claiming territory or about to break into a march." She smiled. "I am grateful that the length of my skirts forces you to use your imagination, Mr. Hastings."

"How provocative of you!" His hands moved faster, the conversation inspiring him as his vision mercifully stayed clear. "I shall imagine that your feet are perfection and allow you to keep your secrets."

"As you keep yours?"

"Mine? I have no secrets." Josiah kept his eyes on the canvas, unwilling to look at her as he spoke such a blatant lie.

"Do you not?"

"If I did, it doesn't seem prudent to admit it, Miss Beckett."

"You never answered my question, Mr. Hastings." She cleared her throat. "About what you find appealing in a woman?"

"You must, of course, vow to keep this information to yourself."

"I promise."

"Well, besides the obvious appealing bits—"

"And what would be obvious, sir?"

"Miss Beckett, please! The obvious would be a sweet nature, lyrical talents, and a constant heart," he teased, dabbing a bit of white paint onto his brush. "Let's see, as a wicked representative of my gender, I will confess that what physically appeals most about a woman is an elusive list. Censoring myself somewhat, I can say I have a personal weakness for the soft curve just at her throat, where her collarbone draws the eyes across to the lines of her shoulders and neck. Not to omit the shape of her ears and ankles, the smell of her skin, and most decidedly, the irresistible grace of the inside of her wrists and that little pulse that can betray her innermost feelings." He sighed. "Better to ask what doesn't appeal, Miss Beckett, for I'm sure the list would be shorter."

She laughed. "What doesn't appeal?"

He shook his head, the idea suddenly sobering him because there was nothing about Eleanor Beckett that didn't appeal. But it went beyond the color and beauty of her form, and he knew it. He loved these impossible questions that made her blush and the even more impossible answers that made him burn for her. He loved the turns of her mind and her naïve and curious nature.

"Don't move, Miss Beckett. Shoulders back, if you please." He did his best to pretend to paint until his nerves had steadied. "If you'd like to take a break . . ."

"No, Mr. Hastings! I would—"

But Escher's arrival with a tray overrode her protest, the older man crossing the room with his usual groaning, unsteady gait. Josiah turned to watch his progress, then shifted back to his work as Escher rested the platter down, his relief apparent. "There's a note, sir."

Josiah glanced over his shoulder at the familiar gray shadow of Escher, but didn't move from his stool. "What does it say, good man?" Josiah asked, dabbing his brush to the canvas.

Mr. Escher rolled his eyes but dutifully broke the seal on the note. "Josiah, our contact at the *Times* reports that a response to our placement has been received. The Jackal has taken the bait and the Jaded are set. His identity remains unknown. No word from Thorne on—"

"That's enough, thank you, Escher." Josiah came back to the present with a quick snap of embarrassment. He'd been so involved in what he was doing he'd sacrificed discretion and included Eleanor on the worst of the Jaded's business. "I'll see to it later."

Escher withdrew with only a few grumbles and closed the door behind him.

"The Jackal? The Jaded?" she asked, her eyes wide with awe. "Are you in pursuit of a spy or a notorious criminal, Mr. Hastings?"

He had to bite the inside of his mouth to keep from smiling. "Not exactly. It's . . . just a bit of business. My friends and I are working on . . . resolving a private matter."

"Is Mr. Rutherford involved?"

"Why?" he asked, oddly irritated by the question. "Are you concerned for Michael's safety?"

"Hardly. But as he is concerned with yours, I would very much want to make sure your protective older brother and nanny is aware of any nonsense you've entangled yourself in that includes jackals and bait," she shot back calmly. "Not that I mean to pry into your personal business."

His irritation evaporated. She was so formidable and so enticing, Josiah found himself wondering how any man withstood the combination of a beautiful woman who possessed such fiery wit. "I am a member of a small circle of gentlemen known as the Jaded, and while it sounds wicked, I think there are knitting circles that get into more mischief."

"Knitting circles aren't generally baiting jackals and placing furtive advertisements in the papers, Mr. Hastings." Eleanor's green eyes blazed with disapproval. "Again, not that it concerns me."

Josiah bit the inside of his cheek to keep from smiling. "I was only guessing since I cannot knit."

"You are a rogue, Mr. Hastings." This time it was Eleanor who gave in to the odd humor of the moment and lost the battle to smile. "And I, for one, imagine there are dozens of knitting circles relieved to do without you."

He waited a few seconds until her shoulders relaxed before he touched the brush to the canvas. "What are you thinking, Miss Beckett?"

"I'm thinking I should have gotten those character references when you offered them to me."

He laughed. "Are you thirsty, Miss Beckett? Why don't I ring for Escher to come back to bring us something to drink?"

Eleanor's face betrayed her confusion. "But he's already brought us refreshments, Mr. Hastings. It's there on the tray, is it not?"

Josiah turned quickly, as if he'd spotted a cobra on the table. "Ah! Yes, so he has! I didn't even bother to look. Shall I pour you a glass, then?"

She shook her head slowly. "No, thank you."

He dismissed the idea of pouring himself a glass, all too aware that his luck hadn't been very solid lately. Josiah wasn't in the mood for another "inexplicable" spill. He picked up a different brush and his palette, reacquiring the point on the canvas he'd been working on and trying to orient his vision. "Back to it, then."

"You are all business today, Mr. Hastings."

"I am a man on a mission, Miss Beckett." He looked up at her. "Hold still, please."

"Mr. Hastings." She sighed. "Why haven't you kissed me again?"

Damn. So much for my peace of mind. . . .

"I'd rather not say, Miss Beckett." He started to lift his brush, but Josiah knew it was a sham. He was seconds away from "obliging" her again, and forfeiting the day.

"You said I could never overstep. And I left yesterday, when you asked, without protest."

"You were—very kind to do so, Miss Beckett. I am in your debt." *God, it's all so formal and I can feel the lightning sparking up my spine because I'm right back where we left off in the park. Because if I know anything of my Eleanor, next comes—*

"I wish you to kiss me again, Mr. Hastings. I wish that you would, if only to prove to myself that it was real." She was blushing so beautifully it made his chest ache to look at her.

He set his brush and palette down, as carefully as he could, and unfolded from his seat. "Let's have at it, then, and see if we can't set all these questions to rest and get back to work, shall we?"

"Yes." She answered breathlessly, waiting for him with eyes that mirrored his every want. "Yes, please."

He went down on one knee on the dais, and without preamble, leaned over to gently pull her into his arms. Whatever light kiss he'd intended was immediately lost as something inside of him broke free and begged to have nothing between them. She sighed at the first touch of his lips to hers, and Josiah let it all go—there was nothing restrained or held back.

Here was a bruising conquest without a victim, for his Eleanor matched his urgency and hunger as the kiss began as if there had been no interruption from the park. He sampled every corner of her mouth and feasted on the sensations and passion she evoked inside of him, her body molding to his as his hands pressed her against his chest.

His cock grew heavy and hard, and he almost shuddered at the churning fire in his blood that coiled inside of him and demanded release. Lust poured through him, and Josiah groaned at the long-lost memory of what it could be to truly drown in a woman's embrace. Eleanor arched against his caresses, her hands frantically seeking purchase on his sleeves and shirtfront, molding her body to his, spurring him on.

He kissed her neck and teased the hollow of her throat with his tongue only to find the sensitive juncture of the trail where her neck and shoulder came together in a firm curve that begged for the playful work of a man's teeth until she cried out to plead for more. His breath fanned the

gentle rise of her breasts just above the gown's décolletage,
sweeping over the modest curves of her body and savoring
the heat of her breasts when she shifted up against him.

Eleanor had never dreamt that every inch of her skin
could become electrically linked to create an overwhelming cascade of tingling arcs that ignored even physics and
gravity. He nipped at her throat and shoulder, and her
breasts tightened until the fiery points of her nipples ached
at the touch of her own clothes. His breath fanned her ears
and her thighs trembled, a coil of tension between her hips
answering every unspoken command with primal promises
of fulfillment.

Josiah found her delectably curved bottom beneath all
the layers of her heavy skirt and petticoats, to lift her up
against him and then allow her to slide ever so slowly back
down onto the fainting couch, pressing her back to recline
against its curved cushions.

Too easily. Too quickly. He was caught up in it, lost to
the sweet discovery that whatever lesson he'd thought to
teach her, he'd forgotten all common sense along the way.

It was too easy to slide red velvet up to give his hands
what they craved. His proper lady wore proper stockings
and flannel drawers, but he sought her flesh through the
opening in her underclothes and found the velvet folds of
her sex, already dripping with honey and slick with want.

"Oh my . . ." she gasped, but it was more of a sigh than
a protest, and Eleanor failed to close her thighs to him before his fingers discovered what he desired to touch most.
The taut little pearl of her clit jutted out from the zenith of
her ripe entrance, and Josiah swept his thumb across it and
experienced pure triumph as Eleanor's reaction was total
and unashamed.

Working that lovely pearl with the dewy issue from her
own body, Josiah marveled that her pleasure had become
his so entirely. Whatever conceit he'd once had for being a
generous lover gave way to a new dedication to pleasing
Eleanor and Eleanor alone.

The rhythm of his fingers escalated with the rate of his

kisses affirming the lesson that she was entirely an inter-woven creature of sinew and muscle, nerves and pulse, and that not one touch of his body to hers would leave any other part of her unaffected. Josiah could sense the build of tension in her frame, and ended a kiss only to look deeply into her eyes to drink the sight of his Eleanor aroused and experiencing the first hints of what pleasure her body was capable of.

This. When there's nothing that I can see, I'll close my eyes and I'll have this.

He dipped one finger into the hot damp of her body and instantly knew he'd gone too far. Eleanor's eyes opened wide in alarm, the green storm immediate and unmistakable. She froze, and clutched at his arm, reaching down to grab his wrist and push him away and end the liberties he was taking with her most private and sensitive places.

The game had gone from passionate kisses and caresses to the threshold of something far more serious. A rogue would have retreated only to try again while she was still off balance and confused—but Josiah Hastings was no rake.

Damn it! She's so close—but only an ass would press his advantage.

Josiah yielded, withdrawing as gently as he could, and watching her as she recovered her senses, ignoring the ignoble demands of his own body.

"Oh my!" She reached up to caress his cheeks, framing his face in her hands. "The effects are—remarkably undiminished, sir. Is that . . . proper?"

"Don't think to apply rules to this, Eleanor." He put his hands over hers and gently pressed them against his chest to cover his pounding heart. "But we should leave off while we can."

"Leave off?" she asked, her voice wobbling with distress. "Yes. I mean, should we?"

He guided her hand down over his stomach slowly, leading her touch toward the stiff heat of his cock, its length pressing his swollen head painfully up against the waistband of his pants. He drew her palm down over the cloth to demonstrate in no uncertain terms the state of his arousal, his flesh jerking as her fingers spasmed in panic. He had to hold her wrist to keep her from jerking her hand away, and he watched her eyes widen in fear at the length and mass of him—the implications for her virginity were all too clear.

"J-Josiah?"

"I don't want to ruin you, Eleanor. Not now, not ever. And for you, is my touch not the very definition of ruin?"

"No! Yes . . . I don't know anymore."

"This is no flirtatious game, Miss Beckett, that ends in chaste kisses." He let go of her hand, hating the taste of defeat. "I know you well enough, Miss Beckett, to know that until you are sure, I have my answer."

* * *

It was a long, lonely carriage ride home. Eleanor was awash in confusion, and even more uncertain of her feelings now that she'd achieved another taste of sin. Her mother had told her that when she met the right man, she would simply *know* and that everything would peacefully fall into place just as it should; that there would be a calm resolution that would erase all doubts.

But nothing about Josiah evoked calm.

He unsettled her senses and challenged everything she knew of reason and balance. He looked at her and she forgot all the rules of etiquette and social restraint that had been drilled into her since she could first walk. Nothing about him conveyed quiet resolve or muted affection. Instead, there was the promise of an exotic sanctuary in his eyes, and when he kissed her, she didn't care about anything else.

She was falling in love. The attachment was overwhelming, but tangible. It just didn't seem to match a single sentiment described by Lady M. Eleanor had overstepped infatuation into deeper waters, and every instinct heralded that drowning was a very real danger. But instead of frightening her away, the acknowledgment made her only want to run like a madwoman back to him and throw herself at his feet and beg him for some merciful resolution that would restore her mind.

Or just beg him to kiss me until I don't care what any of it means. To touch me until there is nothing of this anxiety and hunger left.

From the moment he'd rescued her, Eleanor's ideals of what it meant to be a man had morphed into Josiah until she couldn't see anyone else. Every gentlemanly gesture and charitable act had laid a foundation of trust, and instead of seducing or mistreating her, Josiah had kept himself in check. She was in the odd position of holding the reins on her own fall.

I'd have yielded to him completely today, if he'd pressed me. But he saw the fear in my face . . . and here I am again, sent back to the Grove to recover my senses and decide what to do next.

He'd said he had no secrets. But Eleanor knew better. And it wasn't just that mysterious note about the Jaded.

There was something wrong with his vision. She was more and more sure of it. The intensity of his gaze gave way to the habits of a man who looked as if he were trying to peer around something or constantly working to get something out of his field of vision. Unless something was directly in front of him, it was as if it didn't exist. At any new sound, he turned his head to look, never leading with his eyes.

He'd spilled the paints more than once and overturned more glassware than any man had a right to, and when he'd fallen in the park, it had been another clue. He'd even said something about being more clumsy "these days," as if it were a new experience and not just part of his general physicality.

There'd been a dozen subtle moments where he'd missed something or made references to colors lost or a quest for more light. And the candles . . . as the days had passed, more and more candles had been added until his studio rivaled any cathedral nave for its glow. Eleanor tried to recall every incident where he'd given her pause, worrying over each fleeting memory and its implications.

He doesn't trust me with his secrets, great or small.

Not yet.

A part of her ached to be brought into his confidences and to know more of him if he would allow it. Or did such men only open themselves up to women who shared their beds? Was that part of it—the bond between men and women, sealed with intimacies she couldn't yet fathom?

The carriage stopped in front of the Grove, and Eleanor climbed down with the driver's help and made her way inside the inn's doors.

"Are you all right, then, dear?"

"I'm fine, Mrs. Clay." She started up the stairs and then stopped. "Mrs. Clay?"

"Yes, dear?"

"How . . . often are your instincts about people incorrect?"

"Never, Miss Beckett. Not in all my years have I missed spotting a bad egg."

"How can you be so sure?" The question had a sad, desperate edge to it, but Eleanor longed for a reassurance that only the motherly Mrs. Clay might provide.

"Has something happened, my dear? Has someone—"

"No, Mrs. Clay! Please don't worry. I spoke out of turn. It's just that my instincts have never been very good, and I'm almost afraid to trust my own judgment."

"Aren't you a lamb?" Mrs. Clay wiped her hands on her apron. "Well, I say actions never lie. If you're not sure, then you look at the work of a man's hands and not the prattle coming out of his mouth. Does that help?"

"Yes, I suppose it does." It sounded so simple.

Tally met her on the landing, as he often did, shyly making sure she had light enough to find her way into her rooms and that her fire was tended before withdrawing. Her miniature attendant was naturally quiet, but Eleanor had come to enjoy his companionship and she usually chatted with him as best she could.

But tonight, she was too distracted for conversation and simply handed over a small bag of jellies she'd bought for him. "Here, sweet boy. I only hope your mother doesn't disapprove. . . . I should hate to disappoint. . . . Well, good night."

She closed her door only to rest her forehead against it to wait for her emotions and imagination to settle. She felt feverish and giddy, miserable, and yet, oddly, alive and whole.

Josiah's actions had been honorable and kind. His behavior was faultless. Eleanor accepted that she had been the one to brazenly press him for more kisses and invite every manner of indiscretion. She was having trouble blaming him for any of it, since it was Josiah who had ended it even after her secretly base nature had almost taken over.

Eleanor's heart pounded at the twist.

Almost is a slender thing to hang one's virtue on. I'd no thought of stopping, but then—suddenly I did. But what happened? Is he right to think I still fear ruin?

It hadn't felt like fear, but more like a seizure of uncertainty. When his hand had slid up her skirt, the panic had come not from virginal terror, but from the intensity of her own shameless reaction. For Eleanor knew that for her there were no half measures. One followed the rules completely. Once set on a path, one did not look back. One did their absolute in all things worthy of their time and attention. Eleanor smiled.

My passions and affections for him are becoming extremely absolute. But if I'm mistaken . . . I'll have lost more than my virginity.

He was keeping things from her, his failing vision and this business with his friends. And who knew what other secrets he was shielding from her, or what else he was hiding.

What kind of man pays for a woman's company?

She shuddered as a quieter voice inside of her ruthlessly answered. *What kind of woman takes a man's money for her time?*

She found the contract she'd set aside in her drawer after their dinner together at the inn. She'd avoided it, repulsed by the strange commerce of her life. Then, when she'd become so charmed with his presence, she hadn't wanted to be reminded of it.

But now, Eleanor broke the seal and opened it, forcing herself to actually read it for the first time. She slowly worked through the short document, determined to understand what it truly meant. For here was the work of his hands and a reflection of his true intentions, was it not?

Eleanor read on, her hands trembling as the language of the contract sank in.

It didn't bind her to him at all. In fact, true to his word, it gave her the money, as he'd said, once the painting was complete or by a certain date if he failed to finish. But then she saw it—a last clause tucked in before his signature and the witnessed signatures of his solicitor and a clerk.

Whereupon if Miss Eleanor Beckett refuses to participate in the proposed creative venture, all monies are to be transferred to her immediately. She is to have the full amount, despite any objections she may have, with the understanding that if Miss Beckett doesn't wish to retain the fifteen thousand pounds, she may dispose of it to charity as she sees fit. It is Mr. Hastings's sole wish that she be happy.

"He gave me my freedom. I've been my own woman all along," she whispered.

The paper fell from her numb fingers to the floor, and Eleanor sat down on the floor in a daze.

Chapter
16

He didn't send for her for three days. For three endless days and nights, Josiah worked alone in his studio, a man possessed. Escher brought him meals and trays, only to take most of them away untouched as Josiah poured his heart and soul into every brushstroke.

Everything was coming to a head. The blasted note Escher had read aloud had reminded him that his life was far too complicated to explain to the likes of Miss Beckett and his existence far too precarious; Josiah had barely managed to allow reason to rule over the sweet insanity of kissing the lady.

Why haven't you kissed me again?

He could hear her voice, so innocent and unashamed—and so anxious for affection. He'd been a breath away from every wretched cliché about wicked and wanton artists seducing their heavenly subjects.

But his honor had held.

Barely, but he'd decided to treat it like a solid victory.

All his promises and proclamations of higher morals

tasted like ashes in his mouth. He'd sent her a message via courier that she should wait at the Grove and that he would summon her soon. He'd meant to avert any more misunderstandings, but he wasn't sure how to reassure her when he wasn't sure of any solution that would rein in his feelings. Every time he closed his eyes, she was there, and in his dreams, she was an erotic queen demanding that he experience and survey every colorful inch of her body for all the paintings to come.

Each time he awoke, he'd had to talk himself back into exile. Because he knew if he saw her again, he'd forfeit everything to have her.

Amidst all of his angst, the painting held true. What he couldn't touch in reality, he could create on canvas. Josiah was like a man teetering on the brink of madness. The hours bled away, and the portrait had taken on a life of its own. He'd worked around the fleeting black spots and shadows that crowded into his vision, and worshipped her the only way he knew how—by immortalizing her. For hours, he stood in front of her image and painted, freed by his inner vision from having to perch like a humble supplicant on the floor.

Escher knocked on the doorframe to announce his arrival. "She's come, sir."

"What?" Josiah threw a cloth over the canvas to cover it, unwilling to let some stranger see it. "Who's come?"

"Miss Beckett, of course. She's on her way up the stairs, and bein' that you've been a bit . . . insistent on not being disturbed, I thought you'd want to know."

Eleanor's here. Impossible!

He hadn't sent the carriage, but Josiah realized it was foolish to think the woman couldn't come of her own volition if she wished to. Somehow, he'd been so distracted and lost in his own fog, it had never occurred to him before this moment that she would arrive on her own. After all, the rules of good etiquette forbid an unmarried woman to make such calls or even send correspondence. And if Eleanor Beckett was anything, she was a firm believer in adhering to the rules.

"Thank you, Escher."

"Shall I bring up lunch for you both, sir?" Escher offered. "Rita's most unhappy that you're still not eating."

"No, but thank her for the worry." Josiah ran a hand through his hair. "I'll ring if I need anything."

"As you wish." The older man retreated, and Josiah was left to face the disarray of his studio and the state of his clothing.

"So much for cleaning up and making a better impression. . . ."

"And who would you be trying to impress, Mr. Hastings?" Eleanor asked from the doorway, still wearing her coat and bonnet dusted with snow.

"I wasn't expecting you, Miss Beckett."

"No," she answered him softly. "But I have decided not to always do what I am expected to do."

"Have you?" Josiah thought his heart might pound out of his chest as he came toward her. "I'm not the right man to argue against a good smattering of rebellion, Eleanor. As we've established, I fear I'm a terrible influence on you, Miss Beckett."

She held out an object for him, like an offering in her gloved hands. "I bought you something—a small token."

He took it from her and opened the oblong wooden box as carefully as if it were glass. "What is it?"

"You should look and see."

Josiah lifted the object, his brow furrowed in confusion. "You brought me a spyglass?"

"It's a kaleidoscope. See?" She held it up, directing one end of the small telescope-looking object to the windows to maximize the light. "Won't you please look?"

He held it up to one eye and gasped. "Oh my!"

"It's what I imagine the colors of India would be. I saw a water-colored print in the window at Able's and Black's Bookshop of a palace garden in Bombay. You . . . said you missed that spectrum." Eleanor waited for his reaction, hoping she'd invoked the happier moments of that day before it had been spoiled by her demands for his kisses.

"I did say that. And I can't believe you remembered it."
He put the kaleidoscope back into the box reverently. "It's
the most thoughtful gift I've ever received. Thank you, Eleanor."

"Mr. Hastings?"

"Yes."

"I owe you an apology. I was too forward when we saw
each other last. For all my talk of propriety, I've discovered
that I am . . . less restrained than I thought. Perhaps it's my
impending freedom that's given birth to an impetuous nature." Her voice trembled, but she'd come too far not to give
her heart the full rein it demanded. "Why haven't you sent
for me?"

"Because I don't think I trust myself with you anymore.
Not alone. It's gone beyond . . . I don't think I'll be satisfied
just looking at you, Miss Beckett."

"But the painting—!"

"The work's far enough along that you don't have to risk
pneumonia to ensure the painting's completion." He leaned
against the table, his hands gripping the edge. "You never
need to apologize to me, Miss Beckett, and you were not
too forward. But you should go."

"And if I want to be here?"

He released the table, a tiger stepping out from the shadows, and Eleanor shivered at the latent power that ema-
nated from him. "Miss Beckett. If I may speak freely and
demonstrate what the word *forward* is. I'm going to tumble
you right here if you don't turn around and go back to the
Grove."

"T-tumble?" she asked in a whisper.

"By tumble," he said softly, one hand reaching out to
capture the edge of the ribbon trailing off the wrap at her
throat, "I mean I'm going to kiss you out of your clothes,
Eleanor. I'm going to bare every inch of you so that I can
taste you with my mouth and feel your skin with my hands
until there is no part of you that isn't known to me and open
to me. I'll do everything in my power to get you to beg me
to spoil you, and when you do, I won't hesitate for a single

second to take your maidenhead, Eleanor. Do you understand?"

"Oh!"

"I love the way you politely request kisses, but there is very little that will qualify as polite once I touch you again. No rules, no restraint, and above all, there can be no regrets, Eleanor. So, there you have it. Run, Miss Beckett. Run while you can, my prim and proper muse, and I'll send for you when my blood has cooled. Otherwise, surrender, Eleanor, and give yourself to me."

Surrender. No rules, no restraint, and no regrets.

She nodded, and made no move to flee.

The ribbon caught in his fingers, and he slowly pulled the wrap free from her shoulders to allow it to fall to the floor. "I need to hear you say it, Miss Beckett. I'd not have any misunderstanding between us."

She nodded again, her voice temporarily failing her.

"Say it, Eleanor."

"Yes."

"And what of respectability?" he asked as he began to gently tug off her leather gloves, slowly pulling them off to bare her hands.

"I'll have a lifetime of respectability, Mr. Hastings. A lifetime to reassure me that everything is in its proper place—but for now, I don't want to be proper."

"Don't you?"

"No."

"What do you want?"

"I want to be reckless. I want, just this once, to forget every rule and discover what it is that I've been so afraid of sitting over there, staring at you day after day."

"Aren't you afraid now?" He dropped her gloves onto the floor next to her wrap.

She shook her head firmly. "No. I'm nervous, but I expect that that is perfectly normal, Mr. Hastings, when one is attempting to convince a man to . . . seduce you."

He smiled. "I'd say you're the one actively seducing me, Miss Beckett."

She froze, but a new fire lit her eyes, and Josiah knew he'd hit on the key. The lady liked to hold the reins.

"I'm—no temptress, sir." Her eyes were clear and untroubled as she reached up to remove her bonnet and drop it carelessly to the floor. It wasn't the practiced move of a courtesan, but the maidenly grace of the gesture made every muscle in his body blaze with a flare of heat and desire all the same.

"Like hell, you're not," he whispered. "You're no milk-toast-bland creature to make a quiet bid for a kiss and then lay back."

"And this troubles you?" she asked.

"Not in the slightest, Miss Beckett. I'd not want you if you were any other way."

"Good." She sighed, then blushed. "Mr. Hastings, may we keep one rule as we proceed?"

"One rule. Let's have it." Josiah watched the delicious play of color across her cheeks, but also marveled at the way her impossibly green eyes sparked when she was roused, their shimmer mesmerizing enough to make emeralds seem pale by comparison.

"Promise you won't laugh at me. If I—make a mistake." Eleanor's hands found each other as she nervously navigated the last of the conversation while the desire in his eyes ignited her bones and made her long to have it done with. "My courage may not sustain itself if you . . . laugh."

Josiah had to bite the inside of his cheek to make sure he didn't smile at the amazing sweetness of her request. It revealed so much of her innocence and her fears, but also hinted that if he had the will to gain her trust that there was nothing she wouldn't yield to him. "You cannot make a mistake, Eleanor. But even if you could, I swear on my life and honor, I will never laugh at you."

"Very well, then." She let out a deep breath in relief, a new eagerness entering her countenance. "You should promptly tumble me, Mr. Hastings."

Thank God.

* * *

He instantly closed the distance between them and pulled her into his arms. This, at least, was familiar territory, and Eleanor marveled at the renewed thrill of anticipating his touch. Throwing off the last constraints of ladylike behavior, Eleanor savored the lack of anxiety she had about the act itself. For despite Lady M's vague warnings, she had every intention of enjoying every aspect of Josiah Hastings and the fall to come. She tipped her face up toward his and was rewarded with the kisses she craved.

One searing kiss became a dozen, and she was breathless with the wanton speed of the lust that made her heart race to catch it. She'd yearned for him for three days, and now there was nothing beyond him as the world fell away. The sweet friction of his mouth, the taste of him, the smell of his skin and Eleanor was trapped in a blaze of her own passions.

He abandoned her lips for just a moment and looked down at her with an unmistakable desire, so raw and unbridled that something inside of her tightened and ached with a hunger to equal his. Before she could find her voice, her feet suddenly left the ground and she squeaked in surprise as he lifted her up to carry her up to the dais, past the covered easel, and up toward the waiting couch.

"Mr. Hastings!"

"I do love your formality, my dear Miss Beckett." He set her gently down next to the sofa, then cupped her face in his hands to kiss her again. "I shall never tire of hearing you say my name, woman."

His fingers dropped to trail down her throat, and her breath caught in her throat as they met with the first of the small plain ivory buttons of her blouse. True to his word, he kissed the firm curve of her jaw, then down the pulse at her throat where her modest collar rested.

I am being kissed out of my clothes!

Eleanor gripped his shoulders, not trusting her legs to hold steady while the magical workings of his mouth against her skin forged endless ripples of fevered sensation through her. She was caught up in it, wanting him to hurry, desperate for the game to never end.

The buttons of her white cotton blouse yielded easily to his hands, and Eleanor moaned softly as he pushed the cloth down her shoulders and off her arms to drop it to the floor so that he could place hot kisses along her collarbone and gently bite the crest of her shoulders. Her hold on him tightened, and Eleanor instinctively tipped her head back to give him more access as he slowly undressed her.

Josiah tasted her skin, inhaling the faint fragrance of vanilla and white jasmine, and had to rein in his appetite as Eleanor transformed in his arms into a joyous siren, moaning and sighing her ready pleasure and inciting him to take all that she had to offer. She was both eager and sweet, clutching at his shoulders for balance as she swayed against him, her eyes blissfully closed in surrender.

But the real surrender had yet to come, and Josiah intended to savor every glorious moment of it—and see to it that she did as well.

He reached up to touch the silk of her hair, gently removing the turquoise pins she favored, dropping them carelessly on the floor at their feet. Within a few seconds, the wild, unruly copper curls had tumbled free from her tight chignon, and Josiah was rendered speechless at the sight of his muse unbound. Her hair fell like a thick silk curtain behind her, and the candlelight from the side table made it come alive with shimmering gold in a riotous dance of light and color.

With her blouse dispatched, Josiah wrapped one arm around her waist to lean over and kiss the bare curves of the uppermost swell of her breasts, teasing the soft skin there and using his tongue to elicit little mews and sighs of excitement—even as he strategized the best approach to exposing more of her by dealing with the industrial steel cage of the corset she wore.

He lifted his head to eye it like a general surveying an enemy on the field.

Eleanor started to offer to help, but before she could protest, he simply put his hands firmly around her waist, and in once quick motion as she exhaled, Josiah popped the busk and sprang her free from the corset's hold. "There!" His smile was pure wicked triumph. "So much for wrestling with all those hooks and laces."

"You . . . are a very naughty man."

"It's a compliment when you say it like that, Eleanor." He tossed the bulky undergarment onto the floor off the dais, unwilling to trip over the damn thing later, then turned his attentions back to the reward at hand.

"God, you're beautiful!" he whispered, stroking her through the thin cloth of her chemise, the tiny ribbons frayed and coming loose at the lightest tug of his fingers.

Her breasts weren't overly large, but were like firm, ripe peaches tipped with pert nipples the color of red clay. They jutted into his hands, grazing his palms like hard pebbles, and he gently circled each one with his fingers until Eleanor's fingers entwined in his hair and pulled his mouth down to give them the attention they demanded.

As clear as his vision had been all day, he didn't trust his eyes. He wanted to touch her as much as he could, feeling each move that she made, to map her with his fingertips for a lifetime of nostalgia and longing.

He suckled each one through her chemise, then deliberately pulled the cloth back across each sensitive crest, the cool, wet friction across her warm flesh making her shiver and tremble against his chest. Josiah lifted her again, this time to sit her on the sofa, pushing her gently back against the curve of the fainting couch to recline.

He knelt down next to her and began to unlace her boots, then peel off each woolen stocking in turn.

"Josiah!" She tried to pull an ankle out of his grip, but he wasn't relinquishing any ground he'd gained.

"Shh! I must see these perfect feet of yours. Why—I see no sign of a farm hand! They are delectable, these feet!"

"You cannot be serious!" She was breathing hard, astonished at the effect he had—his hands caressing the sensitive curve of her foot. He lifted one foot to kiss the arch, and she squeaked in protest before moaning in pure ecstasy at the shower of electric sparks that swept up her leg. "I'm sure that this is—highly irregular, Mr. Hastings!"

"Is it? And what of this, then?" He tongued the indent of her delicate ankle only to gently bite the meaty rise of her calf.

"Oh, what are you doing?"

"I am feasting on you, Miss Beckett. I am memorizing you from the toes all the way up to the top of your prim and proper head—although I admit I may be diverted along the way. As promised, I intend to kiss you out of every inch of your clothing until there is nothing of you that isn't bare and offered up to me."

She didn't care anymore. Whatever plan he'd prepared, she knew she had already acquiesced. If any of his "diversions" were half as startling and wonderful as the feel of his mouth as it trailed wet kisses upward along her calf, she had no complaints.

For this was heaven!

He worked his way up from her calves, lingering a bit to kiss the crease behind her knee to make her squeak again in a weak protest. Her skirt and petticoats were pushed up easily as his hands traced the plump curve of her thighs, pillowed and welcoming, and Josiah wondered if his muse had any idea of what the feast's main course would entail.

He parted her thighs and Eleanor threw her head back, riding the sweet agony of anticipation and satisfaction at its bite. Her hips writhed and bucked as she instinctively tried to urge him to hurry. But Josiah was in no rush.

Eleanor was an active participant, following his lead but then pursuing her own passion and virginal curiosity— fearlessly innocent in the game. Touching his hair, massaging his shoulders, and stroking any part of him she could. She was openly responsive to what he was doing, instinctively communicating her pleasure and spurring him on. It was an aphrodisiac he had never experienced before.

He bent over her, unfastening her skirt's waistband and

untying her petticoats, kissed the soft, gentle rise of her belly only to work ever so slowly up her rib cage. His hands began to leisurely trace the lines of her body, circling back to caress her skin, each pass of his fingertips whispers of trespasses yet to come, making her porcelain skin taut and sensitive. Down her arms, over her shoulders, he skirted the rise of her bare breasts only to drop down and press his palms against her ribs to follow the hollows and curves of her frame.

She bucked up, her back arching in frustration at the touch of his hands everywhere but the most sensitive peaks and junctures of her body. She moaned, fighting the rolling wave of raw hunger that threatened to make her come apart at the seams. It was a strange kind of torture to be in the throes of pleasure but to feel denied.

"Josiah!" she cried out, only to add with a whimper, "Please."

And it came to him that his intention to be playful had unknowingly been cruel. He had pushed her too far. She could no more name her desires than describe the dark side of the moon. "Forgive me."

He could smell her arousal as it intermingled with the perfume of her skin.

His beautiful spitfire, so reserved and polite, was molten mercury, volatile and unpredictable. Josiah decided he'd teased her enough for one encounter. He began to unbutton his own shirt when Eleanor's hand caught his wrist.

"Please. Let me."

It was his turn to yield, and the game took a turn he hadn't anticipated.

She sat up to unbutton his shirt, pushing it back off of his shoulders and mirroring the way he'd touched her to explore Josiah's broad frame and lean masculine lines. His skin was hot and the swirls of hair on his chest were crisp like coarse silk. He was muscular, a creature of taut sinew and male strength, and she was breathless with the thrill of touching him at will, electrified by the glory of his form as it was revealed to her.

He groaned as she threaded her fingers through the hair on his chest and then clenched her hand into a fist. "Careful."

"Did I hurt you?"

"No. You can't hurt me, Eleanor. But you can make a man forget himself."

Silence answered him, but she kissed him before he could interpret the fire in her eyes at his revelation. Her breasts pressed against his bare flesh and his body's reaction was primal.

She grew impatient to see all of him. To touch more of him. To taste his skin as he had tasted hers. He was lean and muscular, as if chiseled from warm stones, so different from her own yielding form. She marveled at the earthly beauty of him and relished the appeal of his body to her senses.

"What are you thinking over there, Eleanor Beckett?"

She blushed, and he loved the contradiction of it. She was so naturally earthy and voluptuous, but could still color like a peony just to pique his interest.

"I am thinking that you are the most beautiful thing I have ever seen, Josiah Hastings, and I . . . I don't wish to say any more."

"How do you imagine it, Miss Beckett? Your first time with a man?" he asked, attempting to gauge if she were still fearful or anxious about the moment at hand.

"I never imagined speaking of such a thing. . . . I imagined it would just . . . happen."

"What would happen?"

"You don't know?" she asked miserably.

"I'm extremely familiar with the course of events, Miss Beckett. But I'm asking only in a quest to make sure that my very procedural-minded Eleanor isn't disappointed or shocked."

Her eyes widened as the blush swept up from her breasts. "I sincerely doubt that—I'll be disappointed."

He smiled. "Agreed. We shall make it a goal not to disappoint." *Or delay things any longer . . .*

He pushed her back onto the sofa and returned to his position between her thighs, this time pulling off her skirts and the last layers of her petticoats and flannels to reveal every last inch of her.

She was as exquisite as anything he'd ever seen, and Josiah reveled in the sight of her body, every shade of pink glistening like a flower, her skin tightening and changing color as her sex opened up in front of him. The musky sweet scent of her made patience nearly impossible, and he lowered his mouth to sample the delights of her flesh.

She'd prepared herself for the return of his touch, expecting his fingers and anticipating him to simply pick up where he'd left off three days ago. She was eager to experience the culmination of the arc of electric heat she'd gotten a taste of—but when he exhaled over the wet flesh between her legs, Eleanor was nearly undone. Here was an impossibility she had never envisioned and couldn't fathom that he would actually think to—

It was bliss.

"Th-this cannot be—the usual course of it, Mr. Hastings!" she exclaimed, her hands clutching at the cushions beneath her as he hovered just above her, fanning the flames of her desire with every breath he took.

"There are no rules, Miss Beckett. Lecture me later."

He splayed his hands against the insides of her thighs to hold her in place, and then gently kissed the ripe lips of her sex, his tongue darting out to chart the folds before trailing up to circle her clit. With each pass of the tip of his tongue winding up and around the tiny bud, Eleanor trembled and moaned. He added more pressure, working the sensitive pearl in a dance of unrelenting taste and touch, and lost himself in the quest for her first release. She was ambrosia in his mouth, and Josiah drank in all of it.

Instead of fighting it, Eleanor felt like laughing at the delicious cascade of pleasure he was creating inside of her. "Yes! Please, yes!"

Josiah needed no more encouragement. Impediments would have better aided his cause to make sure that he'd

readied her for what was yet to come, but it took every fiber
of discipline he possessed to keep from rushing things.
Faster and faster, he circled her clit, until she was writhing
against him, held in place by the firm grip of his hands on
her hips.

Eleanor was lost to it. She climaxed in a fast, sharp rush
that opened a thousand doors to a hunger for more. She'd
tumbled over the edge of release before she'd even had the
chance to realize there was a precipice, and Eleanor was in
awe at the limitless passion he'd gifted to her.

She was still coming in a cascade of rapture when he
freed himself from his breeches, intending to take her completely. Eleanor roused, emboldened by the aphrodisiac of
her first orgasm, and opened her eyes to see what had
robbed her of his touch. Her eyes widened in wonder as his
sex sprang free from the confines of his clothes, her hands
filled with the heavy weight of his cock. It was like nothing
she'd expected, and her admiration was as potent as it was
innocent. She gasped at the velvety softness of his skin over
a molten thick core. It seemed massive to her innocent eyes,
and as her fingers struggled to wrap around him, she accepted that appearances weren't deceiving. The head was a
deep color, like a plum, atop the firm column of his sex.
She squeezed him and then ran her fingers gently down its
length to test its resilience, liking the way it jutted and
bobbed at her touch—as if this part of him had a will of its
own. His body's masculine beauty was unparalleled in her
limited experience, and her innermost muscles clenched
involuntarily with the greedy desire to possess him completely.

"Wait, I have . . . French letters."

"Oh." She bit her lower lip. "Do you?"

"Minx! Only because ever since I asked you for that first
kiss and you said no, I had a premonition that nothing with
you would be predictable, and since I would *never* need
them with a proper lady like Miss Eleanor Beckett, I did
the opposite and put a good supply under the cushion here
and in my bedroom."

She laughed, a husky, unguarded sound that made his body vibrate with lust.

He made quick work of it, encasing himself in the condom, and then returning to position himself between her thighs, notching the round head of his cock up against her molten slit, and aligning himself to press up into her.

Total trust. No questions asked, her thighs were parted wide, her ankles digging into the small of his back.

"I want you to forget yourself." She looked up at him, her green eyes clear and beautiful. "I want to forget myself. Let us be lost together."

Let us be lost together.

Eleanor's legs tightened around him even as he began to press forward one slow inch at a time. Josiah's jaw clenched at the challenge of holding himself in check, fighting the urge to just drive forward into the slick, hot well of her core. He had no wish to hurt her.

But he'd underestimated Eleanor's needs.

In one smooth, graceful movement, she arched upward and enveloped his cock in a tight velvet sheath that left him breathless at the carnal grip of her channel. He groaned and she pressed upward again, completing the act as her maidenhead gave way and rendered herself open to him.

He looked into her eyes, and they were free of any pain or anxiety. Instead there was a small glint of mischievous pride that she'd managed it. He kissed her softly, relishing the way she fit him so perfectly, and then moved again, rewarding her for her boldness with deep, long strokes that metered out pure ecstasy. Eleanor instinctively matched his movements, and Josiah rocked into her, driving forward, relentlessly claiming her body and soul with every thrust of his body into hers.

Every internal lecture about gentility was forgotten. There was only Eleanor and his need to possess her completely, to fill her and mark her as his. Harder and harder, faster and faster, the drive to release took over, and at every turn, she was with him, clinging to him and matching his every move with her body's own desire to be filled completely, to be claimed—and to claim him in return.

She cried out again, spending in long, shuddering spasms that pushed him over the edge. Josiah grit his teeth as he pushed past the zenith of sensation, coming inside of her in white-hot jets of crème, the orgasm so strong it was as if lightning had arced down his spine in a storm of pleasure and pain.

It was several long minutes before he trusted himself enough to speak, his breath coming in long, ragged bursts, and he withdrew as gently as he could, rolling over without relinquishing her to cover himself with her body, praying that she was unbruised.

"Well . . ." Josiah closed his eyes. "I am . . . ready for my . . . lecture now, Miss Beckett. What were the rules again? Besides not laughing, of course, which by the way, I think you did at one point, but I won't hold it against you."

She laughed again, and he savored the delight he heard there.

"I have but one question, Mr. Hastings."

He warily opened one eye. "And what is that?"

"As to etiquette—how soon can a person reasonably request you to do that again?"

It was his turn to laugh before he kissed her, a gentle, reverent gesture that reignited and renewed the bonds between them. "Give me a few minutes to rest my eyes, and I'll see if I can't demonstrate a satisfactory answer, Miss Beckett."

* * *

It was a revelation—this lazy spiral of indolent pleasure that kept her in place afterward. Here was something she hadn't anticipated. That the ecstasy of his touch would banish all shame. She was reborn and all the fears that had metered every decision she'd made were gone. Naked and warm, Eleanor stretched against him, pressing herself along his body to absorb more of his strength.

She surveyed him as he slept, noting that in her haze of happiness, she couldn't tell where her own flesh ended and his began in the sweet tangle they'd created together. He looked vulnerable as he dreamt and Eleanor sighed as she closed her eyes. The even cadence of his breathing soothed her as she savored a thousand new sensations.

She'd given herself to him, completely and without hesitation.

Twice.

Here is freedom. Here is more than I thought possible— for such a man to hold me in his arms! I've never felt so cherished. . . .

He awoke and looked up at her, a man content until his brow furrowed. "Did I fall asleep?" He sat up to run a hand through his unruly brown hair. "I'm sorry for that." Josiah reluctantly began to retrieve their clothes. "We should restore ourselves before poor Escher comes up to make a fuss about needing a tray."

"The day is gone." She sighed.

"It is. But don't worry. We'll have you back to the Grove before the dinner dishes are cleared and Mrs. Clay won't lift an eyebrow, I promise."

"Yes, of course." Eleanor closed her eyes, fighting an awkward unhappiness that he'd been so quick to think of her reputation and a return to the inn. Not that she wouldn't have insisted on a necessary retreat, but . . .

It stung to be released so readily.

"What is that face? Are you—displeased to go?"

She shook her head. "No. Embarrassed that I wasn't thinking of poor Mrs. Clay and how disappointed she would be. I was—lost in this a little."

"Eleanor." He shifted to pull her back underneath him, capturing her with the heat of his body and the strength of the unique cage of muscle and bone that held her still. "I would keep you if I could."

"Would you?" she asked softly.

He nodded then kissed the tip of her nose. "Mine. Say that you are mine, Eleanor. Until it's done. Give me that much."

"Yours, until it's done. I shall be completely yours until the painting is finished." She kissed the pulse at his throat. "I could ask for nothing more."

"Mine and make no mistake."

"And what is that?"

"You'll never have to *ask* again for a kiss, my dear Miss Beckett. Never." He leaned over to trail hot kisses against the silken curves of her throat until she sighed and moaned against his touch, arching up against him in an unspoken bid for more.

"Then we shall make the most of the days, Mr. Hastings."

Chapter
17

True to her word, in the following days, she was his completely in a glorious freefall of painting and lovemaking that allowed Josiah to forget the press of the hours. He sent the carriage each morning as early as he could, and then locked them in the studio for privacy as he worked until teatime. They would eat odd formal little picnics on the dais and make love for the rest of the day for an afternoon of pleasure and conversation.

The Eschers instinctively knew to stay clear of the studio, and Josiah was grateful for their discretion. The lovers were left to their own during magical days of creative freedom and erotic discovery.

But Josiah's enjoyment was edged in melancholy. Her every departure was like a rehearsal for letting her go. With every kiss, he had to battle himself and the growing attachment he felt for this fiery woman who privately transformed daily in his presence from an untouchable, proper lady to his own beloved nymph.

As this day unfolded, just four days after her initial surrender, Josiah was struggling to stay in front of the easel. His eyes had been plaguing him unmercifully and he'd finally been forced to forfeit the rest of the morning in the studio to take her downstairs for what he realized would be the first time.

Oddly enough, getting Miss Eleanor Beckett into his bedroom, even after all the intimacies they'd shared, hadn't been a foregone conclusion. After a debate on the improprieties of entering a man's bedroom in which Josiah had cheerfully allowed her the upper hand, he'd trumped her reluctance with a delicious nod to the one trait all women possessed and could never deny: curiosity.

"Do you not wish to see my most private sanctuary and hiding place, Miss Beckett? Are you not . . . curious, at all?" he'd asked—and won the day.

With the curtains drawn, the room was dimly lit with tapers and gave the lovers the illusion of timelessness. The artwork in this room was special, as each piece had been chosen for sentimental reasons and to remind him of better days. He stepped back to let her explore, enjoying the sight of her in his inner sanctum. But Eleanor's curiosity about his "sanctuary" was only piqued as she looked askance at a strange little shrine set on a small table in one corner.

She walked over to inspect it more closely, lifting one of the hothouse roses he'd cut and floated in a small porcelain bowl in front of a bronze figurine. The Hindu goddess was dancing with one leg upraised and her hands spread wide, demonstrating a balance and grace that Eleanor had never imagined. An oil lamp etched with flowers was unlit next to it, and Eleanor bent over to peer into the exotic face and admire it.

"Are you a heathen, Josiah?" she asked, looking at him through her lashes. "I mean, is that—do you pray to this figurine, with the oils and flowers at her feet?"

He smiled. "I meditate sometimes and kneel there on those cushions in front of her. But I cannot claim to worship her in the strict sense of the word. I don't own her. She isn't my goddess. I'm not reformed enough to deserve her, I think. We have a unique relationship, Lakshmi and I, and if I ask her for anything, it's with the understanding that she has other and better petitioners to bother with than my British self. All I can say for certain is that I find comfort in the Hindu customs. There is little to contradict my Christian upbringing in them and . . ."

"And?" Eleanor reached out to touch his hand.

"There aren't a lot of rules." He savored the whisper-light trails her fingers were making on his skin. "Just truths for each man to pursue. And since you know how I hate rules, you can see the appeal. Besides"—he lifted her hand to his lips to kiss the firm, warm well of her palm—"I don't like to leave the house for my spiritual nourishment, and the Church of England refused to install a vicar in my bedroom."

She laughed, playfully pinching him on the shoulder with her free hand; but she didn't pull away from him as he began to unlace the back of her gown and free her from its confines. "You are a wicked man!"

"See? There's a truth!" Josiah leaned over to kiss the curve of her shoulder, mirroring her blow with a more sensual one of his own. "But to answer you directly, no, Miss Eleanor Beckett, I am not a heathen."

"Mr. Hastings?" she asked, her head tipping to one side as she let the dress slide farther down her shoulders.

"Yes, Miss Beckett?" he replied, enjoying the delicious cool formality of her, even as the brush of red velvet against him warmed his blood.

"How is it that you are not married?"

He stood up a little straighter. "Here's a subject!"

She blushed. "Well?"

"How is that *you* are not married?" he countered. Josiah hated how defensive he sounded, but he wasn't sure if one confession wouldn't lead to a dozen others that he wasn't ready to make.

"Me? The only daughter of an eccentric chemist?" She laughed. "If there was a line of suitors, I missed them, and by the time I thought to look . . . well, Fate intervened, didn't it?"

"In this case, I'm grateful to Providence for any path that brought you here, Eleanor." Josiah wrested the gown from her, lifting her out of it so that he could set his chemise- and petticoat-clad beauty down on the side of his bed. "*Extremely* grateful."

"You never speak of your past without me having to pry it out of you, Mr. Hastings, and even then, I wonder at what you choose not to say." She stretched out her arms to ease the ache of inactivity from posing. "Are you deliberately being mysterious to pique my interest? Or have you some dark secrets that you're keeping?"

"This criticism from a woman who has said as little as she can of her life before she stepped into my carriage?" he countered.

Eleanor sighed. "Only because my life before I stepped into that carriage no longer exists. What is to be gained from a tragic account of happier days, or parents reunited in heaven, or a pitiable portrayal of my skills as a seamstress?"

"What of the man that swindled your father? Do you ever think of taking up your father's lawsuit and restoring his name?"

She became very still for a moment, and Josiah's attention was arrested by the strange look on her face. Regret flooded through him. "I shouldn't have asked, Eleanor. I never meant to cause you any pain."

"No. It's not pain I was experiencing." She reached up to press her fingers against her cheek, as if to cool the flush that blossomed there. "It was a guilty conscience. For I once walked past his mansion one evening and . . ."

"And?" he prompted.

"It was too much. Just the luxury of light spilling out from those windows made me feel so cold and alone—and worthless." Eleanor's hand dropped back to smooth out the sheet across her thighs. "I wanted to throw a rock through Mr. Thomas Keller's parlor window, Mr. Hastings. Or just scream my father's name loud enough to shake them from their peaceful perches."

"And did you?" Josiah pressed her gently.

"Of course not!" Eleanor answered in shock. "What is to be gained from that? I'd have been hauled off to Bedlam and my father and mother would still be gone."

"Justice can be a balm to soothe your pain. Perhaps righting things would—"

She shook her head firmly. "No. I may daydream about kicking the man in his shins or pouring a glass of lemonade on his head, but I don't wish to give more of myself to it than that. Crusades are notoriously wasteful and pointless, Mr. Hastings. My father taught me that much."

"So your entire confession consists of you once walking past the man's house?" Josiah couldn't help but think of his friend, Galen, and his difficult lesson on that same subject. Unlike Miss Beckett, Galen Hawke had learned about revenge by embracing it—and had nearly lost everything he currently held dear. "You're a wise woman, Eleanor."

"I'm stubborn, Josiah. There is a vast difference."

"Stubborn?"

"I'll not give any more of my life over to that villain. Keller has already taken too much of me, of my happiness and my future. Why would I give him more of my present mind or spoil the days that I have found joy here with you?"

"Then I won't mention him again." He reached out to trace the ivory lines of her shoulder, indolently pushing the little capped sleeve of her chemise downward. "Ask me something else, Eleanor."

"Tell me why you stopped painting women."

"You don't want to know. It's not a very good story, Eleanor. Ask me something else."

"Not every story has to entertain, Josiah. I would know all your stories, sir, if it meant that I could know more of you."

"Very well." He sighed, lying back on the bed next to her to look up at the ceiling, the memory replaying in his mind's eye. "Though I can't see how this isn't going to make you think less of me and cheat me of an afternoon's pleasures."

"Now you have to tell me!" She pinched his shoulder playfully.

"Ouch! What a bully you've become. . . ." He kissed her on the nose.

"Confess, Hastings."

"Come, then." He rose from the bed and wrapped her in his robe, and before she could ask, he swept her from the bed, carrying her from the room cradled against his chest.

"Where are we going?"

"Shhh! Remember you asked." He knew his way about the rooms without lighting a single candle, every dimension memorized and every step counted and recounted so often he had no fear of stumbling with his priceless armload. He carried her easily, enjoying her weight in his arms and the heat of her body to his with her arms encircling his neck. He pushed the door open to a small, rarely used study with his bare foot and went inside to set her carefully down on a soft chair. It was a windowless room, dark even in the early afternoon. He found the matches in the top drawer and lit a small lamp on the desk. "I can't recall the last time I was in this room."

Instantly, he knew the portrait on the wall would have come to life, and Eleanor's gasp confirmed it. He barely glanced in its direction, the charms of its subject long faded for him.

Eleanor, on the other hand, was just now experiencing them. "Oh my! She's beautiful!"

Posing as some obscure Greek goddess carelessly holding a bunch of grapes, here was a dark-haired woman, lush and lively, happily wearing little more than a scandalous drape of cloth that bared far more of her curves than it covered. Her features were pert and playful, with wide, lovely eyes the color of brandy and a heart-shaped bow of a mouth that was a ripe wine red that begged for kisses.

"Daisy was."

"I'm almost afraid to hear this story now."

"No need to fear her." Josiah closed his eyes. "I grew up in the country, my father being a member of the country gentry, as I told you. The family holdings were ideal, I think, for a young boy, and my brothers and I would often roam wild to escape my sisters. My father swore we had too much freedom, but I, to this day, don't even know what that meant. How can there be too much freedom for a boy?"

Nostalgia gave the memories a softer glow, and he relaxed into a subject he hadn't spoken of since he'd been chained in the dark of a dungeon with Rowan. "There was a girl in the village, and I don't remember a time when I didn't love her. It was ridiculous, but Daisy always seemed so worldly and wonderful to me. She left for London at sixteen, fostered out to a rich aunt who'd requested her company, and I yearned for her."

"That's sweet."

"It wasn't sweet! It was miserable, and I can't believe the hours I wasted pining away for her. Especially since absence does make the heart grow fonder. We secretly corresponded for quite some time until I was tossed out by my father and headed to London to make my own fortunes. I was poor but proud, and when I met her again years and years later, I was completely smitten—all over again. She had grown into a gloriously groomed creature, and there wasn't a perfume-scented ribbon out of place. Daisy had gained polish and I was dazzled."

"What man wouldn't have been?" Eleanor sighed, envious of the woman's place in his heart.

"I begged her to sit for me and I fell in love with her all over again. I imbued her with all the qualities I'd credited her with over the years. I thought she was natural, not shameless. I thought she was innocent and spoiled, not conniving and greedy. I thought I'd found my muse and my future wife. But when I announced as much, she laughed in my face. I was a diversion, a rather wicked diversion, but she had no intentions of shackling herself to a starving artist without the benefit of fortune or family. She'd found a rich patron and was already enjoying his gifts and his bed. She was going to inherit her aunt's house and money and live the jolly carefree life of a courtesan. She said I was welcome to paint her or pleasure her as I saw fit, but that was all she wanted of me."

"Oh my!" Eleanor's fingers covered her lips. "How could she?"

"I threw her out half naked while she was cursing and spitting like a cat coming out of a rain barrel. I made a vow then and there about painting women. I didn't ever want to look at something so false and give that lie to the world." Josiah did his best to look at the portrait, but it was just a gray outline of a figure on a colorless wall. "Not that I proved to be any great moral example myself, but heartbreak does lead to some interesting choices. After gadding about London like a fool for several years, playing the rake to prove that she hadn't hurt me, I left for India and was painting there and playing the fool when the rebellion simmered over and caught us all off guard."

He waited while Eleanor silently looked at the painting, absorbing the story behind Daisy's sultry looks. After all, here was exactly the sort of portrait she'd been expecting on that first day—

"Why keep her on your wall, then? Why force yourself to look at her every day?"

"It was supposed to be a bit of masculine bravado. I think I said something about wanting a reminder of the lesson so that I wouldn't forget it. But I've kept it up for another reason entirely."

"Is she—still in London? Do you see her sometimes?" Eleanor asked quietly.

He shook his head. "She is, but . . . we don't run in the same circles. I heard that she'd changed her name to Delilah and had done a few turns in the theatre. But I never cared enough to seek her out."

"Not all women are so false."

"Time has given me better perspective. Daisy wasn't false. She never presented herself as anything other than what she was. I was the one who saw her differently and punished her for not living up to my expectations. I'd not have you think me that heartless, but I once was. That painting is proof that I'm horribly flawed." He shifted to lift her up and sit her on the edge of the giant desk in the middle of the study and then stood facing her, nudging her soft thighs apart. "But you are not false, Eleanor." *And when you break my heart, it will be for exactly the opposite reasons as Daisy. She had none of your character. But because of that proud character I've come to worship, I care too much for you to humble you with a useless man for a husband.*

I am the one who is false.

The Jackal will be in motion and I'll let Fate intervene.

But today, you are mine, Eleanor Beckett.

He cradled her against his chest, but the tenderness of the scene gave way to the desire to claim her there and banish the ghosts of the past once and for all. Not Daisy in particular, but Josiah had the irrational urge to wipe every woman he had ever known from his mind. Each time he made love to Eleanor, they'd all faded a few more degrees until he was sure that there would be no memory of any woman he had been with—leaving only Eleanor.

As it should be.

He gripped the lapels of his own robe, admiring how much better it appeared when wrapped around Eleanor's alluring body, and used the cloth to pull her close, the backs of his fingers deliberately grazing the peaks of her breasts.

Eleanor leaned forward, increasing the contact as her nipples grew turgid and firm, snaking her hands upward to caress his chest and lick the sensitive lines of his throat. She loved the way his pulse quickened and his warm skin quivered wherever her mouth teased him with her tongue.

His fingers lifted up each lace-edged strap of her chemise to push it off her shoulders, drawing the soft cotton slowly down across her sensitive peaks, and Eleanor abandoned her campaign to kiss his neck so that she could throw her head back and revel in his attentions.

Her breasts were bare, and Josiah tasted each one, tonguing each circle of firm flesh until it pebbled at his kisses. She gripped his hair to beg him to suckle her, and

Josiah obliged her without hesitation. He lathed and licked the ruddy tips of her breasts until she was shuddering and writhing against him. She became the sustenance his body craved, and Josiah's appetite for his beloved Eleanor overcame a world of shadows and made him believe that happiness might be his.

Her hands roamed over him, never still as she sought a way to please him, even as the first hint of her impending climax began to arc from her breasts and radiate out through her limbs. She fanned her hands out to massage his shoulders and map the hardened planes and angles of his chest and back. Eleanor tipped her head forward again, luxuriating in the sight of Josiah at her breasts, and felt every inch the pagan goddess for it.

But the growing ache inside of her demanded participation, and Eleanor wriggled forward to free her hands and loosen his pants. The head of his cock was already straining for release, and Eleanor slid her hand down its length, lifting one of her legs to press her own wet core against the solid heat of him through the cloth of his breeches.

"So beautiful . . ." He sighed, lifting his head to kiss her, shifting his hips forward as well, following her lead to add to the pressure and tease her with his shaft.

The desk's height was ideal, though Eleanor doubted the makers had intended it for such a purpose. But then another wicked thought occurred to her. "All this time, Mr. Hastings, I'd say you've spent far too much time surveying the view."

"And what do you suggest?"

She shimmied off the edge and pressed against him, only to turn him around and guide him to lean back up against the desk. "It is my turn to survey beauty, Mr. Hastings."

She knelt down between his thighs, and kissed the bones of his hips, teasing him as he had her and demonstrating that she was an extremely quick study in the art of love. His pants were already loosened from their love play, and Eleanor eagerly dispatched with the buttons to free his cock for her attentions. The jutting prowess of his erection was a sight to behold, and Eleanor stared at it in admiration and wonder that such a thing existed. She wrapped her fingers around him, testing the marvelous weight and heft of him in her palm. The color ripened at her grip, and Eleanor experienced the thrill of newfound power.

His breath whistled as he pulled it through clenched teeth. "You're torturing me on purpose, aren't you?"

"No, but I might," she said, then leaned forward to gently kiss his swollen head.

She tasted the musk of his skin and boldly sampled the solitary pearl of moisture that heralded his deep arousal, savoring the salty-sweet flavor of his body. His cock jerked against her lips, and Josiah groaned as her tongue found the sensitive juncture at the underside of his swollen head. She licked him there, laving and teasing the taut skin, before she kissed him again, only to take him into her mouth. She moved against him, using her mouth and her hands, instinctively finding the rhythm and pressure to push him over the edge of rapture.

Every texture of his sex, every ridge and silken line was explored. Her hands and mouth moved in a concert of friction and ardor.

For Josiah, it was a glorious combination of heaven and hell. For he had to hold perfectly still while Eleanor took charge, her unpracticed attentions angelic in their perfection. He was a caged beast as every move of her mouth and hands against him stripped him of his control. When she took him inside of her mouth, the velvet pocket of that inner sanctum froze him in place, consuming him with a fever that threatened to wrest his release from his grip. Every kiss scalded him with honey that made his bones ignite with need.

Josiah couldn't take it anymore.

He lifted her up with a groan to pull her onto his lap, throwing her petticoats up to sit astride him, and penetrated her with a primal growl, grinding up into the tight, wet confines of her body in a merciless stroke. He buried himself inside of her, until his cock was nestled up against the opening of her womb and they were both breathless. He began to rock upward, his hands locked onto her hips to seize and savor the white-hot release that danced just out of his reach.

Eleanor cried out, wrapping her legs around his waist, but suddenly, Josiah's eyes opened and he stopped moving, cursing under his breath as their love play took a very sudden stop. "Damn it."

"W-what is it?" She wriggled against him, hoping to spur him on, but Josiah seized her hips and forced her to be still.

"I have no condoms in this study."

"Oh!" Eleanor bit her lower lip in frustration. "Should I—"

He gripped her bottom, cupping her firmly, and Eleanor forgot what she was going to say. "Miss Beckett, hold on to my neck, please, if you don't mind."

She complied, only to find herself lifted up completely from the desk, still wonderfully impaled by his magnificent erection as he stood and began to carry her out of the room.

"J-Josiah?"

"Bedroom," he growled, concentrating on the issue at hand and praying he didn't spill his seed from the delightful sensations of this unique form of transportation. It was an extremely unorthodox stroll back to the privacy of his room, but he was determined to reach his goal.

Within seconds, they were ensconced safely on his great bed and he had withdrawn only for the brief moments it took to secure one of the French letters from his nightstand. "Where were we?"

"You were going to punish me for torturing you."

"Woman. You have *no* idea."

Eleanor laughed as he swept her back into his arms and the "torment" began in earnest until they were both lost in the fires of pleasure and pain. Every stroke and touch pushed them closer to the edge, blurring the lines between possession and surrender.

She threw back her head, crying out shamelessly, and he

could feel her orgasm flow over him, her muscles gripping him with exquisite spasms that sent his own release spinning out through his frame. Josiah couldn't think as searing crème was wrenched from his body, and he plunged into her to ride out each crest and prolong the moment.

Long moments of silence followed as they each tried to recover and collect their thoughts. Eleanor's heart was pounding so loudly she feared if he whispered endearments she wouldn't hear them, but from his own labored breathing, she doubted the problem would arise.

At last, she was confident that her soul was once again safely tethered to her body, and Eleanor curled up against his side, tucking up to absorb his heat and savor his touch.

She smiled up at the ceiling as a new mischievous thought occurred to her.

"What are you thinking, Miss Beckett?"

"I'm thinking you'll recall the last time you went in that study now, Mr. Hastings."

She was rewarded with his laughter, an uncontrolled burst that made her realize how rarely he'd done so in her presence. And Eleanor marveled that victory could be this sweet and come with a simple jest.

I'll win his heart, yet.

Chapter

18

"Here, let me help you with that." Rita's offer was delivered in her usual curt tone as Eleanor dressed to leave, but she was all smiles when their eyes met in the vanity's reflection. Eleanor yielded her fight with her buttons, grateful for the woman's intervention. "You headin' back to the Grove, then?"

"Yes."

"A lot of wasted time, if you ask me, all this back and forth the last few days," Rita said.

"Wasted time?" Eleanor nervously adjusted the ruffles of her shirtfront. "Whatever do you mean, Mrs. Escher?"

"I ain't as young as I once was, miss, but I know enough. There's never enough time to be happy, if you ask me. Mind, I'm no fool. There's always a crowd ready to judge, but they'd do that even if you walked about with a prayer book on your head and never stepped a toe out of line, wouldn't they?"

It was all Eleanor could do to nod mutely in shock. *So much for our secret!*

Rita finished with the last button. "Not that it's my business! Mind, I'm just pleased he's eating!"

"Thank you, Mrs. Escher. I'm—I'm not comfortable staying . . . I'm struggling with my conscience, and as silly as it seems, I have to keep my own rooms."

"Right enough!" Rita stood back, hands at her hips. "Suit yourself. It's all art and mystery around here and I can't keep track of it. I'm no gossip, so you mustn't worry on that account. Mind, I've never been one to exchange banter while I'm haggling over the price of eels. What a bunch of bothersome biddies at that market!"

Eleanor struggled not to imagine what kind of gossip could be heard in a fish market, but kept her curiosity to herself. "I'm grateful to you, Mrs. Escher."

Rita laughed, a rough music that made it clear she wasn't generally a merry person. "I never thought to see a woman take him in hand, what with him holed up like a hermit and avoiding the world all these long months. But I'm sure as much I never dreamt I'd care one sniff for any wench that did. But here you are, all the same! I like you, miss."

"Oh." Eleanor stood to smooth back her hair nervously. "I don't think I—no one is taking anyone in hand, Mrs. Escher. I wouldn't presume to—"

"That's what I like about you." Rita sobered slightly as she located Eleanor's gloves and bonnet. "A tyrant wouldn't suit, and a weak little thing would just grind on the nerves. Love's not a trinket, and you're clever enough to hold your ground, I'm guessing. So there you are and I can't find fault."

"Thank you, Mrs. Escher. I'm grateful for your confidence." Eleanor took her gloves and hat, hating the heat that flooded her cheeks after such a strange and unexpected assessment. "But it isn't what it appears—"

"It's none of my concern," Rita interrupted her easily. "Naming a cat doesn't make him any less of a cat, miss, but if you prefer to stay mum, I'm your gal. I won't mention it again, mind, and Samuel's as dense as a tree and happy to be left by the fireplace all day. I just wanted you to know that while I ain't no ladies' maid, I'm happy to know you, that's all."

"Oh," Eleanor said breathlessly, touched and horrified in the same instant. "I'm . . . happy to know you, too, Mrs. Escher."

Eleanor held her things a little tighter and hurried from the room, wondering if her feelings for Josiah and current predicament were evident for all the world to see or if Mrs. Escher was simply more perceptive than most.

God, am I so transparent?

Her desire for him increased with every encounter, heightened with each passing day. Nothing was dulled by familiarity, but rather sharpened to a razor's edge that cut into her every waking thought. Eleanor wasn't sure how any woman of sense managed to carry herself calmly in the public eye with a storm of want raging inside of her. She feared that her problem was unique since it was hard to imagine the matrons she'd known losing themselves in erotic daydreams or craving a man's touch until there was nothing she wouldn't do for him.

He was waiting for her on the landing to walk her down the stairs to the carriage. Eleanor studied him in an unguarded moment as he habitually pressed his fingers against his eyes. He was leaning against the banister, the very image of masculine strength and beauty, but there was something about him that made her think of a lost boy.

"Josiah, are you . . . unwell?" she asked quietly, praying he would trust her to tell her the truth.

He lifted his head, dropping his hand with a dismissing wave. "Just a headache. I'll have Rita make one of her concoctions and set me right."

"Rita made it clear that she knows about us."

"Did she approve?" he asked with a mischievous smile.

"Wholeheartedly, Mr. Hastings." Eleanor smiled as a curl of fire snaked through her at his playfulness. "It was one of the most startling conversations I've ever been privy to. She thinks I should stay."

It was a bold thing to say, and she knew it. It was a subtle bid for him to agree and to ask her to stay. Eleanor held her breath and waited for him to speak, prepared to cheerfully complete her fall from grace.

"I told you that she was as sweet as a kitten." He pulled her forward, tipping her head back gently. "You could melt the heart of anyone, my dearest muse."

And what of your heart?

His fingers caressed her cheek, and the faint smell of linseed oil evoked a nostalgic urge to lead him back up the studio and make love yet again. "Kiss me, Josiah."

It was a gentle command that didn't require repeating.

His mouth touched hers in a whisper-light caress, teasing her by dragging the silk of his lips against hers. He hovered there, their breath mingling in a kiss of souls that liquefied her core and made her heart race. Eleanor pushed up onto her toes to silently end the prelude and achieve the kisses she desired.

She couldn't get enough of the warm velvet of his tongue, taking control to sample and explore the magic of his mouth to hers and the paradox of endless satisfaction that only fueled a growing hunger to have more of him. Slowly, she leisurely surveyed the power of his kisses, reaching up to run her hands up his chest and absorb the beating of his heart through her fingertips.

It was meant to be a kiss of farewell, but Eleanor conceded that there was very little inside of her that wished to go.

Each kiss began to grow in momentum, and Eleanor recognized the familiar flare of desire that snaked down her spine and made her thighs damp. It was paradise to touch him, and she would have asked for more, but Josiah gently broke away and set her back on her heels with a playful nuzzle against her neck and ears.

"Now, let's get you downstairs before Mrs. Clay sends out the police in search of her new favorite tenant." He nipped at the shell of her ear and then stepped back to straighten her coat collar. "Did you have a scarf, Eleanor?"

She shook her head. "No. I'll—be warm enough."

It was a bittersweet moment when she accepted that there would be no declaration or change in their illicit agreement. They would be together until the painting was completed and then . . .

Eleanor couldn't even imagine what might come next.

* * *

Josiah limped back up to his studio, his blood raging with arousal and his cock so stiff it bordered on pain. He locked the door and then leaned against it with both hands. He'd come within a hair's breadth of forfeiting all his vows for independence and begging Miss Eleanor Beckett of Orchard Street to never leave his side.

Rita had meant well, he was sure, but the hopeful look in Eleanor's eyes had made her departure almost impossible—and had threatened to unman him.

He walked over to the easel and uncovered the painting.

It was nearly done.

Whether he liked it or not, the decision for her to go or to stay was about to be taken out of his hands.

* * *

"You look worn out, miss," Mrs. Clay exclaimed as she helped Eleanor with her coat. "He's a tyrant to keep you so late!"

"No," Eleanor protested quietly as she removed her gloves. "I . . . enjoy the time, Mrs. Clay. It's going by so quickly and I'll—miss it."

"Of course you will!" Mrs. Clay sighed. "He is charming enough to make an old bird like myself remember the thrill of a good man's company. Not that I'd trade in a single day of my dear Mr. Clay's presence, rest his soul, but I can admire the view out my window, can't I?"

Eleanor halfheartedly pretended to be shocked, but she prayed that her dear landlady wasn't about to repeat Rita's endorsement of illicit affairs with handsome painters. The illusion of propriety was a shield she wasn't ready to entirely drop, not without Josiah at her back. "Mrs. Clay!"

Mrs. Clay laughed, then sobered with a flush. "I'm sorry,

Miss Beckett. I misspoke and forgot myself. It's good you're sitting for him, but I didn't mean to sully your ears with a widow's rambling."

"No, please don't apologize!" Eleanor protested in a guilty rush. "It's all—I love to hear you jest. And there isn't a malicious bone in your body, Mrs. Clay, for all your care and kindness! I'm simply tired, I think."

"Would you like me to send up a hot bath after dinner, Miss Beckett?" Mrs. Clay said.

Her first instinct was to refuse the offer, but she knew better. It was not in Mrs. Clay's nature to "not be troubled" when it came to her tenants' creature comforts. And tonight, Eleanor didn't have the strength to fight off her own longing for the luxury of a warm soak and a bit of solitude.

"Yes, thank you, Mrs. Clay, that would be a delight."

Eleanor headed up the stairs, and at the sight of her door ajar, felt no alarm. Tally's workbox was propped against the wall, and the smell of brass polish and lemon wax hinted at his efforts to make her room perfect. Peering inside, she spotted her diminutive friend finishing up and stirring coals in the grate to invigorate their glow.

She walked across to kneel next to him, and was greeted with one of his sweetest smiles. "Good evening, sir."

He nodded, then moved to sweep the last bit of dust from the hearth.

"I'm in love with him, Tally." She spoke aloud, amazed at how good it felt to speak her innermost secrets. "It's all a sordid mess and I should be more ashamed, really, but I've never been happier than the moments I have with him. It's just—not going to last. He doesn't trust me, Tally. He desires me, but not enough."

Tally sat back and put a small decorative screen back in place against the wall, and then looked up into her eyes as if offering his sympathies. He gestured with his hands, but Eleanor was at a loss to understand him.

"Mrs. Escher seems to think I have the helm, Tally. But

I feel like I'm at the mercy of winds I can't even fathom. Have you ever felt like that?" she continued sadly.

He tipped his head to the side as if contemplating her question and then reached out to pat her hand, his manner a perfect imitation of his adopted mother's.

"I shall take what I can, Tally, all that I can, and then pray to Providence that I'll have hoarded away enough of his kisses to sustain me for a lifetime."

Tally nodded, and sat quietly with her while she cried.

Chapter
19

"It's finished."

The words slipped out before he realized it, and Josiah closed his eyes at the bittersweet taste of them in his mouth. He couldn't imagine lying to her about his progress, but a part of him protested that he'd so stupidly forfeited his happiness in a single breath.

The painting was finished. There was no denying it, but hearing it made it a real and implacable fact. He'd spent the last thirty minutes tracing and retracing his own signature in the lowest right-hand corner to delay saying it—to no avail.

"I beg your pardon?" Eleanor asked from her seated pose. "Did you say it was *finished*?"

"I did." He set his brushes down and forced himself to appear to be cheerful. "You are officially immortal, Miss Beckett, for better or worse."

She stood slowly, her face pale. "I'm sure it is for better. Can I . . . see it?"

"Yes." He stepped back as she approached to make room for the bulk of the velvet gown between the easel and the worktable, then held out a hand to guide her into place. "It is . . . as you see."

Eleanor's legs felt numb as she approached, anxious anticipation making her mouth dry. She'd been contentedly perched, watching him work and daydreaming about how they would make love later in the afternoon, when he'd made his announcement and startled her back into the waking realm.

It was midmorning and her world had just come to a jarring premature halt.

She kept her eyes on the hem of her gown as she walked, trying not to trail it in any wet paint on the floor or move too close to the brazier. But at last, she was in front of the easel and there was no more avoiding the inevitable. Eleanor raised her eyes to confront her own image.

Oh, God. Please don't let me cry.

Vanity had no place in her thoughts, but it was hard to recognize herself in the serene beauty that gazed down at her. The woman in the painting was everything she'd longed to be, but transcended even those dreams. That woman didn't aspire to blend in or attain respectability. That woman didn't care what anyone thought or how anyone perceived her beauty. That woman was . . . *invincible.*

"I can hardly believe that this is me—that this is how you see me." She put a hand up to her lips. "I am not that beautiful, Josiah."

"You're far more beautiful, but I'm not that good of a painter. Do you not recognize yourself?"

"That woman is . . ." Eleanor sighed. "I wish I had her courage."

"You do." He stepped up to put an arm around her waist, and the chill that had seized her began to fade. "It is one of your finest qualities."

"Josiah, what happens now?" she asked softly.

"I will pay you as I promised, Eleanor. You are free to leave me." He took a slow steadying breath. "But then, by now, you must have guessed you've always been free. I could never . . ."

"You speak to me of money?" Eleanor became very still and quiet.

"No. That was a foolish thing to say." He turned her to face him. "Anything I say now would be foolish."

"Then don't. Don't say anything."

She reached up to pull his face down to hers, kissing him as she had never dared. She suckled his tongue and tasted the firm corners of his mouth, her teeth capturing his lower lip and tormenting him with the flicker of her own tongue against it. Whenever he kissed her, she always felt the echo of it in every forbidden hollow of her body and she prayed it was the same for him. She abandoned his mouth, only to trail hot kisses down his throat where his pulse jumped at her touch. He moaned and she closed her eyes at the masculine music of it that made her knees weaken. "Josiah, take me. Here. Now."

He was already caught in her spell, and Josiah groaned at the weight of his cock as if filling with hot sand and hardening in answer to her invitation. "I don't . . . have any French letters here. Downstairs—"

She shook her head. "No. Here. Now."

If he'd meant to argue, he forfeited the debate as her hands slid down over the planes of his stomach where his erection was straining against the confines of his pants. She'd unbuttoned just the top two or three buttons, but it was enough to allow his flesh to leap into her hands, her touch searing his spirit as she stroked and squeezed him, the urgency of her own desire fanning his.

"Oh, God, Eleanor . . ."

It would be their last time together.

He moved his hands up her back, over silk velvet, to press her to him, even as his heart finally admitted its surrender. He loved her. He truly loved her. But his excuse for keeping her was gone. It was stupid to proceed without the condoms, but an irrational part of him embraced the risk. She would be *his*, and the thought of a child made him selfishly and fiercely glad. But he didn't want to dwell on his reasoning.

He didn't want to think at all.

Not now. Now there was only Eleanor, and the need that burned between them.

"As you wish." He kissed her, matching the fierce passion of her touch with his own. Josiah lifted her up as if she weighed nothing at all and carried her toward the dais to set her on the couch. "Damn it. Get out of this dress, woman."

She moaned, untangling herself from his embrace to comply. "Yes."

He reached behind her and untied the ribbon that had been tucked into the back, and then firmly wrapped one end of it around his hand to pull it free and unlaced the evening gown in one firm fluid motion.

Eleanor gasped in shock and pleasure, instinctively holding the bodice of the gown to her chest to keep it from falling. "You are . . . quite talented, Mr. Hastings. That— shouldn't have been possible!"

He smiled. "Rita's no ladies' maid and I've been fantasizing for endless days and nights about how easily a man could creatively dispatch with this gown."

"Have you?"

"Yes, but I want you to undress for me. I want to watch you." He deliberately took three steps back, leaving her alone on the dais.

Eleanor stood proudly to face him, looking into his eyes as she allowed the gown to fall to the floor. Without a tremble of shyness or reserve, she moved with an easy grace to loosen her petticoats, kicking aside each layer and watching the stark effects of each discarded item on the man before her. At last, there was only a thin chemise left and she slid it off her shoulders to let it slide from her fingertips to the floor below.

She held her place, as naked as the day she was created but for her stockings, shameless and lovely enough to make his throat close with a thousand unnamed emotions. The red velvet and under things made a sumptuous puddle around her bare feet, and for a moment, he realized she presented an erotic version of Botticelli's *Birth of Venus* arising from a pool of scarlet cloth instead of a shell, with nothing to cover her but her own fiery headdress of untamed curls as it tumbled down her back and the dark auburn triangle of fleece that crowned her sex. Her figure was perfection in his eyes, and all he could do was stare at the lines of her body, the curves of her, so balanced and firm. Instead of a look of serene detachment, his Venus met his gaze with all the knowledge of her seductive appeal.

Eleanor made no effort to hide herself from his gaze, aware of the flush that swept up from her breasts and the taut feel of her stomach and hips as the craving for him whipped through her. She pushed back her long hair to reveal even more of herself to him, basking in his undivided attention as never before. She was rewarded when she heard him gasp with pleasure, and Eleanor seized on a surge of the glorious power she wielded. Lifting her own breasts, her nipples hardening with the turn of her mind, emboldened by the look in his eyes of awe and searing raw lust.

She tipped her head to one side, studying him and savoring it. Impulsively, she pointed a toe and then lifted her foot to balance it on the sofa, deliberately teasing him as she held his gaze and bent over to slowly roll down her stockings.

"God, I love your body."

She gasped, her eyes filling with tears. "Then have it, Josiah. Take me and leave nothing. Don't be kind or gentle. I don't think I could bear it."

Desperation edged their every move, and Eleanor stepped down to rush into his arms. She felt as if she would shatter into a million pieces if he treated her like fragile glass; the ache in her chest was a storm on the horizon, but now there was the temporary shelter of his arms. Tenderness would feel like deception, a promise of a love that he hadn't professed and might not exist. Eleanor wanted to lose herself in the passion that was tangible between them until she couldn't think at all.

He kissed her roughly and Eleanor moaned as she met

the intensity of his touch with her own, biting the corner of his mouth as she tore the linen of his shirt pulling it off his shoulders. He was far too overdressed for the occasion, and the sound of the fabric being rent spurred them both on. She dragged her nails across his skin and then up his back, making him shudder at the fire in her touch. She'd marked him and his soul welcomed it, wishing for a scar to carry like some strange souvenir; proof that she'd once been his.

He lifted her in his arms slightly, her bare feet losing purchase with the floor, and Josiah tried to move back but bumped into the table with its miniature forest of blazing tapers. Eleanor cried out as a few drops of hot wax touched her shoulder.

"Oh, God. Are you burned?" he asked, releasing her instantly.

"No," she answered quickly, then bit his shoulder hard enough to make him shudder. "Do . . . do it again."

He leaned back to look down into the emerald cauldron of her eyes, and within a single heartbeat, he instinctively knew what she wanted. "Yes."

He took one candle and led her naked back to the dais by one hand, his eyes locked onto hers. She followed him willingly, the trust in her eyes so pure it burned. He guided her, pushing her back down onto the sofa, and laid her out, arranging her hair and toying with her position as if he meant to paint her this way. He stared at the sensual feast spread out before him and had the good sense to thank God his vision was as clear as he could ever remember it being. There was nothing marred or clouded, nothing of her he couldn't take in.

Her eyes shimmered with the heat of her desire, and her lips were parted as her breath came quickly in anticipation of what was to come. Her red hair fanned out around her beautiful face, transformed by the candlelight into molten copper, and the cream of her skin was already coated in opalescent dew as if she herself were carved out of pearl. The darker triangle of auburn curls above her sex was already gleaming with her arousal, and as he watched, a single trail of clear ambrosia leaked from her body to crest down her lush thigh.

She held her arms up over her head in a pose of submission, her breasts lifted up and her thighs open so that he could see the ripe color of her sex, her lips swollen and slick with wanting.

He held up the candle and carefully allowed a single drop to fall onto her breast, coating the most sensitive strawberry-tinted peak, then leaned over to blow on the wax to cool it and Eleanor screamed out her pleasure, bucking and writhing beneath him. Her hands gripped the cushions over her head and her eyes fluttered open, searing him with the look of raw satisfaction and hunger he read there.

"Yes." It was one word, but Josiah absorbed a universe of meaning in that instant. *Yes.*

Again and again, he trailed hot wax over her skin, pooling it in her belly button only to finally risk a few drops against her thighs. Eleanor was transformed, a woman unbound, and spread her legs wide for him. The invitation was not to be ignored. He knelt over her, freeing his cock and fisting his rampant erection with one hand, and then dripped one hot line of beeswax up her opening and onto her swollen and ready clit.

She began to come, and Josiah blew out the candle and threw it across the room, refusing to be left by the wayside. He pulled her roughly up from the sofa, only to press her onto her knees so that he could take her from behind, and wasted no time to line himself up with her waiting channel. She was still so tight it took his breath away as he pressed forward to notch his head inside of her. He caressed the underside of her breasts, then squeezed each one, tweaking the hardened peaks in a pinch that made her moan and press back against him, her hips undulating to rub the rich honey of her arousal into his skin.

"Josiah!" She tipped her hips upward, and the sight of her, straining to take him, the strawberry pink gleaming flesh slick for his pleasure, stretching to take him in, was too much.

"As you wish."

He drove forward in one relentless thrust, gripping her hips to hold her in place while he entered with a searing force that made them both cry out. Her delectable ass so perfect in his hands, her skin so warm and firm against his fingers, he had to grit his teeth to maintain control. Muscles gripped him in a molten vise that almost made him spill his seed. But no power on earth was going to force him to forfeit a minute he didn't have to.

There was no gentility in the primal drive to possess her. He took no quarter and showed no mercy. It was a punishing force, thrusting forward up inside of her so completely that she cried out at the culmination of each push, surrendering to him completely. On and on, Josiah relentlessly took all that she offered, his desire fueled by the smell of her sex and the sounds of their flesh slapping together. Eleanor's mews and moans of pleasure were oddly melodious, a sensual siren's call so strong he didn't care if he was being led to his doom anymore.

Pain and pleasure intertwined and Eleanor gave in to all of it, her skin marbling at the intensity of his touch. Her heart was pounding as the ache inside of her turned into a molten coil of tension. It was a glorious fall she'd never imagined. Her nerve endings blazed with a new sensitivity that made it difficult for her to breathe. Even so, she wanted more—so much more. "H-harder! Yes!"

He complied, one hand buried in her hair, riding her, civilization falling away, his cock growing even thicker as his arousal reached its peak. He could feel every inch of her, velvet inside velvet, and the raw pull and grip of her channel against him had him in thrall.

"Josiah, please . . ."

Fingering the small little pucker of flesh forbidden to him, he pressed into her and she screamed as she came at last, in great bucking spasms that forced him to let go of her hair so that he could grip her hips to keep his balance. It was a white-hot ecstasy that erased his sense of self, and he jetted inside of her, thrusting with each wave of his release

until he wasn't sure where her climax had ended or his begun. It was a spiral of release that made him both conqueror
and conquered.

He collapsed next to her, without withdrawing from her
body, unwilling to break the connection or relinquish his
hold, vaguely aware that he'd never fully taken off his
pants. They were both covered in sweat despite the chill in
the room, and Josiah leaned over to rescue the remnants of
his shirt to keep her warm as best he could. But it took long
minutes before his powers of speech returned.

"Eleanor," he began, "that was . . ."

"No words, Josiah. Just hold me. Please"—she sighed,
arching back against him—"just hold me."

He held her, breathing in the scent of her hair and skin,
tasting her arousal on his lips, and then one last thought
echoed in his mind before an exhausted sleep claimed him.

It's finished.

* * *

Afterward, Josiah awoke alone on the dais, surprised that
he'd drifted off at all, and unsure of the hour, only to realize that Eleanor was gone. A quick search confirmed that
the worst had happened. It was still early in the afternoon,
but she had left without a farewell. There wasn't even a note
or a single sign that she'd graced his life beyond the painting that remained.

He had loved and lost.

To add to his disoriented misery, his vision had deterio-
rated. His vision was poor enough to hamper any sudden
moves to action, but he knew it was due to more than fatigue.
He reclaimed his clothes and headed downstairs to his bedroom to clean himself and decide what to do. Josiah briefly
considered drafting her a letter but wasn't sure if his hand-
writing would hold. He was convinced that sending her
some scrawled nonsense in uneven lines wouldn't assist his
cause—and he'd be damned if he was going to dictate his
innermost turmoil for poor Escher to spell out.

It occurred to him that he could summon his solicitor to

try to come up with some excuse to see her. *A new proposal for another work? Or will she recognize it for some weak personal plea to stay awhile longer . . . ?*

Until what? Until my vision fails and I need a cane? Until she realizes her mistake and regrets everything?

He changed out of his clothes and dressed by habit in the simpler darker elements in his wardrobe, ignoring the choices his dressing room displayed for a life he no longer led. Silk coats and tailored waistcoats for parties and social evenings he no long enjoyed. Like the home he'd designed and furnished that now sat mostly unused, Josiah did his best to push aside the ghosts that plagued him and returned to his bedroom.

He paused in front of his makeshift altar and remembered how Eleanor had asked if he were a heathen, as only Eleanor Beckett could. The memory flooded through him and he had to bite his tongue to keep from speaking her name.

Pathetic. I'm already pathetic. This is insane.

Should I send the carriage? Would she come? Or is it worse if I send it and she doesn't. . . .

"Damn it!" Josiah threw the bronze goddess into the corner, the racket of it striking the wall giving him a wicked fleeting satisfaction before the inevitable heartache took its place.

He walked over to retrieve it, and was forced to fumble about as the shadows bled into the gray cords drifting into the right side of his vision. As he searched on his hands and knees with outstretched fingers, a dozen instances when he could have declared his feelings to her echoed in his head—all lost opportunities that a dozen fortunes couldn't gain him. He'd come so close to happiness, but Josiah wasn't even sure that a man could complain of being robbed if he'd deliberately kept his doors unlocked and his most precious treasure unclaimed.

After a few moments, the familiar outline of small woman in bronze came into his hands. He lifted her up and studied her serene little face. "Are you damaged?" he whispered, running his fingers over the statuette. It was intact, and he sighed in relief. "Well, that makes one of us, my beauty."

It was a small thing, but he'd regretted his tantrum instantly. He returned Lakshmi to her place of honor and then lit a stick of incense, centering his thoughts out of habit and taking a few deep breaths.

"So much for wisdom. . . ."

Josiah knelt on the silk cushion and it was a long time before he had the heart to move.

Chapter
20

Later that same evening, Josiah tried to eat his dinner alone in the studio by candlelight, sitting with her painting propped up next to the table. He'd rearranged his food several times, without much hope of deceiving his cook into believing that he hadn't lost his appetite.

He raised his glass to Eleanor's image, whispering in the quiet. "My prim and proper beauty. You're wiser than I to avoid farewells. I'm not sure I'd have had the mettle for it. Hell, I'd say it's a sure bet I'd have forfeited every promise I've made to myself and thrown honor out the window."

"Is this the company you're keeping these days?" Rowan's voice interrupted his thoughts from the open doorway. "I'm not sure I can approve of a man talking to—"

The abrupt end of his speech made Josiah set down his brandy, instantly wary. "Rowan? Are you unwell?"

"Oh, my God! It's . . ."

"Say it." Josiah braced himself for the worst. "Don't let our friendship stand in the way."

"Remarkable!" West walked over, as reverently as a man

approaching an altar. "I've never seen anything like it, but I don't know why. I mean"—Rowan crossed his arms and took another long, hard look—"it's a portrait of a woman in a red velvet dress. But it's . . . compelling and I'm—the colors, Hastings! It's so vibrant and . . . she's sitting still but I swear it's as if she's going to blink at any moment and a man doesn't want to miss it. I thought you were a good painter before, but this . . . my God, Hastings! You've captured her and in a way I would never have imagined."

Josiah lost his voice. All the sarcastic defenses he'd prepared evaporated as the emotional release of a triumph achieved washed over him. *I did it. Hell, I did it and I'm not even sure how. . . . It's my masterpiece and all I want to do is see the thing away and gone because it isn't her.*

"You're not an art critic, West, but I'll take the praise all the same."

"It's done! And so quickly!" Rowan shook his head in amazement. "I'd come to make sure Rutherford had left you be and then was going to compliment you on that frightful-looking troll you've employed downstairs, but if you've finished it . . ."

"I finished it."

"Damn," Rowan whispered, still staring at the canvas.

The painting should have been pure scandal, a woman dressed in scarlet with her hair in wanton disarray, but it was the calm, unflinching fire and pristine self-awareness in the lady's green eyes that defied judgment. Here was a woman refined and proud—who looked out without fear and dared a man to be worthy of touching even the hem of her garment.

"My sentiments exactly." Josiah echoed the curse. "I've never finished a painting with such speed. I never saw a woman with such clarity. . . ."

"Who is she, Hastings?" Rowan asked.

"She is Miss Eleanor Beckett, a true lady and as pure and proper a soul as I have ever encountered." *And the love of my life.*

"A true lady and not a . . . professional model, then?" Rowan moved to the worktable and poured himself a brandy.

"Not that it matters. Cheer up, old friend. You'll have Michael off your back, if that's any consolation. And by God, it's the masterpiece you wanted, Josiah."

"Michael off my back?"

"You promised to dismiss her from harm's way as soon as the painting was finished. And the timing couldn't be better. Did you see the *Times* today?"

Josiah welcomed the change in subject, turning his back on Eleanor's image and its soulful stare. "I didn't. Is it set, then?"

"A week from Friday. Michael didn't want to give him time to regroup or lay any traps. But since his good friend owns the gambling hall we agreed on, I think we'll be safe enough. I'd considered temporarily closing my Wednesday clinic, but Gayle overruled me."

"A wife's prerogative, Dr. West." Josiah could taste bitter envy on his tongue. Rowan had his beautiful young bride, and once this Jackal business was over, he could enjoy his life. But Josiah's pride dictated that he forfeit Eleanor, Jackal or no Jackal, and so it was hard to muster any enthusiasm at all.

The painting was done, and Eleanor Beckett had left him per their agreement. He'd given himself over to the joys of her company and now he was grieving like a lost man in a storm. The real darkness was coming and he hated facing it alone. But there was nothing else to be done. It was best for her, he told himself, but the words held hollow comfort.

"Are you going to show it?" Rowan asked.

"I don't know." He pulled out the soft cloth and tossed it over the canvas, ending the siren's spell. "I'm sure I will at some point. After all, what's the use of a painting in dark rooms, right?"

"Josiah, you did dismiss her, didn't you? Miss Beckett is away from this?"

At first, he couldn't form the words to answer his friend. The wound was too fresh. "She's away. My own poor timing is redeemed."

Rowan continued, as if sensing Josiah's distress. "Call her back when it's finished, Hastings. If you care for her . . ."

"I care for her too much, Rowan." He poured himself another generous brandy. "She is better off out of this mess and clear of me."

"I'm not convinced of that. Every man deserves his happiness and we take what we can. If we learned anything in India, didn't we learn how tenuous and brief life could be?"

"Amidst many painful lessons, yes, Rowan. But this is different."

"It isn't my business, but if—"

"No, it isn't your business!" Josiah set his glass down a bit too forcefully, the amber liquid splashing out onto the wax-covered table. "It's my decision! Not the Jaded's! This is my life and I don't need any more advice on how to live it. I love you like brothers, but all of you need to take a step back. Eleanor is—I'm not condemning her to life with some sort of invalid, and she's too softhearted to refuse me, so I cannot even ask her. Now, please leave, Rowan. Just leave me to it."

Rowan solemnly nodded and walked out, leaving Josiah to wrestle with his demons and the creeping black that edged into the candlelight.

Josiah lost track of the minutes, but when he heard the door open again, he almost threw one of the candleholders at the intruder. "Damn it! Can't a man be alone?"

"I-if you wish—"

"Eleanor!" Josiah was on his feet instantly, rushing toward the welcome sight of her in the doorway silhouetted by the lights in the stairwell. It was only when he came closer, his steps slowed. "What are you doing here? Is everything . . ."

She reached up and slowly removed her bonnet, setting it down on the table by the door. "It's late for a call, I know. Poor Mr. Creed! There is so much activity with all of us paying him no mind at all when he fusses. I passed your friend, Dr. West, on the ground floor, and he was very kind. It seems I'm very brave, Mr. Hastings. I slipped out of the

Grove without alerting anyone, and frankly, am quite sure that this is the most terrifying thing I've ever done."

"Terrifying?" he asked cautiously.

"I should never have left, but . . . it was finished and I thought that it had always been so clear between us, these obligations and agreements that we held to." Eleanor calmly set her reticule on the table as well. "I ran away because I didn't want to hear you say it was over."

He shook his head, unable to speak.

She continued, slowly walking toward him. "But that also means I didn't give you the chance to ask me to stay. I don't think that this relationship has ever been based on obligations, do you?"

Again, he shook his head, the first tendril of hope coming to life inside of his chest. "No, Eleanor. I pray not."

"I shouldn't be here, should I? But I tried to imagine a day where I wasn't here. A day where we weren't together and you weren't painting and we weren't talking, and I . . . couldn't." Her voice was sad, but she looked up at him, smiling through the sheen of tears in her wild green eyes. "I'm under your spell, Mr. Hastings. I hope you don't mind."

"It's late. Mrs. Clay—"

Eleanor placed her hand against his chest. "I left a note in my room that you'd summoned me. If she comes looking and finds it, she can make of it what she will, Josiah. I'll return in a few hours, but . . . I couldn't stay away any longer. You see, I realized something, Mr. Hastings."

"Did you?"

"Not so long ago, I was lamenting that I didn't feel like I had a hand on the helm of my own life, so to speak. I had the ridiculous notion that I was adrift somehow."

"Are you?"

She smiled. "No, not at all. I was feeling sorry for myself, but I am the mistress of my own fate, aren't I? And I am where I want to be, Josiah. You've never pushed, have you?"

He shook his head slowly. "You don't strike me as the kind of woman who wants to be directed or overcome, Eleanor. I wanted to respect your wish for autonomy."

"And so you have." She reached up to touch his face, cradling his cheek in her palm. "Are you glad to see me, Mr. Hastings? Will you . . . ask me to stay awhile longer?"

"I have no right. What I want—is impossible. But you . . . I'm so glad to see you I can barely speak, Eleanor. I want you to stay, but I don't know if I can survive letting you go again."

"Josiah."

"I'm afraid you'll break me, Eleanor."

She kissed him on the cheek, then whispered into the shell of his ear, "Never."

"I don't want to break you either."

"Never," she whispered again, and Josiah pulled her tightly into his arms, banishing fear and ignoring the darkness that lurked in the edges of the room. The heat of her body, the points of her breasts against his chest, and the magic of her mouth against his skin were a deafening symphony of sensations that made the room spin. Josiah inhaled the floral scent of her skin and kissed the warm column of her throat, a fierce joy seizing him.

Mine! She came back because she's mine!

It was the illusion of a happy ending and he knew it.

Can't keep her. Can't even try. Shit.

He kissed her more deeply, and savored the instantaneous power of it, the power that healed the breach and made the world stand back. Eleanor sighed, a soft sound of contentment that made his heart soar. He lifted her against his chest to carry her downstairs, taking her to his bedroom and kicking the door shut with a resounding bang.

He wanted to give her whatever happiness he could, to love her completely without holding anything back and demonstrate a tenderness that had been lost in so many of their recent encounters. Josiah didn't want to be rushed or frenzied in his quest to claim her.

He celebrated that he was still whole in her eyes, and that Eleanor had come to him freely. Once she knew his secret, the path would never again be as clear. Pity and guilt would cloud reason, and he was sure that she would ultimately feel tricked and trapped by a man who had deceived her into loving him.

It was an impossible situation fraught with heartache.

As if she sensed his mood, Eleanor allowed the gentle lull of his slow, studied caresses and tender touches. She didn't press him to hurry, but instead, stood blushing while he removed her hairpins and undid each braid.

She reached up to nervously tuck a curl behind one ear. "It's a tangle tonight. After . . . this morning, I didn't bother with combing it out as I should."

"I'm glad." He led her toward the bed, undressing her as carefully as a man unpacking a china doll, even as she helped him out of his things. Within moments, they stood together without a single barrier.

"Glad?"

"It's a foolish thing, but all this time, I've wanted the privilege of brushing that hair, Miss Beckett. If you'd allow it."

She looked at him warily, but nodded. "Truly?"

"After everything, I marvel that you're still so modest about such things, and then"—he reached out to run the back of his fingers from her collarbone down to the rise of one breast to sweep across them both without touching her sensitive tips—"so naturally shameless and confident in so many other ways."

She blushed. "A woman's right to be contrary, Josiah."

"Amen."

He stepped closer and pressed his lips to her forehead, just skimming the surface before trailing a string of kisses over her face, landing briefly on her cheeks, eyelids, brows, and even the tip of her nose. He followed every touch of his lips with the light brush of his fingertips, memorizing her features with his hands. Josiah finally kissed her mouth, reconnecting with her soul and reminding himself what it meant to be alive. He measured the column of her throat with the span of his fingers and dropped down to lift her breasts, cupping and holding them in his palms until they tightened and hardened in his gentle grip.

He glanced down to note how her nipples had thickened and darkened in response, and he bent over to suckle each one briefly, before gently pushing her down onto the mattress.

Eleanor stretched out on the bedding, her gaze never lowering from his or shying away from his body as he took inventory of the bounty she willingly offered him.

With an artist's eyes and hands, he worshipped all of her. The small of her back, the dimples above her buttocks, the curve of her belly, the slope of her ribs, the shape and width of her hips were all given equal attention. There was nothing of his Eleanor that he wished to overlook. She writhed beneath him and he kissed the underside of her breasts, his tongue following the crease there, while his hands fanned out down her rib cage but didn't yet move below her belly.

Josiah knew if he touched the silky wet folds of her sex, he would forfeit his vow to move slowly and savor her return.

Instead, he lifted her hand and kissed each fingertip and then the palm, her wrist, lingering to inhale the scent there and lick her pulse. Then playfully kissed the inside of her elbow and up to her shoulder, until she laughed at the indulgence of it.

"It's far too one-sided, Mr. Hastings. All this lovely attention," she protested softly.

He shook his head. "How is it that I always know I am in for trouble when you speak of fairness, Miss Beckett?"

"Stop complaining and lie back," she commanded him.

Before he could stop her, she'd shifted away from him and was now the one to press him back onto the pillows. "Quid pro quo, sir."

She explored his body with the same tortuously dreamy pace that he'd applied to her, and Josiah had to bite the inside of his cheek to keep from protesting. The minx began with his ears and then worked her way down, exploring his body and tasting the landscape of his flesh at her every whim and will.

What began as playful revenge turned into something else as Eleanor forgot the game as she admired all the masculine contours of him. She teased his nipples and suckled him, thrilled to note that the effect was very similar, then shifted downward to use her teeth and her tongue on the hard, firm flesh of his stomach. She straddled one of his thighs as she happily labored, then sat up to admire the lean lines of his legs and the rough texture of the dusting of hair on them.

"Are these scars, Josiah?" she asked shyly, her fingers tracing a ridge of lines around his ankles. She hadn't noticed them before, but then in the usual heat and race to satisfy their mutual hunger, Eleanor had never thought to look at her lover's ankles.

"Stories for another day." Josiah pulled her down onto his chest and distracted her with kisses.

One tumbled kiss led to a dozen more, and the slow embers that had glowed between them blazed into life. Josiah couldn't stop kissing her. He didn't want to. But she wriggled from him, and nibbled on his shoulder. "You have too many secrets and untold stories."

Josiah's heart skipped a beat, but he shook his head. "Enough conversation."

He turned her over, delighting in her squeal of protest, but made quick work of ending any wish she had for verbal exchanges. He knelt at her feet and massaged each one until she had given in to the languid tyranny he imposed, then kissed the soles of her feet and ankles. Josiah skillfully rubbed the muscles of her legs and then slid his hands up over her bottom, appreciating the seductive curves of her body before dipping down to stroke her thighs. With each pass of his hands, he "inadvertently" teased the dark pink lips of her sex until she was glistening with her own arousal.

"Josiah, please . . . no more!"

He turned her over to part her thighs and finally kiss her waiting sex, licking the hot bud between her legs until her legs were quivering and he knew she was ready. He lifted himself up to cover her, her thighs parting to accommodate him as his rock-hard cock pressed and prodded her entrance to find the welcome harbor it sought.

He drove forward in one long stroke, filling her completely, and his throat closed at the emotional impact of Eleanor in his arms with her green eyes looking up at him as their bodies blended into one. Her legs wrapped around his waist, and the dance of passion swept them both up, each riding wave after wave of sensation at each stroke, long and slow, deep and strong. As their ardor began to crest, Josiah instinctively shifted so that he was spooning her, neither one dominating the other, but instead, it became a soft tangle of flesh that left them both breathless and amazed.

Eleanor gave in to the primal need for release, the hot coil inside of her springing free in a cascade of mounting ecstasy. She cried out as every part of her felt electrified and featherlight, as if something inside of her had broken free of her body at the moment of climax. Only the heat of Josiah's body and a vague awareness of his answering cry and the searing crème that flooded her core grounded her to her physical being.

She'd returned for this—for him.

Without demands for his declarations or for respectability, Eleanor had returned.

Because she didn't want to live without hope.

* * *

Josiah walked her down the stairs and held the lantern as she alighted the step into the carriage to return to the Grove. He kissed her fingertips and released her, as reluctantly as if she were a soldier heading off to battle instead of a warm, cozy bed and bath under Mrs. Clay's matronly care.

He hated it. Time had always been his enemy but now, it was as if every minute had a new edge to it. He should let her go before this intended confrontation, but he still had some time.

He was borrowing hours from a future that wasn't his to claim.

"Eleanor."

"Yes?"

"Come tomorrow. Will you come back tomorrow?"

For him, it took forever for her to settle into the carriage seat and rearrange her skirts before she answered him.

"Yes. Tomorrow."

Chapter
21

The following morning, she returned, and by sheer habit, they ended up in his studio. It was arranged almost as before, a blank canvas set up before the dais graced this time with only a wooden chair. Eleanor walked over to run her fingers over the chair's curved back. "Would you not like to start another painting?"

He shrugged his shoulders and joined her on the platform. "Perhaps. But, you should think about it carefully, Eleanor, before you offer to sit for me again."

"Why?"

"It's a brush with scandal to sit for an artist once. But it's pure scandal to do it twice and be seen as his *favorite*, don't you think?" He lifted her hand to kiss her fingertips. "It might be more notoriety than you realize."

She leaned against him, resting her head against his shoulder. "I hadn't considered that, at all."

He stroked her cheek and fingered a stray curl that had come loose. "It's a terrible sign that I'm so familiar with the twists and turns of infamy, Eleanor."

She laughed and pushed against him to free herself, looking up to better gauge his mood. His masculine beauty was as striking as ever, but Eleanor's heart skipped a beat at the signs of fatigue she saw on his face. Dark circles shadowed his brown eyes and made Josiah look a bit beleaguered. "You look so tired."

He shook his head. "Ah! That's what a man longs to hear from his beloved paramour!"

Eleanor tried not to laugh but longed to divert him from whatever cares made him press his fingers into his temples and sigh. "Is it so strenuous, then? If painting tires you so, then perhaps . . ." She drew closer to him, to trace her fingers over the strong, beautiful arch of his brows and look into his mahogany brown eyes. "You need to try another perspective."

"Another perspective?"

"Come, why not sit for me?" She led him playfully around to the front of the chair. "Let us set you there and see if I am not inspired to create a masterpiece of my own."

"Ah!" He sat back with an exaggerated pose, showing off his profile. "A masterpiece, you say? Think you it's so easy?"

"How hard can it be?" She climbed down and picked up his palette and a brush, doing her best imitation of his serious looks and then chewing on the end of the brush as she'd seen him do whenever he was lost in thought. "Now, be still, man. You may speak, naturally, but do try not to move too much."

"Are all artists this bossy?" he asked.

"Shhh. I'm concentrating on the geometry of your nose." She tapped the brush tip to her chin, then set it aside to pick up a small charcoal stick. "I shall sketch first and see if I cannot make a go of it."

"You're just going to draw my nose? Any chance the rest of me is going to be in this portrait?" he teased.

"Everything but your hands," she replied. "I have never been able to draw hands, so I will imagine yours are tucked in your pockets—an artist's discretion and vision, sir."

"I can see why the Royal Academy will be on our door-step at any moment, miss. Sheer genius. Why did I never think of pockets?"

Eleanor laughed. "Yes, why when—" She dropped the paintbrush in surprise as a tall, dark figure filled the studio doorway. "Oh!" She blushed miserably to be caught in an unguarded and intimate moment by a stranger.

Josiah was facing her, still unaware of the intruder. "What? Did I move and spoil your efforts to put a wart on my nose?"

"You have a guest."

He stood quickly. "So much for the troll's effectiveness. Who goes there?"

"It is I, unannounced as usual, but don't blame the troll. He was trumped by your dragoness of a housekeeper, who vouched for me and ordered Creed to let me pass." The man came forward, giving every impression that despite the fashionable cut and cost of his clothes, there was nothing soft or spoiled about him. "Have you followed in Dr. West's footsteps and taken on an apprentice to help you buy more coal?"

Eleanor stiffened, unsure in this man's presence. She couldn't discern from his expression whether he was friend or foe.

"I'm no teacher, Galen. May I introduce Lord Winters, Galen Hawke? Galen is a trusted friend. Lord Winters, this is Miss Eleanor Beckett, my muse and inspiration."

Eleanor held her breath at the casual introduction to a peer of the realm, biting her lower lip at the surge of forbidden pleasure that whipped through her at his words. *My muse and inspiration.* "Your lordship, it is an honor to meet you."

"The honor is mine. I didn't mean to intrude, Miss Beckett. I understood you were alone, Hastings, or I would never have barged in."

Josiah sobered instantly. "We've never bothered with calling cards. What brings you here, Galen?"

"Nothing dire. Rowan let it slip that the painting was

finished. He mumbled something about your genius and insanity and then forbid me to come."

"So naturally, here you are." Josiah crossed his arms. "Did he mention meeting Miss Beckett?"

"Naturally." Lord Winters smiled, and Eleanor decided that she liked him after all. "You haven't been yourself lately. And since you are so often absent unless, well, unless someone uses phrases like *life and death*, I thought it time to stop by and make sure . . ."

Josiah finished his question. "I wasn't hiding with some artistic temper tantrum or swinging from the rafters?" Eleanor gasped, but Josiah walked to the table to ring the bell for Escher. "Would you like some refreshments, Lord Winters?" he asked.

Galen shook his head. "No. You have company—and I should go."

Eleanor took a step forward, determined to prove that she wasn't embarrassed to be met in such a place but also hoping not to drive Josiah's friend away prematurely. "Without seeing it?"

Lord Winters stopped in his tracks, a warmer smile banishing the last of his initial icy impression. "That would make me look a bit daft, wouldn't it? If I ran off without even a glance."

"It would make your excuse for stopping by less plausible," Josiah noted sagely.

"Mr. Hastings! You are too abrupt with your friend," Eleanor chided him. "You just said he needed no excuses to call, and I would not have Lord Winters thinking that my presence has made you unkind."

Galen's eyebrows rose in surprise, but Eleanor held her ground. They were both acting like children as far as she could tell.

"Miss Beckett, I think my wife is going to like you."

Josiah playfully rolled his eyes. "There's an alliance you should avoid."

Galen ignored him. "Don't worry, Miss Beckett. I know Josiah too well to worry about his bluster. And you're right.

I would like to see the painting that had the ever-serious Dr. Rowan West spouting bad prose. Lady Winters has the better eye for these things, but I was impatient and didn't wish to wait weeks."

"Is she not in London?" Eleanor asked.

"She is still visiting with my father at our estate at Stamford Crossing. He's ridiculously fond of Haley and has taken full advantage of her good nature to keep her close. I miss her beyond words, but"—he gave Josiah a dark look—"I wouldn't want to risk her health in London."

"You are a considerate man, Galen." Josiah crossed his arms, walked over to the painting where it was set against the far wall, and pulled off the canvas covering it.

"Yes, let's see the painting that has made you absent these last few . . ." His words faded as the work came into view. "Bloody hell!"

"Language, your lordship!" Josiah said sagely. "She's going to think the peerage no better than common dock workers if you're any example."

"I apologize, Miss Beckett. I—forgot myself. It is a remarkable piece of art, isn't it?" Galen stepped closer. "It should be seen by the public."

"Time enough, after . . ." Josiah's words trailed off and he gave his friend an odd look. "Later. Rutherford would spit out a kidney if he heard you considering some kind of public event, Galen."

Galen shrugged. "True, things are not uncomplicated at present, but I'm tired of being restrained at every turn. I don't see it as impudence if we try to live our lives. Hell, I want my wife back at my side where she belongs."

Eleanor's brow furrowed in confusion. The conversation had grown convoluted, as if coded for their ears alone. "What complication is there?"

Josiah waved a hand in the air. "It's nothing. Old business we're muddling through and nothing to do with us."

"I have a few connections, Hastings. A small nudge in the right direction and you could land a place in the Royal Society. You know I'd like nothing better than to balance the scales and do something for a friend. At the very least, the work will sell and you can afford to buy yourself a new coat, Hastings."

"There are no scales to balance, no debts to repay. You already do too much for our motley circle, Galen. And I don't need . . . I don't desire to be . . ." Words failed him. Even weeks ago, he'd never have hesitated if given an opportunity to secure his name in the honored rolls of lauded artists in England. Hell, that had been the whole point, hadn't it? But ever since Eleanor had first sat on that chaise and looked at him, he'd forgotten everything he'd been striving for. All the torture and strain had faded. "I like my coat as it is."

"Fair enough. I'd say with this work, your peers couldn't ignore you any longer, Hastings." Galen winced as his friend covered up the painting, and turned instead to its living reflection. "Miss Beckett, I am sure just from this brief exchange that your presence has improved him."

Eleanor laughed. "I wouldn't presume to boast of it, your lordship."

"No titles, please. They bruise my heart and remind me that I'm no better than the next man and probably worse for the attempt." Galen's dark eyes flashed with a pain that reminded her of Josiah when she asked him of his past. "Get him to show it, Miss Beckett."

Josiah moved away to rearrange the paints on his worktable. "Anonymity suits me."

"I should be going to allow you to talk privately about this unfinished business of yours," Eleanor announced quietly, standing to break the awkward tension between the men. "It was an honor to meet you, sir."

Galen bowed over her hand. "And a pleasure for me, Miss Beckett. But there's no need to rush off on my account. I was the one who interrupted your work, and from the unsubtle look of impatience on my friend's face, I'll remove myself from the fray."

"A wise man," Josiah muttered. "I'll see you at the next gathering."

Galen nodded, bowed to Eleanor again, and quickly withdrew, leaving the pair alone again. Eleanor had to catch her breath as the door closed behind him, amazed at the strange turn in their day. She had expected Josiah to puff up a bit at his friend's praise and reaction to the painting, but instead he looked surly and even more uncertain.

"Why didn't you accept his offer? Lord Winters seems sincere and wishes to see you do well. I thought that's what you wanted, Josiah. Immortality, yes?"

He refused to look at her, his hands purposelessly moving the objects about on his worktable. "Yes. It's what I wanted. But apparently I'd rather die a mortal and be forgotten, Eleanor, than . . ."

"Than what?"

"Than share you. I can't bear the thought of other men looking at you when I—won't always be able to look at you for as long as I want. Apparently, I'm a selfish bastard."

"Language." The correction was whisper-soft, and lacked any teeth. She reached out to brush his hair back from his cheek and capture it behind his ear. "So this is only for your sake, this decision?"

"Besides, you were the one most worried about your reputation, Eleanor. Are you so ready to see your portrait in a grand hall with hundreds of people gawking and commenting on that delectable woman in red?"

"Well, when you put it like that . . ." Her expression sobered.

"There would be no going back."

She became very still, and then stepped closer, molding herself to him, her face nestled against his chest, her head just reaching his chin. "I don't want to go back."

"Eleanor?"

"Yes." Her voice was muffled with her lips pressed against his shirt, and the warm air of her breath sent a ripple of desire across his skin.

"I want you to be proud of this—of me. Are you? If I knew you were, then the weight of the world would fall away and I wouldn't care what awaits me. If I knew that my

Eleanor wasn't embarrassed to be on that canvas . . . or to be in my arms."

"I'm very proud, Josiah. Please show the painting. Promise me that you will."

"As you wish."

"P-perhaps a small gathering though," she amended, a flush creeping up from her breasts as old shy habits reasserted themselves. "I'm not sure I'm ready to face a large public event."

He nodded. "There's my delectable Miss Beckett. Very well, my last great masterpiece will see the light of day, just to please its subject."

"Last? Surely this isn't your last painting?"

"Of course not. I misspoke."

"Can I not inspire you again?" She kissed him, and he savored the sweet fiery lust that came to life as she tasted his lips and opened her mouth to invite more of him to the feast. His muse knew exactly how to arouse him, her teeth capturing his lower lip and gently suckling the sensitive flesh there until every nerve ending was taut and ready for more.

Then he was holding her, trying to catch his breath. He fingered the delicate strand of small pearls she was wearing. A modest thing with a single intricate gold filigree drop bead at its center, it was the only piece of jewelry he had ever seen her wear.

Eleanor is like these pearls. Beautiful and whole, with an impenetrable depth in each one that makes me wish I could see inside of her heart. But there's the inspiration. . . .

"Ah, I think I know just what is needed. . . ." Josiah pulled out a good-size chest from underneath the table. He'd retrieved it the night before on a whim, toying with the idea of showing it to her just to see her eyes light up. But now, the treasure would serve another purpose. "Here, come see what I have." He unlocked it and opened the lid, lifting several long ropes of pearls out for her to see.

"Oh my!" she exclaimed breathlessly.

"I think you will look like a queen wearing them." He draped an opulent offering of lustrous pearls across her shoulders. "These look pink against your beautiful skin."

"I can't wear these! They are far too extravagant, Josiah, and I'm not sure it's appropriate to—"

"Nonsense. Have you ever seen an oyster? They are the most humble and rotten looking things on earth, and you don't hear them fussing about extravagance or what's appropriate."

"I am not an oyster!"

"Just wear them for me, woman."

She eyed him warily. "Like the red dress? Just to wear for the painting?"

"Precisely. No scandalous gifts of jewelry. You can just put them back in the box afterward . . . if you prefer."

She nodded, some of the excitement returning to her face now that a compromise had been struck. "Wherever did you get all of them?"

He shrugged. "Souvenirs from India."

"Souvenirs? Queen Victoria doesn't have a single strand to rival even one of these, Josiah!"

He smiled. "What does she need of more pearls? Whereas my Eleanor"—he leaned over to kiss the warm little indent behind her left ear—"should wear these and nothing else."

"I will not pose without my clothes!" She squeaked her prim protest, but leaned back against him, urging him to brave more of her skin as she tipped her head to one side. "You are . . . a rogue to suggest it!"

"Then I shall find an ivory satin dress to suit the occasion." He sighed, as if conceding a great battle. "Something simple to set you off like a jewel, Eleanor, and I will paint you like a modest goddess if you wish." His tongue teased the lines of her neck until she shivered against him and he added another rope of pearls to the decadent strands already around her throat.

She bit her tongue to keep from laughing. "I will buy my own clothes, Mr. Hastings." It was too sweet a victory that he would agree to work again, even if she suspected that once again she'd been maneuvered into doing exactly what he wanted. The cold pearls had warmed against her skin, their weight hypnotic as the silky soft orbs moved across her shoulders to drape down the sensitive line of her spine. "And I am no goddess. But I think . . . we should put these away, Mr. Hastings. They are too opulent for a woman born on Orchard Street."

"They are not rich enough, Miss Beckett." He spoke against the shell of her ear, sending another shimmer of desire down her back to pool between her legs. "Not opulent enough to match you."

Eleanor guided his hands down over her breasts, the pearls adding to the game, and she closed her eyes at the soft slide of her surrender. "Then you must paint me in pearls and teach me what opulence is."

Josiah smiled and began to unhook the buttons of her dress. "Let the lessons begin."

Chapter
22

Eleanor adjusted her bonnet as she watched the London streets pass. Josiah had urged her to use the carriage for a day of errands and she'd made the most of it, giving in to pick up some new dresses and necessaries. The ivory satin evening gown was safely ensconced in a box on the seat across from her, and Eleanor was doing her best not to look at it since the very thought of the "pearl" dress made her skin tingle. It felt wicked to indulge herself again and spend money without fear, but the lingering anxiety from her recent poverty was finally starting to let go.

Even so, there was one bit of her past that she didn't wish to banish.

Finished with her own requirements, Eleanor had asked the driver to head back toward more familiar streets so that she could seek out Maggie. She had few enough friends in the world, and wanted to assure herself that dear Margaret was well. But the runner she sent into Madame Claremont's confirmed that Maggie wasn't in the shop that day, so she'd started to lament her plans. She'd even had the carriage wait along the route Margaret would take from the shop to the boarding house. But her friend never came. At last, Eleanor had given up on an impromptu reunion and tapped on the roof for the driver to head back to Josiah's.

But as the carriage pulled away down a narrow side street, Eleanor caught sight of a familiar bonnet on the sidewalk. She signaled the driver to stop and launched out of the carriage to catch her friend in the crowd. "Margaret?"

"Ellie! Is that you?" Maggie turned, openly astonished and pleased to see Eleanor, before giving her a quick hug.

Eleanor smiled and then took a step back, some of the joy at the reunion fading as she realized that the state of Maggie's dress bordered on scandalous. Despite the cold bite in the air, the cut of her bodice and blouse invited the eyes to appreciate her bountiful cleavage, and the bright blue and yellow of her skirts made her seem like a bright bluebird surrounded by dark winter pigeons. "Margaret. I was looking for you at the dress shop."

"Oh, dear! I'd have paid to see that dust-up!" Maggie laughed.

"I wisely sent a boy in to ask for you." Eleanor smiled. "I'm not brave enough to face her again. But, are you . . . not in her employ?"

"Madame Claremont turned me out after you left."

"Oh, Margaret! I'm so sorry!"

"Don't be. It was inevitable with her temper, but she was in quite a lather over it all when you kicked her off. The other girls were spiteful to you, I know, but they were secretly happy to see you get away. And when your Mr. Hastings left me that purse, I wasn't sorry to go either!"

Her first instinct was to correct Maggie's assumption about *her* Mr. Hastings, but she bit off the words, her stomach churning. "He left you with some money that day?"

"A generous sum, to be sure. Didn't he tell you?"

Eleanor shook her head.

Maggie laughed. "I think he did it just to goad ol' Claremont for bickering over that red dress! Don't worry, Ellie. It didn't come with a wink."

"Of course not. Mr. Hastings is not that kind of man."

Maggie's smirk did nothing to comfort Eleanor. "As you say, as you say!"

"Are you . . . all right now? Have you found other employment?" Eleanor asked, determined to steer the conversation onto more solid ground.

Maggie laughed. "I'm my own mistress and no complaints!" She touched Eleanor's coat sleeve. "And you? It was a brief meeting, but I envy you your patron. Is he generous, Eleanor? Are you happy, then? I know the sporting life isn't exactly what you had in mind, but a man like that could make it pleasant enough, yes?"

She gasped in shock. "Mr. Hastings is—not my patron. I don't . . ."

Maggie eyed the carriage behind her, her expression chilling at the perceived slight. "Of course you don't. You're a good girl. So, it's another shop you're at, then? Or did you get a position as a governess for a family in Town?"

Eleanor's face blazed with misery. "No. Mr. Hastings hired me, but not—I mean, I am not his . . ." The blush deepened, her conscience screaming at the twists of an impossible situation. *I am not his mistress. I am simply the woman he paid to look at and who now eagerly beds him in a blissful dance of ruin that she never wants to end. Oh, God. How tangled is a life that I cannot describe it to anyone without disgracing myself?* "I model for him. He is a painter."

"Model?" she asked, her tone a bit too neutral. "Well, that's different, then."

Eleanor couldn't meet her friend's unflinching gaze. "It . . . is."

"Well, I'm glad for you. You've kept your feet on the ground, as they say, and not become a light-skirt like some others." Maggie crossed her arms. "You're a lucky girl."

"Yes. I truly am." Eleanor swallowed nervously. "Mr. Hastings is—or rather, was a very generous employer."

Maggie looked at the carriage behind them and the waiting driver. "So it seems."

"I—hope you'll let me—would you like to get something to eat? We can get out of the weather for a bit and—"

"I'm pressed for time today, miss." Maggie took a step back, all bravado as she defensively retreated from Eleanor's charity. "And I'll be warm enough after a toddy or two."

"Margaret, I didn't mean . . . You were always so kind and I would never insinuate that you—"

"My feelings aren't bruised, Ellie. I'm no delicate flower, and I don't want you to worry about me. Another day and we'll sit over marzipan and teacups and talk about the weather. 'Course, if your man needs another model, you feel free to tell him I'm as cheerful as a magpie, yes? I still have his card and I'm not at all shy."

Eleanor nodded, inwardly sickened at the idea of any other woman sitting for him as she did. Irrational jealousy made her even more miserable at the strained meeting with her friend. "Yes. Another day, then."

Maggie sauntered off, her hips swaying provocatively as she walked and causing several men to stare appreciatively. Eleanor could only watch her go and wish that somehow she'd been less like Mrs. Dunleigh and more like Mrs. Clay in their encounter.

* * *

Josiah dabbed another smattering of paint on the canvas. It was all he could do to pray that Eleanor wouldn't get back too quickly and catch him with his nose less than three inches from the surface of his work.

His head was pounding from the strain on his eyes, but once again, he was driven by the idea of capturing his beloved muse in oils. Eleanor in some white organza shift and pearls was an ethereal vision, and Josiah was determined to paint her as an earthbound angel.

Especially since he knew with each passing hour that his angel was bound to fly off. Even without the pressing deadline of the meeting with the Jackal, he would have to face losing her sooner rather than later. Eleanor's nature would not allow her to remain much longer. No matter how liberated the sexual fire was between them, she was still a respectable creature of the world.

How much longer will she allow me to love her as I do?
If only I could marry her. . . .

The fantasy spun out again, and for longer than usual, it held steady in his mind's eye. Eleanor could help him bear the unbearable. The comfort of her presence might make life worth living, even if he couldn't paint again.

Hell, I've money enough to hire an army of servants to free her from my personal care and—

His stomach turned at the idea of being a pitiable object requiring care, and even if his dear wife weren't directly involved, it made it worse to think of Eleanor seeing him that way. Josiah pressed his hand against his eyes, using the heat of his fingertips to try to press away the grim fog.

It was only a matter of time before he would be forced to confess his illness to her.

Perhaps it was better if his last vision of her involved an honest reaction to his malady. Then he wouldn't have to be tortured for the rest of his life wondering if he'd made the right decision.

Or you could man up and end it before it comes to that, Hastings.

His hand dropped and he looked again at the canvas and the first hints of the portrait there. Breaking her heart out of some backhanded effort to spare himself the agony of enduring her disgust or pity seemed cowardly, and Josiah firmly dismissed the idea.

I'll tell her when it's appropriate, and that will be that. If she leaves me before I get the chance, then that will be even better, but I'm not shoving that woman out the door until I have to, damn it! I've hired Creed and I've put new locks on the gate. Escher's been warned not to allow any visitors he doesn't know well and his wife's been careful to source all her ingredients so we don't run afoul of any more poisoners. It's not as if the Jackal is going to draw more attention to himself before the meeting and spoil his chance to get his hands on whatever mysterious trinket he's angling for.

Josiah stepped back to use a rag to clean his hands and surveyed his tools. Escher had left a tray with the day's paper for him, but Josiah hadn't been able to force himself to pick it up. Losing the ability to read had been a stinging blow to his ego and unsettled him more than he wanted to admit. Yesterday, Michael had sent another note, and after several long, unsuccessful minutes of watching the hand-writing on the page slip and slide just out of his field of vision, Josiah had conceded defeat.

Even worse, he'd cut himself shaving no less than three times and was going to add that ignoble request to the list of Escher's growing duties before too long.

It's all happening so quickly now. There's not much time left. But time perhaps for one last grand gesture—a fast private showing of the portrait to prove to her that no mat-ter what else she may come to think of me, I was a man of my word.

The sound of Eleanor's footsteps through the studio's open doorway interrupted his thoughts, and Josiah forced himself to smile as she came into the room. "How was your outing?" he asked.

A lump formed in her throat; the image of Maggie standing on the sidewalk in her garishly bright clothes adrift in the world had nearly broken her heart. *There but for the grace of God, go I.*

"Eleanor?" He caught her hand. "What happened?"

"I saw Margaret from Madame Claremont's on the street. She was the shop girl that you were kind to the day you rescued me. She is . . . living by her wits, Josiah. She is . . . the mirror of the life I might have been forced to have. Worse, I couldn't help but ask what makes me any better? I've sold myself to—"

"No." He cut her off softly. "No, I won't have it, Eleanor. You were neither bought nor sold, and I won't have you casting yourself in that light. What's between us has noth-ing to do with commerce, damn it!" He pulled her to him, his grip on her shoulders firm and commanding. "Look at me, Eleanor. Look at me and tell me that you feel nothing for me and that all of this has been some kind of show."

She shook her head slowly. "I can't."

"Tell me that you are misused or unhappy. Tell me that I compelled you to ruin and that you don't long for my touch, even now. Can you do that?"

"I can't." The warmth of his fingers seared her flesh and awakened an answering heat inside of her.

"Then pity your friend, Eleanor, and be generous to her, if you wish. But don't ever think for a single moment that there is an echo of you in her. You'd have drowned yourself in the Thames, God forbid, before you'd have fallen into the life she's chosen. I know you well enough to know that for certain."

Her eyes filled with tears. It was a wretched truth.

"And here is another thing for certain, my dear Eleanor." He bent over to kiss the crest of her cheekbone and then trailed the magic of his lips against her skin over to her ear, where he whispered, "I could not live in a world that didn't have one impossible beauty named Beckett. I'll march down to Hades to rescue you if I have to, woman. But this isn't ruin, Eleanor."

A moan escaped her lips at the fires he evoked inside of her and the petulant hunger that stirred to demand more of his kisses.

If it isn't ruin, then what is it?

Chapter
23

"Give me a moment to wrestle with my nerves, Mr. Hastings." Eleanor didn't budge from her perch on the carriage seat. "My courage is failing me, sir."

"Nonsense!" he chided her gently. "Just remember that this is your doing. You were the one who seemed disappointed I wasn't showing it." They had arrived together at friends of Josiah's for an impromptu evening gathering to unveil her portrait. Salon parties were notoriously varied in attendance and lively social affairs. It was out of season and Josiah knew it would be a small event. He'd given his host carte blanche on the invitations with only one name added by Josiah on a whim.

Wisdom aside, if Keller shows, I'll kick him in the shins myself.

But he doubted chemistry magnates bothered with art showings and didn't expect any satisfaction. Instead, the evening would be about the two of them. Josiah wanted to please her by giving her a taste for the finer things and to allow himself the selfish indulgence of a public outing and the fantasy that all was right in his world. It was a dream that wouldn't last, but Josiah was too stubborn to let it go. He held out his hand to help her down from the carriage, smiling at the picture she presented of feminine allure and terror.

"You're right." She smiled but didn't quite manage to unclench her hands from themselves in her lap. "You're sure this is just a . . . friendly gathering."

"Completely! Mr. Wall bought my first painting and is known for his lively and varied salon guests. No one will raise an eyebrow in this company! I've seen ballerinas sitting next to bishops and animal tamers trading philosophical arguments with reformists. Trust me, your elegant manners will stand you in good stead in a drawing room or a palace. There is nothing to fear."

She took his hand, alighting from the carriage step gracefully to stand beside him. In a gesture that warmed him to his core, she'd yielded to his wishes and worn the infamous red velvet, aware of the theatrical presentation they would make and the stir it would cause. "Easy for you to say, Josiah. I've never heard you express a single fear of your own."

"That's because you banish them all, my dear Miss Beckett." He leaned over, using the guise of readjusting her coat's mantle to whisper against the sensitive white curve of her ear, "You're a goddess, Eleanor."

"Mr. Hastings! What a shocking thing to say!"

His arm pulled her against him, tucking her up against the warm wall of his chest. "Not at all. And since your followers are about to increase, I'd say that was a prophetic thing to say, woman."

She pushed away from him as they reached the door, blushing but clearly pleased at the flattery.

"Ah! Here is the man of the hour!" Mr. Wall greeted them, enthusiastically pumping Josiah's arm until it ached. Gus was as round as he was tall, and a comical figure, considering his complete lack of reserve—in all things. "Every name you gave me is here with bells on. You've sold it already, Hastings!"

"It's not for sale, Mr. Wall."

"I know, you wicked man, which is making the price absolutely scandalous as my guests fight to convince you otherwise! Very clever, Hastings, very clever—but who is this? Is it possible you have brought the delectable and original Lady in Red to my home?"

"I have. Miss Eleanor Beckett, may I introduce our host, Mr. Augustine Wall." Josiah watched with pride as Gus fell into spasms of excitement at the thrill of meeting the portrait's subject.

"Miss Beckett, you are a dream to behold! You are my guest of honor!"

Eleanor shyly tried to demur. "It is Mr. Hastings who has that place, sir. I couldn't possibly think to—"

"Nonsense! Never argue with a man who is eternally correct and wise! Now, come, escape Mr. Hastings's selfish hold on your arm and come meet my wife and allow her the pleasure of showing you off to our jealous friends and dangerous acquaintances!" He tucked Eleanor's hand into the crook of his arm and led her away.

"But Mr. Hastings—" she began to protest weakly.

"He will have to survive without you for a time. After all, once everyone has seen the Lady in Red, the bidding will become even more frenetic, and Hastings will thank you for it." Mr. Wall was like a general commanding an army, and Eleanor had no choice but to brace herself for the social games ahead without Josiah at her side.

Mrs. Wall was equally eccentric and lively, making the pair both delightful and frightening from Eleanor's perspective. She was as thin and tall as her husband was stout and portly, but Mrs. Wall was just as loud and talkative. Every social rule she'd ever memorized was apparently ill applied when it came to the Walls and their salon. It was all Eleanor could do to keep from laughing and simply hang on as she was whisked from introduction to introduction.

Elegantly appointed with marble floors, it was a large room clearly designed as a private performance hall. Tonight it was transformed with clusters of sofas and chairs throughout into a vast conversation area, with servants offering refreshments and a small trio of musicians playing from a far corner they'd been banished into. For the dais where they would normally perform held a gilt easel with Josiah's painting displayed for all to see.

It was distracting to see herself there in oil paints, brazen and proud, while strangers stood around and openly admired her. The terror that had paralyzed her in the carriage threatened to return, but Mrs. Wall at her side was an unstoppable force, and she caught sight of Josiah across the room, and the calm quiet of his gaze soothed her nerves.

"Have you met the Lady in Red?" Mrs. Wall was asking yet another guest. Eleanor was desperate to ask her to stop using such a scandalous name, but she wasn't sure how to politely suggest that she had a proper name like every other woman in the room and would prefer that Mrs. Wall use it.

"Ah! Dear lady! My husband has fallen in love with you and was just threatening to throw me off if you truly existed!" The lady laughed, as if losing husbands were cause for celebration.

"Mrs. Buchard!" Mrs. Wall clapped her hands, adding to the jest. "Bertram will faint at the sight of her beauty and that's an end to it!"

"Poor man, you are undoubtedly right." Mrs. Buchard sighed. "But how thrilling to meet the model! Aren't you a pretty bird?"

Eleanor did her best to tamp down her ire at being addressed like an ignorant object. "I am no classic beauty, Mrs. Buchard, but I am pleased that you find Mr. Hastings's interpretation enjoyable. He labored tirelessly on the piece and I was merely honored to contribute what I could."

Mrs. Buchard gasped. "Oh my! Why you're no street bird! What a lovely little speech and so refined!" She smiled, patting Eleanor on the hand like a child. "I apologize. You must tell me your name!"

"Eleanor Beckett," she supplied, relieved to finally be on familiar footing with her manners intact.

"Miss Beckett, I vow you'll be the toast of London next Season!" Mrs. Buchard proclaimed.

"And I will have the singular right to boast that I was the first to have you on a guest list," Mrs. Wall crowed.

"I wouldn't wish to rob you of your triumph, Mrs. Wall, but I have no intention of . . . participating in the social season. It would be completely inappropriate!" Eleanor began to explain, convinced that if they knew of her lack of family they would retreat from the subject.

"Nonsense. There is nothing the peerage love more than being inappropriate," Mrs. Buchard said firmly. "Bertram is an authority on being inappropriate, and our social calendar is exhausting. Exhausting, Miss Beckett! But his cousin is one of Her Majesty's favorite ladies in waiting, and I will impress upon her the significance of our discovery so that the lady can make mention of it in court."

"Your discovery?" Eleanor asked, lost at the turn in the conversation and unsure of where it was heading.

"The Prince Consort is an avid supporter of the arts, and once we have Mr. Hastings's latest work pushed under his nose—well, who's to say that I didn't discover him?"

"Mr. Wall may beat you to it, Mrs. Buchard!" Mrs. Wall protested. "You wicked thing!"

A man in an evening coat and dark gray clothes cleared his throat behind the women, and Mrs. Wall recalled her hostess's duties.

"May I introduce you to Mr. Thomas Keller? He is the most serious and humorless young man in London, but terribly clever! His family's fortunes are recently made in the business of apothecaries, of all outlandish things! This lovely woman is Miss Eleanor Beckett, and I am just newly acquainted with her as a guest of Hastings, but I could not be remiss in sharing her!" Mrs. Wall said merrily. "Now, won't you exchange small talk while I excuse myself and Mrs. Buchard to chase down some more wine?"

"Of course," Mr. Keller replied before Eleanor could think of an appropriate excuse to prevent Mrs. Wall from leaving them alone.

Keller. He is so much younger than I imagined him, but for all my brave talk, now that I'm faced with the villain who ruined my father, all I want to do is escape before I empty my stomach on the man's shoes.

"M-Mr. Keller, I . . . am not one for small talk. I apologize—" she began.

"You. Miss Beckett, is it in fact you? Eleanor Beckett?"

It was an unexpected question that caught her off guard. "I suppose I am."

"I overheard you give your name and I couldn't believe the hand of Fate would allow it. Our fathers did business together, I believe, and I can tell by your expression that there is nothing of the worrying matter you are not already familiar with." His voice was low, but gentle, and his face reflected true concern at her distress. "My father died two months ago and I only just learned of his—misdeeds. I made inquiries on Orchard Street, but you had effectively disappeared."

"You made inquiries? Whatever for?" she asked.

"To apologize and to see if there was any chance for amends."

Her mouth fell open slightly in shock. "Truly?"

"I know it seems unlikely, but I had prayed that we would meet. My father spent a lifetime in ruthless pursuit of profit, in neglect of his character. I was in pursuit of a degree in religious studies when I was called to London to his bedside."

"He confessed to you what he did?"

Thomas's eyes reflected a terrible sadness. "No, Miss Beckett. He was proud to the end of his financial legacy. But in his final delirium, he did say something odd about your father, about how the most brilliant are the easiest to trick, and I had my first clue. After he'd passed, I had the accountants begin to dig and the legal documents spoke for themselves."

The most brilliant are the easiest to trick. Father was the cleverest man I ever knew.

"I am sorry for your loss. I should have said it before, but . . ." Eleanor reached out to touch his sleeve, a small gesture of comfort. "We are orphans together, then, Mr. Keller."

"I swear to you, Miss Beckett, I had nothing to do with my father's business."

She smiled. "It seems not. And I'm glad for your peace of mind that you didn't. What little I've gleaned about their partnership has been unsettling, sir, and frankly, once the lawyers had their way, I was almost glad to be done with it all."

His eyes lit with pleasure at her words. "You're too generous!"

Eleanor laughed. "I'm a practical creature, Mr. Keller. I decided long ago that a temper tantrum about matters beyond my control was likely to gain me nothing. Not to say that I wasn't seconds away from kicking you in the shins when Mrs. Wall introduced us."

"My shins and I are grateful for your mercy, Miss Beckett."

"I am relieved not to have to brawl and embarrass my hosts."

He finally smiled, and she could see that he was not accustomed to it. Thomas looked around the room. "I was miserable to be out this evening, but had promised a family friend that I would make an effort to be social after I unexpectedly received the invitation. I have no interest in art, but . . . it is a lovely painting, Miss Beckett."

"You should tell the artist your opinions, Mr. Keller. I'm sure he would love to hear that even a man with no love of paintings managed a compliment."

There was an awkward silence before Thomas changed the subject. "May I get you a glass of warm cider, Miss Beckett? Or another refreshment if you prefer?"

"Thank you. I would love something, if only to have something to hold so that I won't worry about where my hands are." She smoothed out her skirts. "It is my imagination, of course, but I swear everyone is staring."

Josiah appeared between them, masterfully towering over Thomas and stepping up to enter the conversation without any preamble. "They are staring because you're far more beautiful than your portrait betrays, and if they're not staring, it's because they're too busy speculating on who you are. Don't you agree?" he asked Mr. Keller.

"I don't believe we've met." It was more of a statement than a request for an introduction, and Eleanor had to bite the inside of her cheek at the frosty looks the men were exchanging.

"Josiah Hastings, artist." Josiah held out his hand. "And you are?"

"Thomas Keller."

"As in, Keller's Gentle Smelling Salts?" The question dripped acid, and Eleanor instinctively put a hand on Josiah's arm to keep him in check.

"The very same," Thomas replied coldly. "Miss Beckett generously passed on the opportunity to set my coat on fire, but if you'd like to strike me, sir, we could—"

"No one is striking anyone!" Eleanor squeaked out, all too aware at the misunderstanding about to take place. "Thomas's father did business with mine, and—gentlemen, you are drawing far too much attention! I beg you, mind your manners!"

Josiah's fingers covered hers, a possessive gesture that made him marvel at how quickly his simple plans could go awry. He'd meant to allow her to bask in a bit of social glow, and if things went well, hear praise of her beauty and feel some assurances that the artistic exercise between them had been worth the effort. He'd wanted to take pride in the painting and sweeten the experience by having Eleanor at his side.

Instead, she'd been whisked off by their hosts and Josiah had realized that no amount of praise from party-goers was going to improve his mood. Every complimentary word was tempered with insinuations about Eleanor and wicked questions about his "new muse." Their interest in the Lady in Red made him wonder if he hadn't made a terrible mistake and underestimated the worst in people's natures.

Fifteen thousand pounds wasn't enough. Hell, I don't know what amount would be enough to buy back her honor. . . . I'm such a fool!

Worst of all, his vision had started playing tricks and he'd stumbled into no less than three other guests and two tables in less than fifteen minutes of their arrival. Without the subtle guidance of Eleanor by his side, he was a man adrift in a crowd of blurred faces. Humiliation and fury were a terrible mix in the merry atmosphere of the Walls' party, and Josiah had to accept that they would all assume he'd been drinking heavily.

Not that my reputation was stellar to begin with, but I swear, I should have known better than to come out like this.

He'd been working his way through the crowd to retrieve her so that they could leave when he'd spotted her in conversation with a handsome block of a man. Even fighting the poor contrast his vision provided in candlelight, it had appeared like a cozy exchange, and Josiah was sure Eleanor needed a rescue. And then realized it was Keller.

In a crowded salon, he'd effectively made them the center of attention in a strange triangle—and if he punched Keller now, he'd cast himself in the role of jealous lover for all time.

Damn it! In for a penny, in for a pound. . . .

"I'll mind mine," Josiah offered, striving to keep his voice low. "Artistic temperaments being so volatile, I can't make any promises though."

Eleanor gasped at the veiled threat, but Josiah was past caring.

"I was about to escort Miss Beckett home." He kept his hold on her hand to underline his intentions. "A pleasure meeting you, Keller."

"We only just arrived!" Eleanor started to protest but was far too sensitive of the social dangers to put up a fuss. "A-although, I am sure Mr. Hastings is far more experienced in . . . these social matters."

"You'll not stay for the toast to your success, Mr. Hastings?" Keller asked.

"Miss Beckett does not partake, and I find I have a headache. Why don't you make our excuses to the Walls?" Josiah stepped away without even a nod in Keller's direction, forcing Eleanor to mind her skirts and forgo a polite farewell to her newest friend.

The dim room worked against his determination to make a smooth departure, and Josiah had to swallow curses as he awkwardly navigated the furniture and guests in the grand salon. Conversations hushed around them as they moved, and he was wary of the ripples and eddies in their gossip. Still, the damage was done, and he was consumed by the desire to reach the sanctuary of the carriage and home.

In his hurry, he did his best not to pull her arm or make it seem as if he were dragging her out of the house, but it was nothing short of catastrophic when he rushed into one of the servants with a tray of champagne glasses. The sound of shattering crystal echoed off the marble floors, and Josiah groaned at the futility of it.

"Mr. Hastings! You cannot be going!" Gus came forward, signaling for more champagne and ordering the musicians to earn their keep to distract the other guests from the fray. "Only kings will be able to afford this painting if you go now!"

"Gus, please." Josiah took their coats from the footman.

"It's too mysterious! Clever of you, but come, Hastings! Show mercy! By the time you close that door, there'll be a feeding frenzy of delicious gossip, and you know how Mrs. Wall loathes gossip." Mr. Wall managed the lie with a straight face, and Josiah knew he spoke from affection.

"I'm too clumsy tonight, Gus, and not myself. If I stay, I shall only end up setting the drapery on fire. Besides, why deny them their pleasure? Let them talk, Gus. Hell, you can even tell them I mumbled something about being inspired and needing to rush back to my studio to work, very well?"

"That does sound promising!" Gus conceded, shaking Josiah's hand. "And you must come back without your tyrant of a chaperone, Miss Beckett! You must grace my home with your beauty since the foul beast won't sell your likeness!"

"You are too kind, Mr. Wall." Eleanor's voice was far too quiet, and Josiah knew a storm was coming. "Thank you for a lovely evening."

Once he'd helped her back up into the same carriage he had less than an hour before had to coax her to abandon, Josiah sat on the seat next to her and tried to take one last deep breath to steady his nerves. "I am sorry, Eleanor, for spoiling the outing."

"And yet you did. Why?" she asked.

Josiah closed his eyes. "I . . . would rather not say."

Eleanor reached across the carriage and tugged at his coat sleeve. "Josiah! You were the one that insisted I go, that I wear this dress, that there was nothing to fear. I did all to please you, and yet we just left as if the house were on fire!"

"Were you enjoying yourself?"

"Were you?" she countered.

"No!" he snapped, wishing there were a way to explain everything without revealing the worst. "I should think you'd be grateful to escape after running into Keller."

"What just happened? We were just talking and you— nearly punched him?"

"I have an inkling of his villainy from what you've shared. He's the son of the vulture that stole your family's fortunes, and by the looks of him, the apple didn't fall far from the tree."

"By the looks of him?" she asked in astonishment. "Are you mad? I was in the midst of a perfectly civil conversation, when you rattled over like a complete barbarian. Do you know Mr. Keller personally, then? Have you some previous dispute with him besides your prejudice on my behalf?"

"Apparently, I'm the only one to dispute the man! I've never seen a woman act so magnanimously in my life! Was he so charming, then, that upon your first meeting you've forgiven him for growing fat while you starved and for cheerfully spending money that isn't rightfully his?"

"He is not fat! You are positively pouting over there,

Josiah Hastings! Pouting! Are you aware of it? Of how ridiculous this conversation is?"

"I am a grown man and I am most certainly *not* pouting!" He was furious because, of course, the woman was
right. Hell, there was nothing about his actions that he
could safely defend, and he knew it. "Can't a man express
a bit of righteous indignation if he wishes?"

"It's something else, isn't it?" The quiet concern in her
voice froze him in place. "Everyone loved the painting, so
it cannot be that."

He squeezed her hand, aching to heal the rift between
them. "No. It was . . . well received."

"Did I do something to embarrass you?" There was a
catch in her throat, and he knew, even with his muddled
vision in a dark carriage, that she was on the verge of tears.
"Did your friends find me ill-mannered or too coarse for
their company?"

"No!" He left his seat and knelt on the narrow space
between them, pulling her against his chest. "Never, Eleanor! I could never be embarrassed to be in your company.
Not if you'd actually poured a punch bowl over your own
head and attempted opera."

"Then tell me. Tell me what has you so unnerved, Josiah
Hastings, that we are here, like fugitives, and you are looking at me as if you have nothing but regrets?"

"I haven't been out in weeks, months actually, Eleanor.
My social skills are fading and I was—jealous and stupid.
Staying wouldn't have improved things and I didn't see any
choice but to retreat." He caressed her cheek. "Am I forgiven?"

"Almost." She leaned her face into his hand, pressing
into the contact. "Tell me what you want most. Tell me
what you need, Josiah."

"Damn it. Don't ask me that, Eleanor." His voice caught,
the lump in his throat threatening to break him at last.
*Don't ask me because the answer is you, and I cannot have
you, Eleanor. Not forever. I can't give you forever.*

His silence wounded her, but there was nothing more he

could say. He waited for her to strike him, or rail against his cruelty, but instead, she leaned over and kissed him. Gentle at first, the cool blades of her fingers against his cheek soothing as she parted her lips and invited him to taste the sweet confines of her mouth.

But at the first touch of his tongue to hers, Josiah's world spun out of control, the familiar fire of his raw lust overtaking them both. Fevered passion infected them both equally and Eleanor gave in to the moment with total abandon.

Josiah tried to ignore the wave of guilt that tangled with his need to possess her. He couldn't love her more—it wasn't possible. But he was stumbling and ruining what time they had left, and he hated himself for it.

He kissed her harder, as if he could replace the hurt of it with passion, until she could taste how much he needed her. He drank from her lips, as if he'd crossed a desert and she alone could assuage his thirst.

The confined space of the carriage's enclosed interior added to the force of their embrace. It was Eleanor who took charge, moving to slide her hand inside his shirt and then downward to trace the outline of his hard sex through the cloth of his pants. She unfastened his buttons and freed him, eager to hold him. She wanted to break through the wall he'd placed around his heart, but it was his body that she was allowed to touch.

She stroked him, until his flesh was iron hard and responsive at her slightest touch. Her boldness surprised even her, but the notion that all of London passed by within inches of the cramped, curtained world they occupied provided an unexpected aphrodisiac.

She lifted the heavy velvet of her skirts and silk petticoats to sit astride him, a wanton thing unwilling to relinquish this stolen chance for pleasure. Josiah's mind painted the image she made, a scarlet rider against his black evening clothes, and his cock jumped and thickened at the first brush of the feverish silk of her slit against it.

Her sex was already dripping with wanting, and Eleanor lowered herself onto him, crying out at the delicious sensation of being stretched and filled with the raw heat and power of him. He bucked upward, his cock stiffening even more at the delicious grip of her tight channel, her muscles pulsing and squeezing him in rhythm with each thrust. Josiah did his best to let her set the pace but had to close his eyes at the realization that his more immediate concern would be staying close as his body raced and surged ahead of his intellect.

He kept one hand splayed against the small of her back to aid her balance, but the other reached under her skirts to touch her clit, teasing little strokes of his finger, its rhythm adding to the dance. Her thighs rode him, and she gripped the cushions of the seat behind his head, the sounds of her bliss edging him closer and closer to his release. It was like a duel, and neither one of them wished to take more ground than they gave.

"More! Please, Josiah . . . more . . ." She sighed into the darkness, and he was enslaved.

Faster and faster, he moved against her clit, until it was a whisper-light stroke he knew would drive her mad. At last, she cried out with her orgasm, arching her back to yield herself to it, and Josiah pulled his hand away, forced to use both hands just to balance her on his lap and prevent her from spilling onto the carriage floor in her abandon.

Eleanor recovered and began to move, deepening each stroke and touch, increasing the friction of every caress, and tilting her hips forward so that her clit was grazed and pressed by each sweeping lunge of his body up into hers.

But Josiah was unaware of any of it. He drove into her, his own climax fast on the heels of hers. The explosion and pulse of crème came so quickly, he groaned at the force of it.

Eleanor felt the erotic splash of heat inside of her and cried out again softly, gripping the handhold of the carriage for leverage as she rode another release—and she knew she was lost to him. Every illusion she had ever held of her own self-discipline was swept away. When it came to this man, she would never know restraint.

After a few minutes, they each withdrew, quietly restoring what order they could to their clothing, and Josiah did his best to retrieve a few of the tortoiseshell hairpins she'd lost in the melee. They didn't speak as the muffled sounds of the city drifted back through the carriage, but Josiah pulled her back up against his chest so that her head rested against his shoulder. He stroked the soft skin of her face and tried not to think about what the future might hold.

Eleanor sighed, wondering what it all meant. They were bound together by passion, but for her, it was so much more. He'd been jealous. She was sure of it. And she clung to the significance of being seen with him publicly and being introduced to his friends. Surely, he was closer to seeing the truth that was right in front of him.

She loved him with every fiber of her being.

"No regrets, Eleanor," he whispered in the shadows.

"Good. For I have none," she said softly.

Chapter
24

In the morning, Josiah began to clean up his workspace and prepare for Eleanor's arrival. After their late evening, he expected her well after lunch, but it pleased him to be ready should she surprise him. As much as he hated it when she left his bed for decorum's sake, he did enjoy the thrill of her return.

"Excuse me, sir," Escher interrupted from the doorway. "Creed's got a man downstairs. The gentleman's asking to come up, name of Thomas Keller."

"Keller?" Josiah laid a drop cloth aside on the floor. "He's no threat. Have Mr. Creed let him pass and direct him here. Thank you, Escher."

"As you wish. I hope he's fit for the stairs, sir. I swear it's a test for all your nearest and dearest to mount five flights!" Escher shook his head. "But I'll send him up." He left and Josiah smiled as he could hear the unique approach of his houseman to his duties as the man walked down to his own residence only to yell down to Creed that the gentleman was free to come up to the top floor to the studio.

Alas, whenever Eleanor isn't present, we forgo the niceties.

Josiah continued to fold canvas until he heard Keller's heavy footsteps in the stairwell.

"Mr. Hastings? Your man sent me up, and I—what an unusual home you have, sir." Keller was doing his best to catch his breath as he entered the room. "I thought the building abandoned."

"I'm an unusual man, Mr. Keller." Josiah crossed his arms defensively, and silently cursed that the Fates had chosen to put a floating gray blob where Mr. Keller's face should have been so all he could see was the man's body language and the outline of his head. "Can I help you with something? If it's a commission, I'm afraid I'm not accepting any contracts at the moment for—"

"No, Mr. Hastings. I've come on another matter entirely." Keller came into the room, leaving the door open behind him. "It's about Miss Beckett."

Josiah didn't move. "Yes?"

"I shall be direct, Mr. Hastings. After meeting her last night, and after your abrupt departure, I made inquiries. There was quite a bit of salacious gossip and speculation about the nature of your relationship with Miss Beckett. So much so that I feared for her safety and moral state in your company, and I've come as a gentleman to ask you to end your association with her."

The man's tone was crisp and humorless, and Josiah forced himself to take several long, slow breaths to keep his temper in check. At last, he trusted his voice enough to answer as calmly as he could. "Your fears are ungrounded."

"Without family or resources, it would be easy for someone to take advantage and to compromise her reputation. I find it hard to believe that the woman I met would have considered the distasteful choice of modeling for a painter if she'd had any other choice."

"Distasteful? You, sir, are beginning to get on my nerves."

"Have I said something inaccurate? Did she volunteer to sit for you? Was it her brilliant notion alone?"

"I can't believe I'm defending myself against someone partially responsible for Miss Beckett's lack of choices. Wasn't it your father that swindled hers out of the fortune you're now enjoying? Easy to speak of morals and play the pontificate when your own blood did all the foul deeds necessary to build you that golden pedestal you're standing on! Tell me, when your father was laughing about his thievery and filling your purse, did you give him a lecture on morals?"

"I never knew what had happened! Not until just recently after my father passed away, and I'll warn you that you'd best keep a respectful tongue in your head! I'll rectify my father's wrongs soon enough! And I'll begin by making sure that his partner's surviving daughter won't be destroyed by a philandering wastrel!"

A dangerous silence fell over the room as Josiah discovered that he more than disliked the man who had invaded his inner sanctum. He decidedly hated him. "You don't know me, Mr. Keller."

"You are probably right. But here is what I do know. You're not a member of the Royal Society, I've never seen your paintings in a public showing, and I can't recall hearing mention of you, really. Except in the Society pages, if memory serves, attending parties and playing the rogue—I even recall something about a secret club of some kind. The Jaded, was it?"

Damn. Galen was right. How did I ever think that article was a good joke? And why are we under the illusion that there is anything secret about our secret circle?

"Your point being?"

"It is a sick ploy of some kind to play the artist and prey upon innocent women."

"I have never preyed on anyone, Keller. And I do not play either."

"You offered a woman on the brink of starvation and homelessness money if she would compromise her morals and sit for you."

"I'm no villain." The memory of a passionate ride through

the streets of London undermined his confidence, along with a dozen other erotic images that made him wonder where the line between villain and hero had blurred. "Take your gossip and shallow judgment and go bother someone else."

"Then deny what I've said directly. Or can you? How much did you offer her? How much did it take?"

"To hell with you! It's none of your business. None of it! Not the contract between us, not her moral safety or any part of my life falls under your jurisdiction. You have intervened where you are not welcome to do so, and where it is unwarranted. You should leave, Mr. Keller, before I throw you out."

"I will go. But not before I've made it clear to you, Mr. Hastings, that Miss Beckett has no need of your sordid money or your friendship. I will give you the benefit of the doubt and pretend that your interest in her is purely artistic and that you meant to improve her situation and not degrade it, but only if you'll then repay that generosity by considering that I came here today to ask you to do the right thing for once in a life that has apparently been spent in selfish pursuits and pleasures."

He was speechless for a moment. "Has it? I'm amazed at your insight into my existence, sir. All this? Really? From one brief meeting and the vile gossip of equally uninformed people, you've deduced my entire life's path, have you?"

Keller held his ground. "You care for her?"

"I might." He'd be damned if he was going to spit poetry about how much he loved Eleanor to this icy fish!

"Will you offer her marriage?"

"Why would I? According to you, that would be the worst thing I could do, since I've already ruined her and gotten what I wanted, yes?"

"What did you want?"

It was bitter frustration and fury that shaped his words, the sarcasm as sharp as a scalpel. "I wanted a model. I wanted a lovely bit of flesh and bone to use for my latest masterpiece. I wanted something to look at, Keller. I wanted a bit of color in this room and I'd have painted a scullery maid, a whore, or the Queen if she'd inspired me. One is very much like another, are they not? What is a woman to me but a means to an end? All that differs is the price. All that matters is the work and the image I create on the canvas."

The crash of the tray and the sound of shattering glass turned both of them around. Eleanor stood as pale as a ghost in the doorway, her hands frozen in shock as if they still held the offering of tea and cake in ruins at her feet.

"Miss Beckett, I—" Keller began, but it was Josiah who cut him off as he rushed toward her.

"Eleanor, you must believe—"

She turned as if to go, but then didn't take a single step. "Mr. Keller," she said, "please go."

"I'll wait for you downstairs, Miss Beckett." Thomas bowed his head and left without another word, diplomatically stepping over the broken glass, and left them alone.

Josiah took one long, slow breath and briefly tried to hope that the fact that she hadn't bolted meant there was a chance. But that hope died quickly.

"You once advised me to trust my instincts, Josiah."

"I did."

"But I've soundly ignored every warning and cautious advice my head has been screaming at me for quite some time. I let my heart rule my actions and my passions dictate my choices." Her back was still to him, and Josiah closed his eyes at the painful sight of his beloved Eleanor unable to even look at him. "I trusted you."

"I was angry with Keller. I spoke out of turn." Josiah's hands fisted helplessly at his side.

"Did you?" she whispered. "Were you ever going to marry me?"

Defeat tasted like turpentine, and Josiah opened his eyes to take in her silhouette. He wanted to beg her to take him, to throw his fortunes at her feet and win her back with declarations of his love. But a dark cloud in his peripheral vision reminded him that he would be making false promises. He would need a nurse, not a wife, soon enough. And although almost every word out of Keller's mouth had been wrong, he'd hit one truth. Eleanor deserved better in life.

His hesitation sealed his fate.

"I'm a fool, Josiah Hastings. Because I allowed myself to believe that with you, there were no rules that couldn't be broken if I loved you enough. That it would all be righted in the end. But I'm ruined for an eternity, am I not?"

He shook his head, but she didn't see the gesture.

Her voice broke at last. "It would take a blind man not to see it, Josiah."

And she was gone.

Chapter
25

Eleanor wasn't sure how she made it down the stairs, her eyes stinging with tears and the ache in her chest making it almost impossible to breathe.

Josiah's words had hit their mark, and she limped down the last flight in tears only to find Mr. Keller waiting at the bottom as promised.

"Miss Beckett, I have a carriage waiting. Please allow me to see you home."

A rough voice grunted behind them. "Don't know you, gent, so I'm not sure your offer's safe." Roger Creed stepped from the shadows, and even in her agony, Eleanor was forced to marvel at how oddly chivalrous and protective the man was being. "I'll see to a hackney. She ain't gettin' in no four-in-hand with the likes of you, sir."

"M-Mr. Creed, you are . . . so kind to be . . . Mr. Keller is a family friend, so please don't trouble yourself."

Roger touched his cap, his menacing stare never leaving Thomas's face. "No trouble at all. Good day to you."

She let out one unsteady breath and faced Thomas. "Mr. Keller, I'm too upset to argue the matter."

"Then don't," he replied, and held out his arm to escort her out.

She didn't really want any company, longing to be alone where she could give in to the avalanche of grief that threatened to overtake her. But his carriage was waiting, and every second that she lingered was a torment Eleanor didn't want to endure. "Thank you for your thoughtfulness."

His coach was as luxurious as any she had seen, but she was too numb to do more than vaguely appreciate the warmth of its interior.

He took a seat across from her. "Where do you reside, Miss Beckett?"

"The Grove, on King Street, if you please." Eleanor closed her eyes as a mortifying wave of distress threatened to overtake her, and her tears gained momentum. "I can't imagine what you must think of me, Mr. Keller."

"I have only the highest opinion of you, Miss Beckett. You are a woman of conscience, and while posing for Mr. Hastings may have been a grave mistake, I know that poverty and desperation drove you to it. I am the one who should be apologizing to you."

"No. No, Mr. Keller." She readjusted her wrap and averted her eyes, unwilling to even look at Thomas and see the pity in his face. "Please, don't. Our fathers' business is in the past. I can't . . . relive it today."

Several minutes passed in silence, but finally Thomas spoke again. "I am sorry for what has happened, Miss Beckett, but only because of your heartbreak. I cannot help but hope that you will celebrate your liberation from such a man—if not today, perhaps in time. He offered you so little, Miss Beckett."

Eleanor covered her face with her hands, determined not to sob in this man's presence. "You mustn't . . . say such things."

"I think you deserve better, and if you'll allow me, I can—"

"No!" Eleanor's hands dropped and a new fury seized her. "No more offers! I'll not go from one man's attempt at generosity to another! I am not a drowning woman, Thomas Keller. Fool or not, I made my own choices and I'll be damned if I will lean on your arm and wilt in tears and let you think that I—" Eleanor took a deep breath, ignoring the tears that streamed down her face. "All I ever wanted was to live a respectable life and not suffer at the whim of Fate. As much as I hated being hungry and destitute, I thought that if I stayed true to myself nothing could really hurt me. I-I was wrong! But, please—it is too soon to speak of celebrations or my freedom."

I don't want to be free! I've lost my heart to a man who wanted nothing more than a figure to paint, flesh and bone—the muse of the moment. Oh, God. From his own lips, to hear myself so dismissed . . .

Thomas nodded, saying nothing as she lost the battle to control her emotions. Instead, he quietly averted his gaze to give her what privacy he could until the coach pulled to a stop in front of the inn.

She recognized the Grove through bleary eyes but wiped her cheeks firmly. "Mr. Keller? Have you ever felt so defeated that you weren't sure if you could breathe?"

He looked at her in sympathy. "You are not defeated, Miss Beckett, and I stand by what I said earlier. You are a woman of conscience and I am glad to know you."

"It was a pleasure meeting you, Mr. Keller. And I—wait!" She hesitated with her hand on the coach door. "Why were *you* there? Why were you in the studio this morning?"

Thomas's sober expression became almost pained. "I feared he was mistreating you. I called on him to . . . assure myself that I was mistaken."

She studied him for a moment, unsure of her own reaction to his confession. "You were mistaken, Mr. Keller. He never—*never* mistreated me." Her throat closed in agony as a thousand memories of each gentle touch and considerate gesture flooded her mind.

"He isn't what he seems, Miss Beckett."

"H-how is that?"

"It's common knowledge that his family threw him off years ago for pursuing such a . . . an immoral profession. He has wealthy friends, but I must ask, where do his fortunes come from? If he's known no great artistic or critical success, then how is it that he possesses the resources that he has? No one seems to know, Miss Beckett. Do you?"

She shook her head. "It is . . . none of my concern, or yours."

"He disappears into India for several years and then resurfaces without a word to make strangers of almost everyone who knew him beforehand. Hastings is no gentleman, Miss Beckett. He is a pretender and a—"

"Enough! You sully your own reputation when you say such things and dishonor yourself, Mr. Keller. I will not speak of him again. If I was deceived, then I am well clear of it. In a strange way, I should be proud of my gullibility, Mr. Keller. Like my father, I want to believe the best in people and to see in them the qualities I hold dear. It is not a fault I intend to amend. Good day, Mr. Keller." Eleanor stepped down from the coach without waiting for assistance and walked into the inn without looking back.

She was grateful for Thomas's concern but was sure he'd misunderstood both her character and Josiah's. Thomas had exaggerated them each in turn as a villain and a damsel in distress, and she didn't have the stomach to defend either one at the moment. Eleanor surmised that Josiah's gruff behavior at the Walls' had misled Keller, and the disastrous encounter today had surely cemented her role as a helpless victim in his eyes.

As for the source of Josiah's fortunes, it was the least pressing of her worries.

Whatever Mr. Keller's intentions in sharing his fears, it was sordid business that a sober-minded man would wisely stay clear of—and Eleanor did not expect to meet Mr. Thomas Keller again.

Not that it matters.

Michael Rutherford was on the first-floor landing, and she blindly ran into him in her haste, tearfully colliding with him and knocking everything he carried out of his hands. A flurry of paper scattered everywhere and Eleanor knelt to help retrieve it as best she could.

"I'm so sorry!"

"There's no need for that!" Michael knelt next to her, reaching for a copy of the *Times*. "Are you crying? Are you injured?"

"I'm fine, Mr. Rutherford!" Eleanor tried to ignore him and focus on the papers at their feet.

Tally must have felt the commotion through the shuffle of their footsteps and came bounding up the stairs to lend a hand. To Eleanor's surprise, Mr. Rutherford's reaction to their assistance was not what she expected. He seemed to become more frantic in his retrieval of the scraps, wincing as Tally held out one of the sheets to her since she was clos- est. Decorum dictated that she avert her eyes before hand- ing it over to Michael, but something made her look. Perhaps it was the flash of fear in Rutherford's eyes. . . .

Jackal. The word caught her attention, and she quickly read it through damp eyes. *Jackal's set for the Thistle. Fri- day at midnight.* Eleanor shook her head. "Here you are, Mr. Rutherford. Do the Jaded often meet in such places?"

His expression was one of horror as he took the paper from her hand, folding the draft quickly as if to hide it from her view. "There's no meeting. Tally, here, let me have those."

Tally cheerfully handed over the rest of the newspaper clippings and retreated with a bob of his head, unaware of the storm brewing between the two adults.

"No meeting?" Her cheeks were still wet from crying, but she gave him a look of pure scathing derision. "Can none of you be honest when pressed? Is it even possible, Mr. Rutherford, for even one of your little group to speak with honor? Men! What a worthless lot of jaded fools, if you ask me!"

She stepped around him as daintily as a duchess step- ping around a dung pile and slammed her door behind her.

Chapter
26

On Thursday morning, Eleanor sat quietly in her lawyer's office. He'd summoned her about what he described as pressing business, and she'd been grateful for the distraction of an appointment after days of listless inactivity.

"I have the documents here, Miss Beckett, and wished to speak to you in person to convey the remarkable turn of events."

"If it's anything to do with Mr. Josiah Hastings, I won't waste any of your valuable time, sir. My business with him is concluded and I am loath to—"

"No, Miss Beckett. This is another matter altogether and quite surprising since we never pursued an appeal. It seems your father's case has been settled privately."

"M-my father's case? I don't understand."

Mr. Olmstead held out a sheaf of papers for her inspection. "It's quite official, Miss Beckett, and effective immediately. You are a woman of some wealth now. I have the contracts here from the young Mr. Keller, and a bank draft, which his clerk assured me is only the first in good faith that is due you. Similar payments are to be made in the schedule he has included, and there is a legal document entitling you to a good percentage of all future profits made from Keller's Gentle Smelling Salts and all pertinent brands and products. I must say, it is an extremely generous offering!"

"Oh my!" Eleanor surveyed the summary letter and marveled that she didn't feel more elated. After all, this vindicated her father and restored his legacy. "Why? Why would he do that?"

"Who can say? A burst of conscience? A moral imperative? Or more likely, his lawyers have uncovered new evidence that would have exposed him to great liability should it have come to light. In any case"—Mr. Olmstead beamed triumphantly—"justice is served and I cannot think of a better beneficiary than yourself!"

A wealthy woman. All my dreams, dropped into my lap without ceremony, and all I want to do is to cry. The world has righted itself too late to save me, and I'm too numb to feel anything but lost. I have the means to go anywhere twice over, but nowhere I care to go.

"Justice." She repeated the word, standing to shake Mr. Olmstead's hand. "Yes, thank you. I shall be sure to send a note of my sincere appreciation to Mr. Keller for this act and . . ."

"Was there something else, Miss Beckett?"

"No. There's nothing."

* * *

Josiah tried to paint. His imagination and memory sustained an image of Eleanor in pearls, sitting against a wash of green satin, an offering from Poseidon that any mortal would sell his soul to taste. The shadows were worse today, gray and black clouds that loomed in his peripheral vision and then drifted inexplicably in front of him without warning. But he ignored them and painted with his face so close to the canvas that his breath fanned the oils and coated his throat until it burned to breathe.

In his mind, the storm raged. The wise course of action

was to wait to pursue her until this Jackal business was finished and it was safe. Rutherford had made a point of stopping by to underline the matter. Waiting until after tomorrow night, at the very earliest, was a reasonable and sound decision. But every minute that passed chafed his nerves.

Pride be damned. I should just tell her. I should just lay my fortunes at her feet and confess everything.

"You're painting." Eleanor's voice behind him was a stunning revelation. He turned, elated to see her but also surprised. "How . . . ?"

"Mr. Creed knows me enough not to bother with any alarms, and since you still have no working bell, I didn't trifle Mr. Escher." She stepped primly forward. "Your security is quite lax."

"Eleanor." He took a deep breath. "There's so much I should—"

"Wait." She was all business as she opened her reticule and then held out a folded envelope. "I insist on paying you back, Mr. Hastings."

We are back to Mr. Hastings? So formal?

"Paying me back? I don't understand. You don't owe me a farthing."

"On the contrary"—she moved a little closer, her gloved hand still extended with the paper toward him—"I owe you a great deal. Here. The sitting fee, plus an additional sum for my lodging and any incidental expenses you may have incurred on my behalf. Mrs. Clay's estimates were clearly fraudulently low, and I couldn't bear the thought of hurting her feelings by pointing out the obvious, so I hope my best estimation wasn't too far off."

"You're rambling, Eleanor. I don't care for a farthing of it. You earned that money per our agreement, and I don't see why you're compelled to pay back a penny that you don't owe!"

"I have money of my own now, Mr. Hastings."

"Money of your own? From what source?" he asked.

"Mr. Keller voluntarily settled against my father's legal suit and restored my father's reputation." She lifted the paper another inch. "So because of his honorable gesture and generosity, I have money of my own and can now repay you as I always wished."

"With Keller's money, you mean!"

"I have money *of my own*, rightfully earned by my father's hard work. I cannot move forward with my life and be in debt to you."

"Debt? Give it to charity if you don't want it!"

"*You* give it to charity, Mr. Hastings. I can't imagine accepting anyone's gratitude for something *your* money has provided. If you wish to become a philanthropist, then by all means! But I am not going to be your first case!"

"You're doing this out of spite. I asked you to sit for me for a fee and you agreed. The painting was completed and it was—all that I'd hoped. I'm a man of my word. I don't want your money."

"I'm no longer in a desperate position where I need it! Please . . . it was always a ridiculous sum and your friends seem quite convinced that you cannot spare twenty pounds."

"Oh, God."

"Something to do with the state of your coats and the paint on your shirts, I'd guess. And even if you have more money than Midas, it doesn't matter. I want nothing to do with this business. I wish to be free of all of it."

"Goddamn it—"

"Language, Josiah!" She smoothed back her hair out of nervous habit. "I shall leave it on the table, Mr. Hastings."

"Then it will rot there. Take the money, Eleanor! I *need* you to take the money!"

"Why?"

"Because it's the—" He caught himself, a wave of hunger for her nearly unmanning him. "Because it's the only thing I'm free to give you."

The words stung like poisoned nettles against her skin, and Eleanor marveled that she was still standing. "Truly?"

He turned away. "Be merciful, woman, and take the damn money."

"Have you nothing else to say to me? Nothing?"

He had a thousand things to say to her, but he couldn't imagine a man feeling more muted by fate and circumstance.

"Then you don't deserve any mercy, Mr. Hastings. I have already given you too much of myself for too little." She tried to drop the envelope on the table but missed as her eyes filled with tears. Somehow the sight of her offering pitifully fluttering to the ground was the last straw. "Good-bye, Josiah."

She made yet another emotional escape from his presence, resenting the crushing pain this last encounter had caused. She'd vowed not to cry again, or forfeit her dignity, but Eleanor knew that the money had been a flimsy excuse for her visit.

She'd wanted to hear him say that he'd missed her. She'd wanted him to beg her to stay and admit that he'd made a mistake. She'd fantasized about how he might sweep her into his arms and banish the hurt of these last few days.

It's the only thing I'm free to give you.

Because he could not give her anything else—not his name or his heart, not a single promise of fidelity or a future—not even his trust.

I failed him somehow. There was something in me that didn't seem strong enough to him or reliable for the hardships to come. Something . . . but what else could I have done or said to convey to him how very much I care?

Or did he speak his mind to Mr. Keller that wretched morning when he said women were interchangeable? That I was nothing to him?

How could that be true? If he didn't care, then how could he have been so tender and caring, so generous and thoughtful? How is it that every fiber of my being is so hungry for him, even now?

After everything that had passed between them, it had all come down to a transaction completed and money in her hands in exchange for her innocence.

It was over.

Chapter
27

It had been a long, restless, sleepless night, and Friday morning dawned with a biting cold in the air. Eleanor listlessly rearranged the food on her breakfast tray to avoid a long sigh from Mrs. Clay, but finally gave up the attempted subterfuge. She'd made halfhearted plans to go out and look into securing different lodgings. She had money enough to take a home in Town if she wished, but nothing felt settled. *I wonder if I could get my father's house back? Would I want to be there alone now? Or is it haunted with too many bad memories?*

The Grove had become home in the last few weeks, but its association with Josiah was unacceptable. She looked over the pile of offerings from the solicitor's office that had been deemed suitable. Mr. Olmstead had attached a note advising her of a reputable hiring agent so that she could acquire a staff when the time came. She fingered it and then set it aside. She gathered all the papers into a leather packet and headed down the stairs, only to find Mrs. Clay sweeping out the entryway.

"Are you off today, miss?" Mrs. Clay asked. "You'll want to be wearing your warmest woolies, if you ask me. But Mr. Hastings's carriage hasn't arrived, so if you'd—"

"I am not . . . I am no longer employed by Mr. Hastings, Mrs. Clay," she said, cutting the older woman off.

Mrs. Clay's look was pure surprise. "No? Truly?"

"Truly."

"Well, there's a turn! I hope it wasn't—" Mrs. Clay's cheeks grew ruddier with emotion. "Was he the reason you were asking me about judging a man's character? Was Mr. Hastings unkind to you, Miss Beckett? Is it even possible?"

Eleanor shook her head. "No, Mrs. Clay! It's just that the painting he was working on . . . is quite finished. It was— unthinkable for me to continue . . . modeling. I made an exception for Mr. Hastings, but it isn't a very reputable pursuit for an unmarried woman." Eleanor winced, disliking the prissy tone in her voice. "I'm sure you understand."

"I suppose. I'm too old to keep up." Mrs. Clay sighed. "He's a dear man. I've always liked him, miss."

"As you should, Mrs. Clay. Mr. Hastings is a perfect gentleman."

The older woman smiled. "No man is perfect, but Mr. Hastings's greatest fault only adds to his appeal, don't you agree?"

"His greatest fault?" Eleanor asked, dreading the conversation. Josiah was a topic she'd hoped to avoid, but it had taken no less than twenty seconds for his name to take hold. "What flaw is that?"

"Pride! He's terribly proud, isn't he? Before he left for India, he was as poor as a street urchin and I knew it! But he had every tailor in Town vying to dress him and delighted in playing along with his betters. It was all a game for the handsome rogue, but I can spot a man who's missing a meal. Even so, would he take a dish for charity here when offered?" Mrs. Clay shook her head. "Not once! Not once did he take advantage and ask for a crust of bread on credit. But if ever I needed anything after losing Mr. Clay, rest his soul, there was my artist ready to lend a hand or just bring in his rich friends to make sure my common room was lively and my accounts sound."

"Proud." Eleanor repeated the word softly, absorbing this new perspective while struggling with the feeling that she'd just missed an important clue.

"Too proud for his own good, I'd say, but then, it's not my place." Mrs. Clay returned to her chore, working the mud out of the corners with her straw broom. "Far too proud. Something happened in India, and the fact that he's never said a word of it only makes it certain in my mind."

"Perhaps." Eleanor put a hand on the banister to ground herself as the nagging sensation grew stronger. *There's something there. I've missed something important in all of this.*

"When he introduced me to Mr. Rutherford, I knew. His concern for his friend was striking, but whatever tiger had taken the snap out of Rutherford's eyes, it didn't fail to take a bite out of Mr. Hastings, too, did it? Mr. Clay's father had that look about him after the war, but he was a proud man, too. My Mr. Clay, rest his soul, said a man's pride dictated silence and was the mark of scars you can't see with your eyes." Mrs. Clay kept sweeping as she talked. "He had a way with words, didn't he? Perhaps he did possess a bit of gypsy blood."

"Yes, your husband was very eloquent." Eleanor took a deep breath. As interesting as it all was, she wasn't sure how Josiah's silence about the Troubles had much to do with his dismissal of everything that had happened between them. "Mr. Hastings's pride being what it is, I cannot make a complaint of it. I can assure you, Mrs. Clay, he was always considerate and put me first in all his . . ." The words trailed away and the world retreated a single step as if into a fog.

He's losing his sight.
And he's proud.
It was never about trust. Why did I think it was trust? All this time, trying to earn his confidences when that wasn't the problem at all. He's thinking of me—as always.

He's protecting me and I reinforced it with all that non-sense about security and wanting the future I'd lost. I was so determined to keep my respectability so that my life could be restored, and he heard that, knowing that a life with him wouldn't restore my life, but change it altogether.

He doesn't think less of me.

He thought more of me than I did.

"Mr. Keller!" Mrs. Clay's greeting interrupted her thoughts. "I'd just meant to tell Miss Beckett that you'd come by while she was out yesterday, and I'll confess right away that it had slipped my mind. I am so sorry!"

Thomas nodded solemnly, shaking some of the snow off his coat onto the freshly swept floor. "Do not trouble yourself, Mrs. Clay. It seems the lady is here, and unless I've arrived at a bad moment, all is well." He turned to Eleanor. "Miss Beckett? Were you on your way out?"

"Yes, just."

"Can I offer you the use of my coach?" he asked.

"You're too generous, Mr. Keller." Eleanor hated the awkwardness of it all. When she'd seen him last, she'd just had her heart broken and hadn't been very gracious. And this was their first meeting since the legal settlement, so Eleanor didn't want to appear ungrateful for what he'd done. But after the revelations following Mrs. Clay's maternal nudging, she wanted nothing more than to think for a few minutes in peace. "Yes, thank you, Mr. Keller."

He held out his arm and she allowed him to escort her out to his waiting carriage. Once they were both inside, she took the fur he offered her and laid it over her lap to stay warm. "I am still in shock, Mr. Keller, at your generosity."

He held up a hand, waving off her words. "I received your note after the settlement. A better man would have forfeited all of it, for the sake of morality, but I couldn't betray all of my father's ambitions. I'd hoped you would understand that adhering to their initial agreement as partners and the division of profits your father signed seemed like an acceptable middle ground."

She nodded, numbly trying to take it all in. "Of course.

I never wished to see your family impoverished at my expense, Mr. Keller."

Thomas smiled, leaning back against the upholstered seat. "You've forgiven me again, and I'm immeasurably grateful to Providence, Miss Beckett. To meet you by chance that night and to win your friendship, by any means, is more fortune than I'd hoped for." He eyed the leather packet in her hands. "Are you out on business, then? Can I direct the driver somewhere on your behalf?"

Eleanor took a deep breath, aware that his simple offer was perhaps a turning point, and her choices in the next few minutes were far more critical than they might appear. "Mr. Keller? May I ask you something first?"

"Yes, of course."

"If I remember you rightly, you said that it was an unexpected invitation to the Walls'. Yes?"

He shrugged. "Yes, your memory serves you well, Miss Beckett. I was invited by Mr. Wall to his salon gathering. A pleasant surprise, to be sure, but finding you made it even more of a revelation, Miss Beckett."

"Are you not a close acquaintance of Mr. Wall?" she asked.

"Not at all!" he scoffed. "Frivolous pursuits have never appealed, and by reputation, the Walls do nothing that isn't silly, from what I could see."

"So why do you think he invited you to his party?" she pressed. "If he didn't know you?"

Thomas's naturally serious countenance grew even more somber. "I'm sure I don't know. Social ambition? Curiosity? An assessment to see if I might qualify beyond my fortunes for their circle?"

Eleanor nervously smoothed back her hair. "Mr. Wall is a close friend of Mr. Hastings."

"Is he?" Mr. Keller seemed genuinely shocked at the notion.

"Mr. Wall could have done it at Josiah's bidding. It was Josiah, all along, do you see? He meant for me to have the chance to give you the cut direct, if I wanted to, I'm sure of it. A chance to fuss a bit and feel better, I think, for all that had happened between our fathers."

"Hardly an admirable gesture, Miss Beckett, to unknowingly set you up for a public confrontation. I'm glad your better nature didn't succumb to the temptation to call me out in front of all those people."

"As I am that your better nature preferred justice over greed. But don't you realize what it means?"

Keller shook his head.

"He's done nothing, absolutely nothing, since the instant I've met him that wasn't motivated by his desire to make my life better. Even letting me go."

"As well he should. As I told him, it's the only honorable course and—"

"As *you* told him?"

"I offered him the advice of a man with a better vantage on the situation. After all, an artist is hardly a respectable choice for any woman, much less one in your position. He was taking advantage of you—perhaps for the money all along! As you say, he did arrange to make the introductions between us. He might have hoped for the very outcome we achieved, and then thought to benefit with you as a patroness to support his lackadaisical—"

"Mr. Keller." She cut him off, her hands clasped as her nerves kicked in. "What exactly did you tell him was the honorable course?"

"I told him that he should end it. I pressed him on his dishonesty and he lashed out, just as you heard."

He lashed out. Eleanor marveled that she might have missed so obvious a step, but then refocused on the next obvious thorny question. "Mr. Keller, what is your interest in me? I mean, beyond correcting your father's mistakes and amending the financial hardships that were inflicted; you have now interfered on my behalf without being asked twice. Is there some cause?"

"I . . ." Thomas was stunned into speechlessness, his naturally somber expression giving way to confusion and then determination. "You are very . . . beautiful, Miss Beckett.

It's clear your father mistakenly educated you far above your station, but I find you utterly charming. And while Hastings has nothing but notoriety to offer you, I have measured my life by the respectable choices I have made. You are an extremely proper young lady, despite your unfortunate associations with a painter; you would suit the restrained nature of my personality and the requirements of my domestic life. I realize this is sudden, but as you asked me directly—my interest in you has become very personal, Miss Beckett."

Eleanor pushed the fur off her lap. "I am flattered, Mr. Keller, but please understand that I cannot allow a misunderstanding between us. I am, most decidedly, less proper than I appear and my interests lie elsewhere."

"With Hastings?" he asked, a bitter edge betrayed in his tone.

"A friend advised me to judge men on their actions and not their words, Mr. Keller. Please don't make me amend my good opinion of you. However, if you spitefully withdraw your legal actions to atone for your father's crimes, I shall make a point of never speaking your name in public. I don't wish to be your enemy, Mr. Keller. I simply cannot be more than your friend." Eleanor opened the carriage door and alighted unaided. "Mr. Hastings was in love with me, Thomas. He loves me and he gave me up to prove it."

She turned and held her head up proudly as she walked back into the Grove.

And I was the one who was too blind to see the truth.

Chapter
28

Eleanor returned to her room, pacing the hours away as the day slowly faded. It was only the memory of the note that Michael had dropped that kept her from running over to Josiah's. No matter how she felt, whatever business was pressing down on Josiah and his friends, tonight was the night of its completion, and Eleanor doubted that it was fair to confront him on such a day. The unknown enterprise was fraught with tension, and she was no fool to insert herself into it.

Even so, the temptation to—

A gentle knock came at the door, and she wasn't entirely surprised to see Tally there with a dinner tray she had never sent for. Mrs. Clay wasn't one for letting meals be missed, and Eleanor smiled as she let him in.

"Thank you, Tally. Please tell your mother I said thank you." Eleanor did her best to signal her gratitude with the sign Mrs. Clay had shown her, but she suspected she'd made an awkward show of it. She'd learned just a few of his signs and suspected that her young teacher was not only extremely forgiving of her ignorance and lack of coordination, but also had invented a few signals just for her ease and use.

She touched her lips with her fingertips, as if taking a bite of bread. "Will you eat with me, Tally? Are you hungry, young sir?"

He shook his head and rubbed his belly with a smile.

"Your mother spoils you!" Eleanor teased him.

His expression was pure mischief as he protested and made as if to beg for the sign he'd taught her for sweets.

"You imp! I suppose it's me who's spoiled you, then." She crossed over to retrieve a small brown bag from her top drawer. "I may have saved a few licorice bites for just such an occasion."

She handed them over and was rewarded with a fierce hug as Tally threw his arms around her waist. She stroked his white blond hair and struggled to keep her emotions in check. He was such a dear boy, like a younger brother she had never had, and Mrs. Clay had become the mother she'd lost. She closed her eyes and took a steadying breath. Josiah had said he was fortunate to be able to choose his family, and Eleanor realized that she had managed to do the same.

"There, there." Eleanor stepped back and made sure that all was well. "It's only licorice, but you must promise not to eat it all in one go. Please?"

Tally smiled, then blushed, and then made a quick wave she interpreted as *Good night!* He turned in the blink of an eye to attend whatever tasks awaited him in the downstairs kitchen and dining hall, and she watched him from her doorway skip down the stairs with a child's enthusiasm.

She shut her door and settled in with her tray by the fire, contemplating family lost and gained and the twists and turns that made up each life's path.

Suddenly, someone was pounding on her door, the sound startling her into crying out and overturning her dinner tray with a horrible crash. Eleanor ran to the door and threw it open, only to see a complete stranger standing there.

He'd obviously been out in the weather with the snow melting off his oilskin coat, his sodden boots and clothes splattered with mud from a hard ride. He looked cold and miserable, but the fierce intensity in his dark green eyes was compelling.

"Can I help you, sir?"

"I-I'm looking for Rutherford. It is most urgent."

"His door is the next there." Eleanor pointed across the way to Michael's apartment.

"Of course, how stupid of me! I'm fatigued and apologize for the intrusion." The man nodded, adjusting his collar and bowing awkwardly to end the conversation before he immediately began repeating his efforts to rouse Michael Rutherford by banging his fist on the door she'd indicated. Eleanor almost shut her door to dismiss the situation, but there was something in the stranger's demeanor that made her linger. "Should I summon the landlady?"

It took a moment for him to cease, before he replied, "No. That won't be necessary."

"Are you sure? Is something wrong, mister . . . ?"

He looked at her as if he'd only just realized that she was still there. "Mr. Thorne. Darius Thorne. Pardon me, but it's nothing to concern you, miss." He turned his back on her, only to lean against the doorjamb, his eyes closed to either think or prepare himself for falling over into an exhausted heap.

It would have been all too easy to demur, but something in her refused to budge. "It might. I am Eleanor Beckett."

He opened his eyes, looking at her again as if for the first time. "I'm sorry, but I'm not familiar with the name. Do you know Mr. Rutherford, then?"

"Only in passing. Are you one of the Jaded, sir?"

He shifted his weight, suitably uncomfortable. "I don't know you well enough for confidences, Miss Beckett, and I'm out of time. I must urgently find my friend. If you'll excuse me—"

"Is there some danger?"

"I'm sorry. I shouldn't be indiscreetly blurting out my

private business." He touched his hat and nodded, turning on his heels to leave. "Again, my apologies for—"

She caught his arm, uncaring for the niceties of introductions and first meetings. "You are pounding on these doors as if there's a murderer at your back! Please!"

He freed himself gently from her grip. "Miss, if I've given you that impression, then I am at fault. But I'm in a great hurry and simply don't possess the time to stop and divulge my business to a complete stranger."

"If it's to do with the Jackal, then I believe they're meeting him tonight, are they not? At the Thistle?" Eleanor's hands fisted at her hips. "By all means, Mr. Thorne, don't divulge anything, but do not presume to tell me what is and is not my business! If any of you had any sense at all, you'd think of a better name for your club and better methods for communicating than pounding on doors!"

His jaw dropped open for a moment before he recovered his composure. "I see. Well . . . Have you seen Michael recently?"

"Not since yesterday."

Mr. Thorne looked stricken but he took the news in stride. "I'll make a point of not pounding on too many more doors and pass along your suggestion."

"And there's no danger?" she asked him again.

He shook his head. "No. I can't believe I'm having this conversation, but, no, there shouldn't be. Everyone is diverted but Rutherford and I'm confident I know where to find him since he's not here." He bowed again and tipped his hat. "It was a unique experience meeting you, Miss Beckett. I hope to have the pleasure again soon."

He left without another word, and Eleanor pressed her hands against the fiery warmth of her cheeks.

I was a tyrant to a complete stranger and I'm not even sure if I said too much or helped at all!

She returned to her room and began to pace. It was just after eleven o'clock at night, but she couldn't help feeling that something was wrong. None of the men or their previous conversations had ever seemed so weighted. Josiah's friends were notoriously cavalier about dropping in on each other without warning, from what she'd seen and from Mrs. Escher's comments. Josiah had cut off Escher when he'd read that first note aloud and then tried to divert her from the subject.

He'd unsuccessfully tried to make it all sound ordinary and unimportant.

But this meeting was different than any his "knitting circle" may have enjoyed previously because they had some dark business with a Jackal. By the way Mr. Rutherford had also reacted when she'd seen the place and time of the gathering, there was no doubt in her mind that the meeting was supposed to have been an absolute secret.

If there is no danger, then why was Mr. Thorne looking so pale and exhausted—and frightened?

Enough is enough.

There was a ghost of a thought about the scandal of calling on a man at such an hour, but it was the last fading echo of the old Eleanor Beckett, the one who would never follow her heart if it meant stepping off the respectable well-worn path of a modest young lady.

Eleanor grabbed her reticule from the inside of her doorway and raced down the stairs. Her coat was still hanging in the foyer, and she retrieved it to run out the door into the icy cold night air. Whatever had driven Mr. Thorne to haste, she wasn't sure, but the anxiety of the unknown fueled her own frantic need to take action and personally confirm that Josiah had, in fact, been successfully diverted from the gathering.

She was lucky enough to find a hackney for hire near the Grove, and set off without looking back to see Tally standing in the doorway of the inn, waving farewell.

*   *   *

The carriage made good speed to Josiah's home, and Eleanor ordered the driver to wait, then made her way inside. Mr. Creed was nowhere to be seen, but even he wouldn't have slowed her down. She'd grown used to the climb up several floors and was barely winded when she met Mr. Escher on the third-floor landing.

"Miss Beckett?" Escher held up an oil lamp, dressed in his long woolens, a tattered nightcap drooped over one ear. He was a comical sight in his robe and slippers. Clearly, the hour for visitors was long past. "Miss Beckett, h-he's out."

"Out?" Eleanor slowed, a cold stone settling in her stomach at the word. "He's out?"

"Rita's to bed, but you can wait for—"

"Did a man named Darius Thorne come by earlier? Did Josiah have any callers this evening?" she asked.

"No callers. A note came an hour ago, but Mr. Hastings had already left so I just set it aside."

"Where is the note?"

Escher blinked in surprise but answered dutifully. "On the table where I always set them, by the door in his apartment. Although, the way he's been holed up in that studio these last few days, I should probably have—"

Eleanor didn't wait for him to finish. She picked up one of the lamps set in one of the windows and continued past him up the stairs. Her speed barely kept pace with her fears as she gathered her skirts to make it easier to run.

His door was unlocked, as always, and she had to bite the inside of her cheek at the foolishness of men who played dangerous games but refused to lock their own homes. *Hire a bodyguard and leave your doors open. Where is the logic in that? He's being careless as if to prove he's invincible.*

There was a small disorderly pile of unopened correspondence in a stack on the table just inside the entryway, but the one on top was the one she seized. The handwriting was rushed and uneven.

It's from that man! I would stake my life on it!

It was pure instinct, and what she did next was equally driven by a growing sense of dread. She opened the seal and guiltily read the letter from Darius Thorne. While it was incomprehensible for the most part, there was no mistaking that the tone was dire—and she hadn't underestimated the danger that Josiah faced.

Don't go to the Thistle.

There's a third party involved from Bengal, and I suspect even our enemy has a more powerful enemy that has been watching the exchange in the papers. My contact in Edinburgh said that an inquiry was made from London a few weeks ago about a sacred treasure, and it was accompanied by a threat. Something about the Seeker being cursed. They hate English hands on this thing, but apparently some mystic somewhere predicted the treasure would journey across the seas. But somebody is making a distinction between exactly which English hands get to pocket it. So long as the current holders keep it from the hands of the Company—the Jackal as we've taken to calling their representative—no blood will be shed. Here's a quote though, "But if they think to hand it over to this Demon, then none of them will emerge alive."

All bets are off, Josiah.

We've suspected all along an agent of the East India Trading Company was our nemesis. But we never thought to look beyond him. We can't give the Jackal what he wants—or we've got a bigger problem on our hands. We must deny the Jackal his victory, or face a worse hell.

D

Escher came up behind her, limping with fatigue. "Off to see his friends, he said, Miss Beckett. Were you to wait?"

"No. No more waiting, Escher."

Eleanor pushed past him to return down the stairs to the waiting carriage, the note absently tucked into her pocket while an impulsive plan formed in her mind.

* * *

The private meeting room at the Thistle was on the second floor, accessible only by a rear staircase hidden by a door on a long hallway near what Josiah suspected were bedrooms for the patrons of the tables below to avail themselves of the charms of the various hostesses below. It was a rustic establishment, but he had to admire Michael's choice. He'd arrived hours early, within minutes of Rutherford, only to be trapped in a long, anxious wait as the appointed time for the meeting approached and none of the other Jaded had appeared.

"Where the hell is everyone else?"

Darius came pounding down the hallway and stumbled into the room, out of breath. "Hastings! Didn't you get my note? What the hell are you doing here? Michael, it's off!"

Michael was on his feet instantly. "Off?"

Josiah also stood, a bit more slowly as the shock of Darius's announcement sank in. "Why would the Jackal call it off? After all his efforts to—"

"Not the Jackal," Darius explained, even as he continued to try to gesture his friends from the room. "We're to rendezvous at the brownstone to regroup. I'll explain it in the carriage, but we have a new problem to—"

Screams from the ground floor cut him off midsentence, and Michael Rutherford instantly transformed into the soldier they knew well. He moved around the table, past Thorne, to open the door and assess the situation. The smell of smoke was already toxically dense on the stairs, and Michael slammed the door closed.

"It's a fire," he said calmly. "One way or another, Darius is right and the meeting's off."

Josiah marveled at the lack of fear he felt at the announcement. "Darius, the others are safely away?"

Thorne nodded. "I sent runners with notes to everyone and thought I'd managed to get my message to all, except Michael. But I knew where you lived and meant to catch you there. It's just us, gentlemen."

"Shall we go?" Josiah turned back to Michael. "Yes?"

"Yes, but let's hurry. I chose the Thistle because I knew we couldn't be ambushed, as there's only one way up to these rooms, but . . . my strategy seems to be flawed." He shrugged his shoulders, then took a deep breath. "Take in what air you can and we'll head back down single file."

Darius rushed to the sideboard and poured water from a waiting pitcher onto some cloth napkins. "Here, take these to cover your mouths! It will help with the smoke."

Josiah cursed as he missed the handoff of the moist cloth, but Darius pressed another into his palm and they were ready. For Josiah, there was a moment of déjà vu as they stumbled out into the now smoke-filled hallway. It reminded him of their clumsy escape from their earth-bound prison in Bengal. With noise and chaos echoing nearby, they were once again following each other in the dark on instinct alone toward safety.

The smoke was too thick to see clearly where they were going and they could hear the fire crackling and roaring beneath their feet. It was horribly disorienting and Michael hesitated. "Damn it! It's burning fast!"

"Who was that?" Darius gestured to the opposite end of the hallway. "Did anyone else see that?"

Michael coughed before answering. "Couldn't be anyone! There's no exit that direction and we're the only ones on the second floor! I checked it when I arrived!"

Josiah shouted, "Enough discussion, men. Six doors to the left, count them and stay low and then the stairs will be there! Darius, take hold of the back of my coat, and Michael, you hold to his, and let's get out of this!"

They made their way to the door to the narrow staircase, practically forced to crawl after opening it as black smoke and vapors poured up the structure like a newly vented chimney. They'd gone less than a dozen steps down when Josiah realized that there was someone below them on the landing.

It was a tall, broad-shouldered figure swathed in a black coat still wearing his top hat, the dim, smoky stairwell masking his identity. But one thing was clear. He held a pistol in his hand pointed directly at their midst. "At last, we meet again."

Michael was furious. "Why burn us out? You'll never get what you want, Jackal, roasting your opponents!"

"I didn't start this fire! You did!" The man roared back over the din of the fire. "To hell with you! You're the ones with everything to gain if you trap me in a public blaze! I should have known it was a trick!"

Darius stayed low against the walls, coughing, but managed to call out, "No tricks! We never—"

"Shut up! We'll meet on *my* terms next time!"

"Your terms? Knife-wielding assassins, poison, and burglary? Your terms are shit, if you don't mind me saying it," Michael growled. "We'd have played nice if you had the courage to face us in the light of day, Jackal."

"The time for negotiation is over! You'll give me what I want and what's rightfully mine! No more middle men or emissaries, old friends. I'll deal with you directly from now on. But here's a bit of an advance payment for my troubles so you'll remember to respect your betters in the future."

"No!" Josiah knew it was up to him to avert the shot that was surely coming, but with his failing eyes, he felt helpless. He lunged forward as Rutherford grabbed Darius and tried to shield him from harm with his own body. Josiah instinctively moved to close the gap between himself and the shooter, but the world slowed to a nightmare crawl of flickering images that flashed in front of him in rhythm with his heartbeat.

He saw all of it in a strange cascade of horror: the dull gleam of the gun barrel and the flash it made as the man pulled the trigger just as he struck his wrist upward. The noise was deafening and Josiah fell to the floor, the momentum of the blow and his efforts to stop the Jackal forcing him to his knees. By the time he looked up, his ears ringing, the Jackal was gone.

"Thorne? Rutherford?" He looked back at his friends, hating the acrid taste of fear and smoke in his mouth. "Is anyone shot?"

Michael reached up to wipe blood from his cheek. "No. I think my face is cut from the splinters that went flying when that ass shot the wall next to my head, but I'd say we survived this round."

Darius straightened up from where Michael had pushed him down onto the stairs. "If no one is shot, then I suggest we keep moving! I swear, for men of action, you are wasting a good deal of time in discussion while we suffocate in this stairwell!"

"The professor's right!" Michael said, his humor returning. "Lead on, Hastings!"

Josiah stood and realized that it wasn't just smoke obscuring his vision. His ears were still ringing and the adrenaline from their confrontation with the Jackal made the world skewed and strange. But the worst of it was that he couldn't really see anything. All he could do was feel the warm weight of the tangle of Darius and Michael behind him as Michael put a hand on his shoulder. "Yes. We should go."

The staircase was too narrow for Michael to get around to take point and Darius was nearly incapacitated with smoke, so Josiah's first priority became getting them out alive. He counted the steps and tried not to fall, ignoring everything else, and just as the timbers of the old hall began to creak and sway, the men reached the first floor, tripping over overturned chairs and tables.

"Where's the door?" Darius called out.

But Josiah didn't have the breath to answer him. Instead, he grabbed Thorne's coat, trusting that Michael wouldn't have let go of the chain, and used the map in his head he'd habitually constructed upon arrival to lead them in a race toward safety.

Flames licked up the walls around them and the noise was deafening, but at last, the haggard group limped out of the front entrance and out onto the street, where citizens were beginning to bring what buckets they could to help until the fire brigades arrived.

"My God! What a nightmare!" Darius exclaimed, his voice ragged from the smoke. He began to cough as his lungs seized on the fresh night air. "Damn!"

Rutherford pounded him on the back, doing what he could to help his friend clear his lungs. "What the hell was that man saying? 'We meet *again*' and something about being 'old friends'? Do we know him? Is that possible?"

Josiah pressed his fingers into his eyes, uselessly trying to see if his condition were temporary. "Not a chance of it! I've not a friend in Christendom who would go to that kind of trouble to—"

A man approached their small band and interrupted the conversation as Darius staggered over, doubled with coughing from the smoke. "Rutherford! You're safe, thank God!"

"Lawrence! What happened?" Michael answered, then turned to his friends. "Lawry owns the Thistle and was in my regiment an eon or two ago."

"I can't say the cause of it," Lawrence answered, his eyes turned back to his beloved Thistle's ongoing destruction, but then his gaze narrowed and his focus returned with renewed concern. "Did the young lady find you? Is she with you, then?"

"What young lady?" Josiah asked, his head snapping up at the unexpected question.

"A woman arrived a while ago and asked for the Jaded and knew of the meeting, so I assumed it was all right. I directed her up to the room but couldn't leave the card tables. Did you not see her?"

"What the—" Josiah started, but Michael stopped him with a firm hand on his shoulder.

"Red hair? Very pretty?" Michael asked.

"That's her. I sent her up just twenty minutes ago, but—"

"The hallway. Darius thought he saw someone. It's Eleanor!" Josiah pulled away from Michael's hold on him and sprinted back inside the building, ignoring the roar of disapproval at his back.

"Damn it! Wait!"

But Josiah wasn't going to wait, not if the Devil himself tried to bar the door. Nothing could stop him, and as Darius had reminded them, there was no time for debate and discussions.

The fire was growing worse by the second, and the roaring howl of it made it hard for a man to think. But he could hear the faint alarm bells of the fire brigade and took some comfort in the notion that help might not be far off. He raced through the deserted ground floor and returned to the stairwell leading up past the first floor to the second, where they had hoped to have their momentous meeting. The smoke was thicker, but Josiah hardly noticed it. He crouched low to the ground where the air felt a little cooler, and began to recite an ancient Hindu prayer as he made his way up through the unsettled, swaying structure.

O God, lead us from the unreal to the real.

He closed the door behind him and knelt in the hallway to regain his bearings. She had never come to the room they were in, which eliminated it as a choice. Josiah knew she must have mistakenly been waiting for them in another private meeting room and wracked his brain to recall which direction Darius had been looking when they'd stepped from that doorway and seen someone.

O God, lead us from darkness to light.

The smoke was growing thicker and it was harder and harder to breath, forcing him to accept that there wasn't much time left. But at last, logic overpowered terror and he surmised that she'd have been nearer the staircase since they'd been at the far end from it when Darius had spoken. "Lawrence directed her and the last door on the left could have been misunderstood as the first door," he ground out, the sound of his own voice steadying his nerves. "Come on, Hastings. Try it and then try them all if you have to."

O God, lead us from death to immortality.

He moved to the first door across from the stairwell, but it was locked. The next, the same. Josiah dropped back to his knees and crawled across to the right side of the passage, a wave of nausea from the smoke making his stomach churn and his hands shake. At last, he'd found an open door.

"Eleanor!" Josiah called out her name, his hands outstretched into the stygian gloom only to be rewarded with a brush of textured gabardine from a woman's skirts. "Eleanor?"

He found her hands and then her face, and pulled her to him, relieved to find her warm and pliant, if unresponsive. She'd fainted from the smoke, but was alive, and for Josiah, it was enough.

He found the damp cloth that Darius had given him and tied it around her face. He then hauled Eleanor unceremoniously over his shoulder and mentally prepared himself for the gauntlet of destruction awaiting him, remapping his path and counting the steps. The entire building creaked and moaned again, and Josiah abandoned his preparations and moved into action.

A wall of heat and smoke nearly knocked him over when he opened the door to the stairway, but as Michael had said, here was the only exit. The steep stairs had transformed into a deadly chimney. Speed was his greatest objective, and he ran down, taking multiple risers at a time in a strange off balance juggling act between the forces of gravity and the need to keep himself upright. Josiah fought off the surreal effects from oxygen deprivation that made the walls seem to dance and fall away.

He'd reached the first-floor landing when a small explosion on the floor above rocked him down to his knees. The concussion from the sound and force of it made his ears ring harder, and for the space of a breath or two, he wondered if he hadn't allowed his own blind stupidity to lead to both of their deaths.

"I should . . . have let . . . Rutherford . . . get you. . . . He can see, dearest . . . but . . . pride goeth . . . before the fall." Josiah readjusted his precious bundle, fighting the sensation that he'd just lost all, and staggered back up to fight his way down the last of the stairs.

The ground floor was an inferno, but Josiah managed a grim smile as the oven-hot blaze warmed his face as he squared up in the doorway. "Here," he said, his lungs miraculously opening up, "is where it's an advantage to be blind because I'm betting a hundred sterling a sighted man wouldn't be able to take a single step forward, Miss Beckett."

The pinpricks of light were frightening enough to give him an idea of what lay ahead, but Josiah ignored all of it, unwilling to trust himself to spots of vision no larger than halfpennies. He pulled her from his shoulder to cradle her against his chest, unwilling to allow fiery debris to fall onto her or to use her in any way as a shield. Josiah ran forward, darting as best he could away from the worst of it, as even the columns that supported the ceiling were now burning like Roman candles.

It was only seconds, but he could hear Rutherford shouting encouragement from the steps of the Thistle just outside its open doors, and it was the lifeline he needed. Josiah followed the sound to safety and the instant relief of the wintry night air on his face.

"You're insane! You realize that, don't you?" Rutherford said, guiding Josiah down the stairs back toward a tree stand across the street. "Is she—is she all right?"

"I don't know." It was only with Michael unknowingly guiding him that he stayed upright until they were a good distance from the chaos. Josiah stopped, kneeling on the sidewalk to assess the damage and face his worst fears. "I can't see! Is she breathing? Is she burned?" Josiah desperately tried to ascertain the extent of her wounds, taking slow breaths to calm himself, and tried to concentrate using touch alone to feel for the telltale wet of blood. "Rowan! Goddamn it, where the hell is Rowan?"

"Not coming. Told you. None of you—" Darius had to stop, a coughing fit seizing him and doubling him over again for a minute. "Were to be here. I sent notes by courier as soon as I arrived in London but—I thought it was only Michael—I hadn't reached."

Behind them, the Thistle collapsed to the ground in a grand rush of flames and timber, and each of them shuddered at a grim end they'd missed by minutes.

Michael knelt next to Josiah. "Hellfire, my fault! I dropped those damn papers and she saw the Thistle in my notes—"

"Shut up!" Josiah cut him off ruthlessly. "Listen to me, Michael. I can't see. I can't see a damn thing. I'm literally blind! So help me find out if she's hurt and make sure she's breathing properly!"

"Blind," Darius said. "How did we miss that?"

"Blind." Michael echoed the announcement in whispered shock, but instantly moved to help his friend and the young woman he cared for. "All right." His search was efficient and quick, turning her on her side to see if the lining of her coat might be stained and give them some clue. "I don't see any sign of burns or injury, but I can't imagine she can breathe easily in . . ." Michael's speech trailed off uncomfortably.

"What is it!"

"Her clothing and her corset. I can't see how anyone could breath in that steel cage, Josiah, much less a woman with scorched lungs. Perhaps we should get her somewhere where we can get the damn thing off and—"

"You are *not* removing one single stitch of my clothing in public, Josiah Hastings! We have an agreement!" Eleanor struggled to sit up, affronted to awake to a discussion about her unmentionables. "I may have compromised my principles slightly for the sake of art, but—"

He swept her into his arms, ending her adorable lecture about the improprieties of rendering first aid on a street corner, a groan of relief wrenched from his lips. "Oh, God . . . what a delectable prig you are!"

"I am *not* a prig! Now, kindly let me up. . . ." She blushed at the word, aware of the unique nature of his endearments.

"Go slowly." Michael tried to intervene. "There's no telling how much damage your lungs have suffered after all that smoke. You'd fainted, Miss Beckett."

"Oh." She glanced down and winced slightly. "I never faint, Mr. Rutherford." Then she smiled. "Despite my industrial foundation garments, I am relatively unscathed. But what have you gentlemen to do with all of this? Did the Jackal come?"

"And on *that* note"—Michael shifted his weight onto his feet and stood, an oak tree unfolding from the ground—"I'm retreating for the night. I have an idea I'm to blame for the lady's presence and will therefore make a strategic retreat. I'm off to see the others at the brownstone and make sure that no one else had an equally adventurous night. And to make sure Rowan looks at poor Darius."

"I'm fine. . . ." His protest was cut off by another coughing fit, but he waved off their hands. "I'll go with you and explain what I think prompted our 'adventurous night.'" Darius brushed some of the soot from his pants. "Josiah, I suspect Miss Beckett will want to see you safely home and that will give you time to answer all her questions."

"And what of *my* questions?" Josiah asked as he helped Eleanor to her feet.

"I'll call on you tomorrow afternoon and make sure you have all the information as well. Be safe." Darius waved. "Come on, Rutherford. My hackney is there, but I'm sure if we walk a bit, we can find another one easily enough. Let's yield it to Hastings so he can see Miss Beckett out of this."

The men left the pair without looking back, determined to complete their mission to ensure the well-being of the others, and Josiah shook his head in wonder at it.

That was it. I told them and the world didn't come to an end. No coddling. No inquiries. No pity.

Telling his friends in a moment of pure necessity had been painless. But now he would have to tell Eleanor everything, and pray that between knife-wielding assassins and her aversion to controversy, she might forgive him before they parted.

I am finally and completely out of time.

Chapter
29

The carriage ride back to his home was surreal. The smell of burnt wood and oil clung to their skin and clothing, and all he desired was to hold her hands in his, kissing her palms and absorbing the fact that she was still alive, still there, and miraculously still with him. Here was a good-bye he'd never imagined, and Josiah wasn't sure he had the stamina for it.

"What just happened, Josiah? Did that . . . man burn down the Thistle to hurt you and your friends?"

"It seems so, but he accused us of the deed and got off a shot before we could stop him." Josiah pressed her palm against his cheek, savoring the luxury of its healing powers. "And so the Jackal lives to bother us another day."

"It's like a penny novel! I just don't understand any of it."

"It's a puzzle for another day, perhaps." Josiah kissed her fingers. "I don't want to think about him anymore."

"I'm such a fool. I didn't realize—I was simply going to find you and make sure that you were safe. I thought I'd arrived ahead of you somehow when the room they said you were in was empty, so I was just waiting. . . ." Eleanor shuddered. "But then there was the smell of smoke and people were screaming, and when I finally worked up the courage to escape, I heard a gunshot and lost my nerve. I shall have nightmares for the rest of life, I'm afraid."

"Damn, I'm so sorry that you were involved with this mess, Eleanor. They all warned me to be sure you were clear of it, before—I was going to come to you once we'd finished with this villainy."

"Josiah, I need you to tell me what just happened and the truth behind this Jaded nonsense. Please confess it."

He found her hands to hold them gently, drawing her closer. "My small circle of friends earned a silly nickname after we'd returned to England. I think it was Ashe or myself who said something about how nothing engendered interest more than a lack of it, and since we were irrevocably jaded from the twists and turns of our adventures, we were doomed to live the rest of our lives in defiant isolation and arrogant ignorance of the rules of civility. A woman of rank overheard it and dubbed us the Jaded. It was . . . quoted in a paper, and for complicated reasons, we decided to let the name stand."

"It is a wicked name, Josiah."

"I know, but honestly, it's grown on us. And I thought nothing of using a public mystery as camouflage to hide our real secrets. It was all a lark, Eleanor, until Galen came under attack, Rowan's house was broken into, and then someone tried to poison Ashe and nearly murdered his wife instead. It's been a jumble of assassins and veiled threats and—I should never have turned my back on the danger. Michael accused me of being selfish and heartless for bringing you into my life."

"No! But why would anyone want to hurt you or your friends?"

"That man, that *Jackal*—believes that we have something, a sacred treasure from India, that he is entitled to. He's been trying to draw us out with notes and threats, and we've been trying to discover how to satisfy him or destroy

him, whichever is possible. But none of us have yet surmised what that sacred treasure is or how it is he knows so
much of us. Unless Darius solved the puzzle and uncovered
a clue in Scotland amidst the gem brokers and that's what
he was trying to tell us before all hell broke loose."

She shook her head. "He found out about the ambush,
and that there is another player in the game. It's this unknown that may have caused that fire—not the man you
were facing. And the fire must have been set to stop him
from acquiring your . . . treasure."

"How do you know all this?"

"Mr. Thorne sent you a note." Her voice dropped, and he
recognized the sweet shame he heard there.

"You're reading my correspondence?"

"I was worried!" Her voice rose defensively, the lilt like
music in his ears. "Mr. Rutherford was being a bit too se-
cretive about this Jaded business, and when your friend Mr.
Thorne came by the inn earlier, I began to fear that something had happened . . . even to you. So I came to your
house . . . and read the correspondence he'd left for you."

"And then set out to rescue me—alone?"

She shifted next to him. "I'm not sure if *rescue* is the right
word, but I had hoped to warn you. And I wasn't completely
impulsive to come alone! I would have dragged Mr. Creed
along, but he was nowhere to be found when I left." Her
gloved hands smoothed over his and squeezed his fingers
gently. "I knew you couldn't have read Mr. Thorne's note and
I was terrified to think that you might be hurt."

The carriage came to a halt, but he made no move to exit
it, signaling the driver to wait. "You knew I *couldn't* read
his note?"

"Naturally. I may be a prig, but I'm not an unobservant
prig, Josiah Hastings."

"You know? About . . ."

"Your sight? Of course." She touched his face, tracing
his jaw with the soft cup of her palm. "It's failing, isn't it?"

He nodded. "It is." He took a deep breath. "I don't think
I can face going in. Not just yet."

"Then we'll wait until you're ready."

Josiah took another deep breath, holding it until his lungs ached before letting it go, and then glanced out the window at the dark looming shape of the ruined factory's shell that was home. "I can't see a single light. It's as if the house isn't ready for my return either."

"No, Josiah. There are no lights. You mustn't torment yourself to—"

"No lights?" he asked, the hackles on the back of his neck rising. *She'd said she couldn't find Creed, but how is that possible? He'd never have left his post. . . .* "Look again, Eleanor. On the third and fourth floors and at the gate. Creed will have his lantern, and the lamps are always set at the gate and the stair landing when I'm out at night. And the Eschers . . . they'll have waited up. Look again."

Eleanor dutifully looked again. "No, Josiah. The house is dark."

Josiah banged his fist on the roof of the carriage and opened the window to lean out. "Driver! Take this woman to the Grove and see her safely in."

"Josiah, no! I cannot go! You cannot—"

"I cannot see you in harm's way again, Eleanor. It may be nothing, but I can't risk it. Go to the Grove and wait for me there. I'll follow as soon as I can." Josiah shut the carriage door. "If I'm not at the Grove in an hour, send a runner to Dr. Rowan West on Charles Street. The Jaded will come."

"Josiah, I beg you!" Eleanor clutched at the lapel of his coat through the window, desperate to keep him close. "Send a runner yourself and wait for your friends! You *can't see*! Why go in alone if there's danger?"

"Because Rita and Samuel are in there. They're the only family I have, Eleanor, and I have to be sure that they're safe. I can see well enough, yet." The last was a lie, but he refused to risk her. He pried her fingers loose from the wool cloth and kissed the palm of her hand, only to release her. "I love you, Eleanor. Farewell."

"Josiah! No!" She tried to grab hold of him again, panic seeping into her voice, but he stepped back and turned to the driver.

"Driver, move on there! A sovereign to deliver her safely to the Grove!"

The carriage pulled from the curb quickly, sweeping Eleanor out of his reach and leaving him alone to face the darkness.

*   *   *

Damn!

Creed's moan of pain echoed in the vaulted and open ruined factory floor, and Josiah put out his hands to try to avoid falling as he made his way toward the sound. He found Creed next to one of the milling machines but only after the man moaned again in pain and unwittingly helped Josiah narrow his search.

"Roger?" Josiah knelt down. "Are you injured, then?"

"My head . . . Some bastard tried to open my skull. . . ." Creed whispered, the weak rasping sound of it only feeding into Josiah's awareness that his illusion of his home's invulnerability was forever shattered.

Josiah took off his coat and laid it over the bodyguard. "Here, stay still and I'll see about getting you some help."

"The Eschers . . ."

"I'm on my way up. There's nothing you can do, so try to stay warm and I'll be back as quickly as I can, all right?" Josiah put a hand on the man's shoulder. "Do you need anything?"

Creed turned his head away. "A reference . . ."

"You won't need one. You're not fired, Mr. Creed."

"I ain't?" he asked dumbfounded. "But . . . I . . ."

"You're human and I'm the one to blame for this, so I'd have you stay if only to let a man redeem himself in your eyes."

Creed groaned. "I never thought—thank you, Mr. Hastings."

"All right, then. We'll talk about fixing up old factories and making good another time. You'll stay still."

Creed grunted his assent, and Josiah stood to make his way carefully back across the floor and then up the stairs. He didn't bother with stealth, but took the stairs two at a time, hating the idea that he'd find the Eschers in a similar state of injury on his behalf.

And for what? A sacred treasure I don't possess—or the stolen treasure I do?

He was on familiar ground and moved confidently without bothering with any lights. He tripped over Escher on the third-floor landing, cursing as he fell. "Damn! Escher, are you all right? Did I break your ribs?"

Escher could only mumble and Josiah discovered quickly that his houseman was bound and gagged.

"Here, let's have you out of this! Are you hurt?"

"Mr. Hastings!" Escher spoke once his gag had been removed. "I'm fine, but my wife! They went inside our rooms!"

Josiah untied his legs and helped him to his feet. "Stay behind me and we'll find her together. Don't worry, Samuel. If they trussed you up, I'm sure they paid her the same courtesy."

Escher lit a lamp and followed behind him, unaware of how little the flame helped Josiah find his way. Even so, both men followed the sounds of banging and thumping coming from inside the kitchen pantry and found the poor woman on the floor, tied just as her husband had been.

"My beauty!" Samuel knelt next to her and freed his beloved wife. "Did those bastards bruise you?"

"Did you see who it was?" Josiah added.

Rita shook her head, her cheeks streaked with tearstains. "It was like ghosts! I never saw 'em! The lights went out and it happened in a blink! Not a word or a whisper spoken and my poor man nowhere to be found! I was in a terror for you!"

Mr. Escher stroked her face. "I was trussed up, too! But what's all this worry for me?"

"Well, mind"—Rita's bluster returned, betraying her

emotions—"I'm not the one with the aching bones. You could catch your death on a cold floor! I'm so sturdy they could have hung me out the window by my ankles and I'd enjoy the fresh air."

Rita relit more of the lamps and then turned back to them. "Oh, Lord! You're a sight! Have you been cleaning chimneys?"

"Never mind that." Josiah shook his head, enjoying the odd humor of his cook and housekeeper. "Creed was struck on the head and will need some attention."

"I'll see to him," Rita offered.

"You'll *both* see to him," Josiah amended, intervening before his bruised and elderly houseman volunteered to help him search the rest of the house. "I'll search the house and make sure our guests have gone."

"We should send for the watch!" Escher growled. "They'll have robbed us blind!"

"No. I'll see to my own house, and I don't want the authorities on my doorstep. Not tonight. Not after—please, both of you, just trust me. If someone is threatening the house, I need to see to it."

Samuel nodded and then got up to rummage through one of the drawers in the china cupboard. "Here, take this, then." He pressed a revolver into Josiah's hand. "I had it for protection. . . ."

Rita snorted. "Well, *that* came in handy!"

"Be kind, woman! A man can't shoot ghosts in the dark now, can he?" Escher countered defensively.

"We'll argue the points of home defense later," Josiah said, ushering them both to the landing. "Please, see to Creed and wait for me downstairs."

"You're sure, then?" Escher asked again. "Not that I don't think you can manage, but a good pair of eyes couldn't hurt, could they?"

Wonders never cease. The old bird's known all along.

"I'm grateful for the offer, but I'd rather face a dozen armed robbers than your wife if I put you in harm's way or accidentally shoot you, Escher."

Escher laughed. "All understood, sir! We'll wait below and I'll hold off until you signal."

* * *

Josiah moved by touch alone.

A man can't shoot ghosts in the dark. Escher's prophetic words made him smile in the inky black. *Not to mention the idiocy of a blind man carrying a gun in the first place. . . .*

Josiah set the revolver down on a small table inside the first set of double doors leading into the apartment. At best, it was a useless object, and at worst, a deadly thing he'd use and only succeed in killing himself.

He moved quietly and with practiced confidence. It was his house and sanctuary, and he had been living without light in the evenings for many weeks to accustom himself to it. It was only Eleanor's arrival that had changed that.

But old habits died hard, and Josiah was pleased that he wasn't forced to crawl or stumble about with his hands held out in front of him. *Not here. Maybe everywhere else from now on, but not here, damn it.*

He expected to trip over upended furniture or to come across some sign of mayhem from a violent search. After all, he suspected that whoever had done this must have come looking for the sacred treasure, and a polite search didn't seem possible after Creed's fate.

All the doors were open to each and every room, but as he methodically walked through each room, Josiah made the same discovery again and again.

Nothing is touched. Nothing out of place.

A chill slid down his spine at the strange idea that it had been ghosts, but Josiah shook off the sensation. "Come out, come out, wherever you are," he quietly commanded, to be answered with a silence so loud it made his chest ache.

In his bedroom, Josiah began to cross over to his dresser only to trip over an unexpected object someone had deliberately set in the middle of the floor. He knelt down and realized it was the ornate wooden jewelry chest set. Heart pounding he opened it, only for his fingers to encounter the smooth, unmistakable weight of rope after rope of pearls and the silk bags holding the loose undrilled larger orbs he'd saved for barter.

It's all here. As if these were useless trinkets. . . .

Josiah lifted a handful of the cold pearls to the throbbing heat at his temples, trying to soothe the storm of his thoughts and emotions.

No sense. This doesn't make any sense. Why carry it downstairs?

But then a new thought seized him.

Josiah retraced his steps, racing up the stairs to the studio, his fingertips gliding along the banister. The pitch-black didn't hinder him, but he slowed as he reached the landing.

The painting. If it's destroyed, then so am I.

The door to the studio was wide open, a soft glow emanating from within. Josiah deliberately moved toward its source, experiencing in a new way the challenges of the solid black curtain that obscured his vision. Slivers of light revealed the direction of his steps until he finally surmised the details of the surprise waiting for him.

It was the small bronze statuette of the Hindu goddess perched on a wooden platter in front of a single dancing flame, while behind her, one of his canvases served as a backdrop. He tilted his head to try to be sure he wasn't hallucinating.

My shrine. My little makeshift shrine is . . . here? They've moved it and lit the oil lamp and even the flowers. Why?

"Thank God!" Escher's voice interrupted his thoughts and Josiah didn't have the energy to chastise him for ignoring his express orders to remain below stairs.

"Yes. A miracle they didn't take anything."

"Not that, sir. The paintings. They didn't spoil them. Although I'm not sure what this lot is doing up here out of your rooms. But look here. Miss Beckett in the pearls! Oh, dear!" his tone changed, dismay flooding his words. "They smudged it, those ghostly devils!"

"Smudged it?" Josiah scanned the work, unsure of what Samuel was seeing. He was fighting to translate what little he could and ignore the habit of a lifetime that dictated that he should look directly ahead to achieve his goals. "Where?"

"There! Right on her dear face! What a shame!" Escher sighed.

Josiah finally managed to see it by turning his head and glancing sideways, imagining that in doing so, he probably looked like a very bad imitation of a sly villain on the stage.

On her face. That's not a smudge. But that's impossible. . . .

The work in progress had barely started to take shape, as he'd sketched out his lovely Eleanor in pearls and layered in a few rudimentary colors. But a single delicate red smear in the shape of a man's thumb print now rested on her forehead between her eyes. His English lady had been transformed into a Hindu goddess with the single touch of a stranger's hand.

"You can fix it, can't you?" Escher asked at his elbow.

He shook his head. *It's the sign of a blessing—not a curse.*

"I wouldn't remove it for all the wealth of India, Mr. Escher." He crossed his arms, lost in a new meditation. "Please leave me for now. Make sure your wife has Creed in hand and send for Dr. West if need be."

"And you, sir?"

"I—I'll be going to the Grove."

"Yes, sir. Give the lady our very best," Escher said and stepped back to allow Josiah to move past him. "Will you be fetching her back with you, then?"

The question made every nerve ending in his body ache for a moment.

Will I be fetching her back?

So much has already been lost—and here is the crux of it.

If I'm to win her back, I'll have to lose one more thing.

"It will be up to the lady, Escher." Josiah began to walk down the stairs. "We'll see."

Chapter

30

Getting to the Grove proved nearly as challenging as surviving the Thistle, much to Josiah's chagrin. He'd forgotten that he'd sent Eleanor back with the hired carriage. Unable to see very well on a dark London street, hailing a cab was nearly impossible. The humiliation of finally having to call for Escher's help was a bitter taste of the daily medicine Josiah feared he would learn to take in the weeks ahead.

Alone inside the carriage, Josiah realized he'd stubbornly then left Escher behind and was now faced with getting from the carriage safely inside the Grove, navigating its unfamiliar interior and finding Eleanor—forcing him to rethink his impulsive fantasy of demonstrating to her how capable and whole he still was.

There goes my argument about being as much of a man as any other and winning her back in some smooth, seductive maneuver.

As the horses pulled to a stop, he tried to take a calming breath to steady his nerves and instead realized that Rita hadn't been exaggerating. The smell of charred wood and wool still clung to his skin, and when Josiah reached up to push a hand through his hair, the unmistakable sensation of soot on his scalp made it clear he probably looked like an oversize bootblack.

Josiah put his head in his hands and wondered if any man had been asked to do more to prove his love. *I've been shot at, nearly roasted alive, had my house broken into, and damned if my ears aren't still ringing, which makes me think I might be deaf and blind before dawn if my luck holds.* A grim smile tugged at his mouth and Josiah's humor finally reasserted itself. "In for a penny, in for a pound."

* * *

"There, there, now!" Mrs. Clay soothed, gently placing an arm around Eleanor's shoulders. Dressed in her nightgown and robe, she'd intercepted Eleanor downstairs and escorted her with motherly concern up to her rooms. Apparently, she'd been waiting all along after Tally had come to fetch her following Eleanor's panicked departure, keeping watch for her safe return. Now, the woman stayed to offer what comfort and counsel she could as they waited together for Josiah.

"Why wait an hour? I should send word to his friends now and get back to him as quickly as I can!" Eleanor nervously touched the pearls at her throat. "It's ridiculous to wait an hour. Why in the world do men say such things?"

"Ah! If I knew the answer to that, I'd have more power than the Queen." Mrs. Clay sighed. "And I don't think she knows either! Her Majesty's probably just as puzzled on occasion by her dear Albert as you are by your man."

Eleanor shook her head. "Has it been an hour yet?"

"He'll come, just as you said, and then we'll see what's what. Mr. Hastings is a man of his word and . . . well, I won't lie, miss. I can hardly wait to hear about these misadventures and see him for myself! What a hero to save you as he did, and what a delightful ruckus!"

"Delightful?" Eleanor asked woefully. "How can you say such a thing?"

"Well, everyone's no worse for it, and a good story like this will get a man a few free pints in any common room in England if you ask me!" Mrs. Clay smiled. "Not that it's clear what anyone was doing at such an establishment as the Thistle at this hour, or how you got into the thick of things, but I'm glad to see you safe."

Eleanor stood, gently disengaging from Mrs. Clay's maternal grasp. She moved to the washstand and poured out some fresh water to wash her face and hands, groaning at the sight of gray ash clouding the water and staining the towels. "I must look a fright!"

"No worse than Tally after he dropped that can of ash in Mr. Rutherford's rooms," Mrs. Clay assured her and crossed to tug at the bellpull by the fireplace. "I'll have one of the kitchen maids bring up some more coal and a nice hot toddy to put a little bit of color into your cheeks."

"Please don't awaken anyone at this hour! There's plenty of coal, and honestly, Mrs. Clay, I've no interest in any more roaring fires." Eleanor finished drying her hands, and then found herself unexpectedly bursting into tears. "He won't come! S-something has happened, I just know it! The house was dark and . . . even if it was nothing, he's too proud to come now! He's thought it through and he'll make a noble gesture to sacrifice—"

"To sacrifice his pride?" Josiah supplied the ending from the open doorway. Tally peeked out from under his winter coat and then guided his charge into the room. "For I swear, my pride is the only casualty of the evening, apparently."

"Josiah!" Eleanor rushed to him, heedless of any thought but Josiah and his safety, openly weeping in relief. "Thank God! Was everything all right? Are you injured?"

"I'm all right." Josiah retrieved a handkerchief from his pocket. "Here, dearest. I'm not sure how clean it is after what we've been through tonight, but I cannot have you crying on my account."

She took it from him, and then turned away to wipe her face, blushing. "As I told you the day we met, I am not a woman that cries often, Mr. Hastings."

"It's one of the things I admire about you most, Miss Beckett." He started to shrug gingerly from his coat, wincing a little. "Though apparently, while I avoided injury, my poor fitness from so many hours standing at an easel has guaranteed me a few aches in the days to come. Someone will have to tell me again why I insisted I didn't mind stairs."

"And the Eschers and poor Mr. Creed? Were they unharmed? Was it burglars?" Eleanor asked, her composure recovered as she tucked his handkerchief away in her pocket.

"Nothing was taken," Josiah assured her. "But there were intruders all the same. But it's a matter for another day, and Rutherford will take over the subject tomorrow as soon as he gets word. The man lives for a chance to protect his friends."

Mrs. Clay's reaction was almost as dramatic as she clasped her hands in joy. "Oh, Mr. Hastings! Oh, dear! You look—dreadful and as dirty as a stray dog after a mud bath! But I'm so pleased to see you're here to relieve my poor Miss Beckett's worries." She readjusted her mobcap and walked over to pat him on the shoulder. "I'm going downstairs to start the water heating for a nice hot bath. Trust me, Mr. Hastings. I'll see to everything, and my Tally and I will leave the two of you in peace for a while."

"Thank you, Mrs. Clay," Josiah said, releasing his gentle hold on her son and accepting the welcome gift of privacy. "You are the kindest woman I have ever known."

"It's hardly appropriate for—" Eleanor began and then stopped herself. "Thank you, ma'am."

"And I must thank Master Tally for his assistance. I'd have hated to burst in on the wrong guest room and been arrested as a burglar myself if left to my own devices." He knelt down to try to look Tally in the eye. "Thank you, sir."

"Come, Tally! Leave the man to his lady!" Mrs. Clay blushed and retreated to the door, with a grinning Tally in tow. "Nonsense! Now the two will sort it out so that I can begin with the congratulations!" She shut the door before they could answer, and Eleanor's cheeks felt warmer than they had at the Thistle at the realization that everyone had known of their relationship all along.

"So much for all those carriage rides home to keep up appearances," she said, pressing her hands against her face to try to stem the pink that was flooding her cheeks.

"As tempting as it is to wait for this bath and the ministrations of my beautiful attendant, she's right in that we should sort out this business between us, Eleanor."

"Josiah!"

"It was pride, Eleanor. I should have told you about what was happening to me, but I didn't want you to stay out of guilt or pity. It was stupid. I see that now," he confessed, his back ramrod straight.

"I should have seen it. I thought you didn't trust me. I thought I wasn't good enough to earn your love and respect—that I'd failed to reach you."

"You've had me from the first moment I saw you, Eleanor. You've been the mistress of my heart from that first day when you clutched that pitiful jewelry box and refused to come home with me."

"Then why did you say nothing? Even when I came that day . . . the money was meaningless. I'd only wanted to hear you say that you cared. Was it pride then, too?" she asked, taking a step closer to him.

"As you can see . . . pride is a luxury I've lost. I haven't any left."

"I don't believe you."

"Look at me, woman! I'm filthy! I've got twelve-year-olds leading me around like a large, sorrowful dog to make sure I don't think too highly of myself. I have little to recommend myself, Eleanor. Blind artists aren't exactly sought after."

"Blind? You said your sight was failing but that you could see well enough! You sent me off in that carriage and you faced intruders by yourself *blind*!" Eleanor was furious. "How could you?"

"It was my last deception, and a necessary one. But I swear, I won't ever lie to you again, Eleanor."

She stepped up to him, placing her hand on his chest as if to assure herself that he was real. "You swear it?"

"Here's my final bid, Eleanor. When the world went dark in that stairwell, I wasn't even thinking of the paintings or colors or any of the earthly sights I'm going to miss. I was just thinking of you. And when I realized you were in that blaze, nothing else mattered. Not my pride, not legacies and ridiculous quests for immortality or truth and beauty; just you. You are everything I want, and without you, there's nothing but darkness."

"And with me?"

He smiled, a flash of his old humor returning. "I shall just cheerfully pretend I can't afford candles and distract myself by endlessly exploring your body with my eyes closed."

She gasped, but he recognized the spark of heat that flared between them as she reached up to touch his face, the cool blades of her fingers soothing his skin. "How bad is it, honestly?"

"It's like a black cloth over my head, but there are small holes in the fabric. Here and there, I can see perfect little spots of the world, but they are too small to serve. I'm not sure . . . I'm wrenching my neck in every direction to try to peer through and see what's in front of me, but—it's bad enough, Eleanor. It's bad enough to render me useless."

"You're not useless. You can paint."

"I cannot think of it now. No, I can't paint."

"You must."

"Why?"

"Because I want you to. If you can see anything, then you can see enough to try, Josiah Hastings. Promise me that you'll at least try."

"And my reward for risking abject humiliation and committing aesthetic suicide?" he asked warily.

"Me."

He tightened his arms around her, reveling in the feel of her against him. "I'd try sharpshooting for a reward like that."

"I love you, Josiah Hastings."

"Even if I'm blind?"

"What difference does that make?"

"Doesn't it make some difference? If you're to master your own fate, it hardly seems fitting to tie yourself to—"

"The benefits far outweigh the disadvantages, Mr. Hastings. I won't have you speaking meanly of yourself . . . and stop quoting me! It's very cheeky of you, sir!"

"What benefits?"

"Well"—she paused as if to organize her thoughts—"you won't see me age, so I will always be young in your mind. And since at least some of that pride is sure to linger, you'll want me with you more often than not. I can be quite helpful at making sure you don't purchase any more chestnuts for a guinea."

"I meant to do that!" he protested lightly.

"You did not!" She pressed a finger against his chest. "Josiah, may I remind you that seconds ago you swore not to lie to me ever again?"

"Very well, I didn't, but that's not to say that I want to condemn you to a life of being chained to me like a dog, Eleanor."

"I . . . am . . . *not* . . . a . . . dog." Each word was underlined with a brisk tap of her foot. "Did you come here to win me or not, Josiah Hastings? I said I loved you and have received nothing but arguments for it! You speak of sacrificing your pride, but I swear you are digging in as if to prove that you're impossible enough to frighten me off!"

He released her and stepped back to put a blackened hand on the back of one of the chairs. "I am making a mess of it, aren't I? I was going to declare myself and beg you to marry me. But I can't even see your face and I'm distracted by all of it—the smell of smoke, worry over your safety, and this Jackal nonsense and the price of chestnuts." His grip tightened until she could see the white of his knuckles. "You said you loved me, Eleanor. It's all I've wanted for weeks, but finally hearing it . . . I've never been so terrified in my life. And I'm including over a year in an Indian dungeon and this evening's insane mishaps."

"Terrified?" Eleanor asked, gently moving closer to place her hand over his, soothing the tension of his hold on the fabric. "Am I so frightening a proposition?"

"I can't see what's ahead of me, Eleanor. Literally and figuratively. What promises can an honorable man make? That day when Madame Claremont accused me of selfishly taking you for my own wicked ends, I hated her because a small part of me knew she was right. You were rightly suspicious of me, Eleanor. And now that this darkness has caught me at last, I'm afraid because I don't know how I'm going to . . . be. A lifetime of practices and habits have deserted me."

"What are you saying, Josiah?"

"What if I turn into a humorless troll? Banging about my factory building and bemoaning my fate?"

Eleanor acted without thinking, moving on an impulse of raw, emotional reaction.

"Ouch!" Josiah reached down to hold his shin. "You kicked me!"

"Oh!" Eleanor was as shocked as he was, but she held her ground. "Josiah Hastings, you are being ridiculous! No man can see ahead of him or promise a future! You've lost none of that impossible pride if you think for one second that you alone controlled the universe when you *could* see! I . . . I . . ."

"Yes?" he asked, stifling a laugh as he accepted just how foolish it all was. He loved her. She loved him. Where was the problem? The path ahead looked crystal clear.

"I have become a bully." Her voice was filled with misery.

He pulled her back into his arms, wrapping her up to press her against his chest, savoring the way she fit against his frame as if some unknown sculptor had crafted her to his measurements. "I love that you bully me, Eleanor. I love you when you take charge, and while I must ask you to refrain from kicking me on a regular basis—I deserved that last blow. I was being a whining prig."

She tipped her head back to look into his face and was rewarded with a kiss.

The world fell away and he closed his eyes and forgot everything but the miracle of Eleanor Beckett loving him. He tasted her sweetness, and the hunger he'd spent so many days and hours trying to ignore nearly unmanned him. Gentleness fell to the wayside as both lovers sought to regain the ground they'd lost. Passion wiped away reason, and Josiah lifted her up. "They'd best hurry with that bath or I'm ruining those sheets, Eleanor."

"Josiah Hastings! You'll do no such thing!" she admonished him, but nibbled along the strong line of his jaw to find the sensitive pulse just beneath his ear. "Not without locking the door. . . ."

"I love you, Eleanor."

"So you'll paint?" she whispered against the shell of his ear.

He nodded, his expression solemn. "I'll try."

"You'll try until the door is completely closed and there's no light at all. I refuse to let you give up."

"If you wish it. And when there's no light?"

"There are worse things, Josiah Hastings. We'll go to concerts and lounge in the countryside and listen to our children laugh and play."

"Are we to have children?" It was a stunning thought and one that made him feel suddenly fiercely joyous and hopeful. "Are you marrying me, then, Miss Beckett?"

"I am." She brushed his hair back from his face. "It is only proper to do so, Mr. Hastings."

Epilogue

From the London Times, *June 14, 1860*

**The Premiere Showing of the
Royal Society of the Arts**

*Mr. Josiah Hastings had an unusual debut at the Society
with what can only be described as a striking and boldly
brief offering. The reclusive Hastings agreed to reveal
only two paintings this evening. Some critics, who had
accused the artist before the premiere of hubris, withdrew
their complaints and stated instead that if an artist can
demonstrate prowess and skill with only two paintings,
they are keen with anticipation to think what more lies
ahead.* Lady in Red *had been rumored to be unparalleled
in beauty, and at last, the public can judge. The second
work in question,* Lady in Pearls, *is equally unforgettable,
but has stirred controversy with its otherworldly and en-
chanting presentation of an English beauty as an exotic
and foreign goddess. Rumor has it that the lady in both is,*

*in fact, Mrs. Josiah Hastings. Hastings has refused com-
ment and was unable to attend the unveiling ceremony at
the museum. To date, neither painting is available for
sale, and at the end of June, both portraits will be withdrawn to return to the artist's private collection.*

Keep reading for an exciting excerpt from
the next Jaded Gentleman novel

Obsession Wears Opals

Coming December 2012
from Berkley Sensation!

Somewhere a drum was beating.

Isabel groaned in frustration at its insistence, at its intrusion on the numb, cold peace that had finally overtaken her. She'd lost track of time. She didn't know how far she'd ridden, but the gallop of yesterday had long yielded to a slow crawl through the night, and Isabel couldn't remember seeing the sun rise. She had ridden until exhaustion and the wintry lash of wind and icy rain had woven together into a tapestry of deadly quiet.

Except for that infernal drumming.

The rhythm was steady and slow. But loud enough to draw attention, she thought, because now there were voices. Someone was screaming and then there was an exchange, distant and anxious. Hands were touching her with muffled questions she couldn't understand. And then someone was lifting her from the frozen, wet ground.

I was on the ground? Did I fall from the saddle? How is that possible—Samson would never let me fall. . . .

Isabel's anxiety bloomed at the thought that something

had happened to her faithful stallion, that she'd ridden him beyond the limits of his strength, but then her ankle was being freed from the stirrup where it had caught and she was being pressed against someone and cradled in a man's arms, wrapped in a coat and blankets. She struggled to open her eyes, aware for the first time that she must have closed them.

The voices were closer, the vibration of the deep timbre of his speech touching off a spike of agonized fear that jolted her back to reality.

The drumming was my own heartbeat. God help me, I was praying for it to stop.

Numbness fell away in a single breath and Isabel cried out at the cruel loss. She didn't want to feel—anything. Not the fiery bite of the sleet against her cheeks or the warmth of his frame against hers; or the horrible return of memory and terror that had driven her to try to escape.

"I've got you," the stranger said softly, and something in her ached at the gentleness but despised the pain that it evoked.

You have me.

And what would you say if I just begged you to leave me as you found me?

There was a flurry of activity, and Isabel became more and more aware of what was taking place as her weightless state gave way to sodden skirts and labored breathing. A woman was hovering behind them and making an awful keening fuss as they crossed the threshold and the warmth of the house enveloped them all. "Is she dead? Oh, God! A dead woman in my winter garden! I'll be haunted all my days!"

"She's *not* dead." He shifted her carefully and began to make his way toward the heart of the house. "Calm yourself, Mrs. McFadden. Fetch Hamish and ask him to ride for Dr. Abernethy at once."

"No," Isabel croaked barely above a whisper, wincing at the agony of speech, but her terror overrode everything. "P-please, I beg you. N-no . . . a-authorities. . . ." She looked up at him and tried not to cry as desperation bled into her words. "P-please, sir. I c-cannot . . . go back."

"What's that she's saying?" the woman screeched from the kitchen doorway.

Isabel held her breath, praying for mercy in an unmerciful world, and nearly broke when she saw the flood of compassion and comprehension in his green eyes.

"Forget the doctor," he amended, raising his voice slightly and turning back to his housekeeper with authority. "Tell Hamish to tend to that horse and make sure the upstairs blue bedroom has enough firewood. Our guest will recover there, but for now, I'm taking her to the library where it's warmest. And hot broth, blankets, and dry clothes, Mrs. McFadden, as soon as you can manage it, please."

"Yes, Mr. Thorne."

Her terror retreated slightly as the threat of a doctor faded and she was carried through another doorway into a small library. He knelt and then with his free hand, yanked the cushions off of a nearby chair to make a nest for her in front of the fireplace. His hands were efficient as he rolled her gloved hands in his, warming the leather enough to peel the gloves from her fingers. He spoke pleasantly, as if they were experiencing an ordinary introduction.

"My name is Darius Thorne and you must forgive my housekeeper, Mrs. McFadden, for her reaction. I'm apparently such a dull man that she's grown unused to any excitement at all." He laid the gloves aside and then sat back on his heels to address the jet buttons on her riding coat. "Pardon my familiarity, but if we don't get you out of some of these soaking wet layers, then I won't be able to keep my word and will have to send for Dr. Abernethy after all."

She nodded, weakly trying to help him with her jacket but failing as her fingers refused to obey her commands. "Thank you. Sh-she has every right to complain. P-people r-rudely landing in her k-kitchen g-garden." Isabel's teeth chattered as she spoke. "I-I'm ruining these cushions, t-too."

He smiled, apparently ignoring that she'd not offered her own name in return. "No worries. I'll make sure she knows

I'm to blame since I've long disliked that chair with its embroidered scene of some idiots cavorting about and shooting deer." He undid the last button and drew the sodden coat from her shoulders, replacing it with the blanket that had fallen off her frame; a temporary aid to ward off a chill. "Let's get your boots off then."

Her extremities had begun to warm, and with the return of her circulation, her skin began to burn as if pricked by a thousand needles. She winced as he pulled off her boots and forgot modesty as he made quick work of her stockings to toss them on the stone hearth.

"Damn," he muttered beneath his breath, and without preamble, began to vigorously rub her feet and calves.

"It hurts!" she protested, but she stopped when she saw the pain in his face.

"I'd not hurt you for all the world, but we must get your blood flowing to ease your injuries. Please forgive me." He returned grimly to his task, and she nodded slowly, acquiescing to his good sense. But there was more to it.

Isabel paid no heed to the tears on her cheeks as she studied her rescuer for the first time. The sincerity in his face was a strange balm that removed her from discomfort. By the firelight, his wire-rimmed spectacles gleamed like copper and his handsome features were accented by the glow. He had the soulful look of a poet with arched eyebrows and sweet eyes, but his face was chiseled as if nature had hoped to fashion him for war. He was calm and careful as his strong hands gently worked over her flesh until the pale skin finally began to glow pink and become pliant to his touch, and when he looked back up at her, Isabel's breath caught in her throat.

"Better?" he asked.

He'd said he'd not hurt her for all the world, but it made no sense in the world she'd experienced to believe him. Still, she was sitting in front of a fire with her bare feet tucked into his lap, half frozen and miserable—and inexplicably feeling safe for the first time in months. It was impossible, but she trusted this man.

She nodded and opened her mouth to answer him, but a crisp knock at the door ended the spell.

"All's prepared upstairs, Mr. Thorne. I've a roaring fire going and a tray of hot broth and fresh pastries to follow, but I thought I'd see her up and settled first."

"Yes, brilliant, Mrs. McFadden." He stood unfolding from the floor, and Isabel winced out of habit at the sudden movement. "Are you unwell?"

She shook her head. "N-no. I don't think so."

"Here, let me help you." He lifted her up effortlessly as if she were a small child and moved toward the doorway and his impatient housekeeper. "Lead on, Mrs. McFadden."

Isabel closed her eyes and swallowed any protest she might have made. Pride urged a lady to insist that her legs worked and that she couldn't allow him to exert himself on her behalf, but a small, practical voice inside of her won the day by noting that she couldn't really feel her toes, that every part of her ached, and that the room was starting to spin.

The haze of exhaustion reasserted itself as they moved up the staircase and Isabel fought to stay alert in his arms. The transition to his guest bedroom was smooth and well choreographed by the firm instructions of Mrs. McFadden as he set her down on an upholstered couch at the foot of the bed. The room was as warm as toast, and while Mr. Thorne waited dutifully outside the door, Mrs. McFadden efficiently saw her out of every stitch of her wet clothes and into soft woolen stockings and several layers of an old flannel nightgown. Then Mr. Thorne returned and lifted her up to carry her to bed as Mrs. McFadden removed the bed-warmer and turned back the covers.

Ensconced under mounds of bedding, Isabel sank into the feather mattress and lost the battle to keep her eyes open.

"There you are," he said softly, before he retreated. "Safe and sound."

Safe and sound.

Isabel slid into the darkness that opened up around her, welcoming oblivion before one last thought bubbled up.

I'll never be safe again.